─────────────── ★ ───────────────

"Sit down." The voice startled her so much she almost
fell. An eyeball stared at her through the doorknob
hole. She sat and listened as something rattled on the
other side of the door. She had a screen door at home
with one of those hook latches on it. This sounded the
same. Except that there were three, maybe four of them.
Each one alone sounded insubstantial. But together, they
would provide enough of a barrier to prevent her from
breaking free.

A heavyset figure wearing a ski mask pushed the door
back against the wall, as if to be sure nobody was
hidden in that neglected corner. Fat chance.

The good news was that the masked man didn't carry
any weapons. The bad news was that he—or was it a
she?—had sturdy bare hands that looked strong enough
to throttle her.

"Who are you?" Annie asked. "Why am I here?"

Nothing. The figure just stared at her.

─────────────── ★ ───────────────

D1440615

INDIGO
AS AN IRIS
FRAN STEWART

W**O**RLDWIDE.

TORONTO • NEW YORK • LONDON
AMSTERDAM • PARIS • SYDNEY • HAMBURG
STOCKHOLM • ATHENS • TOKYO • MILAN
MADRID • WARSAW • BUDAPEST • AUCKLAND

To Kathi Moon,
for reasons obvious only to the two of us,
and to the memory of
Hot Cocoa
and her two kids.

Recycling programs
for this product may
not exist in your area.

INDIGO AS AN IRIS

A Worldwide Mystery/May 2012

First published by Doggie in the Window Publications.

ISBN-13: 978-0-373-63628-0

Copyright © 2008 by Fran Stewart.

All rights reserved. No part of this book may be reproduced
or transmitted in any form or by any means, electronic or
mechanical, including photocopying, recording or by any
information storage and retrieval system, without permission
in writing from the publisher. For information, contact: Doggie in the Window
Publications, P.O. Box 1565, Duluth, GA 30096 U.S.A.

This is a work of fiction. Names, characters, places and incidents are
either the product of the author's imagination or are used fictitiously,
and any resemblance to actual persons, living or dead, business
establishments, events or locales is entirely coincidental.

® and ™ are trademarks of Harlequin Enterprises Limited.
Trademarks indicated with ® are registered in the United States
Patent and Trademark Office, the Canadian Trade Marks Office
and in other countries.

Printed in U.S.A.

My Gratitude List for Indigo

Alicia Kessler, a flight attendant I met on my way back from a book tour. She said she'd be happy to lend her name to one of my characters. I do hope she'll forgive me for the one I chose for her. Believe me, the two women, one real, one fictional, are nothing alike!

Billy and Kimberley Campbell, who founded Memorial Ecosystems and established Ramsey Creek Preserve near Westminster, South Carolina. Their work is an inspiration indeed.

Dan Barber, my trusty auto mechanic, who advises me of all things car-related in my books. I think I got it right, Dan. If not, it's my fault, not yours.

Dylan Caldwell and Logan Caldwell, who delighted in showing me their three pet goats, particularly the one who liked to stand on the picnic table. Hey, guys, I hope you don't mind that I borrowed your goats' names for this book.

Fallon and Chris Phelps, whom I met briefly at an IHOP one Saturday morning. They sat next to me playing 20 Questions with their aunt and uncle, and I eavesdropped shamelessly, then stole one of their games and their creative solution for Glaze and Biscuit to play.

Jill Sensiba, a woman I met in a Florida airport when I was flying home from a speaking engagement at Edison College. Jill has turned out to be my plant researcher, and she came through when I asked her to recommend a plant someone could fall into face-first without getting cuts and scratches. Also a pink-flowered, spring-blooming perennial that would need to be deadheaded and that would sprout easily from seeds. Jill is amazing, and I'm so glad I struck up a conversation with her in that airport.

Joan Maloof, author of Teaching the Trees: Lessons from the Forest, wherein I first learned about the healing nature of the air in old-growth forests.

Mandy Latimer, of Latimer Luck Acres in Watkinsville, Georgia, who gave so generously of her time and shared her expertise about milking Nubian dairy goats and caring for nineteen of them. And "Hot Cocoa," who tried to eat my notebook and who let me feel her babies kicking.

Nanette Littlestone, my incredibly talented editor, who is both patient and exacting. What would I ever do without you, Nanette?

Traci Smith, dear friend and Pampered Chef Lady par excellence, who introduced me to the outrageous dessert I used for the bed-and-breakfast.

Yonette Rooker, who told me who to call to find out about dairy goats.

And, of course, my deepest gratitude to the wonderful folks at Doggie in the Window Publications, who encourage me and listen to me and who see my vision for the Biscuit McKee series.

PART I

WEEK FOUR

MONDAY

She came to with her ankles hobbled and her hands tied behind her back. She had hated playing Blind Man's Bluff when she was a kid, and she liked blindfolds even less now as she lay in the back seat of a car, bumping over a rutted gravel road that threw stones against the undercarriage. Her own car, no less. She knew that because she smelled the cinnamon buns. She'd bought some at the Delicious to drop by her aunt's house in Hastings, a spur-of-the-moment visit designed to save gas and kill two birds with one stone. A bad analogy under the circumstances. She should have called first. Then somebody would have expected her to be someplace. That's what she'd been putting in the car when somebody cracked her over the head. The cinnamon buns. Now they filled her car with their smell of homespun comfort, the aroma of a leisurely breakfast.

Why would anybody knock her out and steal her cinnamon rolls?

A child's voice said, "Mommy, is that lady sleeping?"

"Yes, Willie. Don't you worry none about her. You just finish that sticky bun I brought you."

Well, then. It was all right. She was tied up and blindfolded and her head hurt like the dickens, but a little kid had the cinnamon buns.

She was obviously losing her mind.

PART II

WEEK ONE

MONDAY

I HEARD MARGARET CASPERSON'S 1933 Duesenberg pull up in front of the library where Sadie's yellow Chevy usually sat. The day was mild enough for open windows, and Marmalade and I happened to be close to one in the Reference section, straightening up the Funk & Wagnalls Encyclopedias someone recently bequeathed to the Martinsville library. That is to say, I was straightening the books while Marmalade sniffed around the bottom of the shelf.

A bug is under there.

As Margaret trudged up the walk, I opened the heavy front door and stepped out onto the wide porch, that standard feature of all the gracious old houses in town. And some that weren't so gracious, if truth be told.

She paused to pat the stone lion on her left and grinned up at me. "Are you ready for a surprise?"

"Sure. I love surprises."

She rummaged in a dark blue gift bag and pulled out an envelope. "Here's yours, Biscuit. Wait. Don't open it till I get up there." She reached for the wrought-iron banister and hauled herself up the few steps.

"Are your feet bothering you more today?" My feet hardly ever hurt, but when they did, it was awful. I couldn't imagine walking around in pain all the time, and Margaret was only in her early forties.

"Oh, after a while I get used to it. Doc gave me some pain pills and I've been taking those pretty regularly, but today they don't seem to be helping much." I bit my tongue to keep from telling her what I thought about pain pills in general.

"Okay," she said. "Open it up."

A rubber-stamped boat, or rather a ship, graced the ivory envelope in the upper left corner. Margaret may have had enough money to buy her own ocean liner from her petty-cash account, but she still took delight in simple crafts. Everything she'd given me, except the stone lions, sported a rubber stamp of some sort on it. She stood there leaning over my arm like a kid at somebody else's birthday party. I had to smile. "What could this be?"

"Oh, quit stalling. Open it."

There were three lines of names on the invitation. "Margaret, this is beautiful. You used your computer to make this up, didn't you?" Margaret disliked computers even more than my mother-in-law did. "The font is pretty." Pretty flowery, if you asked me, but that was okay, considering what it said.

Dear Annie, Biscuit, Dee, Ellen, Esther, Glaze, Ida, Irene, Madeleine, Maggie, Margot, Melissa, Miss Mary, Monica (love you, Mom!), Myrtle, Rebecca Jo, Sadie, and Sharon,

I've put all of you in alphabetical order, so nobody would get her feelings hurt. Take a look at the enclosed brochures. Join me to celebrate my 42nd birthday. Limousine to the Atlanta airport Cruise through the Caribbean for a whole week Return the following Saturday

All you have to do is let me know if you can make it. I'll foot the entire bill.

Love, Margaret

"Well," she said, "can you come?"

"I'd love to. Here I am fifty years old, and I've never been on a cruise before."

What is a kruse?

Margaret smiled down at Marmalade, who had just uttered a funny gurgle, unlike her usual rumbly purr. "They're lots of fun. The food is magnificent." She handed me another brochure. "Here. Look at this."

I glanced at the title. "What's a genealogy cruise?"

"That's the best part of this. I've already reserved twenty spaces for us with this group. They schedule speakers and classes for us to learn stuff about genealogy while we're at sea. You don't have to take the classes. You can sit in a hot tub the whole time if you'd like. But I figure we can learn a lot about our town history if at least a couple of us take each class, and then we can compare notes over dinner. What do you think?"

"I don't know, Margaret. With my vitiligo, I sunburn so easily."

"So sit in the shade. There'll be plenty of umbrella tables."

I went back to the first brochure and looked at the pictures. Sea, sand, smiling faces, tropical birds. "Birds on a cruise ship?"

"No, silly," she said. "You'll see the birds when we visit the jungle on one of the islands. There are lots of side trips we can take while the boat's in port."

The next page showed the food. "My gosh, Margaret, I'll gain twenty pounds. Look at this feast."

Is there any chicken for me?

She stepped back and looked me up and down. "You don't have a thing to worry about. You stay so active."

My husband, Bob Sheffield, was the Martinsville town cop. When we married last year I'd kept my maiden name of McKee, primarily to avoid an unfortunate monogram. Of course, I already had an unfortunate monogram. Oh, well. Bob once described me as a comfortable armful. I did keep active, though, gardening and walking mostly, and climbing the three floors in the library. My weight hadn't changed much in the past twenty years, although I'd gained some when my first husband died seven years ago. I had depended on comfort food—a lot of it—to get me through that horrible time. Food and good friends and family. I finally walked and gardened off most of the excess pounds once I recovered from Sol's unexpected death. I still missed looking at the stars with him. Sol's last name was Brandy. That was why I'd kept the name McKee through my first marriage. Biscuit Brandy? It sounded like a snack and a shot. No, thank you.

"...if my feet didn't bother me so much, but I

suppose I won't have to walk too much on the boat. Especially if I take all the classes." I tuned back in to Margaret's monologue. She followed me through the massive front door, and Marmy wandered back to the encyclopedias. "Did you order those new computers yet?"

"Yes. I sent it in on Friday morning. You should get my thank-you note today when Celia makes her rounds." Margaret quietly put her scads of money to good use. She'd benefited the town in countless ways, and now the library would be brought up-to-date with a computerized system. The lovely old Millicent Mansion on Third Street had been willed to Martinsville several years before, on the condition that it be used as a "fine town library." The ponderous multi-drawered card catalog, its light oak darkened with age and thousands of fingerprints, used to be at the elementary school, where some of the original library books had been housed.

My job is to kill the intruders.

"I'm going to miss being able to thumb through those cards," I said and pulled out a tissue so I could pick up the slightly munched cockroach Marmalade had just deposited beside my foot.

"Ha! Bet you won't miss having to type them up."

"You do have a point there, although my Petunias usually do that job." I dumped the bug in the wastebasket and tapped the edge of the invitation. "Let me talk it over with Bob. Not that we have anything special planned, but I'd feel better discussing it with him before I give you a definite answer." I looked at the list. All three of my volunteers were on there. Hmm. "With no Petunias available, I'd have to close the library for a week. Have they all accepted?"

"I'm headed out on my rounds to deliver these. You're my second stop. Mom already has hers, and she said yes. I'm pretty sure most everybody will want to go. Especially the ones that enjoy charting their ancestors."

That would be practically everyone in Martinsville, I thought. If there was one thing people in this town knew about, it was who was related to whom, no matter how distantly. "I'll need to think about this, Margaret. Is that okay?"

"Fine." She pulled a dark blue notebook from the same bag. "I'll put you down as a definite maybe. Uh...Biscuit?" Biscuit had been my nickname since grade school. My mother, a potter, named her two daughters Bisque and Glaze. It was a good thing she hadn't had a son. He probably would have ended up being called Kiln. His brother, if he'd had one, could have been named Wheel. We'd need an Urn and a Mug and a Plate to complete the set. Maybe we'd call the youngest one Teapot.

"Yoo-hoo. Biscuit?" Margaret called me back from my daydreaming. She was used to my habit of tuning out of a conversation while my mind reeled away in a different direction.

"Sorry, Margaret. You know me."

"That's okay. I wish I had your imagination. I've always wondered why you call Sadie and the others your Petunias."

"It's because the first time I ever saw them, when they came to volunteer to help me with the library, they were all lined up in a row, each of them wearing a flower-print housedress. They reminded me of a flower bed. I couldn't very well call them my Pansies or my Zinnias or my Johnny-jump-ups, so I settled for Petunias." What would I ever have done without my three elderly library volunteers? Between us, we managed to keep the library open three and a half days a week. I was going to have to figure out a way to include some evening hours, but that was more than I could face at the moment.

A cruise, though. I could face a cruise, even if it meant closing the library for a week. The town would understand.

"Can I share a room with Melissa if I go?"

Where will I sleep?

"I think they call them staterooms, and of course you can."

"Then change that definite maybe to a yes." One

thing I loved about my husband was that, unlike many men, he never expected me to ask permission to do what I wanted to do. I knew he'd be okay with my going, but I would need to let him know the dates so he could plan ahead.

WEEK ONE

TUESDAY

Dear, dear Margaret,

You are so kind to invite me on your birthday cruise. Especially one centered on genealogy. I'm fairly sure of my Russell family background, but I'm certain I could pick up some pointers.

Ordinarily I'd love to say yes to the cruise, but with Wallace the way he is now I just can't plan too far ahead. So you and the other girls have a fine trip without me. I'd hate to be in the middle of the ocean and find out that Wallace needed me. I'm sure you'll understand.

If you ever have another one, let me know.

With love,
Sadie

P.S. Have it pretty soon. I'm in my eighties after all.

JEFF WINSLOW PAUSED until the prison guard strolled past, out of earshot. "I tell you, she's got more money than anybody can count. Got it when she was a little girl. Been swimming in it ever since. She won't even notice a quarter of a million gone. And she's real good friends with my girlfriend's sister."

Jeff's cellmate had one eyebrow, a solid expanse of bushy brown hair that stretched in an unbroken horizontal line above his eyes. He raised one end of it. "You mean your ex-girlfriend, don't you?"

"I don't need a wise guy. Are you in or not?"

"We're splittin' this even, right?"

"You betcha. Fifty-fifty."

Gordon Harvey furrowed his forehead in a parody of thinking. "There's two of us and only one of you. I say we divvy it up in threes. My sister's going to do the hard work, and I'm the one who's gonna have to tell her how to do it. That won't be easy. They watch us pretty close on visiting days."

"Tell you what." Jeff spread his hands, palms up. "I'm easy to get along with. I'll give you the best part of the deal. We'll divide the money into four parts. Four's more than three, see? You and your sister take two of those, and all I'll get is what's left over."

Gordon licked his thin lips. "Okay, sounds good that way."

"Yeah. You do most of the work, you get most

of the cash. Maybe we'll even divide it into fives. That way you and your sister each get fifty thousand dollars. What do you think about that?"

"Okay by me."

"It's a deal, then?"

"Sure thing. Now, how's this gonna work?"

"I already told you. You get your sister to nab my girlfriend. Then she writes a note and sends it to the librarian, telling her to pay up or lose her little sister."

"How's she gonna know who to nab?"

"That's easy." Footsteps. The guard returning. "That's easy," Jeff repeated slightly louder. "You just stretch all the way up as high as you can reach, and then you bend over real slow, and bingo, your back doesn't hurt as much anymore." He stood and demonstrated the stretch.

The guard tapped on one of the cross bars with a billy stick as black as his uniform. "You turning into the resident doctor, Winslow?"

"Just passing on a little helpful information. You ought to try it, too, next time your back goes out."

"I'll keep that in mind." His footsteps receded.

Jeff lowered his voice again. "It's easy to find Glaze. Nobody has a head of hair like her. You can spot it a mile away. All your sister has to do is hang around Martinsville for a day or two until she finds a short, knockout woman with white hair. That's the one. I don't know exactly where she's

living now, but check out the librarian's house on
Beechnut Street and watch the library, too. She's
bound to be at one of those places."

"Lotsa old ladies have white hair."

"She's not an old lady. Got that? But her hair is
pure white."

"What didja say her name is?"

"It's Glaze. Glaze McKee."

"What kinda name is that?"

"It's just a name, okay? You sure your sister can
take care of her end?"

"Don't you worry none. Wilena works in Martinsville now, so it won't look funny for her to be
driving around there." His upper lip curled into
what might have been a smile. "She's built like a
tank. She hits your lady friend over the head, she'll
be out for the count."

"Don't kill her. She's not worth anything to us
dead. Anyway, I want her to come to and find out
I'm rich. Then we'll see what kind of tune she
sings. Bet she'll want to change her mind then."
Jeff flexed his forearm to set the skull tattoo grin-
ning. "I'll have to decide whether or not I want
her back. Do her good to do some begging. You're
sure that cabin is well hid?"

"Wouldn't nobody find it if they didn't already
know it was there. When's the date?"

"It has to be at least a couple of days before I
get out of here. That gives me a perfect alibi. All

locked up by the great state of Georgia. You, too. We'll both be safe. Few days after we get out, we pick up the loot and hightail it."

"What's her name again?"

"Glaze. Like a pot."

"Wouldn't know about that. I never did pot."

Dear Margaret,

Thanks so much for inviting me. I really do appreciate this. Unfortunately, I have to say no. I'm embarrassed to admit that the store hasn't been doing as well as I hoped, so I can't afford to close it for a whole week.

My brother's been sick a lot, and I drove to Atlanta several times over the last year to be with him, which has cut heavily into my profit margin. I don't mean to be complaining, but that's just the way it is. I hope you'll understand.

    Sincerely,
    Annie

"HOT DOG! A CRUISE!" Ida Peterson practically crowed as we all filed into Melissa's kitchen for our usual Tuesday night gab fest. Tap-dance class had gone well. In fact, we'd invited the teacher, Miss Mary, to join us at Azalea House for the first time ever. Guess we were keyed up enough to be able to stand her exclamation points for another hour or so, although I did wonder privately why Margaret invited her on the cruise. Could we bear her strident enthusiasm every day for a week? Who on earth would be willing to share a room, a stateroom, with her? Our tap-dance class had swollen to seven in the past few months, and Dee, the newcomer, was working hard to pick up the steps. I had to admit I appreciated the review, since I still tended to get lost somewhere between the Buffalo and the Cramp Roll. Our oldest class member, Sadie, was eighty-two. She knew the steps better than any of us, so she didn't need to review. Which was just as well. She'd chosen to stay at the hospital this week with her husband, Wallace, who had taken a turn for the worse.

Marmalade, my orange-and-white tabby cat, had met us after class on the sidewalk outside the dance studio. I'd taken her in when I first moved to Martinsville…

Excuse me? I chose to live with you, Widelap.

…to take the job as librarian. I later found out that I was the only applicant. Marmalade was the library cat, in charge of exterminating the vermin that overran the old Millicent Mansion. She'd shown up one day and started killing mice as if she'd been hired to do it. It was quite a job, but she was amazingly efficient. There were still a few mice occasionally, and she always set the dead ones, like little fur-wrapped gifts, on the floor next to the old rolltop desk. We knew that desk had a secret drawer in it, but we'd never been able to find it. Anyway, once Marmalade had the mouse population under control, she started walking home with me, and now she was a regular feature in my life. I couldn't imagine life without her. It seemed as if everywhere I went, she trailed along, almost like a dog.

A dog? Mouse droppings!

Marmalade snorted, sounding surprisingly like my grandma Martelson. Marmy was a regular visitor at Azalea House anyway, from what Melissa told me.

I would like some chicken, GoodCook.

Marmalade preceded me through the door and ducked under the long kitchen table. She headed for Melissa's fridge, purring loudly. I learned to love this homey kitchen with its bright white counters and high ceilings during the year I lived with Melissa Tarkington when I first moved to Martinsville. She'd become a dear friend. I was going to put her on my gratitude list. Again.

Ida slumped into the closest chair and frowned. "A paid-for cruise, no less, but I'll never be able to take that much time away from the grocery store. Ralph would have a fit."

Annie McGill circled the table and sat in her usual chair at the other end. "At least you have him to run the place while you're gone. I can't just close up the herb shop. There's nobody but me."

"I keep telling you, you need an assistant. Some-body who could take over when you have to be gone."

"Now, how on earth would I pay an assistant, Ida?" Annie had seemed so subdued, so quiet when I first met her. The tap dancing must have sparked some sort of feistiness inside. "The shop gives me a fair living," she went on, "and my costs are low because I live upstairs, but when I shut that door, there's no income."

Melissa pulled tea out of the fridge and poured it into an ice-filled pitcher that she handed to my sister, Glaze. I watched her cut up something—it looked like chicken—into a saucer. She set it on the floor in front of my cat and turned back to wash her hands at her immaculate porcelain sink.

Thank you.

Why Marmy didn't weigh a ton, I'd never know.

I walk a lot.

Miss Mary sat next to me. "Goodness, girls! Do you bicker like this all the time?"

"Only when I'm right and she's wrong," Annie said with a bit of a snicker.

Ida glared at Miss Mary. I entertained a brief vision of Ida standing at the back end of the cruise ship, dumping our tap-dance instructor overboard. Goodness gracious, what an awful thought.

"Do you even get a chance," Glaze asked, "to go to the bathroom during the day?" Leave it to my sister to think about a thing like that.

Annie rolled her head around in a cross between a nod and a shake. "I stick a little card on the counter that says BE RIGHT BACK. So far nobody's run off with the cash register."

"Which is nothing but a puny cardboard box you've got under the counter." We all looked back at Ida. "When are you going to get a real cash register?"

"When I can afford one," Annie snapped, "and not before." Annie had such a sunny disposition, she didn't frown very often. Now she looked as if she was living up to the stereotype of a hot-tempered redhead.

Melissa placed a plate of her Parmesan cheese straws on the table next to the cinnamon rolls Dee had brought. Dee was my ex-sister-in-law, if there was such a title as that. She'd recently divorced Barkley Sheffield, my husband's younger brother. She told me once that it wasn't only his cheating that instigated the divorce. "The cheating wasn't the problem in and of itself," she said. "It was just a pretty obvious symptom of a much deeper problem. Our marriage was over years ago." I had to admit, I liked her a lot more than I liked Barkley.

Melissa sat down between Glaze and Dee and wiggled her fingers in Ida's direction. "What about that old cash register?" she asked. "Did you save it when you went all fancy with the new computer setup?"

We all turned and looked back at Ida. She and Ralph not only installed an ATM on the wall outside their grocery store, they had those scanners that made the checkout go so much faster.

"Well, I'll be doggoned. I do still have that old thing. You want it, Annie?"

We might as well have been watching ping-pong.

What is a peeng pong?

Once that was settled, Ida asked, "Have you seen that new woman in town?"

"Who?"

"Which one?"

"Who are you talking about?"

"Hush up, all of you, and I'll tell you. She's got long black hair. I swear it's longer than Annie's."

"Not possible," Glaze said. "Annie grows hair better than anyone."

Annie halfway stood up and bowed over the blue-checked tablecloth, swinging her long red braid like a baton.

"Yes, it is," Ida insisted. She stopped to look at Annie. "Well, maybe not quite as long."

"What's she here for?" I asked.

"Don't know. She's staying up at Alicia's." Ida waved down the table at Melissa. "Sorry. Alicia grabbed another one of your potential customers. It must be that sign she has at the end of her drive-way."

"It's a cute sign," Glaze said. "But I think it's more that people have to pass right by Alicia's on the road down from Braetonburg. They can't miss it. They don't see Azalea House, though, unless they're driving around in Martinsville and just happen to make it all the way down here to Magnolia Street."

I was constantly amazed when new people found their way to Keagan County. The Metoochie River Valley ran quietly through an out-of-the-way fold of the lower Appalachians. Only one access road, running through a gap in the cliffs that surrounded the valley, connected us to the rest of Georgia. The people who found us usually had chosen to leave behind the high-pressure atmosphere of city life. There was no major industry in the county, un-less you counted two car dealerships, a catalog company, a gadget manufacturer, and a fertilizer outfit that shipped bat guano harvested from the extensive caves along the east side of the upper Metoochie. Fortunately, the harvesters couldn't reach the Martinsville caves. At this end of the valley, the caves were largely inaccessible....

I was born in one of them.

Bob and his two best friends used to explore them when they were kids, but now the caves seemed to be the sole property of the bats, who kept the bug population of Martinsville under control.

They eat flying bugs. I kill the cockroaches.

"You know what you need?" Ida wagged her finger at Melissa and brought my wandering mind back into the conversation. "You need better advertising." The last time she'd said those words, she and Sadie ended up launching a highly successful ad campaign for getting new library patrons.

"Don't worry about me, ladies." Melissa set her cheese straw down on a blue-and-white-checked napkin. "We've both got more business than we know what to do with. Most of Alicia's guests are the drop-in variety. Mine are the long-term, come-back-on-a-regular-schedule kind. I don't consider us competitors."

"I buy my honeysuckle soap from her," Annie said.

Glaze pointed across the table at me. "That's her favorite soap. She smells like honeysuckle all the time now." Glaze, on the other hand, always smelled like a cookie because of her favorite vanilla perfume.

Annie smiled at me. "You're my best customer for that soap. Alicia's sister makes it by hand, and Alicia delivers it to me, so I've never seen her place, except from the road. Is it nice on the inside?"

Melissa nodded. "It's quite homey. Her guest rooms are all upstairs and they're light and airy-looking. The bottom floor of the house is built right up against the cliff, so only the front rooms have windows. But the top floor is deeper. It stretches back over the ledge."

"So, the bottom floor is more like a basement?" Dee shuddered. "Yuch."

"Only at the back. It's just that it's built on such a steep hillside." Melissa scanned the group. "You can all go look, if you want to. But send your friends to stay with me when they come to visit."

I like visiting you.

Marmy let out the cutest little yawp just then, and we all laughed.

My Gratitude List for Tuesday
Five things for which I am grateful:
1. Tap dancing.
2. All the women in the class, especially Melissa. And Annie. And Ida. And Glaze.
3. This quiet valley, even with the wind that's howling outside right now.
4. This handmade quilt Annie gave me for my birthday. It looks so good here in Bob's and my bedroom. And it's extra cozy on a rainy night like this.

5. Margaret's generosity. I wonder if I can get by with my old green swimsuit on the cruise.

I am grateful for
Widelap
the bird feeder
food from GoodCook
this soft bed while the wind is noisy
claws to scratch that itchy spot under my chin

WEDNESDAY

Margaret dear!

I couldn't possibly leave my little dance students for a whole week! It was sweet of you to think of me, though! I have to admit that sometimes I've felt like I was on the outside looking in, if you know what I mean. Everyone here seems so close-knit. I've been teaching that tap dance class for almost a year now, and last week was the first time (!) they ever invited me to join them for their gathering after class. Maybe there's hope!

I wish I could take you up on this cruise idea! If you plan any other kind of party, please keep me on your invitation list! I'll be happy to join in as long as it's just a one-day thing!

Thank you again!
Miss Mary

GLAZE OPENED HER SQUEAKY kitchen door. "We're just about ready," she said around a yawn. "You're early."

Dee stepped inside and inhaled. "Did you go and buy cinnamon rolls again?" Without waiting for an answer, she nodded at the coffeepot on the green counter. "Did you make it or did Madeleine?"

"I've been warned away from the coffee making, thank you very kindly. You never have to risk drinking mine again. You know where the cups are." Glaze headed back to the bathroom, still yawning. Doodle-Doo had started crowing way earlier than usual, and once Glaze was awake, she never could get back to sleep.

While Dee poured half a cup of the rich brew, Glaze brushed her teeth and ran a hairbrush across her head. Thank goodness she didn't have to fiddle with her hair, otherwise she'd never make it to work on time. Glaze was blessed with genes direct from her grandma McKee. Her hair, silver since she was twenty-one years old, fell in gentle waves around her face with no prompting whatsoever on her part. Everyone always thought she dyed it. She'd let her roommate dye her hair once with one of those do-it-yourself coloring kits, soon after her hair started turning white, but it ended up a yellowish orange, rather like the middle line on a highway. Sharon Armitage told her that she could do it right, but Glaze wasn't that trusting anymore, even though Sharon was a professional. Never again.

Madeleine's voice drifted down from the top of the stairs. "I'm coming, I'm coming!"

"Don't hurry yourself," Dee called up to her. "I want to finish my coffee."

"Turn it off, will you?"

"Already did," Dee hollered back. "Wouldn't want my personal coffee shop to burn down while we're at work. Can I have one of the cinnamon buns?"

Glaze stuck her head out of the bathroom to answer, but Dee hadn't waited. Glaze watched her lift the heavy glass cake plate cover, inhale deeply, and scoop a roll onto her saucer. Glaze almost hated to interrupt her reverie. Almost, but not quite. "Are you going on the cruise?"

"Who, me?" Dee's cat-like eyes closed briefly as she savored the first bite of rich cinnamon. "The cruise? I think so. I'll have to combine some of my sick days with the rest of my vacation days, but I'm pretty sure I have enough." She licked her fingers. "What about you?"

"Can't. Hank won't let us change our vacation time."

"That man's a monster."

"Who's a monster?" Madeleine lifted her purse

from the newel post as she reached the bottom of the stairs.

"Hank. He won't let Glaze change her vacation, so she won't be able to go on the cruise."

"That stinks."

"Are you going, Maddy?" Dee took another bite.

Madeleine threw her arms open and set her purse swinging in a wide arc. "In a heartbeat. I've never been on a cruise before. Blessings on Margaret and her millions."

"Kazillions, you mean," Dee said.

"Okay. Bless her kazillions as long as she shares some of it with us." Maddy pulled off her glasses and squinted at them. "Fingerprints. Rats!"

"Maybe she could buy out Hank and we could set our own vacation schedules."

"Why on earth," Glaze asked, "would Margaret want to buy CelerInc? Let's go. We don't want to be late. Leave your glasses alone, Maddy. You can clean them in the car."

"Miss I-have-to-be-everywhere-on-time strikes again." Madeleine wagged her fingers at Glaze and grinned.

THEIR CARPOOL ARRANGEMENT had worked out better than Glaze had anticipated. They'd talked about how lucky it was that without really planning it they'd all ended up working in the same town within a block of each other and with similar work hours.

Madeleine Ames, sister of the town priest, wrote copy for the catalog listings at Wish Fulfillment, a company in Russell Gap that had experienced explosive growth over the past few years. Dee served as the assistant manager for Wish's shipping department, a job that kept her on her feet most of the day, but they let her wear tennis shoes. Glaze had gone from a moderately good-paying job in Philadelphia to being unemployed when her company downsized. Now she was a glorified secretary at CelerInc, a small manufacturing concern located on the other side of Wish's parking lot.

Glaze was matter-of-fact about her modest income potential. She'd wasted a lot of years wallowing in the swamp of an undiagnosed bipolar disorder, what everyone used to call manic depression, but very few doctors knew how to diagnose. Before she got help, her depression-induced low self-esteem had ranged on some days from mildly blue to who-gives-a-hoot, and on others from absolute despair to suicidal. It was something of a miracle that she survived long enough into adulthood to be diagnosed. Then, over a course of several years, a strict regimen of medications and therapy pulled her through. That and her own determination to live despite the pain.

There were still days when she felt blue, still days when her world went black, but they were few. She tried every so often to go without her meds, hoping that somehow her body had learned how to create the brain chemicals she needed, but that never worked. Still, she kept hoping that someday she could be med-free.

She set down the hairbrush and leaned against the squat bathroom cabinet, which, thanks to Madeleine and her paintbrush, was as red as the cardinals at the bird feeder. The last time Glaze had stopped taking her medications, that creep Jeff Winslow, her ex-boyfriend, moved right back into her life. When she finally left Philadelphia, the scumbag followed her to Martinsville, terrorized her and her sister, and finally, thank goodness, got himself arrested after he broke into Doc Nathan's office and trashed the place. "I wonder when he's getting out," she asked her reflection in the mirror.

"Not for a long time," the other Glaze answered back.

Satisfied, she fluffed her silver hair with her hands, firmly ignoring the small voice inside her that said, "His sentence wasn't that long." On her way outside, she lifted a jaunty pink cap from the hook behind the door, picked up her purse, and closed the door behind her without locking it.

"WHAT'S THE HAT FOR?" Dee asked. "You having a bad-hair day?"

"She never has a bad-hair day," Madeleine complained. She climbed into the back seat and curled her legs beneath her before she fastened her seat belt. "Not like me. I should wear a hat every day just to cover up my cowlicks."

"Your hair always looks fine, Maddy." Glaze plopped into the front and set her purse on the floor.

"So, why are you wearing it?" Dee persisted.

"Hair?"

"You're nuts. Why are you wearing the cap?"

"Do I have to have a reason? I walked past the door and it caught my eye. That's all."

Dee edged her dark blue sedan away from the curb, but threw on the brakes when Sadie Russell steered her yellow Chevy past at a crawl. "What's she doing on Upper Sweetgum?" Glaze asked. "She never drives this street. It's too narrow and the corners are too sharp."

Dee looked askance at Glaze. "I'd say 'never' is an exaggeration, since she's driving it now."

"Maybe she had to go all the way around the block because she missed her parking place," Maddy suggested as Dee pulled out behind Sadie. She looked at her watch. "We have plenty of time to get to Russell Gap. You could have downed an extra cup of coffee, Dee."

"Wish I had."

Glaze kept her eye on Sadie's car as it wove from one side of the street to the other. Thank goodness most of the cars were already gone for the day. Sadie avoided a mailbox, skimmed just outside a gaudy splash of nasturtiums that spewed onto the pavement from their curbside flower bed, and narrowly missed somebody's rear bumper. Glaze and her friends watched in disbelief as Sadie shot across the T-bone intersection at the bottom of Upper Sweetgum Street. Her solid old Chevy hopped the curb, plowed down several dark green azalea bushes, and rolled into the funeral-home lot. It slowed and stopped a foot or so short of the white column that held up Marvin Axelrod's portico. A dozen feet more and she would have hit the side of the hearse that Marvin had left standing open, ready to receive who-knew-what or whom.

Dee swung right onto Third, then left into Marvin's parking lot, and sped toward Sadie's car. She slammed on her brakes; Glaze and Madeleine piled out and ran to see about Sadie. Dee was close behind them. Glaze got there first, hauled open Sadie's door, and screamed. Madeleine took one quick look. "I'll call an ambulance," she said and ran into the funeral home.

Glaze had never seen so much blood, not even that time when Jeff beat her up so badly he'd broken her nose and two of her front teeth. Sadie sat there with her head forward against the steering wheel, one hand clamped over her face. Blood dripped steadily around her fingers and onto the lap of her yellow skirt. Glaze turned to Dee. "I don't know how to handle this," she said. "Do you?"

Dee pushed her aside and laid a hand on Sadie's shoulder. "We're getting help for you, dear," she said. Glaze thought Sadie nodded, but she couldn't be sure.

Marvin scuttled out of the funeral home. "I'm coming, Sadie! I'm coming!" He careened around the front of the Chevy, skidded to a halt, took one look at Sadie, and fainted, toppling into Glaze on his way down. She collapsed with the undertaker draped across her lap. Dee swore softly; Madeleine stopped dead. Sadie lifted her head from the steering wheel.

"You'd think an undertaker would know what blood looks like," she whispered into the silence.

"You're alive!" Madeleine gasped.

"Well, of course I'm alive," Sadie snorted. "Didn't you ever see a nosebleed before?"

"We called an ambulance for a nosebleed?" Dee asked in the general direction of the open hearse.

"We might need it anyway," Glaze said. "Marvin looks pretty gray, and I can't feel a pulse. Anybody know CPR?"

Dee rolled him off Glaze's lap, checked his airway, ripped open his white shirt. Buttons flew every which way. She laid her ear against his chest.

"Is he okay?"

"Can you hear anything?"

"What should I do to help?"

"You could shut up so I can listen better." Dee's fingers felt along the side of Marvin's neck; she listened once more. "Call them back. Tell them we have a probable heart attack." Madeleine took off running again. Dee listened again and swore loudly this time. She bent over him and forced two breaths into his mouth, then started pressing rhythmically on his sternum. Twenty compressions, two quick breaths. Twenty compressions, two breaths.

Glaze had never known time to pass so slowly. The ambulance, staffed by people from the fire department, was only three blocks away, but there was no telling how long it would take them to get to Marvin's parking lot.

Dee kept pumping and blowing, paying no attention to Glaze dithering away beside her. When Glaze saw the white vehicle pelting up Third Street, she waved her arms in the air to direct them into the parking lot.

One of the attendants wrapped a blood-pressure cuff around Marvin's arm. Glaze had seen him in the deli once or twice, laughing with friends. He had a nice laugh. How, she wondered, did you keep laughing when you dealt with fires and car wrecks? Or a heart attack? He moved in to take over the chest compressions while the other person fitted an oxygen mask onto Marvin's face and asked Dee how much time had elapsed since Marvin collapsed. The driver, a barrel-shaped woman with her uniform sleeves pushed up above her elbows, pulled out a narrow bed on wheels. It took several precious seconds to lift Marvin onto the gurney and into the ambulance.

"Ohmigosh," Glaze said. "We forgot about Sadie." She shouldn't have worried. Madeleine held Sadie's nose in an expert pinch. With her free hand she wiped at the blood that painted Sadie's cheeks and pooled in the deeper wrinkles around her mouth.

Madeleine nodded toward the funeral home. "Go grab some wet paper towels."

"Just don't get a winding sheet," Sadie said. "I'm not ready to croak yet."

Dear Margaret,

How sweet of you. I talked this cruise idea over with Ralph, who wasn't that keen about it, but when I asked if I could have it as a birthday present, he said yes. Funny how I can talk him into birthday presents all year long!

Then I talked to Sadie. I didn't want to

leave her alone, what with Wallace the way
he is, but she said to go on and eat lots of
chocolate cake for her as well as for me. So I
guess my answer is yes.

Hooray!

Love you,
Ida

"Good morning, KorsaCat," I said to Nathan
Young's office kitty, a white-and-gray feline who
filled the job of official greeter, comforter, foot
checker, and chair warmer. Marmalade walked
in behind me and stationed herself on the corner
of the green rug in front of the fan that purred
gently in the corner.

Good morning, GrayGuy. Good morning, Helper.

"Doc's not in yet...."

I call him GoodHands.

"He's doing his hospital rounds up to Garner
Creek." Polly Lattimore, Nathan's nurse, office
manager, receptionist, and comforter herself, shuffled some papers. She looked down at Marmalade,
who purred in a rhythmic rumble. "You didn't
have an appointment, did you?"

"No. Neither one of us did." I laughed and offered her a bundle wrapped in a tea towel. "I came
by to bring you some fresh bread. Made it this
morning."

"Oooh, it's still warm!"

It's impossible to make just one loaf of bread. Sometimes I felt as if I was feeding the whole town of Martinsville two or three loaves at a time. "It's the dill bread you like so much. I brought some for Nathan, too. How long will he be?"

"He should be back soon." Polly buried her nose in the tea towel. "This smell always reminds me of my aunt Betty's kitchen."

"My grandma and my mom both made bread. I think I absorbed the skill as I grew up and never forgot it." I took a deep breath. Doc's office, a homey-enough place to begin with, felt even more welcoming now as the rich smell of yeast blended with the soft background music.

Polly quit her inhaling. "Did you hear? Marvin Axelrod suffered a heart attack this morning."

"Marvin? He's too young for that. Is he okay? Will he be all right?"

"Looks like it. Dee was there when it happened and started CPR right away. Thank goodness she moved here. She probably saved his life."

The open door behind me swung wider and I moved out of the way.

"Saved whose life?"

"Hey, Margaret," Polly said. "How you doing?" Naturally, she didn't wait for an answer. "Dee Sheffield saved Marvin. He had a heart attack."

"What did she do?"

"CPR, right in the funeral-home parking lot until the ambulance could get there."

"Goodness," Margaret said. "I'm glad I wasn't there. I wouldn't have known what to do." She smiled down at KorsaCat, who sat down, oblivious to the conversation, leaning against Margaret's sturdy shoes. "Sure does smell good in here."

"Biscuit brought me some bread."

"I hope it's my turn soon," she hinted rather obviously.

I did a quick calculation. "Next week," I said. "I promised some to Sadie. But you know me. I always make three or four loaves at a time."

Margaret grinned and went back to the exciting news. "So Dee saved Marvin's life. I wonder what she was doing at the funeral home. What about you, Biscuit? Do you know how to do that CPR stuff?"

I nodded, but then thought better of it and shook my head.

What is a seepiyar?

Marmalade let out a squawk, almost as if she were answering the question. We all laughed. "I took a Red Cross course," I said, "but that was ten or fifteen years ago. I doubt I could remember any of it."

"How did you hear about it, Polly? Did Clara call you?" Clara Martin, married to the chair of the town council, was the self-appointed town crier.

She spread every bit of news, often with her own unique interpretation of it, and prided herself on always being the first to know anything of import. Thank goodness Margaret left her off the cruise invitations.

"Nope. She missed it. Nathan called me a few minutes ago from the hospital. He said Marvin was stabilized."

"Did he go up with the ambulance?" Margaret asked.

"No. He was already there checking on Wallace when they brought Marvin in." She paused. "You know it won't be much longer for him. For Wallace, that is. Nathan said he wants to come home to die, so they're arranging for hospice help."

"Good," I said. "Those hospice people are wonderful."

Margaret shuffled over and plopped herself into one of the green plaid armchairs, followed closely by KorsaCat. "Poor Sadie," she said. "They've been married such a long time."

I thought for a moment and sat down myself. This bum knee of mine. "Sixty years, I think."

"Hmm. You're right. I wonder how she'll get along without him to take care of?" We were silent for a few seconds, each of us reviewing what we knew of Sadie and Wallace. I, for one, wondered about mortality in general. We always assume we'll have at least seventy or eighty years, but here I was at fifty— with well more than half my life gone. Good grief! What had I accomplished that was worth much?

I love you, Widelap. You take good care of me.

Fortunately, Margaret interrupted my thoughts. "I need to make an appointment, Polly."

"What for? You ailing?"

"It's these feet of mine. I need to get a new prescription for those pain pills."

"If your feet are hurting so much, Margaret," I said, "why did you come over here? Why not just call?"

"I couldn't," she said. "The phone line snapped last night when a big branch fell across it. Guess we're low on the totem pole for getting service."

If the phone people realized she had enough money to buy the whole company, they would have fixed her up a lot sooner, I thought. Of course, Margaret may have inherited a fortune, but you'd never know it to look at her or talk to her. Just a regular person. Come to think of it, she'd probably saved Marvin's life as much as Dee had. We had a fire in town last year and the volunteers couldn't get there fast enough, so Margaret went into action and funded a full-time fire department. She threw in an ambulance while she was at it.

"Did you walk over?" Polly asked.

"Not a chance. Sam's tinkering with the Duesenberg again, so I drove his car. I wasn't about to walk." Margaret shifted one foot out from under KorsaCat and rotated her ankle, examining it as if she'd never seen it before. "Not with these feet and this warm weather." She'd been having trouble with her feet for several years, and it seemed to be getting worse. "About those pain pills," she started, but Polly cut her off.

"Now, Margaret, are you telling me that you ignored what Doc told you to do?"

Margaret hemmed and hawed a bit. "He wants me to see that chi-ro-practor up in Garner Creek." She sounded as if he'd asked her to have all her toenails ripped out with pliers.

Ouch.

I was distracted by another loud meow from Marmalade. Was something wrong with her? She looked comfortable sitting there in front of the fan, with the hair on her back ruffling gently in the artificial breeze.

Polly, never one to pull her punches, wagged her finger at Margaret. "A chiropractor will do you a lot better than getting yourself hooked on those pain pills. If you'd get your back straightened out, your feet wouldn't hurt nearly so much."

Margaret clinched her jaw and shook her head. She looked like my grandpa's old mule. "I don't want my neck cracked. You never know what's going to happen. They could break my neck."

"Margaret." Polly shifted to her Patience Voice. "Doc Nathan goes a couple of times a month. He wouldn't recommend anything dangerous, and you know it."

"I've heard horror stories about those chiropractors." If I hadn't known Margaret was in her forties, I would have thought she was a paranoid old geezer, stuck to one idea and unwilling to consider alternatives.

Polly shook her finger at Margaret again. "Medical doctors used to bleed people to let out the bad humors. But they don't do that anymore. Chiropractic has come a long way in the last fifty years, and it's a darn sight safer than all those drugs people seem to want nowadays that just cover up the symptoms."

"Well, I saw an ad on TV..."

"Ha! Just what sort of medical value do you think those things have, for heaven's sake? They're written by ad agencies to talk you into asking your doctor for an expensive prescription!"

Polly might have gotten even more heated, but KorsaCat chose that moment to stand up and give a very loud meow. "Look there," Margaret said. "You're scaring KorsaCat."

"Sorry, Korsi." Polly reached behind her to turn up the classical music playing in the background. Korsi, named for Nikolai Rimsky-Korsakov, settled down and resumed grooming his front paw. I could have sworn he was licking in time to the Flight of the Bumblebee, as music filled the awkward silence.

"Well," Margaret conceded, "maybe I could give that guy a call."

"I'll go with you to your first appointment if you want me to," I volunteered. "I'd like to check out the place myself."

"Good," Polly said. "While you're there with Margaret, ask him to look at your knee."

Dear Margaret,
    Yes—yes—yes. The sea, the sand, the food—I can't wait. Thank you for including me.

    Love,
    Maddy

My Gratitude List for Wednesday:
1. Polly.
2. Margaret.
3. My healthy feet.
4. My healthy heart.
5. Marmy, who is pl   ite
    with it! Whoops!   aying with this pen as
    I try to wr

I am grateful for
toys
leftover chicken
GrayGuy who watches over GoodHands'
house
humans who pet me nicely
fans

WEEK ONE

THURSDAY

Dear Margaret,

Two trips in less than a month? Whatever am I thinking of to say yes? But of course, I have to say yes. Think of all the people on that boat who might need a Realtor. Did you know I'm specializing in nationwide relocation deals now? I even have an international deal in the making, but it's hush-hush, so don't say a word.

I don't want to make a business trip of this, like the convention I'm going to in a couple of weeks, but if I just happen to take my cards with me, there's no telling what will come along, right?

Count me in.

Love you bunches,
Ellen

THE STURDY YOUNG WOMAN standing in front of me in the grocery line had to be the "new woman" Ida mentioned at the tap class, the one staying at Alicia's bed-and-breakfast. The Rooster and Biscuit. I liked that name. It was cute, but it made me think of waking up way too early, perhaps because my neighbor Maggie Pontiac's rooster, Doodle-Doo, was particularly vocal at sunrise. As roosters were inclined to be. Maybe this "new" woman was an early riser, though. That hair of hers was truly magnificent. There was one person in line ahead of us. I didn't recognize her. She might have been someone from that new development just north of town. She definitely didn't have a library card. Must have had kids, because her cart was loaded. I should have brought some of those flyers that told about the children's story hour. The long-haired woman took a step forward and the kiddies went out of my mind. I watched in fascination as her hair rippled like a lustrous black waterfall, all the way down to her knees. I couldn't help wondering if anyone with magnificent hair like that was ever approached with anything but awe. Of course, Annie's Irish-setter-red hair was just as long. Even when she braided it, it hung well below her waist, which was still long enough to impress anyone, but I'd long ago stopped identifying Annie by her hair. She was just Annie. Sweet, irrepressible, slightly mischievous Annie. Of course, the first time I met Annie, I'd been fascinated by the sheer volume of her hair.

The black hair ahead of me shifted slightly, and I wanted to touch it, to run my fingers from the top of her head down the three-foot length of silk. It had to feel as good as it looked. Nothing coarse could possibly look that smooth or reflect those blue-black highlights. I inched closer and just happened to brush my hand against it as I reached for the plastic divider to put between our purchases. It was cool, like the waterfall it resembled, like the clear water in the creek that flowed through my backyard.

She turned around and looked at me.

"I'm sorry," I said. "You're probably tired of people like me, but your hair is so striking, I couldn't resist." I wilted a bit in the face of her blank stare.

"If it weren't for my hair"—scorn fairly dripped from her voice—"you never would have noticed me."

I looked at her. Nothing particularly definitive there besides the hair. She wasn't old enough to have grown much character in her face. There were no lines or hollows or sags that spoke of years of laughter. Or tears. Still, she would have looked pleasant if she hadn't been glaring so hard.

"I do notice people." I don't know why I chose to defend myself. Maybe it was guilt over having taken what I admitted to myself was an impertinent liberty. "I'm the librarian in town, and I know that you don't have a library card. Neither does the lady standing in front of you."

That woman looked up from stuffing her change into her wallet. She opened her mouth, glanced at the black hair, and shut it again. There was a whole happy conversation in the look she gave me. I knew I'd see her in the library soon, getting her card.

Black Hair wasn't aware of the exchange. She wasn't through with me yet. "If I'd been particularly heavy-chested, would you have wanted to touch that part of me?"

"That's sheer nonsense," I said. "Hair is different. Hair isn't…isn't so…so intimate."

"It is to me. It's my hair, and I have a right to some privacy. I get tired of being identified as nothing but the woman with the hair. I'd like someone to see me for who I am."

"Why don't you cut it off, then?" The words were out before I could swallow them. I was usually a diplomatic person, but her snippy tone pushed a button I didn't even know I had.

She stared at me long enough for me to sense the hush that fell around us. Why did today have to be a busy grocery-shopping day? Everyone within earshot was listening. Ida wasn't even pretending to be discreet. My new library card hadn't moved a step. Perhaps my voice had been a bit loud. I'd been as rude as she was—maybe even a tad more. I backed up a step. She was strongly built.

"I swore when I was a child that I would never cut my hair until I found my father and made him apologize."

"Apologize? For what?" Good grief, Biscuit. I shook a mental finger at myself. That is no business of yours. I didn't listen. "What did he do?"

She blinked—hard—and straightened her shoulders. "He left us before I was born."

Before I could think of a thing to say—and what could I have said?—she moved forward and nodded to Ida. Ida met my eyes briefly before she picked up Black Hair's plastic-wrapped sandwich and waved it through the scanner.

Dear Margaret,

I wouldn't miss this for the world. Can't wait. Do we have to dress up for dinner, though? I don't have a lot of fancy duds. Let me know so I can plan ahead.

—Dee

BOB AND I WERE BOTH fairly self-sufficient. After all, he'd been divorced many years ago, and I'd been widowed for five years before we met. It wasn't as if we couldn't make do without each other. But having him as my husband for a year now, well, it just felt good knowing I'd wake up next to him. Unfortunately, he was planning to be in Atlanta for two whole weeks at a police training, sponsored by one of the big gun manufacturers. Not a comforting thought. It was a special one-week course designed for small-town cops. Of course, except for five or six cities, most of the state was small towns. Then more arms training for another week.

Softfoot has two arms.

"You won't have a chance to miss me that much," he said when I complained. "It'll just be during the week." He finished his coffee and set the mug out of his way on the windowsill. "They don't hold classes on the weekend, so I'll be home Saturday and Sunday."

We'd eaten dinner at the small round table that snuggled into the bay window on the north side of the house. Dusk fell early in Martinsville because of the tall cliffs that surrounded the town to the west and south. I was so seldom aware of that moment when the world shifted from day to evening, but I looked outside at the sunset-orange clouds above the forest that filled the block behind our backyard. Almost the next moment, the clouds grayed, and the light in the kitchen dimmed. I could hardly see Bob, much less the big calendar that hung on the far wall, until I stood and switched on the small yellow lamp on the counter. "The circus will be in the valley that weekend at the county fair-grounds. Do you want to go?"

"I think I'll pass on that." Bob carried his plate and mine to the sink.

What is a sirkuss?

I loved the thought of a circus. I hadn't been to one in years. Of course, they didn't come here very often. The ones that did come were awfully small. Not even any elephants. Guess we were too far off the beaten path. Keagan County, which consisted of the six towns along the Metoochie River Valley, was so small that most of the rest of Georgia didn't even know we existed. Martinsville was the southernmost town, bordered on the east by the river, with the cave-riddled hillside beyond it and towering cliffs on the south and west. A narrow mile-long gorge funneled the river away at the south end of the town. Huge boulders at the opening prevented any sort of boat traffic on the Metoochie.

Bob ran water over our plates. "I've worked too many county fairs to enjoy a circus much. I'd spend the whole time looking for pickpockets. Why don't you go with Glaze? You can do that after you take your walk."

Glaze and I usually took a long walk around

town every Saturday morning before I had to open the library. But our Saturday afternoons were for Bob and me, just the two of us. "Don't you want us to do something together on Saturday? The Petunias are going to run the library, so I don't have to go in."

He shook his head. "I'll drive back up after class on Friday. Be home pretty late, so I'll probably want to snooze in. You go ahead to the circus with your sister. I'll get up real slow and go tie some flies after breakfast. Maybe we'll go out to dinner Saturday night."

I thought about the popcorn and the cotton candy. No, I'd avoid that stuff. But then there were the pretzels and the fried dough and the hot sausage sandwiches. And the ice-cream cones. "Uh-uh. I don't think I'm going to want to ever eat again by the time I get home."

"Do you intend to stuff yourself, Woman?" He wrapped his arms around my shoulders and pulled me back against his chest. Then he did some delicious little maneuvers that involved his face and the back of my neck. And I promptly forgot to call Glaze to ask her about going with me to the circus.

Dear Margaret,
    I've never been so depressed over something. Well, I have been (you know my story).

I'd truly love to go on the cruise with all of you. That stupid job of mine is in the way, though. I just can't get the time off that week. You wouldn't happen to know of another job available, would you?

Sadly,
Glaze

FRIDAY

Dear Margaret,

Joy's expecting her first. It will probably be twins, of course. She's due around about cruise time, and I need to be here with her just in case. Then I'll be up to my eyeballs for a while with the new kids. Wish I could take you up on your generous offer, but I'll have to pass this time.

The blackberries are ripe and luscious. Send Sam over, and I'll load him up with enough for you two and your mom also.

Maggie

"SO THAT'S THE DEAL, SEE?" Gordon Harvey leaned closer to the heavy mesh that separated the prisoners from their visitors. His sister was frowning, rubbing her hand back and forth along the cold steel counter between them. "It's easy. Really. You nab her, take her to the cabin, and hold her there. Lock her in the back bedroom."

"That's Willie's room."

"So move him out of it. And you nail some of that plywood we got up on the windows so she cain't climb out."

Wilena rolled her sleeves down. She glared at her brother through the wire mesh. "I don't want to hurt anybody."

"You don't hafta hurt her. Just be sure she don't get away. Then you send a note to her big sister, the library lady. Here's the address. They hang out together a lot."

She glanced around. Two guards were still over by the back wall and one by the door to the visitor's room. "How am I gonna know who to take?"

"It's easy. She's got hair that stands out a mile. He said she's the only one in town with hair like that."

"Does she have kids?"

"'Course not. She ain't married."

Wilena raised an eyebrow at her brother. "Neither am I."

"You know what I mean."

"Did he say what her name is?"

"Gale or something like that. Just look for somebody with the library lady. Somebody with hair."

"Hair?"

"Yeah. Stand-out hair."

"What's her last name?"

"How would I know?"

"Gordon." She gave him that sister look he hated. The one that said she thought he was dumb but wasn't going to rub his nose in it. The look was just as bad as saying something, though. "What am I supposed to do with Willie while all this is going on?"

"He won't notice anything," Gordon said. "He's just a dumb kid."

"He is not. He already knows his ABCs."

He balled his fingers into a fist. "Tell him a story or something. Dump him with a babysitter." It wasn't exactly a snarl, but close to it.

"You know I've got nobody I can leave him with except for day care when I'm at work. There's nobody lives close except our crazy landlady on the other side of the ridge. She's always got a shotgun with her every time I've seen her outside."

He leaned closer to the wire mesh that separated them. "Don't you screw this up, Wilena. This is worth a lot, and you're gonna make it happen."

"Yeah? What'll I get out of it? Just for me? So far all you've talked about is you."

"We're splitting everything."

"This better work. I don't show up for my job, I'm gonna lose it."

"Don't you worry about that crap job anymore. You and me get the most of the money 'cause we're doing most of the work." He lowered his voice even more. "You still got my gun?"

"I'm not using a gun for this."

"You still got it, though?"

She nodded. "It's hidden on the top shelf of the kitchen cabinet. I don't want Willie to find it."

"You worry about that kid too much."

She looked at him long and hard before she stood up to leave.

My dear daughter,

I've already told you yes, but I thought I would be terribly proper and send you this note. In fact, I already spoke with Rebecca Jo and Esther. We'd like to room together on the boat, so count all of us in. I'm assuming there will be a room big enough for all three of us to fit in. Who are you rooming with?

Have I told you lately how proud I am of you? I think what you're doing for Tom is just wonderful. Don't worry. I'll keep it a secret, just as you asked.

Love,
Mom

FRIDAY EVENING AT CT's Restaurant was a habit for Bob and me. Occasionally I wondered if Bob got just a wee bit tired of the soups and breads

I always served. Putting together what Melissa called a "real meal" was never a strong point for me. Soup and bread were my culinary accomplishments, and thank you very much, that was quite enough as far as I was concerned. Put soup and bread together, and there's a full meal. With chocolate for dessert, of course. I did enjoy eating other things, though, as long as somebody else cooked them. Especially if that someone was Tom Parker. Tom had been Bob's best friend since childhood. He'd made a name for himself in New York, finally sold his fancy restaurant there, and made over his family's old house on the corner of Third Street and Magnolia into a restaurant for gourmet delights. I could always count on exquisite food served beautifully. Yum.

"Hey there, Bob. Hey, Biscuit. How's it going?" Sam Casperson motioned us over. "Sit with us while we're waiting. There's quite a line tonight."

Margaret patted the cushion beside her. "We'll let the men have those chairs. This is more comfortable."

I disagreed, but good manners kept me from mentioning that most couches were way too deep from front to back. Without two hefty pillows behind me, I had to practically lie down to put my back up against something. Lacking pillows, I perched sideways on the edge and leaned against the armrest. "How's the cruise crowd shaping up? Have you gotten a lot of answers?"

"A few. We're keeping Celia busy, that's for sure. The first three notes I got said no, but now I'm getting some good answers." She held up her fingers one at a time. "You, Ida, Madeleine, Ellen, and Dee, and your three library ladies. That's eight."

"I'm sure you'll hear from more people soon." I looked around at the unusually large number of people waiting for dinner. "I wonder why it's so busy tonight."

Sam pointed a finger at me. "You mean you haven't heard?"

"Heard what?" I looked at Bob, but he shrugged.

"Tom's added a new menu item. He was advertising it in the *Record* this week. All the spaghetti you can eat."

"Spaghetti? Here? At CT's?" Chef Tom's was the most upscale restaurant in the Metoochie Valley. It was Tom's baby. I couldn't imagine something as mundane as spaghetti on the menu.

Bob leaned forward. "You sure you read it right, Sam? That doesn't sound like the sort of thing Tom would serve."

Margaret spoke up from the depths of the couch. "He's been saying things were going to change around here."

"But CT's has always been so"—I hated to use

the word *snooty*—"highfalutin. Spaghetti seems a bit plebeian for his taste. What's gotten into Tom?"

"Maybe he's getting tired of serving the same old boring stuff month after month."

Margaret nodded. "To the same old boring people, too."

"Boring?" I tried not to roll my eyes, but couldn't help it. Eggplant and curries and imported cheeses and gourmet sauces were hardly what I'd call boring. And now spaghetti? All you can eat?

"Well, not boring exactly." Sam looked around at all the new faces filling the lounge. "Maybe he thought his fancy menus scared some people away."

I looked at a large group gathered nearby. "Yes. I see what you mean." More metal studs and rings on ears and eyebrows than I could count. Who on earth would want to stick themselves like a pincushion? Their IQs probably matched their ages, somewhere between twenty-five and thirty. At least they were well behaved, though.

Doreen picked up a stack of menus and motioned the group to follow her. As they walked by I heard snatches of their conversations. "…cellist played magnificently…" "…market's heading for a down trend if you ask…" "…don't care if it's the latest, I don't…" So much for my IQ estimate. I was truly going to have to stop making snap judgments based on the amount of body piercing.

Bob raised one of his un-pierced eyebrows at me. "The spaghetti sounds like a good business decision. I just hope all these new customers don't make us have to wait too long to get served. I'm starving."

As WE LEFT AFTER a satisfying dinner—no, I did not eat the spaghetti, but Bob did—Tom pulled us aside and handed me a small paper bag. "A little leftover salmon for the furball. What did you think of the spaghetti?"

Bob saved me. "Good idea, Tom. Looks like it's going to pull in plenty of new customers for you."

"That's the plan. I hope they'll eventually try things other than spaghetti."

"Give it time," Bob said. "It'll work out."

Tom looked over at me. I tried to lower my eyebrow in time, but I think he spotted it. "Good family-style cooking has a lot going for it, Biscuit," he said.

"So does your coq au vin."

Dear Margaret,

Well, doesn't this just beat all. How'd you know I've been wanting to go on a cruise? Carl doesn't think much of boats, so I know I'll have a much better time with you than I would with him, even if I could talk him into it, which I know I couldn't.

Thank you, thank you, thank you. You're a gem. Yep. You're a gem.

Sharon

P.S. Do you want a new hairdo before we leave? Let me know.

My Gratitude List for Friday
1. Willingness to learn. Please don't ever let me get stodgy and stuck in my ways.
2. Marmalade. She was cute playing with her feather toy when we got home from CT's.
3. Bob. He's so sweet to make fun toys for Marmy.
4. Sam and Margaret. It's good to have friends.
5. CT's—the spaghetti did look good. Maybe I'll try it next time.

I am grateful for
the feather toy
this warm bed
bug sounds from the outside
treats from Fishgiver
Widelap and Softfoot

WEEK ONE

SATURDAY

Dear Margaret,

Well, now, aren't you just a dear to invite all of us on a cruise. I'll get my column written up ahead of time. I haven't missed a deadline in over fifty years, and I'm not about to start now.

Maybe I'll find something exciting on the cruise to write about. I like the idea of journalism at sea.

Thank you for including me.

Myrtle

I POKED MY HEAD around the kitchen doorway and motioned at Glaze with my head. "Come on in."

"Ready to go before it gets too hot out there?"

"Not quite." I looked her over. "You put on lipstick for a walk around town?"

Glaze grinned. The bright red contrasted nicely

with her white teeth. I knew the front two were caps from the time Jeff Winslow, that old boyfriend of hers, punched her in the mouth and broke two of her teeth, but they didn't look fake. Just pearly, like all the rest of her teeth. Mine were sort of an off-white, though. I couldn't wear white shirts without my teeth looking dirty.

"It's called Wildfire," she said. "Do you like it?"

"On you, yes. On me, probably not. I'd look like I'd just eaten a fresh carcass."

"Baloney! You ought to try it sometime."

"Not a chance. Come in the kitchen. I still have to find my other shoe."

"Where'd you put it?"

"If I knew that, I'd have it on my foot already."

"Good morning, Marmy." Glaze bent down and stroked between Marmalade's ears.

Good morning, Smellsweet.

"You look quite elegant on that blue towel."

Thank you.

She looked up at me. "You're giving her your bath towels to lie on now?"

"Not really. That one has a big stain on it. Verity snuck the food coloring into the bathroom when she spent the night here last week." I moved to the left of the sink and checked in the alcove below the window that overlooked the back of the wraparound porch. Still no shoe.

"Oh, dear. Food coloring?" Glaze pulled me back to the conversation.

"Yes, and she did it right under my nose. I'm going to have to be more alert where that child is concerned."

"Not another one of her 'experibents.'"

"I'm afraid so. She thought purple bathwater would be fun."

Glaze nodded like a palm tree bending in the wind. "And of course her Grannie taught her that red and blue mixed together…"

"Yeah, but I forgot to mention that there was value in putting the caps back on tightly."

"Your fault, then, wouldn't you say?" She gave one more pat and straightened up. "At least Marmy got a new bed out of it."

A nice bed.

"Well, it started out in her basket over there, but I guess she wanted it closer to the window."

"She pulled it over here herself? I'd expect that of a dog, but not a cat."

Excuse me?

I looked out on the back porch, thinking I might have left my shoes out there. But the one I was wearing had been on the mat inside the back door this morning. I could have sworn that was where I'd left them both. I opened the pantry and looked around. This was ridiculous. If we didn't leave soon, I'd never make it to work on time. Luckily,

Esther and Rebecca Jo both had keys, and they probably never lost their shoes.

"Still no shoe? Why don't you ask Marmy? I bet she knows where it is."

"That would make sense if I thought she could answer me."

"Of course she can. I bet she understands every word you say to her."

I had to admit, I did think Marmy was a remarkable cat, but understanding English? Come now.

"Dare you. She probably even knows what you're thinking."

I took a deep breath and caught a faint whiff of my sister's vanilla perfume.

Smellsweet is right.

"Okay," I said. "Marmalade, do you know where my shoe is?"

"Your missing shoe," Glaze added helpfully.

Yes.

"See, this is getting us nowhere. All she does is purr."

"Well, maybe you should ask her to show you where it is."

This was fun, but faintly ridiculous, like a Ouija board at a seventh-grade slumber party. "Marmy, would you show me where my missing shoe is?"

She stood up, turned around once. Looked at me. Purred up at Glaze. When we didn't do anything, she pawed at the bunched-up towel. My shoe was underneath it.

"See?" Glaze said. "I told you so." She scooped up Marmy and crowed a bit while I slipped into my shoe.

"She was just keeping it warm for me."

WHEN I STEPPED ONTO the front porch, a stray breeze whiffled my hair and blessed my nose with the sweet scent of the *Viburnum carlesii*. No wonder they called it a Korean spicebush. Sweet and tangy at the same time. Instead of using the stairs, I chose to wind my way down the wheelchair ramp Bob built last November for his sister's occasional visits. Glaze chose the steps, but waited for me. "Which way?" I asked at the end of the front walk. Marmalade had elected to stay behind. The fresh chicken I'd put in her bowl may have had something to do with her decision.

"Uphill," Glaze decided. We both turned right. Made sense. Last week we'd headed downhill. Wouldn't want to get into a rut. "Twenty questions," she said, starting one of our favorite games, one we'd played a lot as children. Now that we'd reconnected as adults, the game still felt fresh and fun.

"Would it fit in a breadbox?" I asked.

"Um…yes."

"You're not sure?"

"Is that one of your questions?"

"No." I looked around at all the things it might possibly be. The list was endless. "So it's smaller than a breadbox. Is it outside my house?"

She looked down at her feet before she answered. "No."

"Good. That narrows it down a bit. Is it in my kitchen?"

"I don't know."

"What do you mean, you don't know?"

"Is that another one of your questions?"

I scowled at her. "No. Okay, is it in my bedroom?"

"I don't know."

"What on earth is going on? You'd have to know, if you know it's in my house. How can you not know where it is?"

"Is that your next question? If so, you're disqualified, because I can't answer it with a yes or a no."

"You're nuts."

"You've only asked three questions. Seventeen to go. Or do you give up?"

We walked half a block while I thought about it. The chickens in Maggie's backyard cackled in the background as we walked past. "You smarty-britches!" I finally said.

She laughed. "You figured it out?"

"Is it alive?"

"Yes."

"Is it Marmalade?"

"You win."

SHE ASKED NINE QUESTIONS before she guessed the mailbox. I couldn't get the ducks that live in that Memphis hotel, even though I snuck in two extra questions. Then I stumped her with her own hair. It was a draw. "So," she asked me, "did you ever patch things up with Sally?"

"Sally?" My younger daughter's opinionated face with its square jaw came to my mind. "How can I patch things up with her when she won't even talk to me?"

"Have you called her?"

I took a few more steps. "Not lately."

"Have you offered to babysit?"

"Are you kidding? Jason's mother has a hold on that baby that would gag a maggot."

Glaze took a few more steps. "You're not being rational, sis. Whatever on earth does that mean?"

"What it means is that Sally's decided she doesn't like her own mother and nothing I do or say is likely to change that."

"Slow down. We're not in a footrace here."

I moderated my stride. "She is the most unreasonable, demanding, self-centered, narrow-minded…" I couldn't think of any more adjectives.

Glaze kept looking straight ahead. "You two need counseling."

"How would you know?"

"I've been through it, remember?"

"Yeah, but that was something else altogether." She pursed her wildfire-red lips. "Pain is pain."

"I'm not in pain, thank you very much."

"Horse feathers! Your own daughter won't talk to you. You're too ticked off to call her or write her or drop by for a visit. Why don't you offer to help her with the flower beds? She can't be keeping up with the yard, what with a brand-new baby."

"What would you know about that?" As soon as I said it, I could have kicked myself. Glaze was in her mid-forties. Never been married. Starting early menopause if her hot flashes were any indication. Now here I was lording my mommy status over her. Not that I'd done a great job as a mother myself, come to think of it.

She took a slow breath. In through her nose, out through her mouth. It was a breathing technique I'd taught her, for criminy sakes. "Like I said, you need counseling."

We kept walking because that was what we'd gotten used to on Saturday mornings. Bob was off doing his guy stuff—getting a haircut, tying flies in the little workshop behind his old house, stopping by CT's to razz Tom about whatever men talked about. Eventually we circled across Fifth Street and turned down Willow toward the river. I'd always wondered why the street names in this town sounded so distinctly non-Southern. Of course, nobody really knew where Homer Martin, the founder of Martinsville, came from originally. Or so Bob, my favorite local historian, always said.

I knew I was going off on a tangent so I could forget about what Glaze had just told me. She wouldn't let me bypass the issue, though. "So…" She sounded tentative. Good thing, since she'd ticked me off royally. "So, don't you think your relationship with your daughter is worth salvaging?"

"Good grief, Glaze, what is there to salvage? I always thought we had a good relationship, and now I find out it's all been pretending on her part and sheer ignorance on mine. She's always been prickly. All her life. But it never occurred to me that she hated me. How do you go about healing something like that?"

Half a block later, she answered me. "It's like this walk we're taking. One step at a time." Another half block. "Why don't you talk to Auntie Blue about it?"

Margaret,
   How long do I have before I absolutely have to let you know for sure? Right now I don't have any B&B guests lined up for that week, but I'd hate to miss out if someone wanted to make a reservation. I depend on the repeat

guests, you know. Also on word of mouth. If I turn people down too much, they'll give up on me and start going to Alicia's. Could you list me as a maybe/probably for a couple of weeks?

It sounds like such fun. If I do go, I want to room with Biscuit. Did she say anything yet?

Love you, special lady,
Melissa

My Gratitude List for Saturday
1. Glaze, even though she makes me face some hard stuff.
2. Bob, who cooked dinner this evening!
3. Marmy.
4. Living in a town that's small enough to walk around easily, even if we don't know where the street names come from.
5. Verity, despite the messes.

I am grateful for
Widelap
Smellsweet
Softfoot
Fishgiver
sunshine on my blue towel bed

SUNDAY

"THE TOWN WENT and told me to hire a deputy, and all of a sudden there's nothing for him to do." Bob ran his free hand, the one that wasn't scratching Marmalade's back...

That feels good.

...through his hair. The result was a husband who looked like a disheveled black-maned lion rather than his usual well-groomed panther guise. He was going to have to comb his pelt before we left for church. "No traffic accidents," he went on. "Not even on the road up to Braetonburg."

That is good. Accidents hurt.

"Isn't that a good thing?" That treacherous stretch of narrow road wound between overbearing cliffs on one side and a sheer drop to the Metoochie River on the other. Even with guardrails, it had claimed several lives in recent years. The blind driveways here and there didn't help any.

He nodded. "Doesn't leave me much to train

him on, though. No fights, nobody missing, nothing stolen or lost. Not even any bad weather." He paused, and I knew he was remembering that body trapped in the storm wreckage of the town dock last November. "Not that I'm wishing for any of this, mind you."

So LITTLE EVER HAPPENED in Martinsville that it sometimes seemed silly for the town founders to have put in the town charter that the town had to maintain "an officer of the peace and a town jail." The town jail was one room in the basement of the town hall. Of course, there had been a couple of murders recently, which was why the town council finally coughed up the money to pay a deputy. I wondered idly if Margaret was funding the position. Probably. Now, with Bob headed off for two weeks, it was comforting to know there would be a peace officer on hand, even if we didn't need him.

Marmalade slithered off Bob's lap—he'd stopped scratching her—and hopped into mine. "Reebok is so earnest," Bob said. "So ready to help, and so utterly proud of that badge your sister designed."

I helped her.

Bob, Martinsville's only town cop for the past twenty years or so, just as his father had been the only town cop for twenty years before that, had never worn a badge because there wasn't one. Last fall Glaze decided to change that. She found a book in my library and looked up the town motto, designed a badge, and arranged to have two of them tooled by one of the machinists at CelerInc.

We decided to give Reebok his badge at what we called our family Christmas party. Of course, our "family" stretched far beyond just the relatives. Bob's mom, who happened to be one of my three Petunias, was there, and her daughter Ilona. They'd driven up from Athens, where Ilona's husband worked for the University of Georgia. Bob's brother Barkley didn't show up, which was just as well. Bob's mother hadn't forgiven her younger son yet for cheating on Dee. Even before the divorce was over with, Dee left Atlanta and moved in with Rebecca Jo, who considered her a second daughter.

It was a lively group indeed. The women from the tap-dance class brightened up the gathering. So did Father John, the town priest, and his sister Madeleine. My parents, son, and older daughter came to the party, bringing my two grandkids with them. So did Auntie Blue and Uncle Mark. My younger daughter, Sally, and her husband, Jason, didn't show up. They had the new baby, of course, and didn't want to expose him to our germs. The germs at Jason's mother's holiday party were acceptable, apparently, but I wasn't going to dwell on that.

There were two things that made the party special. The first was the wheelchair ramp that Bob constructed for his sister. She was delighted with it and considered it her own personal Christmas present. In a way, I suppose it was. He'd spent most of November working on it, but I think he got more value out of it than she did. Sometimes hard physical labor was the best way for a cop to deal with some of the things he had to face. Anyway, she appreciated it.

Then there was the badge for Reebok. Glaze had made a gift card with a watercolor sketch of the town hall on the front. Marmalade's paw print graced the bottom corner of the card. We all laughed at that. "She walked through the paint," Glaze explained, "and I thought it looked cute." Marmy sat like a relaxed sphinx on Ilona's lap, with her front legs draped half over the arm of the wheelchair, accepting everyone's congratulations with aplomb.

Bob was duly appreciative of his own badge, but Reebok was ecstatic. Watching his round-eyed glee just about eclipsed the rest of the holiday celebrations. At some point in the evening he whipped out a handkerchief and polished off the fingerprints we'd thoughtlessly bestowed on the shiny metal.

Even without Sally and the new baby there, it still was a lovely party.

Bob slurped down the last of his coffee, and the noise brought me back to the present. He tilted his chair back onto its rear two legs. If I tried that, I'd end up flat on the floor. He didn't seem to have noticed my wool-gathering. "All he's had to do since I hired him is drink gallons of coffee, ride around town, and polish that silly badge." Bob sighed. "Something has to change."

"REBECCA JO," I SAID, before she'd even breathed a hello, "is there a chance you could open the library for me tomorrow?"

"My goodness, you're in a hurry." She waited, as if hoping I'd fill in the reason why. When I didn't say anything, she added, "Of course I can. I was planning to sit with Sadie and Wallace for a spell, but I suppose that can wait. He seems to be on hold."

She still didn't ask me what my problem was, but I could hear the question in her voice. "I need to run up to Auntie Blue's around ten. It may take me a couple of hours. As soon as I get back you can leave."

"Nonsense. You know I enjoy working there. Now that Dee has that job in Russell Gap, I get a bit lonely during the day, and the library fills the bill. Before she moved in, I never bothered much about being alone, but now I guess I've gotten used to the conversation."

Good grief. She was my head Petunia and my mother-in-law to boot, yet I almost never thought to call her or to drop by. I hoped my children never treated me like that once I got old. Of course, they seldom called me now unless they wanted something.

"…coming in every Monday. No need for you to be there all by yourself."

I'd tuned out, in that too-frequent habit of mine, but at least this time I could figure out where the conversation had gone. "You don't have to do that, Rebecca Jo. Monday is always a slow day."

"Good. Then I can get a lot more done upstairs." She paused. "Is Beulah doing all right?"

"Auntie Blue's fine," I said. I'm the one who's a mess, I thought, but I didn't say it out loud.

"What about you? Are you taking care of yourself?"

I briefly considered confiding in her, but didn't want to sound petty. She had a great relationship with her own daughter, Bob's sister. She might not understand my problems with Sally the way Auntie Blue would. My aunt Beulah knew Sally. "I'm doing fine, Rebecca," I said. Fine. That good old Georgia word that masked every ailment known to mankind. Womankind. "I'm just fine."

"That's good, dear. If you ever need to talk, you let me know."

She obviously didn't believe me.

WEEK TWO

MONDAY

I CLOSED THE REFRIGERATOR. I was out of eggs. I needed milk. Sandra was bringing the two girls over the next day. I'd be able to get by without eggs. No, I wouldn't. We were going to make cookies, a fun proposition with Verity, who was five. Her little sister, Angela, though, almost three, was bound and determined that she could do everything her big sister could do, including cracking eggs. Maybe cookies weren't such a good idea. Maybe we'd make butter instead. I'd been saving the cream, freezing it in small batches, and I was pretty sure there was enough for one small batch of butter. I still needed eggs, though. I looked at the clock. Plenty of time before I was due at Auntie Blue's house.

I picked up a little swirl of cat hair from under the edge of the cabinet and tossed it in the compost bucket, wondering idly if earthworms ate cat hair. It was natural, so why wouldn't they? I dialed

Maggie's number. "Sorry to call so early. Can I drop by for some eggs and milk? Angela will be here tomorrow, and her mom wants to get some milk, too. Would you have three quarts? One for me and two for Sandra?"

She sounded out of breath. "Sure, sure. Moonbeam and Noel are producing plenty. Come on through the house to the backyard. I'm just heading out to gather eggs. You can help if you want to."

"Are you laughing at me?"

"Heck, no. I know you're scared of the chickens." Even over the phone I picked up Maggie's frown. "I just keep hoping I'll be able to change your mind. My chickens really are sweet, you know."

"Uh-huh, so you say. Couldn't prove it by me. See you shortly."

I picked up a lightweight sweater and invited Marmy to accompany me, but she was curled up on her towel. "I'm off to Maggie's," I told her. "Come on up if you feel like it." That cat door we'd put in was so convenient.

No, thank you. I am comfortable for now.

It was a straight shot from Maggie's front door through her wonderful-smelling house to her back door. Easier to go that way than try to open the gate in the fence that surrounded her spacious backyard. No chickens around, at least not near the back door. I could see Moonbeam munching hay up near the squat brown enclosure. Nearby, Noel stood on top of a picnic table. The sun backlit both of them, and the little swirl of hair that stood up in the middle of Moonbeam's shoulders looked almost like a bright-winged fairy. Doodle-Doo perched on the fence, fluffing his tail feathers. He spread his ample wings and I was reminded of one of those Renaissance paintings of angels. Fergus, lounging in the dirt beside the small barn, the very picture of doggie contentment, scratched idly at an itchy spot on his furry white neck, his ears flopping like two sails as he did so. While I admired the scene, Joy pranced up beside her sister and leaned against her, nibbling at Moonbeam's neck. It had taken me a while to get used to the taste of their milk, but once I did, I wouldn't trade it for anything. Especially since it was so fresh, and I knew the goats it came from. Little Angela had so many allergies. I'd stopped buying cow's milk, except for buttermilk, which I wasn't about to give up, particularly in the summer. But for the most part, switching to goat's milk made my life easier whenever Angela and her sister came to visit, and I never had to worry about growth hormones or other ghastly additives.

"Come on over," Maggie hollered. Her square face radiated contentment. How anyone could be content in the middle of a flock of chickens was way beyond me. "You're safe," she added. "I locked up Almyra."

I looked at the chicken house on wheels that Maggie and Norm built for their brood so they could move it easily with their garden tractor. Chickens, she once told me, needed to be rotated to new pasture every few days. She considered it a crime the way most farms treated their chickens. Here the chickens, who tended, as chickens apparently do, to stay close to the hen house, followed it to a new spot every other day or so. They ate bugs, scratched up the dirt, consumed weed seeds, and fertilized behind themselves as they strutted around. Maggie planted her garden in stages as the hen house moved. It must have worked, because her vegetables were prolific, and she never used fertilizers or poisonous sprays. The chickens took care of the bugs and weeds.

I was all for ethical treatment of chickens. I just didn't want them pecking at me. Almyra, the largest and most opinionated of Maggie's brood, had her own ideas about who should be allowed in her empire. I knew this from personal experience, having been chased a number of times. There is nothing quite so ignominious as being run off by a foul-tempered fowl. She had a strange arrangement of black feathers on her head. It looked like a hood, so I privately called her Vampirah, but never admitted as much to Maggie, who had an insane devotion to every single member of her flock, the bloodthirsty ones as well as the less-demented few.

I eyed the hen house. "She can't pick the lock, can she?"

"Don't be silly. She's only a chicken."

"That's like saying, 'It's only dynamite.'"

Maggie grinned at me and hefted a good-sized basket that I could see was practically overflowing with eggs. "They're laying real good."

"I'd be happy to take a dozen off your hands, and could you spare another dozen for Sandra? She said she was running low."

"Of course I can. My babies just keep laying, whether I sell the eggs or not. I'm happy they're getting used." She bent down and patted one of the chickens. I kid you not. She patted it. Her. Whatever.

Her airy kitchen welcomed us with the smells of coffee and something I'd noticed earlier as I walked through, but couldn't identify. "What is that? Smells like…blackberry jam?"

"You're close. It's pie. I gathered the berries this morning." She knew better than to offer me pie, after all the lectures I'd given her about how I never combine fruit with carbohydrates. "Sit down while I clean off these eggs." She pointed to the chair at the end of her spacious kitchen table. "Do you want some berries for you and the grandkids?"

"That, I'll willingly accept." Visions of the succulent, purply-black fruit practically made my head swim. If I hadn't been sitting by that time, I probably would have fallen over from the richness of my imagination.

Maggie brushed some feathers and something even less appetizing off one of the eggs before washing it and setting it in a blue-ringed bowl. "I saw Wallace yesterday. Have you heard how he's doing this morning?"

"No. I'm planning to stop by there in a little bit, just to check on them. I know Ida's been spending the nights there to give Sadie a chance to rest."

"You remind them I'd be happy to set a spell if they need somebody else. If you're going by there anyway, would you take them some berries? I have plenty. Those bushes just keep on bearing."

I looked at where she pointed across the pond. Even from this far away I could see the lush berry patch with the canes trained along three strands of wire, making the berries easy to reach without impaling one's fingers. Everything around Maggie seemed to produce. Her goats gave milk, her poultry gave eggs, and, of course, she ate the chickens when they reached the end of their lifespan. She killed them herself, quickly and efficiently. She'd told me once she couldn't imagine sending her sweethearts—that's what she called them— to a slaughterhouse. They'd be so frightened, which would send fear hormones all through the meat, and she didn't want to ingest fear with every mouthful. I wondered idly if the road rage cropping up in cities could be blamed on the steady diet of fear hormones from beef and chickens. Something to think about.

Maggie's pole beans were magnificent. Her squash, four or five different varieties, were prolific. The only thing she couldn't seem to produce was a baby. Doodle-Doo and Vampirah and all the rest of that brood seemed to fill the bill, but I sometimes wondered if she yearned in private. She'd mentioned to me—only once—that she and Norm hadn't been able to start the family they'd wanted.

As if she'd read my mind, she cleared her throat. "Would you be willing to write me a testimonial?"

"What do you mean?"

"Norm and I, well, we've decided it's time to adopt, and we need to fill out enough forms to paper a parade float on the Fourth of July. I figured a letter from the town librarian attesting to our good character would help a lot."

"I'd be honored, Maggie. Thank you for asking." As long as I didn't have to mention Vampirah, I'd be able to write a glowing recommendation.

"We don't want a baby. Or rather, we do, but we decided that since everybody else wants babies, we'd have a better chance of getting our own child if we said we'd take someone a little older." She wiped the last egg and set it down carefully. "There are a lot of older kids around who never got adopted."

Good Lord, I thought. What's she getting into? "That sounds wonderful, Maggie."

"We thought an older child could begin helping us with the animals. Maybe that would be real healing."

"As long as you don't get one who's afraid of your chickens."

"Oh, honestly, Biscuit." Maggie was almost as good at rolling her eyes as Glaze was.

We chatted for a bit. I paid her, and she sent me on my way laden with a reinforced cardboard box full of heaven. Two dozen eggs, three quarts of Noel's and Moonbeam's special milk, and two fat tubs of blackberries. I should have walked down the street and put it in the fridge, but I was only a block away from Sadie's, and the weather was pleasant. Not too hot. Not too windy. Just right. I wondered if Wallace was still interested in food or whether he'd quit eating as his body slowly shut down. I'd read the pamphlet that hospice had given Sadie, so I knew that toward the end the body stops needing nourishment.

MARMALADE MET ME as I crossed Pine Street. She looked as if she was headed to Sadie's, as well. Part of her mooching routine, I supposed. I paused in the front yard, looking at the myriad bird feeders. I could see that Easton had kept them filled. As much as I disliked that woman and her flirtations all over town, I had to admit she'd done a lot to help Sadie. "Marmy," I said as a chickadee swooped over our heads and onto the bottom of the nearest feeder, "you leave those birds alone."

I do not chase birds. I do not want feathers in my mouth.

I'd never seen her chasing birds, but of course she was often out of my sight. She meowed at me and padded up the steps ahead of me. I knocked softly, not wanting to intrude, just wanting to keep Sadie company for a bit and deliver the blackberries. I could see her through the glass, sitting beside the hospital bed they'd installed in the living room. She motioned me to come in.

I used my elbow to push down on the brass handle. Door handles make so much more sense than doorknobs. If my arms are full—whether it's eggs and goat's milk, or anything else for that matter—I can simply use my elbow to push, rather than having to set down everything to get a hand free to turn a knob.

Sadie's yellow door swung soundlessly inward. Marmalade stepped in as if she owned the room. Sadie often told our tap-dance class how much fun it was to sit on the front porch and watch Wallace hold Marmalade on his lap. Treats of cream were a frequent ingredient in those idyllic pictures, too. But Marmy didn't seem to have cream on her mind this time. She sat beside me, curled her tail around her feet, and waited.

I set the food down on the wide table by the door, slipped off my tennies and hung my sweater on the ancient hall tree. I picked up one of the tubs of berries and padded across the square of oak flooring and onto the bright yellow carpet. The bed was the only piece of furniture that wasn't yellow, but Sadie had swaddled Wallace in a soft yellow comforter. His pajama-clad arms lay quietly across the coverlet. I was surprised to see a blue quilt draped over his legs. Nobody knew why Sadie always surrounded herself with yellow. Or why she seemed unable to keep her shoelaces tied. But I'd never heard of any complaint from Wallace about the unicolored house. Maybe the blue quilt was his one rebellion.

The couch, end tables, and chairs squatted around the perimeter, pushed aside to make way for the intrusive but necessary piece of equipment. Wallace could no longer breathe when he was lying flat, but he hadn't wanted to stay in the hospital. Margaret and Sam rented a hospital bed for him. That meant he could come home to die.

Wallace lifted his eyes. I saw, or thought I saw, a flicker of recognition in them, although I wouldn't have been surprised if he hadn't known who I was.

Sadie was my friend. Wallace was her husband, nothing more than that to me. He'd already had a stroke by the time I moved to Martinsville, so I'd never known the man about whom I'd heard so many wonderful stories. I'd never seen his quick wit. Or his fishing expertise, even though I knew Bob admired him more than almost anyone else in town. Sadie rose halfway, but I motioned her back. "No, stay there. I just came by for a moment to bring you some blackberries from Maggie's place."

Wallace lifted his left hand. "Blackberries?" he said slowly.

"Yes," I said. "Would you like some?"

He dropped his hand and closed his eyes. I took that for a no. Marmalade jumped up onto the yellow blanket.

Hello, SlowWalker.

I reached out to pull her off, but Sadie stopped me. "Wallace loves her," she said. "He'll welcome the company."

Thank you, LooseLaces.

Ida stumped her way out of the kitchen. "Hey there, Biscuit. How you doing?" Not waiting for an answer, of course, she plowed ahead. "We've had quite a parade today. The hospice nurse was here this morning. Said it wouldn't be too much longer. Everyone's dropping in to say good-bye. Guess the word is spreading."

"Dying." The word creaked out of Wallace like a rusted hinge on a squeaky gate.

Ida nodded. Sadie pursed her lips. I didn't know what to say. Here I was fifty years old, and I'd never watched anyone die except my first husband. Usually, though, right up toward the end, people—at least people in my family—were always saying things like "Don't worry. He'll get better." The platitudes didn't work, I guessed, since everyone I'd known who appeared to be on the way out ended up dying anyway. But I'd usually heard about the death after it was already a fact. Various aunts, uncles, and my grandparents on my dad's side. Melissa's nephew, of course, the one who'd been hit by a drunk driver. Sol, my first husband, had been in intensive care for four excruciating days before he quietly slipped away. Thank goodness I was there with him. I wasn't functioning very well that week, so I remembered surprisingly little except for his final words—"I love you, Biscuit McKee."

Ida reached out and touched Wallace's left foot beneath the blue quilt that draped across his lower legs, and went on in a normal voice. "You're doing fine, Wallace," she said. "It's okay to let go whenever you're ready."

Sadie nodded, but didn't speak. I looked a question at Ida, who glanced at Wallace and back at me. She shook her head and ran a hand over Marmalade's back. "What's that you've got there?" she asked.

"Blackberries. Maggie sent them. I could take them in the kitchen for you."

"You do that. Get yourself some sweet tea. It's on the counter. Then come back and sit a spell."

JUST IN CASE, I put the eggs and milk in Sadie's old-fashioned fridge. When I returned, Ida had stationed herself next to Wallace's left hand. Not knowing what else to do, I went back to the foot of the bed and rested my hands lightly on the two lumps of his feet. There didn't seem to be much reason for me to say anything. His left hand, lying limply in Ida's grasp, contrasted strangely with her dark olive skin tone. His fingers held a distinct purple tint. The rest of his skin had gone from the yellowish-pink shade I'd seen yesterday to a yellowish-ivory with tinges of green. How, I wondered, does one paint death? Are the colors the same as those of life, only washed-out, muted down? Or is there a death shade that never appears on any palette except that of a master artist? I tried to remember if I'd ever seen a painting with that particular greeny shade. If so, I couldn't recall it. That gorgeous, big art museum in Raleigh had a family portrait by John Singleton Copley. It was some old rich guy with lots of double letters in his name. The first time I saw it, I thought it was awful. The woman sitting beside her husband, with children playing around them and a couple of dogs at their feet, looked like a ghost. No color to her at all. Then I found out—thank goodness for signs in museums—that she had died two years before the portrait was commissioned. Copley had chosen to show her as if she were still there, still with her family. Pepperrell. That was their name. Copley foreshadowed her death brilliantly, though, with that washed-out face of hers. Obviously on her way out, I remembered thinking at the time.

Wallace was different, though. He didn't look washed-out. Every color on him was more intense. His right hand plucked at the blanket, then settled like a mottled brown bird folding in its wings. The flap of his pajama pocket fluttered above his struggling heart.

"We've had so many good times, Wallace." Sadie's voice cracked a bit as she reached for his right hand. She cleared her throat and stroked his purpled fingers one at a time. "I don't think I ever thanked you for taking such good care of me."

He turned his head toward her and blinked slowly. "You were so pretty," he said with an effort that seemed to drain him.

"I loved you all the time," Sadie went on in a soothing tone. "When you went to war, I knew you'd come home to me. I never doubted that, because I knew we'd grow old together." She paused and lifted his hand to her corrugated cheek. "We made it, Wallace. We're both old now. Ida and Ralph are going to help me, so you won't have to worry about anything." She kissed each of his fingertips. "I'm going to be just fine."

Wallace squinted at her. "You aren't pretty anymore," he said. The words came out of the side of his stroke-slackened mouth. Each one was an effort. Sadie didn't reply, but her faint eyebrows contracted and the lines around her eyes tightened, as if to hold in a hurt. Wallace turned his hand and drew one finger along the line of her jaw. "You aren't pretty," he repeated slowly. "You...are... beautiful." For a fleeting moment, I thought I saw the young man he once was. The one Sadie married sixty years ago.

I might have felt like an intruder except for the minor fact that neither Sadie nor Wallace, nor Ida for that matter, paid any attention to me. I was a witness, nothing more, there to offer quiet support, to stand at the foot of his bed and watch death close slowly over him.

He turned away from his wife, his beautiful wife of so many years, and looked in my direction. Not at me, though. He focused somewhere over my right shoulder. "Hello there," he said with such a surge of welcome in his voice that all three of us looked to see who had come into the room without our knowing. All I saw was an empty space between me and the whatnot shelves that held Sadie's collection of salt and pepper shakers. Behind me, the yellow couch sat against the front wall in solitary golden splendor, its crocheted yellow doilies spread meticulously along the back and over each armrest. "Hello," he repeated. I looked back and found myself smiling at the look of pure joy that suffused his face. He nodded twice.

"Good-bye, Wallace," Ida said.

Sadie stood up and leaned across to kiss his cheek. Her tears, coursing through the grooves on her cheeks, dripped from her chin onto his shoulder. He took a deep breath, arched his back, and as we watched, all three of us holding our breath, he sighed a sound like the wind rustling through the maple tree at night and gave a gurgle like the creek where it dropped into the culvert beneath Second Street. Although his head sank back onto his pillow and everything about him relaxed, let go, I sensed, just for a moment, a…a lifting, as if something…something…rose and hovered a moment…and was gone.

Some time ago Nathan told me that it can take as long as twenty minutes for all the cells of a body to cease functioning. I had no idea if he'd told the same thing to Sadie or Ida, but without discussing a reason for it, Ida and I stood there, and Sadie sat there, for half an hour, stroking his hands, touching his feet, easing him on his way,

and absorbing quiet comfort from each other. Ida
pushed a sparse lock of white hair off his forehead.
Sadie laid her hand on his chest, still now. His face
had gone from yellowish green to an indigo-shad-
owed alabaster. Ida brushed her hand down across
his eyes and the lids lowered halfway. Eyelids do
not close in death. They hang there, a half-open
doorway, a half-closed gate.

I stayed with Sadie a bit longer while Ida called
the hospice nurse and Doctor Nathan and Reverend Pursey and the funeral home. Marvin wasn't
back at work yet after his heart attack, but someone must have answered the phone. I listened with
only half an ear to Ida's instructions. Life had to
go on. For now, though, Sadie didn't say a thing,
and Marmalade simply lay there with her head on
Wallace's knee, purring her little heart out.

"Auntie Blue?"

"Yes, sweetie? Did you get lost?"

"Well, no. Can I take a rain check? Sadie's husband died a few hours ago."

"That poor woman. Well, you just go on up
there and see what you can do to help."

"No, I just left there. I was with Sadie when
he… I didn't even know him that well, but I…
This is ridiculous." I groped for a tissue.

"Go ahead and cry it out, sweetie. We all have

to go sometime, but that doesn't make it any easier on the ones left behind. Did he die well?"

That made me stop my sobbing. I'd never thought of death as something we could make a choice about. "Yes," I said, and my answer surprised me. "Yes, he did die well, like somebody walking down a staircase and opening a door at the bottom...a door with a friend on the other side."

"That's good. You go make yourself a nice cup of hot tea now, and let me know whenever you're ready to come visit."

"It's more than just a visit."

"Of course it is, but you take all the time you need."

GLAZE DROPPED MADELEINE and Dee off in front of Sharon's Beauty Shop after work and drove quietly up Pine Street by herself. There were four or five cars parked near Sadie's house. She supposed that people were taking the time to drop in and say good-bye to Wallace. Everyone said he wouldn't last another week. Maybe she'd stop by on her way to Biscuit's for dinner. She had at least an hour before she needed to leave. Plenty of time. She hated rushing. Of course, she hadn't known Wallace very well, hardly at all in fact, but Sadie was a dear.

She turned right onto Upper Sweetgum and pulled in to the curb. Bob's old house sat there, as it always did, looking faintly surprised. Maybe it was the two front doors that gave the house that wide-eyed look. They never used the door on the right. It was much friendlier to walk right into the kitchen. That was where everyone gathered anyway, no matter how crowded it got.

She and Maddy had shared the house long enough to feel comfortable with each other. She chuckled as she recalled the awkward moment at Biscuit's house last year when they'd discovered that Biscuit had agreed to rent Bob's old house on Upper Sweetgum to Glaze, and Bob had already told Maddy he'd rent it to her. Luckily, their trial run turned out for the best. Madeleine was a good person, perhaps a bit overly dramatic at times, but heart-of-gold-good nevertheless.

She pulled the mail out of the box and thumbed through it at a leisurely pace. Maddy's mail was on top. Some junk and two letters. Glaze checked out the return addresses. Maddy would not enjoy the one from her battleship mother. She never did. What was her brother doing writing to her? He lived all of two blocks away in the rectory next to St. Theresa's. Glaze shrugged. She'd find out soon enough. Maddy loved sharing her letters, investing the ones from her mother with all the drama at her disposal. Her extensive repertoire made her mother's words sound like a cross between Lady Macbeth and Cinderella's stepmother, with just a touch of Lucretia Borgia thrown in for good measure. Well deserved, from what little Glaze knew about that woman.

Glaze plopped her purse down on the counter and turned to her own mail. More junk, a couple of bills, and a creamy envelope with no return address, postmarked Martinsville.

Dear Glaze,

I hope you won't think I'm being presumptuous, but I'd like to make you a proposition. Would you be willing to stop by Wednesday evening? Better yet, come for dinner. It won't be fancy, maybe just a nice stew.

Call me, please, and let me know if you can make it.

Love,
Margaret

Glaze read the note twice. What on earth was Margaret planning? She called and told Margaret's answering machine that she'd be happy to accept. Soup on Monday—she was sure Biscuit would serve soup—and stew on Wednesday at Margaret's. Two dinners out this week! Glaze was always happy to eat someone else's cooking.

TOM CALLED THAT EVENING as I rinsed the blackberries. "Are you sure you feel up to making dinner?" he asked.

"I have to make dinner anyway," I told him, "and I think I'll feel better having friends and family around tonight."

Glaze walked in through the archway. "I came early to help. Oops! You're on the phone. Sorry."

"No. It's Tom. Here, talk to him while I finish these berries."

She picked up one of the largest and no doubt the juiciest ones. "I love snitching food." She crossed her eyes and smacked her lips. "Mmm-mmm, that's yummy." She listened for a moment.

"You need Tom to bring anything?" I shook my head. "No," she said to the phone. "Just yourself." Nice of her to put words in my mouth. When she put the phone down, she reached for another blackberry. "I feel almost guilty eating these," she said.

"Why? Blackberries are healthy and delicious, and I have plenty of them."

"It's not that. I stopped by Sadie's house on the way here to say good-bye to Wallace."

I wiped my hands on the green-striped tea towel and laid it on the counter. "Oh, I'm sorry. You didn't know. I should have called you."

"That's okay." She looked at the berry she held. "I just felt a bit awkward, barging in like that, not knowing he was already dead. Sadie spent so much time trying to make me feel better, when she should have been taking care of herself. She offered me a bowl of blackberries."

"Sadie will mourn him in her own way," I said. "She may still be in a state of shock, even though it was wonderfully gentle."

"Gentle?"

"Yes. I was there with Sadie and Ida when he died, and it was pretty obvious toward the end. Of course, he's spent the last few weeks being on his last legs, but he managed to keep going day to day. It must have been nerve-racking for Sadie."

Glaze set the berry back in the bowl. "Was Ida there the whole time?"

"I think she's pretty much lived there for the last few days."

"Sadie's lucky to have her." She lifted the fat berry from the bowl again and popped it in her mouth.

Bob and Tom walked in about the same time. Contrary to Glaze's instructions, Tom brought a bottle of blackberry wine. Glaze pulled out the tall glasses that Ida and Ralph had given us for our wedding. I fiddled some more with the tray, and we sauntered out to the side porch. Bob picked up my glass, which made the tray easier to balance. I should have put one of those nonskid mats on it. As it was, the dish of blackberries careened around, bumping into the sugar bowl and the dessert cups. I wasn't as steady as I thought I was. Tom handed Glaze his wine glass and rescued the tray. Glaze and I took the swing. Marmalade jumped up between us. Tom sat on the glider, and Bob chose a rocking chair.

"Hope you're not in a hurry to eat," I said. The blackberries really didn't need sugar, but I passed it around anyway. Tom took some. Bob didn't. Glaze sprinkled three or four spoonfuls. Why even bother with berries?

Chicken is better.

"Half an hour to wait?" Tom looked at his watch.

"Uh-huh." Bob wagged his spoon at me. "I thought you were mildly nuts when you first told me about this food-combining stuff. But I have to admit, I feel better eating this way."

"Plus," Glaze added, "you get to eat dessert first."

"Only if it's straight fruit." Why was I preaching at them? They knew the food-combining rules as well as I did. "Think you could get your customers at CT's to go along with a schedule like that?"

"Fruit half an hour before carbohydrates or four hours afterward?" he said. "Not likely. People around here do like their apple pies right after dinner."

"Wallace…" I choked up, but everyone waited without saying anything until I went on. "Wallace didn't get to eat any of the blackberries Maggie sent him."

Tom ran the side of his thumb back and forth on the rim of his wine glass. "Was it hard watching him go like that?" Bob must have filled him in on the details. I'd called Bob as soon as I got home.

"No. No, Tom. It wasn't. It was peaceful somehow. Sad, but peaceful. I'm glad I was there."

Me, too.

"I've never seen a peaceful death," Tom said, and something in his voice reminded me that he'd gone to war soon after high school.

"Was it hard? Watching all that happen?" I asked him.

He looked inside his almost-empty wine glass, as if the last few sips held an answer. He shrugged. "There aren't words for it." He looked up. Not at me. Not at Glaze. But at Bob. Bob, who'd gone through the same war that Tom had. "There just aren't any words." Bob returned from Asia uninjured physically. Tom, though, spent months in a rehab unit after one of the men in front of him stepped on a mine. I couldn't even begin to imagine it.

"But hey," Tom said, "that's all behind us now."

He finished his wine and set the glass down. "Does Miss Sadie need anything for the funeral arrangements? CT's would be happy to help out."

With the women of this town marshaling themselves behind her? "I wouldn't worry about that. Everybody will want to bring a dish, and Clara will probably mastermind the whole shebang."

"Well," Tom said, "if you think of anything Sadie needs, let me know."

We rocked and swung and glided in companionable silence for a few minutes. The Lady Banks Rose wasn't blooming yet, but I could hear tiny rustles in the leaves as an otherwise imperceptible breeze stirred through the branches.

It is not a breeze. It is a cockroach.

Marmalade hopped down off the swing and wandered toward the end of the porch. I caught Tom watching Glaze and saw that she studiously avoided eye contact. I wondered when I'd find out what was going on.

"I'm headed out of town at the end of next week," Tom said.

"Where are you going?"

"Memphis. It's a convention for restaurateurs."

"Why don't you call yourselves res-tau-*ran*-teurs?" Bob stressed the third syllable. "You run restaurants, and there's an *n* in there."

"Hey, I don't make the rules. It's French, and who knows how that's put together."

What is a french?

"Why Memphis?" I asked. "Why not New York?"

"We were there last time. New York, that is."

Bob waved his wine glass in front of him. "I'd be willing to bet the organizers this time are Elvis fans."

I like fans.

"See?" Tom said when Marmy meowed again from under the rosebush. "She agrees with you." He set his bowl back on the table. "I like country."

"You and ninety-eight percent of the population of this state." Bob laughed. "Clara just about has a conniption every time she walks into Town Hall and there's a radio playing."

"She doesn't like Elvis? I knew she was un-American." Tom smiled over at Glaze, but she'd found a spot on her fingernail that needed addressing.

I spoke into the silence. "How long will you be gone?"

"That depends," he said. "The convention's four days, but I may need to stay longer than that. I'm waiting to hear something from someone."

"Oh?" I couldn't very well ask him if the person he was waiting to hear from was sitting beside me on the swing.

"Be sure to call the station," Bob said. "That'll

give Reebok something to do. I'll be gone all that week. I'm sure Reebok will put your house on some sort of checklist." He reached down to pat Marmalade as she walked past his chair. "I think he just may be planning to live at the station while I'm gone."

"Polishing his badge the whole time," I said.

Tom nodded. "Things pretty quiet around here?"

"You could say that." Bob stopped patting Marmy, and she sidled up to Tom and laid a dead cockroach at his feet.

"Thank you for the gift, Furball," Tom said with more enthusiasm than I would have had under the circumstances. Beside me, I heard Glaze give a grunt.

He rubbed his hands on his knees. "I should get my answer in a few days. You'll all be the first to know."

I should hope so. The wedding march started sounding through my head. I was definitely going to get that matron of honor dress at Mable's.

What are you talking about?

My Gratitude List for Monday
1. Sadie and Wallace.
2. Ida.
3. Bob.
4. Glaze and Tom.
5. Life itself—may I never take it for granted.

I am grateful for
LooseLaces
SlowWalker
the flyers
my humans, even if they are confusing
the swing and bugs

THAT NIGHT, I WOKE to find Bob sweating and swearing and shaking. I held him for a long time, daring the devils that plagued him, trying to banish them with the sheer force of my love for this good man. I wondered whether Tom was awake and who could help when the war memories threatened to overwhelm him.

WEEK TWO

TUESDAY

Moonbeam nibbled between the fence rails at the hay Verity held for her.

"Me, too." Angela wiggled to be let down. "Me, too." Why did I ever try to carry that child when she was much happier running around on her own? She grabbed a handy tuft of green and pulled up the hapless grass, roots and all. "Doat pood. Doat pood."

"Yes, sweetie pie. The green part is probably good food for the goats, but Miss Maggie said that goats like their food to be clean, so they might not want the roots." I might as well have been talking to the wind. Angela waited for Noel to take one tiny nibble, then dropped the grass and bent to watch a grasshopper.

"Grannie?" Verity tugged at my elbow. "Why are their eyes so big?"

I turned from Angela and looked with Verity at the sloping foreheads of the goats, the long noses, and the prehensile lips. "I guess it's because their eyes have to fit their faces."

"Yes," Verity said with five-year-old certainty. "They fit fine." She bent and reached through to grab another handful of hay. "Here, Moonbeam. Here, Noel."

Moonbeam, the larger of the two, raised onto her back feet and rested her front legs on the top rail where Doodle-Doo had preened. Was it only yesterday? The fence groaned in seeming protest. Verity giggled.

Maggie walked up beside me and stroked the side of the goat's head. "You're a good girl, aren't you?" She glanced at me. "Can you stay a bit longer?" I nodded. "Verity," she said, "do you and your sister want to watch me milk the ladies here?"

"Isn't this kind of late for milking? I thought you did that first thing in the morning."

"Goats are a bit more user-friendly than some other animals, kind of like a cross between a horse and a dog. As long as I milk them twice a day, they aren't too particular about the timing."

"Are you milking Joy, too?" Verity pointed to another goat who wandered around the pasture with the rest of the herd, followed closely by Fergus, the Great Pyrenees watchdog.

"No. She's expecting some babies, so I can't milk her."

I did a quick head count. One child, one dog, multiple goats, two women. "Where's Angela?"

Verity pointed.

Naturally it had to be the black-hooded Vampirah that Angela had chosen to pick up. Why that bird wasn't pecking her eyes out, I had no idea. Maggie grabbed my arm and held me back. "You'll scare the child if you panic like that, to say nothing of what you'll do to my chickens if you take off running at them." She waved to Angela. "It's time to set the pretty chicken on the ground, sweetheart, so she can go lay some more eggs."

Surprisingly, Angela did what she was told. Vampirah fluttered a bit, cackled twice, and stretched her wings out to the sides. She looked as if she was ready to pounce on my grandchild, but little Angela laughed, her unpecked eyes sparkling. "Wuvs me. Wuvs me."

"Yes, she does," Maggie agreed. "She does love you. Thank you for being so gentle with her." When she was sure I wasn't going to bolt, she let go of my arm. "You okay?"

"I should think you'd ask if Angela's okay," I said.

"Don't get in a twit. That child's in her element. You're the one I wonder about. Anybody that likes eggs and doesn't like chickens needs to have her head examined, if you ask me." I didn't ask you, I thought. But I didn't say it out loud. She narrowed her eyes at me. "Maybe you should consider counseling."

First Glaze, now Maggie. Why did everyone think I was the one who needed help? "Do they have chicken psychologists?"

Either Maggie didn't hear my sneering tone or, more likely, she chose to ignore it. "Well, a phobia is a phobia. So what if you're afraid of chickens or heights or water or airplanes? It's all the same thing."

Not when Vampirah's in the picture, I thought.

She tilted her head to one side and looked at me. "I can't believe it's just the chickens. There has to be a reason why you want to overprotect your grandkids."

Before I could retort with a completely unjustified comment, she called out to the children and ushered them into the barn to watch the milking. I followed close behind, certain that if I stayed outside, Vampirah would bypass her head-chicken duties to chase me away. I gradually forgot about the bloodthirsty hen, though, as Maggie huddled on a stool beside Moonbeam and squirted milk into a sparkling-clean stainless-steel bucket with a half-moon opening through the lid. Angela laughed, Verity giggled, and Maggie smiled. So did I. Why, I wondered, had Maggie's question bothered me so much? Why did I feel overly protective of the two girls? I sat down on a hay bale and chewed over the thought. Glaze came to mind, Glaze at five years old. Glaze needing to be protected. Glaze, who trusted me. My little sister, and I'd led her into danger. I hadn't known what I was doing, but still...

Maggie shifted slightly and aimed a squirt at one of the barn cats. Verity and Angela giggled more as Calico stood on her hind legs and intercepted the warm milk. Why couldn't we be more like cats? Why couldn't we simply do our part exterminating mice, relishing spots of sunshine, and reveling in warm milk when it came our way? Glaze had forgiven me, but I must not have forgiven myself yet, because I held so much fear for what might happen to Verity and Angela. I watched them pat the goats and laugh. I didn't see any particular reason for the laughter. But that was the way it was with children. They laughed hundreds of times a day. I would happily kill anyone who messed with my grandchildren. Glaze's childhood face came back to me. Quiet, contained, sorrowful. It was my fault she'd lost her laughter.

I still didn't trust chickens, but at least I had the answer to the other part of the puzzle. I was simply going to have to lighten up. Something cackled from the open doorway behind me. Vampirah. Obviously testing the strength of my new intention.

TAP-DANCE CLASS WAS mighty thin that evening. Sadie, naturally, was gone, and Dee had a bad cold, which left just Melissa, Annie, Glaze, and me. Ida came late, just as we were huffing and puffing our way through the Broadway routine.

"Ida!" Miss Mary effused. "We're so glad you made it! Just in time for the very last set! We'll all want to know about how Miss Sadie is, but I'm sure you'll wait till we finish our routine!"

That wasn't my opinion. I was ready to stop the class and hear about Sadie, but Miss Mary had a certain force to her personality. It was hard to go against her militant exuberance.

Ida stood up and flexed her feet in the black tap shoes. She nodded. "I need to work the kinks out. This will feel good after four solid days of sitting by a hospital bed."

"Yes, well, you just get in that line there between Biscuit and Glaze. That's right! Let's start the music again. From the top! Arms out! Smile, ladies! One. Two. One, two, three, go!"

We glided into the center from both sides of the room, three by three. Shuffle, ball-change, ball-change, step, step, and a shuffle, ball-change, ball-change, and a stomp. Arms out to the side, dancing as if the world hadn't ended. Dancing as if there weren't any tears anywhere. Dancing as if that's what life was all about—music and movement.

Shuffle, shuffle, step, step. Smile. Miss Mary filled in the empty spot where Sadie should have been.

LATER, AT AZALEA HOUSE, we let Ida talk it out. Sadie was fine, she said, considering. "Margaret and Monica came by to sit with Wallace's body so Sadie could get some sleep. I didn't want to leave, but Sadie said to tell all of you she'd try to be back next week."

"What a trouper." Melissa sat down in her usual seat next to Glaze. "You really think she's holding up well, or is it all just a façade?"

LooseLaces is very sad.

"It's not like she hasn't known it was coming," Glaze said. Marmalade, who'd walked with us up the hill to Melissa's as she usually did, purred loudly and jumped into Glaze's lap to be patted. Glaze stroked all along her back, and Marmy arched into the contact.

Annie shook her head. "We all knew it was coming." She wiped the back of her hand across her eyes. "That doesn't make it any easier."

We waited a moment to give Annie time.

"Marvin was there this evening," Ida said.

Melissa sent the iced-tea pitcher around the table. "So soon after his heart attack?"

"He wasn't moving fast, that's for sure. But they'd made most of the funeral arrangements a long time ago. All they needed to do was firm up a couple of options."

Annie ignored the tea as usual and stood up to get a glass of water. "Options? Like what?"

Ida downed almost half a glass before she answered. "Gosh, that tastes good. I feel like I'm dried up from all that sitting and waiting." She motioned for the pitcher, and it made its way back to her end of the table. "For one thing, he offered to pick her up in the limousine for the viewing, but Sadie pooh-poohed the idea." She gave a fair imitation of Sadie's high-pitched voice. "'I'm not going to have my first limousine ride be for my Wallace's viewing.'"

"You sound just like her," Melissa said.

Ida hadn't finished her impersonation. "'You're going to make me ride in that thing Friday, and I'll let you get away with that, but Thursday I want to ride with my friends.'"

I will ride with her if she asks me.

"Why are they having the visitation at the funeral home?" Annie asked. "He's laid out now in the front parlor."

Ida smiled down the length of the table at Annie. "Everybody in town will want to attend. Sadie doesn't have room at her house."

"I'll go by tomorrow to sit with him," Annie said. Outside of the valley, people seemed to have forgotten the old way of sitting with the body, usually two friends at a time, so the person who'd died wouldn't be left alone and neither would the family who'd been left behind. Here in the Metoochie River Valley, we kept to the old ways.

"Marvin's going to move him to the funeral home tomorrow morning," Ida said, "and put him in a special coffin to keep him fresh. I'm sure you can sit with him there after Marvin's through with the arranging."

"I didn't know Marvin was back at work," I said.

"Oh, he's not. Not really. But his doctor told him he could ease back into his regular routine gradually, as long as he didn't do any heavy lifting."

I looked at Ida, and she looked at me. We both about split a gut trying to contain ourselves. It seemed dreadfully irreverent, but I couldn't help myself. Neither could Ida.

"How," she gasped, "how can a mortician possibly not do any heavy lifting?" Gradually everyone around the table figured out what we were guffawing about. "Don't you ever wonder what they do down there in the nether reaches of the funeral home?"

What is a nether reach?

"They must have all sorts of contraptions," Glaze said. "You know, for handling bodies that are stiff with rigor mortis?"

Melissa lowered her voice to horror-movie tremors. "Or floppy once it wears off?"

"Maybe they have cranes," I suggested.

"Ramps? Slides?"

The hilarity couldn't last long, though. This was Wallace we were talking about. Annie came to reason first. "I don't think this is funny," she said. "Well, that is, it is funny, but it's not funny, if you know what I mean."

We did. I felt faintly ashamed, but only for a moment. It was a way to deal with our sadness about Sadie's loss.

After a moment, Annie cleared her throat. "I've been spending some time recently getting to know Pumpkin. She's a lot of fun, and I think she'd fit right in, so I'd like to invite her to join the tap-dance class. Do you think it's too late for her to start?"

"Of course not! She'd be more than welcome!"

"This way," I said, "we get to review more, right?"

Melissa pointed her finger at me. "You would be happy reviewing for the next ten years."

I stuck out my tongue at her.

"Oh, don't you worry about that, Biscuit! She'll pick it right up!"

I wasn't worried. I was hopeful.

"There's room for two more chairs here,"

Melissa said. "Can we think of somebody else to invite?"

Ida reached for the last cinnamon roll. "No, but it was nice of you to get such a long table, just in case we find someone else."

Annie shifted the tone. "So Marvin will be directing the funeral?"

"Yes," Ida told us. "He won't be moving too fast, but he's really excited about the new green cemetery."

"I like that idea," I said.

She raised one eyebrow. "I have to admit, I wasn't so sure about it at first, but it's making more sense. I read all the articles about it. I even went to the town-council meetings and heard all the arguments. I have to say, Marvin's got me convinced."

"What convinced me was the idea that we wouldn't be putting any more formaldehyde in the ground." I shuddered. "I also like the idea of protecting all three sections of the Old Woods by converting them to a conservation zone."

Annie let out a whoop of agreement. "Those woods have been there forever. It's a wonder they didn't get cut down long before this. We have Sadie to thank for that, you know."

I'd loved Sadie even before I met her because I'd seen a news photo of her with her arms wrapped around one of the big, old oaks whose roots were splitting the sidewalk on Juniper Street. She was facing off with a thoroughly disgruntled Hubbard Martin. Sadie won, and she'd extended her protection to every old original tree in town. A truce of sorts, hammered out at numerous town meetings, had protected the trees, but now, with the Green Cemetery Act, there was some sort of irrevocable trust that held the trees safe from people like Hubbard who would just as soon have cleared the land and added houses.

"Pass the cheese straws up here," Ida said. "Did you know that Sadie's mother fought off Obadiah and Leon Martin both to save those same trees?"

The position of chairman of the town council was hereditary. I don't think it was written down anywhere. It just turned out that way, from Homer Martin right down to the present, always passing to the oldest son. "Did they have chain saws like Hubbard's?" I said, remembering the dangerous-looking implement Hubbard held in the news shot.

Ida grinned. "Plain old handsaws, sharp as the dickens," she said. "But they were no match for Emma Russell. She passed her genes right down to Sadie, too." She nibbled off the end of a cheese straw. "Those trees are safe forever now."

"What I don't understand," Glaze said, "is why a funeral director would agree to change his whole way of doing things. Surely he won't make as much money this way."

"He's a responsible businessman," Melissa said. "He wouldn't take too grave a risk."

"A grave risk?"

"Shh! Quit that, Ida! Don't you get us started again."

"Do you think he'll sell all that embalming equipment at a rummage sale?"

I laid a hand on Ida's arm. "You're losing it. And we're being irresponsible and undignified."

"Quit being so stuffy. You think it's funny, too, and you know it."

It was Melissa's turn to rein us in. "I always thought Sadie wanted Wallace buried in her family plot, next to her brother and little Sam. That way she can visit them all at once."

"That's the beauty of it," Annie said. "Sadie showed me where Wallace is going to go. You know how their plot is right at the top of the cemetery? And the Old Woods are there next to Eustace?" She looked at me. "Eustace was Sadie's younger brother."

"I know that," I told her.

"Well," she went on, "trees are a big part of any green cemetery."

Melissa paused on her way to refill the pitcher. I was going to have to make a pit stop before I walked home. "Why?" she asked.

"The bodies are placed about three and a half feet deep in hand-dug graves, right among the trees. That way you don't have heavy equipment in there compacting the ground around the roots. It's all part of the natural cycle of life. The bodies feed the trees. There aren't any of those nasty chemicals that poison the soils in regular cemeteries."

"What about the caskets? Don't they take forever to decay?"

Annie shook her head. "No caskets. We'll wrap Wallace in…" Her voice petered out, and Ida took up the story.

"Sadie asked Annie if she could bury Wallace in the blue quilt Annie made for him years ago when she was just a young thing." It couldn't have been that many years ago, considering Annie's age, but I supposed such things were relative. Ida turned to look at me. "You saw it, Biscuit. It's the one we had over his legs there at the end. He'll be wrapped in it tomorrow morning, when Marvin takes him to the funeral home. Then he'll put Wallace in a special coffin they have for the green burials, to keep the body cool." She turned back to the others. "Friday morning, Carl and Ralph and Bob and Tom are going to dig the grave, right there under that pretty dogwood tree on the edge of the Old Woods. When we get to the cemetery, some of the men will lift him out of the coffin, quilt and all. We'll each have a chance to say good-bye, and then they'll lower him down into the hole." She stopped. "The best part is that we'll help cover him up then."

"With the quilt, you mean?" Melissa asked.

"No, sweetie. With dirt. This is the way people were buried for thousands of years, with respect and love. We're returning him to Mother Earth. We'll tuck him in." She reached for the tissue box in the center of the table. And then she passed it to her left. We all took a handful.

WEEK TWO

WEDNESDAY

"DID YOU KNOW his middle name was Douglas?" I waved the Keagan County Record in the general direction of Bob's coffee cup.

"I don't think I ever thought much about it, Woman." He'd called me Woman, so he probably wanted me to be quiet so he could finish reading the front page. I was on the obituaries, usually flowery affairs that extolled the dead person in such a way that the deceased was sometimes unrecognizable as the cranky, cantankerous old skinflint who had actually done the deceasing.

"Did you know he was born in that very same house and lived there all his life?"

"Uh-huh."

"Who on earth would name anybody Gilbert Phylosthenies?"

Bob rotated page one down onto the kitchen table. "I thought you were talking about Wallace."

"I was," I said. "This says his father's name

was Gilbert Phylosthenies Masters. His mother was a Breeton."

"Gilbert's?"

"No. Wallace's mother. She was a Breeton. And listen to this…" This article was just too sweet for words. "He was a 1927 graduate of the Martinsville Grammar School, top in his class of seven students. He went on to graduate from the new Keagan County High School in 1931. Seven students in grade school. Can you imagine that? And it's hard to think of that drafty old high school building as ever being new."

"Most buildings were at one time or other."

"You sound grumpy. Should I be quiet?" The pause that followed my question went on just a hair too long, and I felt I had to defend my chattiness. "These obituaries are fun. They make the dead person sound so likeable."

"Wallace *was* likeable." Bob scratched his upper lip where he was trying to grow a mustache. He'd only gotten to the itchy did-you-miss-your-upper-lip stage and did not seem to appreciate comments about it, so I kept my mouth shut and watched him run his fingers back and forth as if he could conjure up more hair faster that way. "I assume you're going to read it to me anyway," he said.

"Just a bit of it. It's so sweet. It says he took over the hardware store his grandfather founded." I skipped a bit where it got rather wordy, talking about how he had to sell the store after his first stroke in 1987. And then it mentioned woodworking and fishing and card games. "Here it is. Here's the sweet part. 'He touched our hearts and souls in a special way and all loved to be around him. His legacy to this community is the many fine, upstanding young people he mentored over the years. His quiet, humble, dependable, caring, good-natured spirit will be sorely missed.' Isn't that lovely?"

A nonspecific murmur came from behind the front page. Our breakfast conversation appeared to be over. "We should send a check to the Audubon Society," I said. "That's what they're asking for, in lieu of flowers." My only answer was another brief mumble. Oh, well. So much for communication. At the bottom of the obit page, a small box announced:

Axelrod's
The Funeral Home with a Heart
Ecological Burial in
Martinsville's Green Cemetery
(the first in Northeast Georgia)
Caring for you and your loved ones since 1946
Marvin Axelrod, Funeral Director

SADIE LET OUT A BIG SIGH and leaned back into my Buick's well-padded seat. "Thank you for driving me today, dear."

Before I could answer, she clenched her age-spotted hand into a fist and pounded on her left thigh three times. "I lost my nerve when I ran over Marvin's azalea bushes. That stupid nose-bleed scared me so much. I've never had an accident in all these years since I started driving in 1952...."

There were plenty of close calls, I thought.

"That was the first year we could afford a car, you see. Wallace bought a turquoise Henry J. It was such a sweet little car. And he taught me how to drive." She pulled a yellow-flowered hand-kerchief from her capacious purse and blew her nose—a healthy honk coming from such a diminutive woman.

"Doctor Nathan said I needed a rest," she went on. "That's ridiculous, though. I feel like I've been doing nothing but resting lately. Everybody's helped me so much over the past few months as Wallace got harder to care for. Now, with him gone, there's nothing much for me to do during the day, especially since I'm afraid to get in my own car."

"I know you were a big help to him these last few years," I said.

"He would have done the same for me if our situations had been reversed. I'm just glad that he went first. I don't think he would have been too happy being left alone." She sighed again and turned her head toward the side window. "He did like my company, and we loved to cuddle. As he got older we couldn't always…well, you know. But I loved to have him hold me."

I wasn't sure what to say, but before I could think of something, she plowed ahead. "It would have broken his spirit to have to go into that nursing home. I think that's why he finally went so fast. One day he was sitting out on the front porch watching the birds, and then there was that second stroke, and it just hurt his heart to think I wouldn't be able to take care of him. I think he chose to pass on."

"I'm sure he's not hurting anymore."

"Oh, he's probably running races with the angels. Did I tell you he used to be a champion runner in high school?"

The little time I'd known him, I never saw him move faster than a slow shuffle. "It said that in his obituary, but I'd never heard it before."

"He always did love to run," Sadie said. "The first time I ever saw him, he was pelting along the dirt road in front of my house. All the roads in town were dirt back then. Oh, I must have known him before that—we grew up together, you know—but the first time I remember him, he was running lickety-split, with his hair flying backward off his forehead and his shirttails flapping around his knickers. He wasn't even in long pants yet. I think I fell in love with him right that moment and never forgot the feeling." She sighed again, brushed at her nose with the back of her hand, and lapsed into silence.

"He was a champion," I prompted.

"Oh, yes. The fastest runner Keagan High School ever saw. There's a certificate with his name on it in that big showcase right across from the front doors. He was so proud of that piece of paper. Nowadays they give trophies for everything. You don't even have to be very good at something to get a huge trophy. But back then, we had to know ourselves that we'd done a good job. The certificate was just a way of showing that other people noticed. You should look it up sometime."

I pulled up in front of her yellow house. "I'll do that," I said.

"Don't bother seeing me in," she said. "I can manage just fine here, and you need to get to the library."

"No. I put a note on the door saying we'd be closed this week."

"Don't you do that. Wallace always loved to read before his eyes got too bad. Annie comes over—well, she used to drop by to read to him. He'd like the library to stay open, I'm sure."

I nodded. "Esther was planning to work there

for a while today anyway, so I'll head on over and be sure the door stays unlocked."

"You do that." She opened the door and picked up the towel-wrapped bundle beside her. "Thank you for the fresh bread."

"You're welcome," I told her. "You be sure to take that rest."

"Doc wasn't talking about naps, dearie. He wants me to get away somewhere." She shook her head. "He knows Margaret is getting together that group to go on a cruise, and he wants me to go along."

"Sadie! That's a wonderful idea."

"Do you think I could sign up this late? I already told her no, but I think I'd like to change my mind. Will people think it's odd for me to go? It'll be only a few months after the funeral."

"I know she'd be delighted if you joined back up."

"Are you going, too?"

"If you're going, then I'll definitely say yes."

She smiled at me. "Nathan wants me to go see that new massage therapist, too. Have you been to see her?"

"Not yet, but it sounds heavenly. I've never had a real massage. Just what Bob does."

Sadie nodded. "Wallace used to rub my back for me, but then he'd find one spot that was sore and he'd push at it and push at it until I thought I was going to get a bruise."

Kindred spirit. "Bob's the same way. I love it when he's real gentle, but he somehow gets off track and thinks he has to force my muscles to relax."

"That's men for you," Sadie said. "They're all about fixing things."

I thought about the bookshelves Bob worked on last month. "Thank goodness," I said, and Sadie laughed.

"So will you go for a massage sometime?" she asked.

"Probably."

"You'll like her. I knew Amanda when she was growing up here. She moved away after college, but I guess she's come home now." She frowned. "I'd love to go get me a massage, but I'd need to bother somebody for a ride."

"It's not a bother, Sadie. You go ahead and make an appointment and there'll be somebody who has the time to drive you. We're all friends. That's what friends do for each other."

Sadie reached out and patted my cheek. "Thank you." She hoisted herself out of the car and trundled up her walkway. At the bottom stair she turned and waved. I waited until she was in the front door, then drove toward the library, already planning what to wear on the cruise. Sandals. My muumuu. Soft tee-shirts and my long, cool, swirly broomstick skirt that never wrinkled. A sweater for evenings and early mornings. Nothing I had to fiddle with. Comfort clothes. I could hardly wait.

GLAZE HAD NO CLUE what Margaret's proposition could possibly be. She walked, more slowly than usual, along Fourth Street and finally stopped halfway between Juniper and Dogwood. One particularly stately tree grew on the edge of the Old Woods near the street, standing like a grandma with open arms. In this case, a grandma with palm-shaped green leaves for hair. Glaze never bothered to remember what kind of tree it was, although she knew from Biscuit's frequent comments on their Saturday walks that this stand of trees was one of three groves of original trees in Martinsville. In an age when people believed in clear-cutting the land for timber to make room for crops and to eliminate possible hiding places for predators—both the human and the non-human kind—the founders of Martinsville, back in the mid-1700s, preserved these trees. She took a deep breath and felt some of the tension drain out of her shoulders. What on earth could Margaret want?

The late-afternoon sun, diffused by low clouds, threw Glaze's pale shadow toward the base of the green-haired grandma where a feisty grayish-brown squirrel clung head down, twitching its tail.

"I'm not after your acorns, you silly creature." She wondered if this particular squirrel was one of the tribe that regularly attacked her bird feeder. Sadie had suggested several kinds of squirrel guards, but then admitted that none of them worked for very long. She'd have to get something to save her sunflower seeds from depredation. As if he were arguing the point, the squirrel chattered at her.

One more deep breath—the air felt somehow cleaner near these woods—and she walked on. Now she needed to hurry so she wouldn't be late. Glaze hated being late.

Margaret and Sam's small house nestled near the base of the cliff on a cul-de-sac at the south end of Fourth Street. They lived next door to Margaret's parents, separated only by two garages and two driveways in a town where almost nobody had a garage. Of course, nobody else had a 1933 Duesenberg Town Car, either. All the talk about Margaret's millions certainly didn't reflect in the house Glaze approached. It was a simple brick structure with quite ordinary windows and a modest front porch, where a knee-high concrete elephant guarded the two brick steps. Glaze patted the uplifted trunk, mounted the two stairs, and knocked on the bright red front door.

"Come on in," Sam boomed, "and set yourself down." He swung the door wider. "Margaret's fiddling with something in the kitchen." Sam's ruddy square face beamed with welcome and goodwill. Glaze had never seen him in a bad mood. If he'd been twenty years older with white hair and a beard, he would have made a great Santa Claus.

Margaret bustled in from the kitchen with two glasses of iced tea. "This'll keep you from getting parched."

"Thank—"

"Dinner's almost ready. Your lovely sister brought me some fresh Italian bread this morning. Don't you just love that stuff?"

"Yes. I—"

"I hope you like garlic bread, because that's what I'm doing with it."

"Sure. It's—"

"I'm so glad you accepted my invitation."

"My pleasure. I—"

"We're going to have to wait about business, though, until after we eat."

"That's fine with—"

"Sam, why don't you show Glaze to the table? I'll be right back. Don't forget to take your tea with you."

Sam looked at Glaze with a merry twinkle. "Margaret's something, isn't she?" He waited for Glaze to respond with a nod. "I almost lost her last year. You know about that, don't you?" When Glaze nodded again, he went on. "When she was in that coma, I swore I'd never again get upset with her chattiness." He looked toward the kitchen. "She's my kind of woman."

Santa and Mrs. Claus, indeed. Glaze felt a pang of...something. She couldn't quite identify it. Why did such a simple statement of affection hurt?

The meal was as unpretentious as Margaret herself. Glaze wasn't a big eater as a rule, so she surprised herself by taking a second helping of the succulent stew.

"A meal in a pot," Margaret proclaimed over the empty bowls. "Now Sam and I are going to carry these in and set them soaking, and then we'll get down to business. You can go freshen up. The powder room's thataway."

Glaze was used to powder rooms tucked in out-of-the-way corners, like the little room in her own house with a sink over the cardinal-red cabinet, or Biscuit's blue-and-white tuck-away room that nestled under her stairs. This room, though, was the only indication she'd seen that Margaret was indeed a wealthy woman. A larger-than-life-sized swan tucked its bill under a wing with feathers so detailed Glaze couldn't resist stroking them, surprised to find cool porcelain instead of a warm swan body. A beautifully finished, dome-topped chest stood beside the swan. The lid, propped open, was lined with an opulent silky fabric in a deep grayish blue. Indigo would be the best name for that color. Again, Glaze touched; this time her fingers were rewarded with a warm, slightly nubby texture, padded with some rich underlayer. The trunk held stacks of luscious, thick towels. Bath towels, hand towels, washcloths, all as white as the swan that embraced them. Glaze laid her palm on the top bath towel. Its warmth surprised her.

"MARGARET? HOW DO YOU get the towels to be warm?"

Margaret laughed and Sam beamed. "That was Sam's invention. You wouldn't have noticed from the street, but on the back side of the roof, the south side, we have solar heating panels. They provide our hot water year-round. Sam figured out how to run circulating lines of hot water under the floor. He can turn them on or off depending on the weather."

"So we don't roast in the summer," Sam said.

"But how does that warm the towels in the trunk?"

"He put loops in the line. One comes into the powder room through the floor. Sam drilled a hole in the bottom of the trunk and laid a special pad in the bottom and sides. The solar hot water heats some jelly—"

"Gel," Sam corrected.

"—in the pad, and that heats the towels. We have a bed warmer in our room and one in the guest room that works the same way. Sam's a genius."

The genius ducked his head and blushed. "Some people in town think all I ever do is tinker on the Duesenberg, but I've always liked to invent things."

"I've never met an inventor before," Glaze said.

"Sure you have. Bob invents those incredible fishing flies and cat toys, too, from what I've heard." He grinned over at Margaret. "Biscuit invents new kinds of bread every week. Madeleine, that friend of yours, invents stories. Sadie and Wallace invented more kinds of bird feeders than you can shake a squirrel at."

Glaze laughed. "I never thought of those as inventions."

"They're creations of the human mind. I'd say that qualifies them as inventions."

"And that," Margaret said, "leads us right into why I've asked you here tonight."

She and Sam settled back into their easy chairs. Glaze inched forward until she perched on the edge of the couch. Yet another glass of iced tea sat on the coffee table in front of her. She'd be up all night if she ingested this much caffeine, but she didn't suppose Margaret could whip up a milkshake.

"I'm fairly sure you know I have lots of money," Margaret said. "It's something everybody in town seems to know, but everybody keeps it kind of secret from outsiders. I think they're protecting me from the hordes of leeches who would show up if my wealth were public knowledge. Believe me, I'm truly grateful for that."

"How do you keep it secret, though? I thought you owned a big corporation. Surely the records are public?"

"That's one of those misconceptions that people got their brains around and they can't seem to let it go. No, I didn't inherit any of the business side. Just the personal fortune, and believe me, that was plenty. The investments are run by a staid, stuffy and thoroughly dependable management company, and they just deposit a check for me each month." Margaret shifted to a more comfortable position. "It's fairly substantial."

Sam chuckled. If what Glaze had heard was even halfway true, Margaret's comment was the understatement of the century. "What does this have to do with me?"

"Well, dear, I've been using some of my money to help out around the town…"

"I know about the library and the ambulance."

"Yes, well, there are a few other projects going on, and I need someone to oversee them all."

"Me?" The word came out like a squeak. Glaze swallowed. "Me?" she asked again.

"Yes. When you wrote me that you were wish-

ing for another job, I saw that you could truly help
me out. You see, I have a hard time saying no to
people who ask me for money. There haven't been
many who've taken advantage of that, but there
are some."

"And the numbers are increasing each year,"
Sam said.

"But how could I help? I don't think I'm qualified."

Margaret tilted her head to one side. "You're in-
telligent. You're well-read. You know the people
in this town without being related to half of them
the way Sam and I are. I have the feeling you'd
know how to set up some sort of rules to govern
the selection process."

"You'd get to invent them," Sam said.

Glaze gulped. "What about my job at CelerInc?"

"You could keep it for a while and do this part-
time. Or you could quit that job and concentrate
full-time on this."

"I don't think I could afford to quit my job."

Sam and Margaret exchanged a long look.
"Well, dear," Margaret said, "I doubt I could afford to pay you much more than…" She paused
and then named a figure that took Glaze's breath
away.

"Ohmigosh! Are you serious?"

"Uh-huh."

Glaze looked around the living room. There

were line drawings over the fireplace. The central one was Don Quixote on a horse with Sancho Panza and the windmills in the background. Talk about an impossible dream. She took a deep breath. "I can't, Margaret. I don't have any background in stuff like this."

Margaret looked over at Sam, who remained silent. "We figure you'd hire an advisory committee. There would be a budget for salaries and expenses."

"A budget?"

"Yes. I want this to be done in a completely official way."

Sam nodded his agreement. "She wants it off her platter, so she won't have to worry that everybody who says hello is angling for some money."

"That means…" Glaze paused and drew in a deep breath. "That means that I'd be the one worrying about that."

Margaret laughed and waved her hand in a dismissive gesture. "That's the advantage of having a committee, dear. If there's a regular process for applying for grants, it'll slow a lot of people down."

Sam reached for Margaret's hand. "Honey, let's give Glaze a chance to absorb this. It's a big decision."

Glaze inhaled. The smell of yeast bread and stew still wafted around the homey living room.

The smell of money somehow simmered beneath it all.

Sam went on. "How about some ice cream to settle our stomachs? Or would you like a milk-shake? I've got a pretty mean blender that works wonders."

A job offer and a milkshake on top of it. The temptation was powerful, but she'd simply never had any experience with anything like this. If she did it and failed... She didn't even want to think about how awful that would be.

"You don't have to give Margaret an answer anytime soon, no matter how much she'd like to hear a yes right now." Sam stood and headed for the kitchen. "Milkshakes coming up."

"He's right," Margaret said. "He usually is. I need to stop pushing. You can let the idea settle in for a day or two and let me know then. Okay?"

Sam stuck his head back around the archway into the kitchen. "She can take a month if she needs it."

Glaze did manage a grin, even if it was a trifle lopsided. "Is this supposed to be a big secret, or could I talk it over with Biscuit and Bob?"

"They're fine. I know they can keep their mouths shut. But I wouldn't want it to get out to others just yet. Not until you've decided to take the job."

"Not until she's decided whether or not to take

the job," Sam hollered from the kitchen. "If she doesn't want it, you'll have to find somebody else."

"Yes, Sam." But Margaret winked at Glaze as she said it.

"HEAVEN KNOWS I DON'T LIKE the thought of her driving." I waited until Bob finished rinsing out his mouth. "But it hurts to see Sadie too frightened to get in her own car."

He tapped the toothbrush on the edge of the sink and slipped it into the ceramic holder where it nestled against mine. Such a romantic thought. "Maybe it's just as well. It's just a matter of time till she causes an accident."

"Not if she won't get in her car." I picked up the hairbrush, then set it down again. The memory of her pounding her fist against her leg in such impotent anger flared up in front of me. "Poor thing. It doesn't seem fair."

"She doesn't want your pity, I'm sure."

"This isn't pity. It's empathy. I can't imagine what it would be like to be used to puttering around on your own one day and then overnight have to be dependent on the goodwill of others."

"I wonder," Bob said in the velvety-soft voice that I loved.

"Wonder what?"

He moved aside so I could get to the sink. It seemed a shame to disturb Mr. and Mrs. Toothbrush, but my teeth felt fuzzy, so I lifted the missus out of her companion's wet embrace. I definitely had too much time on my hands if I was inventing blather like this.

Bob's reflection met my eyes in the mirror. His mustache was at the Rhett Butler stage. I hoped he'd let it get thicker and bushier. His thick black hair, touched with wisps of silver, parted on the left in the mirror instead of on the right. His once-broken nose headed in the opposite direction to what I was used to when I looked at him head-on. Face-to-face. Hmm. My mind wandered a bit, and I almost missed his next comment. "Do you think we could talk her into taking that defensive-driving course the Senior Center is sponsoring?"

This man I married was brilliant. "Of course we could," I said. But then I thought about it and backtracked. "I don't know if she'd do it. She may not honestly know just how bad her driving is."

"We could tell her she'd get a credit on her car insurance if she took the course."

"Would she?"

"Yeah." He picked up the hairbrush I'd abandoned and swiped it a couple of times through his thick hair. "It's only a few dollars, but every little bit helps."

"It might keep her from running off the road..."

"Or over somebody's mailbox."

"Let's do it," I said. "I'll get the dance class to give her a certificate for the course."

"Your turn."

"My turn?" I put my toothbrush back next to his. "For what?"

He stepped behind me and stroked the hairbrush from the crown of my head to the ends of my ash-brown hair that hung between my shoulder blades. It was just right.

WEEK TWO

THURSDAY

"MARTINSVILLE POLICE department. Sheffield here... Hey there, Brighton. What can I do for you?... Week after next?...Got it. Will you be leaving that Sunday?...I'll tell Reebok to keep an eye on your house...Yes, I'll be gone, too. It's that training program for small-town police officers...." Bob picked up a sticky pad and jotted himself a reminder. "Well, thanks. I appreciate the vote of confidence, but we can all use some new ideas once in a while...Yeah. I'll sign him up for one of these sometime. Right now he's still learning the basics. You have a good trip." He hung up and stuck the note on the corner of his desk. The basics, he thought. How can Reebok learn the basics when nothing ever happens around here?

"ONE CINNAMON BUN, please," Annie said. "I seem to be addicted to these."

"While you're at it, Margot," I said, "I'll take

two of them." I smiled at Annie. "Bob and I are both addicted, too."

Margot lifted a wide swirl of cinnamon roll from the deli case and eased it into a waxed bag. "Are you going on that cruise, Annie?"

"No. I don't want to close the shop until I have to visit my brother. You know how he is."

"That is not what I would call a vacation." Margot spoke with hardly a trace of an accent, but she tended not to use contractions, the result of her Scandinavian upbringing, I supposed. She put two rolls into a second bag and handed it to me. Yum.

"Bob's headed to Atlanta for two weeks," I offered, "but it's not a vacation."

"He is, and so is everybody else."

"What do you mean?"

"Leaving town." Margot waved her tongs in the general direction of north, which was the only way to go if you wanted to drive out of this dead-end valley. "Irene Pursey is headed out tomorrow to visit her sister in Ohio."

"She'll enjoy that," Annie said. "Doesn't she go up there every year or so?"

"Every other year. Remember her sister was here for a week last year?"

"Who else is leaving?" I asked.

"Ellen Montgomery is on her way to Florida week after next." She handed me my change.

"Vacation?" I asked.

"She has a Realtor's convention going on. Brighton is tagging along just for the sun and the fishing, probably."

"What about Ariel?"

"She will stay here."

I didn't like the sound of that. "Alone? She's only seventeen."

Margot waved her hand, dismissing my concerns. "No, no, no. Pumpkin is there." I wasn't sure just what sort of chaperone quality a twenty-two-year-old manicurist would provide. Still, Pumpkin was pleasant, fun even. She'd been dating my son for several months, and that was going well. "That way Ariel will not be alone at night," Margot added.

"When you see her, tell her if she needs anything to give me a call." I planned to call Ellen myself and tell her to post my number on the fridge as a backup contact.

Annie walked out the door ahead of me. "Are you headed back to your shop?" I asked.

"Yes."

"Can I walk along with you? I need more soap and some tea. Might as well pick them up now."

Neither one of us said much on the walk down to Heal Thyself. We mentioned how good it was that the water level in the Pool, a wide pond-like section of the Metoochie River, was back down to normal after the recent floods; we nodded and smiled at the few people who passed us; we looked at the new display in the window of Frank's Frame Shop, but that was about it. What inexpressible comfort to be able to simply "be" and not feel a need to chatter. Of course, chattering could be fun, too. Our Tuesdays at Melissa's certainly proved that. But this felt good. I was delighted that Annie and I, despite the disparity in our ages, had developed a real heart-to-heart connection. Women need women friends.

ANNIE PUSHED OPEN the door and flipped the BE RIGHT BACK sign around to OPEN—COME RIGHT IN. "You want half of this cinnamon roll?" She pointed to her bag.

"No, thanks. I bought my own, remember? You go ahead and eat. I'm going to be a while." I found a couple of things that weren't on my list. Then I dithered around trying to decide whether to get two packages of the licorice-root tea or one of that and one of the hibiscus-flower tea. "What do you think, Annie?"

"Get two of each," she said. "I may have to close up my shop for a week or two, so you'll need plenty to last. You can't drink the licorice root more than five or six days in a row because it might increase your blood pressure. If you have something to alternate it with, you'll be able to enjoy it longer. And the hibiscus tea is almost as sweet as the licorice root. At least, that particular blend is. Be sure you keep them in the fridge. They'll stay fresh longer."

"Thanks. I appreciate the advice." I plopped all four boxes down on her counter beside the stockpile I'd already started. Shampoo, handmade soap, flower-essence cream, organic toothpaste. "This should do it, unless you have something that'll get rid of fleas. Marmalade's been scratching a lot."

"Get a flea comb. Ida carries them in their pet-food section. Comb her every day. And try garlic."

"Garlic?"

"Feed her some chopped-up garlic, just a little bit with every meal. It gets in the bloodstream. Fleas and ticks don't like that taste. Of course it might not be fleas at all. It could just be some dry skin. But the garlic won't hurt, and it might help."

"Will she eat it?"

"Hopefully. Dogs usually like it. Cats go fifty-fifty. Try mixing it with some chicken."

"Annie! You're a vegetarian. Why would you suggest chicken?"

"Cats aren't vegetarians, and we can't expect them to be."

"Oh. Would salmon do, then? I have some left from last night."

"Yeah. Salmon is good for dry skin, too, in case it's just that." She rang up the total on her new cash register.

I pulled out my wallet. "Why are you closing your shop?"

"My brother the complainer," she grumped. "The one I was telling Margot about. For as long as I can remember, it's been one ridiculous medical problem after another, and every time he has another set of tests done, he expects me to baby-sit him. Well, this time I told him I didn't think I could be there, but I did agree that I'd drive down if he really needed me. Which he doesn't, but he thinks he does." Annie was usually so calm, except at tap-dance class, when she became as animated as a circus performer. It was sad to hear her spouting with anger like this. "I've closed up my shop so many times and run to Atlanta to take care of him for nothing whatsoever. Just his overactive imagination. He is such a hypochondriac. You'd think nothing in the world ever happened to anybody except him. Now he thinks there's something else major going on, and he wants me to go down there and hold his selfish hand."

"Don't you and he have other relatives who could help?"

She shook her head. "We have aunts and uncles all up and down the valley, but most of them are in their fifties or sixties. Too old to be of much use."

Stop, Biscuit, I told myself. Fifties? Old? Land's sake, whatever was the child thinking? Of course, I used to think her way, too, when I was in my twenties, as she was now. The older I got, the farther old age receded into the horizon line. "Yes," I couldn't help saying. "Yes, I see what you mean. That's really old."

She had the good grace to look abashed. "I didn't mean it like that. I mean, you're not old. You take tap-dance lessons and everything." She tossed her heavy braid back behind her shoulder. It had a tendency to migrate forward. "You don't act old the way my relatives do. You'd think the world was ending if they miss one of their TV shows. Still, they don't seem to care that I have to close my shop every time I go down to my brother's. That means no income, but I still have to pay the mortgage on this place."

"What sorts of problems has he had? Your brother, I mean."

"That's just it. It's never been anything conclusive. He's gotten every test in the book, and they all amount to nothing."

"He must have symptoms, though, for them to be willing to do tests."

"He's been saying lately that he has horrible headaches. I think he's making it up to get attention." She picked up one of the quilt squares that lay in a pile on the counter and twisted it in her hand. "He's been like this since he was a baby— always needing to be the center of everything. I'm sick and tired of being the one he always calls on.

Why can't I just stay here and quilt and dance and run my shop? Or get in my car someday and start driving and never stop. Just run away."

I could hear the pain twisting her voice. I could see it in the tension of her hands tearing at the fabric. "Sounds like you need a big sister to spoil you."

"Fat chance," she said. But then her eyes lit up. "Are you volunteering?"

I thought only for a moment. It did sound like fun. "Why not?" I said. "Glaze and I are going to the circus next week. Do you want to go with us? We're awfully old, I know." She laughed and slapped at me across the counter. "I'll even buy you some…" I almost said *cotton candy,* but Annie, a vegetarian and health-food nut, would never sink so low as to eat that sugary stuff. "Popcorn," I said.

She put down the ruined quilt square and reached out to shake. "It's a deal!" She started putting my items in the cloth bag I always had with me. Annie did not approve of plastic bags. She'd made sturdy cloth tote bags for every one of her regular customers. If we didn't bring them with us, we were out of luck.

One more thing. "Are you going to the funeral tomorrow?"

"Is anybody in town not going to be there? As

far as I know, everybody's closing their stores. It's going to look like we evacuated Martinsville."

"I hardly knew him. I'm going primarily for Sadie's sake."

"I did know him," Annie said. "Quite well." She sniffed at the soap and added it to the bag. "Love this stuff."

"That was the last one on the shelf."

"Thanks. I didn't realize I was low." She absent-mindedly twiddled her braid with her right hand while she jotted a note to herself. Annie made her own notepads by tearing up paper that had been printed on one side already. Always the ecologist. "I'll call Alicia to get some more," she said. "Her sister makes the soap."

"Alicia the bed-and-breakfast lady?"

"That's the one." She tucked in the shampoo and returned to our talk about Wallace. "He was almost like a grand-daddy to me. He used to play catch with us kids up at that vacant lot on Willow. He taught everybody how to fish, and you'd think he had all the time in the world anytime we wanted to talk to him. He never tried to do three things at once. He just listened." Her hands hovered above the bag, fingers wiggling in the air. "I was afraid of the worms we used for fish bait right at first. But he never would bait the hook for me. He always said if I was going to kill something, I had to have the decency to put some real effort into it. I asked him if he was talking about the fish or the worm. And he said…" Her voice sank to a near whisper. "He said, 'They're both living creatures, don't you think, Little One?'" She looked up at me through a veil of tears. "That's what he always called me—Little One."

"I'm sure he loved you very much."

"He and Sadie lost a son years ago. Did you know that?"

I nodded. "I don't know the details, though."

"Neither do I. I never wanted to pry, and they didn't seem to want to talk about it, especially when I was so young. But I often wondered if all of us were just there because he couldn't make up for what he'd lost." She pushed the bag across the counter to me. "Still, it sure felt like he loved us."

"I don't think you can fake love, Annie. He may have missed his son dreadfully, but that doesn't mean he loved you any less."

"I hope not," she said. "I hope not."

I turned to leave. "You'll be at the viewing tonight, right?"

"Yes. I need to say good-bye, although Melissa stopped in earlier and said that people were in and out of Axelrod's all day. Wallace hasn't been left alone even for a moment."

"I'm surprised. Funeral homes usually have set hours for the viewings."

A slow smile spread across Annie's face. "Marvin really liked Wallace. And he's had such a change of heart recently. It's amazing to think of how different this funeral is going to be."

The bell on the door tinkled and Pumpkin breezed in. She nodded to me. "Don't want to interrupt. I had a few minutes between nail appointments and I thought I'd look around some more. Is that okay?"

Annie smiled. "Of course. Let me know when you have more questions."

Pumpkin headed toward the back. "I'm going to start where I left off yesterday."

Annie smiled again and lowered her voice. "She's so interested in all the products. I feel like I'm teaching an herb class whenever she stops by."

"It must feel good to know that someone is so intrigued by your work."

"She's a natural at it. She wants to come up with a whole line of organic, healthy products she can get Sharon to use in the Beauty Shop. I guess I'd be sort of a wholesaler for those."

I thought of the wave of chemical smells that wafted out onto the sidewalk whenever anyone opened Sharon's shop door. The baskets in the small gift shop that adjoined the beauty parlor always smelled faintly of hair spray and coloring agents. "Good idea. Think she'll agree?"

Annie shrugged. "It's worth a try. And it would generate some more income here."

Pumpkin bounced back in our direction. "Did I tell you I've been doing some research? I found a really good line of nail polishes that don't have any toluene in them." She squinched up her nose and looked at me. "That's short for toluenesulfon-amide formaldehyde resin. Nasty stuff. It's in em-balming fluid." She swiveled back toward Annie. "Do you want to carry them? They'd be much healthier for everyone. The clients, and me, too."

"I don't know how you manage to breathe that stuff all day long," I said.

"It's pretty awful. Same with the hair-care prod-ucts Sharon uses. We need to change this whole industry. It's a living for now, but I'd like to see some big improvements made." She looked back around at Annie's peaceful shop. "I'd love to have my own shop someday, but I have a lot of saving and planning to do before that's a reality. Whoops! Look at the time. Hafta run. See you!"

The bell sang out again, and Annie shuffled a few display products from one side of the counter to the other. "You know what I'm wondering?"

"I think I can guess. You might be able to train Pumpkin to fill in for you now and then?"

"I don't know if it would work. There's not a lot of extra money. But she has some good ideas for bringing in extra customers. And this idea of hers to sell worthwhile products to beauty salons? What do you think?"

"Sounds like it's worth a try."

"I think I've been too scared for too long." Annie smiled. "Way too long."

Dear Annie,

We'd all have much more fun if you came along on my birthday cruise. I don't want to offend you, dear, but would you consider allowing me to reimburse you for the cost of closing your shop for the week? It would be an honor for me to help you in this way.

Please don't be upset with me. I acknowledge how well you have done, setting your goals and opening your shop. You have made it a place of beauty, and I love the products you sell. I want to make sure that you thrive in your business. This would be my gift to you, but you can call it an indefinite loan, if you want to. I wouldn't need to be paid back until I ran out of money—and we both know that'll be a LONG time coming.

Please take me up on this. I want to see you dancing across the poop deck (is that the right term?) with that red hair of yours blowing in the Caribbean breeze.

With great respect for all you've accomplished,

Margaret

My Gratitude List for Thursday Afternoon

It seems important somehow to be more grateful than usual, so I'm doing two lists— one now and one later tonight.

For now:

1. Annie, definitely!
2. My new shampoo.
3. Hot tea.
4. Comfortable shoes.
5. I wonder if I'll ever put busybody Clara Martin on this list? Probably not, although I suppose every town needs one like her.
6. That wasn't really number five, so I'll add: Cinnamon rolls. And honeysuckle soap.

I am grateful for
sitting on LooseLaces' lap
my catnip in the garden
pens to play with
my new comb
the salmon, even though it tastes funny

AXELROD'S WAS PACKED that Thursday evening. Even with their big parking lot, it was a good thing that practically everybody in town walked everywhere they went, except for Margaret, of course, because of her feet. She'd come in the Duesenberg, bringing her mother and several of the truly elderly townsfolk. Ida and Ralph had picked up Sadie and planned to stay with her the entire time.

We met up with Henry and Irene Pursey at the guest book. Irene handed me the pen. "I hear you're leaving for Ohio tomorrow," I said as I signed and passed the pen to Bob.

She nodded toward where Sadie stood near the door. "Not now. I'll stay for the funeral. Anyway, my sister's miserable with a rotten cold, so I'm going to wait another week before I go up there."

"Those summer colds can be bad news," I said.

"You're right. So can the autumn ones and the winter ones."

"And the spring ones?" I finished for her.

The next stop was at a rectangular table that held squares of white paper and a variety of colored markers. A small sign proclaimed:

COFFIN NOTES
Write a short message
to accompany Wallace on his way home

I picked up a green marker and wrote *I wish I could have known you sooner and better.* Bob's marker was red. We traded our pieces of paper, and I read: *You taught me so much about so many things. I will always treasure our friendship. Rest well.* We each placed our note in the big fishbowl that sat in the middle of the table and moved closer to where Sadie greeted people.

Sharon and Carl Armitage stood right before us in the informal line. Sharon kissed Sadie's cheek and said a few words.

Carl shook her hand and patted her on the shoulder. They walked past the banks of flowers to the casket, and it was our turn. Sadie was quietly composed. We hugged. I thanked her for allowing me the honor to stay with her there at the end. She nodded, but I had the feeling she wasn't sure what I was talking about. She probably didn't even remember that I'd been there when Wallace died. Bob leaned way over to murmur a few words in her ear and kiss her cheek.

Right behind us, Maggie and Norm Pontiac waited their turn. I took Bob's arm and we moved ahead to admire the floral arrangements. No matter how often people say *In lieu of flowers, please send a donation to our favorite charity,* there were always those who kept the florists in business. I was on the verge of whispering a snide comment to Bob, when I noticed one particularly striking piece with daylilies and daisies and even a big floret from a joe-pye weed. It looked somewhat like my wedding bouquet. Out of curiosity I peeked at the card. *In loving memory of a dear friend.* It was signed *Biscuit and Bob.* I poked his arm and changed my comment to a question. "What did you do that for? They said no flowers."

He leveled a glance at me and folded his hand over mine. "Doesn't matter. I sent a check to the Audubon Society, just like they asked. But I also know that flowers mean a lot. She'll look at the cards afterward and know we love her."

"It takes more than flowers at a funeral to show that." I was mildly ticked at him.

"Don't you like the flowers I picked out?" he asked, and he brushed his broad, gentle fingertips over the ring on my fourth finger.

"Maybe it wasn't such a bad idea after all," I admitted.

We moved on over near Sharon. "He's cool," she said. It took me a moment to register that this was not a phrase out of the fifties. She meant it literally. She picked up Wallace's hand. It had lost its purple tinge and looked soft. "Here, feel it." Instinctively I backed away, remembering the time I was ten years old and my grandmother tried to kiss a dead body in a casket. The look on the funeral-parlor lady's face was enough for me to know that my grandma was messing things up big-time.

Sharon laughed at my expression. "This is the nicest thing about not having somebody embalmed." She smiled down at Wallace, who, I had to admit, didn't have that stretched, artificial look that corpses usually had. His wrinkles had eased away. "They have to keep the body refrigerated. This is a special coffin just for that."

I reached out, tentatively at first, and laid my hand on his. It did feel cool. It felt soft, too, and incredibly flexible. I could almost imagine him sitting up and inviting us all to go fishing. Bob stepped around me and laid his hand on Wallace's chest. "Thank you for teaching me to fish," he said. "Rest well, friend."

Maggie nudged my right arm. "Take a look at that," she said and pointed at the floral arrangement that covered the bottom half of the casket. It looked like a two-foot square of meadowland where a fisherman dropped his tackle box. There were weeds and grasses, some tiny white daisies and a few buttercups. There was even a pine branch complete with cones, and a couple of dandelions. A bright orange tackle box on its side spilled lures and hooks and a spindle of spare fishing line onto the patch of moss in the center of the arrangement. The ball cap I'd seen Wallace wear was perched there beside his tackle box. A slogan on the brim said *Old fishermen never die. They just smell that way.* There was a wooden fold-up ruler. One side of it had regular inch marks. On the other side the marks were squeezed together, so that a nine-inch fish would register a foot and a half long.

Ida walked up beside us. "Wallace would have hated one of those formal floral sprays, don't you think?"

"This is just right," I said. "Just exactly right."

My Second Gratitude List for Thursday
1. My wonderful husband—may we have many years together.
2. My wonderful sister—ditto.
3. My dear friends—ditto again.
4. Roger, who is so dependable with his garbage route.
5. This creaky old house where I feel safe.
6. The joy of seeing that "meadow" on Wallace's casket AND—
7. The idea of a green cemetery. I think it's about time!

Oh, heck, I need a number 8, too. Combing Marmy. I've always brushed her, but this is better. She curls her little head around and licks her tongue in and out while I'm doing it. She must really enjoy it. I haven't found any fleas, but I've gotten out a lot of extra fur. That much less for her to shed on the bed. And the couch. And the chairs. And the floor. Good grief, Biscuit. Stop writing and go to sleep.

I am grateful for
eating
running
sleeping
playing
stretching
and being combed by Widelap

WEEK TWO

FRIDAY

AMAZING GRACE, AS MY FATHER, a high school music teacher, once explained to me, uses the pentatonic scale. It's a far older scale than the do-re-mi folderol. That's why the melody is so haunting. Maybe that's one of the reasons it's so overused at funerals. My dad taught us to play it on the black notes of the piano. Just those five black keys, and all the pain, all the sorrow, all the anguish comes rolling out. Also all the hope and the wonder. Maybe not so overused at that.

Easton Hastings sang it, standing beside the open grave with her luscious voice spilling the music onto the forest floor in front of us. "...was blind, but now I see."

How often, I wondered, had I been blind, blind to the beauty around me? Blind to the heartaches of other people? How often did I forget to reach out or was too busy? How often did I not acknowledge the thoughtful things Bob does for me—

the orange juice in the morning and the way he brushes my hair? Who else did I pass over on a regular basis?

You are a good human.

I slipped my fingers into the crook of Bob's elbow. He folded his large, comforting hand over mine. Marmalade rumbled her loud purr beside my left foot. Just beyond her, Glaze stood quietly, absorbed in her own thoughts. I saw Tom reach out and take her hand. She let him, and I sensed her body lean a bit closer toward him. That was well, then. I glanced over at Sadie. Marmalade walked away from me and leaned against Sadie's left leg, as if to comfort her friend. Ida stood behind Sadie on her right. Comfort in stereo.

Easton repeated the first verse. "'I once was lost, but now am found, was blind, but now I see.'" The notes faded slowly. She lowered her head. Easton had changed a lot in the past six months. At least, I hadn't heard any of the wives in town complaining that Easton was still chasing their husbands. She still had that volcanic head of hair, like a flow of new lava erupting in a halo. That woman certainly didn't deserve a halo, but she did look angelic standing there with her hair cascading down her back. Maybe I'd been unfair. Maybe—as Sadie always did—I should see the good in her, see the woman who'd struggled with a difficult childhood and lived to come through on the other side of it. See the woman who loved birds as much as Wallace had. Then she raised her eyes and looked at Bob. My Bob. So much for grace, amazing or otherwise. She hadn't changed a bit. I tightened my hold on his arm. Bless him. He hadn't noticed a thing.

Henry said a few more words, but I wasn't listening. Like a lot of people there, I wondered what would come next. None of us had ever experienced a green funeral before, and all we had to go on were Marvin's quick instructions at the start of the service.

There were two stark mounds of dirt sitting on blue tarps behind the open grave. Three shovels stuck out of the larger mound on the left. Henry stepped away from the grave and stood next to Sadie. He nodded at Bob. Bob looked at Tom. Together they walked to the lightweight cardboard casket that sat on two fabric-covered sawhorses. While Roger Johnson and Ralph Peterson held the coffin steady, Bob and Tom lifted Wallace's body gently, reverently, and carried him to the open grave. He was wrapped in the blue quilt Annie made for him years ago. In the past few days, she had sewn the sides of it together, to make a sort of pouch to hold his body. I noticed that in the three days since he died, Wallace had begun to look more like a shell than anything else. Even though his body had been cooled, he'd somehow sunken in, as if something vital had left. I wondered if that would make it easier for Sadie to let go.

The dogwood tree, as if it had rehearsed a script, rustled in the breeze and then was still. Henry escorted Sadie forward. Roger stepped to the side of the grave and picked up an old-fashioned yellow mixing bowl, filled to overflowing with yellow rose petals mixed with all the "coffin notes" we'd written yesterday. He held it while Sadie sprinkled about half of the contents into the grave. She kissed Wallace's thin cheek and swayed against Henry, who led her back to the chair. Ida laid a hand on her shoulder. Marmalade leaned back in close.

Bob took the full weight of Wallace's limp body while Tom knelt down. Bob passed the body to Tom, then knelt himself. Together they eased Wallace into his final resting place. Annie stepped forward then and went down on her knees. Tom held her around the waist while she leaned way forward and placed a large quilt square over Wallace's face. There was a heart in the center of it. Maggie brought a blackberry-laden branch. She handed it to Tom, who reached down and rested it on Wallace's chest. Roger brought a short bamboo fishing pole. Ralph offered a bunch of bananas. "He loved bananas," he said when we laughed. One by one, Wallace was showered with simple gifts, not so much, I thought, to ease him on his way, as to honor him for Sadie's sake and to ease our own knowing of his passing. At the end, Sadie stepped forward again and scooped up the remaining yellow rose petals and handwritten notes and showered them onto the body, onto the gifts, onto what was left of the man she had known for almost her entire life, the man whose bed she had shared for sixty years.

Those of us who chose to stay took turns shoveling the dirt gently back into the hole, forming a burial mound over him, starting with the heavier subsoil that sat on the left-hand tarp. Ralph and Roger finished the effort, ending with the lighter top-soil that had been kept separate on the right. Ida nestled a small azalea bush into the mounded dirt. Maggie offered it a drink from a green watering can. Bob and Tom replaced the leaf litter from yet another tarp. They had scraped it up earlier, before the grave was dug. The azalea looked right at home. The dogwood tree rustled one more time, and it was over.

On the way to Sadie's after the funeral, Bob and I dropped by Town Hall so he could pick up his pager. I walked in with him simply because it beat standing on the street. We rounded the corner into Bob's office rather abruptly and caught Reebok polishing his badge. He didn't look the least bit put out. I couldn't help but wonder if he would ever have any real work to do.

"Thanks for filling in for me today," Bob said. He moved to a corner of the room where there was a small sink and lathered up his hands. The dirt, all that was left of the end of the burial, washed away, down the drain.

"Happy to help, Sir." He always called Bob "Sir," and it always sounded as if he'd capitalized it. Reebok slipped his polishing handkerchief into his back pocket. "You can call on me anytime."

"I think for now, having you here nights and weekends is more than enough. It's a real luxury not getting calls in the middle of the night."

A shadow clouded Reebok's sunny face. "There haven't been many calls at all, Sir."

"That's a good thing, Garner. We'd like it to stay that way as much as possible."

"Yes, Sir," he said, but without conviction. "Did the funeral go okay?"

"Nobody fainted and nobody got run over. It went just fine." Bob sounded brusque, but I was pretty sure he was just holding in a lot of sorrow. He walked around the desk and slid open the top drawer. "Forgot my pager," he said. "Glad you didn't need to reach me."

Reebok moved his oversized coffee mug to one side and aligned the notepad that rested beside the phone. "I can handle it, Sir. You can count on me."

"I'm sure I can. I'll be at Sadie's house if you have to reach me. Then we'll head home after that."

"You have a good rest of your day."

"I'M SURPRISED HE DIDN'T salute you," I said. Our footsteps rang on the polished floor. A few voices in the background chatted, laughed. Somebody sneezed. Somebody else coughed. Normal sounds for a workaday world, but this wasn't a regular day. This was the day we'd helped lay Wallace in the ground. "It seemed so much more civilized this way," I said.

Bob knew what I was talking about. No wonder I loved him. He took my elbow as we walked out the imposing front door and down a short flight of steps. "You're right. I don't ever want to see one of those barbaric funerals again."

"Why do you suppose Marvin agreed so readily? This is a complete changeabout."

"His dog died a while back," he said.

"What does that have to do with anything?"

Bob let go of my elbow and took my hand. "Bear with me, Woman." As we walked toward Third Street he lifted his other hand in a greeting to the group of firefighters lounging on lawn chairs outside the station. "Quiet today?" he asked them.

The man on the left nodded. "Yessir. Not a single call."

"One call," the woman next to him said at the same time.

"That's still pretty quiet."

"Now, wait a minute," one of the other men chipped in. "Wilena's right. We did get that one call from Orrin, but it wasn't anything important."

"Orrin thought it was." The woman used a bantering tone, but I thought she meant it.

"I mean it wasn't anything we needed to do anything about. He just wanted to know what time the funeral started."

"Library closed today?" the first man asked.

"Yes," I said. "It didn't feel right to keep it open the day of the funeral."

"I hope Miss Sadie understands why we missed the service."

"You needed to be right here," Bob said. "Just in case. Miss Sadie knows that."

The woman sitting in the group looked me up and down until one of the others elbowed her arm. "You haven't been here long enough to know about Orrin," he said. "He calls all the time."

I'd never met Orrin. He sounded like a pain in the butt, but maybe he was just lonely. It seemed that each one of the firefighters had to put in a comment on how slow the day was and how often Orrin called the station.

Bob waved again. "Keep up the good work." We veered right at the corner onto Third Street. "Marvin and I were talking at Larry's one day," Bob finally said. "We were both of us waiting for haircuts. He told me his dog died the week before and that he dug a grave in his backyard. Hey there, Matthew," he called out to our neighbor as we crossed over Beechnut Lane. Matthew stood at the railing of his front porch, fanning himself with his straw hat. "Some funeral, eh?"

"Sure was," Matthew agreed. "About the nicest one I've ever seen. Hey there, Miss Biscuit." I nodded and he went on. "I'll be on up to Sadie's in a few minutes. I stopped by to check on Mr. Fogerty and give him some clean water. He's been losing too many feathers lately. I'll have quite a few to give you for those cat toys you're making."

"Thanks, Matthew," Bob said. "We'll pick them up on our way home from Sadie's."

We walked a few more steps before Bob continued with his story. "Marvin said he saw how he'd been robbing people of a lot of joy. A chance to touch and hold and say good-bye in a way that really meant something. He didn't ever again want to push a family away from a grave so he could lower some cranks and dump a truckload of dirt…" He paused. "Well, you get the idea. He just all of a sudden got fed up with it all. And that's when he heard about green cemeteries. There aren't many of them, yet."

"Well, now there's one more than there was before. You don't think it'll hurt the Old Woods, do you?"

"No. You should have seen the care we took on that grave, being sure we didn't sever any big roots. It was a work of art by the time we got done." The quiet pride in his voice made me rummage around in my purse for a tissue. The rest of the trip to Sadie's was quiet, except for our footsteps on the sidewalk and a few sniffles from me.

THE HOUSE WASN'T AS CROWDED as I'd thought it might be. Oh, there were plenty of people, but most of the store owners had gone back to their shops right after the graveside service. People from offices up the valley headed back to work. I wasn't sure whether the crowd at the cemetery had been there because of Wallace's popularity throughout his life, as reflected in his long obituary, or whether everyone attending was simply curious to see the first green burial in Northeast Georgia. Regardless, good manners kept the casual onlookers away from Sadie's house once the funeral itself was complete. Marmalade, I noticed as I walked in, was already installed on Sadie's lap, enjoying the petting.

I am keeping her warm.

I almost envied her ignorance. Even though she'd followed us to the funeral, she was still a cat, and a cat wouldn't understand what was going on.

SlowWalker is gone and LooseLaces is sad.

Clara, naturally, ran the post-funeral show. I paused in the archway to the dining room and watched her adjust an oversized vase—a lovely deep indigo color. It was filled to overflowing with every kind of yellow flower imaginable. That had to be the vase Margaret had commissioned from Connie, the glassblower who lived on Willow Street. I was going to have to meet that woman. The vase truly was a work of art. Clara stopped fussing with it and directed several people toward the small plates stacked in a pile at the far end of Sadie's long dining table. As if we couldn't see the plates ourselves. I did notice that the bread I'd delivered earlier was sliced and artfully displayed in a lovely handmade basket. Clara's back was to me. I looked at her stocky frame. A belt that would have looked better hanging from a saddle pinched her polyester dress in the middle. She looked like an overstuffed scarecrow, but who was I to judge?

"Whatever you are thinking about that woman," Melissa whispered in my ear, "you better wipe your face in case she turns around."

I pulled my grimace into a semblance of sweet gentility, or as close as I could get considering the view in front of me, and raised my voice. "Shall we go see if we can find the plates, Melissa?"

Clara whipped around. "Right down that way, Biscuit, darling. On the left."

"Why, thank you, Clara."

Melissa pulled me away before I could sharpen my claws.

The hospital bed was gone from the living room, and one of the big couches had been moved out to make room for a number of folding chairs. We gathered around in small groups, chatting quietly, laughing occasionally as someone remembered a story about Wallace and shared it with the group. Gradually we rearranged chairs until most of us were sitting in a big circle, each of us listening to the reminiscences of the others. Sadie told us about how she first fell in love with him. I'd heard the story before, but it felt good to listen to it again. Roger Johnson mentioned how he'd learned to fish, following Mr. Wallace down to the pool in the Metoochie River most summer mornings. Annie recounted the worm story. Matthew spoke of how often Wallace had visited Mr. Fogerty, who liked to perch on his heavy glasses and preen Wallace's eyebrows. Ralph about broke us up when he relived how Wallace caught him and a friend of his years ago trying to shinny up the flagpole in the town park.

Marvin had been standing on the outside of the

circle all this time, but he cleared his throat and stepped between Glaze and Tom. "I'd like to say a few words."

"There's a seat for you over here," Matthew said. "Might as well be comfortable while you're talking, eh?"

"Thank you." Marvin folded his considerable height down onto the chair. "I know I mentioned this up by the gravesite, but I'd like to stress it one more time. I'd like to thank the town council again for agreeing to the formation of a conservation area so we could have burials in the Old Woods. That was a very forward-thinking move. Too bad Hubbard couldn't be there for the votes." He nodded in Clara's direction. She looked as if she'd just bitten into a lemon. "I'm glad to hear he's doing well after his hemorrhoidectomy."

He paused for just a moment. There simply were no secrets in a town this size. Melissa leaned close to me and whispered, "If that man hadn't been in the hospital, the vote never would have gone through, and Marvin knows it."

"Yes, but no sense mentioning that here."

"He doesn't have to—we all know how Hubbard stands on anything ecological."

"Shh!"

"I'd also like to thank Miss Sadie for allowing me the honor of inaugurating the Green Cemetery today by agreeing to have her beloved Wallace put to rest in a way that may have shocked some of you at first." He looked around the circle. Several folk didn't meet his gaze. "I'd like to explain why I did this, if you don't mind. I don't mean any disrespect at all to Miss Sadie, if you'll forgive me. She's heard this story. That's why she agreed to have Wallace be the first. You see, my family's dog died a while ago. I dug a grave in my backyard." He looked around the circle and nodded to a few people. "Some of you had kids that were there at the funeral. Remember how Becky and Cindy picked those flowers and dropped them in the grave? We wrapped Buster in an old baby blanket, and everybody cried and got to pet him one last time and hug him before they said goodbye. Then we each placed some dirt over him, real gently, like we were tucking him in for the night."

Ida turned away, picked up a tissue box, and started it around the circle. All the women took one or two. A couple of the men did, too.

Marvin's voice was quiet. "I had one of those whatdya-call-'em moments."

"An epiphany?" I offered.

"Yes, ma'am. One of those. I saw that I'd been holding people away from their loved ones. I'd been buying into the system that sterilized death and kept people afraid of it. Before today, how many of you ever had the chance to hold the hand of a dead person, a person you loved?" He ran his hands back through his hair. "Doggone it! It's wrong what we've done over the years. We took something that used to be beautiful and meaningful and…and sacred…and turned it into a show. A show designed to make money off people who were so tore up they couldn't stand it." He looked down at his shoes. "I didn't see it that way, of course. I thought I was helping all of you by being sure the service was just chock-full of dignity…. Oh, there was plenty of dignity, all right. But there wasn't nearly as much heart as there could have been." He rubbed his hand across his chest. "Yes, heart. That's what I've been holding away from you."

Clara sneezed. A chorus of bless-you's came from all around. Marvin waited a moment for the ripple of laughter to clear. "Do any of you, and I have to apologize for bringing this up while some folks are still eating, but do any of you know how many hundreds of thousands of gallons of embalming fluid—of poison, that is—get put underground every year in cemeteries? Or how many tons of concrete? Do you have any idea how the graveyards across this nation are polluting…" Marvin stopped. "I'm sorry," he said. "I'll stop right there. I just need to say that I've done a very great wrong. I did it with the best of intentions. But I know better now, and I'm not ever going to bury a single one of your loved ones any more in a way that hurts you or the earth." He looked around one more time. "I think you'll thank me for this someday." He unfolded himself, rather like the fish ruler we'd placed on Wallace's grave, and left the room. Just before the front door closed, Bob started clapping. After a second's hesitation, Sadie joined in, and then we all whooped and hollered as if we'd just been handed a winning lottery ticket. Even Clara, I was surprised to note. Marvin must have heard us, but he didn't come back in.

My Gratitude List for Friday
1. Annie. Sadie said she's the one who created the meadow for Wallace's casket. What an amazingly talented young woman she is. It's going to be fun getting to know her better. I wonder if she'll ever marry. Maybe Roger? With his red hair and hers, they'd have gorgeous kids. How could I get the two of them together?
2. Sadie.
3. Whoever invented green funerals. Reinvented them, that is.
4. Glaze and Tom, Ida and Ralph, and Melissa.
5. Marvin. I admire his courage.

I am grateful for
Widelap
Softfoot

Smellsweet
Fishgiver
LooseLaces

WEEK TWO

SATURDAY

THE DELISCHUSS, a town fixture for the past two decades, served the best hot chocolate on the face of the earth. In my opinion, that is. Hans and Margot Schuss started their deli as newlyweds. His German pastries and her Scandinavian sandwiches educated the taste buds of the fried-chicken Southerners. Then Hans discovered a flair for making good ole Georgia-style barbecue that he ladled over corn bread as good as any my grandmother used to make. You'd think he'd been raised on it. Now we could have regional and international fare at one friendly, convenient spot. And, of course, the hot chocolate, which had recently supplanted my tendency toward hot tea.

Glaze and I often stopped there on our way home from our weekly walk around town—a habit we'd gotten into shortly after she moved to Martinsville. Bob had his own Saturday routine, but he'd mentioned this morning that he planned to go into the office for a few hours. "With Reebok there haunting the place," I'd razzed him.

"No. He's doing some yard chores for Myrtle today, so I'll have some peace and quiet."

Glaze and I alternated our routes each Saturday morning, but we almost always ended up at the Delicious, as everybody called it.

Our favorite booth was over by the big windows. Ariel didn't even ask anymore. She just brought a vanilla milkshake for Glaze and a big mug of foaming, hot heaven topped with swirls of whipped cream and a drizzle of hot fudge sauce for me. Two sips, and we continued our conversation where we'd left off. "Why on earth," I asked her, "does he make everybody take their vacations at the same time? Wouldn't it make more sense to keep the office open?"

"Not if you're a control freak." Glaze pointed at her upper lip and then at me. My napkin, when I finished wiping, had a healthy smear of fudge sauce. I should have licked before I wiped. A shame to waste that extra calorie or two. "Hank," she said, "thinks he's the only one who can make day-to-day decisions, and he's nitpicky as heck. He's constantly looking over our shoulders and poking his nose in where it doesn't belong. If we try to suggest an improvement, he nixes it before we can even explain." CelerInc made gadgets of various sorts. Most often, their inventory went di-

rectly into the warehouse next door and was ped-
dled by Wish Fulfillment, the strangely named
catalog company my son worked for. She pushed
her straw out of the way and drank directly from
the frosty glass. "We scurry like crazy to get a
surplus of product built up and basically don't lose
anything by closing the doors for two weeks while
Hank heads off to the Caribbean. If that's where
he really goes." She wiped off her own mustache,
then stuck her nose down in her glass and inhaled.
"Love that vanilla smell."

"Doesn't he show pictures from his trips?"

"Nope. Never. And he comes back without any
kind of tan."

"Maybe he burns badly." I spoke from experience, since I had no pigment in my skin, a condition called vitiligo. There was no melanin to rise to
the surface in response to the sun's rays, so I never
could tan. It started with one dime-sized patch of
white on my face when I was pregnant with Sandra, my oldest, and eventually spread everywhere.
White legs, white arms, white face.

"Then why would he go south for a vacation?"
Glaze asked. "Why doesn't he go to Vermont or
Seattle or Minnesota?"

I nodded, not having an answer for that one,
and looked around at the other tables filling up
with the predictable late-morning rush. Mostly the
usual folks, but a few new ones sprinkled here and

there. A man in an oversized cable-knit sweater, too hot for this time of year. A hole near his elbow suggested that he might have snagged it and kept walking. Ariel refilled his coffee cup. "Anything else, Mr. Orrin?" she asked. So that was the lonely Orrin the firefighters had discussed. Behind him, a blond woman juggled a coffee cup and a baby. Cute kid, but more drool than I wanted to look at. Off to my right sat a stocky woman with her sleeves rolled up to her elbows, nursing what looked like a glass of ice water. She looked vaguely familiar, but I couldn't place her. The little boy who sat beside her on a booster seat had a mop of dark brown hair. Another cute kid. No drool on this one, which made him considerably more acceptable. His milkshake was almost as big as he was. Beyond the boy I could see a young fellow with his eye on Ariel as she worked the tables with her coffeepot. Over in the corner, Susan of the long black hair sat with a mug in her hands. Hot tea, I'd bet. No, she was more the coffee type. She'd braided her hair and wrapped it around her head. It looked like a crown. A diadem. Not a word I used very often. Not a word I ever used. But in this case it was just right. Even with her hair confined and tamed, the hair was still what I noticed. She had a point. People would automatically identify her by her hair. I did wonder how she'd ever found Martinsville. Our dead-end valley was certainly not a tourist destination. Unless that father she was searching for lived here. Now, that was something to think over. Who could he be? I glanced around the Delicious. The man in the holey sweater looked too old, but I couldn't discount him completely. I did a quick survey of all the other men in the room. Hans Schuss, Margot's husband, stepped from behind the deli case and wiped a cloth over a corner of the glass, probably erasing fingerprints. He was a possibility. Their daughter Miriam was college-aged. I'd have to think about that.

Henry Pursey, the minister, sat in his usual booth near the back across from Father John. That was unusual. They generally met in the afternoon, and here it was only nine-fifteen. Father John's infectious laugh poured out across the room. Henry had that smug look that some people get when they say something funny and don't want to be guilty of laughing at their own jokes. Susan, like most of us, looked over at Father John, but then she glanced around, met my gaze, and shifted her eyes quickly to her mug.

"Earth to Biscuit."

"Sorry, I tuned out there for a minute. What were we talking about?"

She grimaced. "Hank sticking his nose in everywhere."

"So your boss doesn't run the company. He just works there."

"What do you mean?" She adjusted the brim of that ridiculous pink hat she'd taken to wearing everywhere. At least it matched her lipstick of the week. With her yellow blouse, she looked like an Easter egg.

"If he truly ran his business like a business," I explained, "he'd hire people, train them to do the job right, delegate responsibility. Like Margot here. Cory's the one who suggested the espresso machine, and he was in high school at the time. Miriam, Cory, and Ariel all know how to run this place from opening to serving to cooking to ordering to closing. You've seen how good they are at it." Margot and Hans took high school students for after-school and weekend jobs, trained them, in many cases helped them with college plans, and advised them on starting their own businesses. They'd done that for Annie McGill, before she opened her herb-and-natural-products store just down the street.

"Uh-huh," Glaze said, "but Hank won't delegate anything, much less trust us for a whole two weeks. People have tried to suggest that he take a few hours off each day, but he just says nobody understands how hard it is to get people to do things right." She rotated her straw and gave a big slurp.

"Delicious. Some of those people have been working there for fifteen or twenty years."

"He still doesn't trust them?"

"Like I said, he's a control freak. He always grumps about the business not growing, but it can't with the stranglehold he puts on it. He wants to be rich, but I think he just wants the money to fall out of the sky and happen to him."

"You mean like Margaret and her millions and millions?" I'd found out recently that Margaret had quietly initiated a babysitting service for all the town employees, and then she expanded it to a full-fledged day-care center. Anyone who lived or worked in the south end of the valley qualified. If you were a town employee, it was free. If not, it was still unbelievably reasonable. She'd done it with no fanfare, though. I guess most of the long-time residents knew what she was doing, but we tended not to talk about Margaret to the newer residents, for fear of bringing crowds of money-hungry parasites to her front door.

"Yeah, I guess. But all that fortune hasn't spoiled her. She's still a truly nice person." Glaze went all misty-looking for a moment. "Can't you imagine what we could...I mean what she could do with all that dough?"

I wasn't sure if the day care that Bob had mentioned to me was public knowledge. To be on the safe side I said, "Well, she bought the town a new fire truck, and she sure has helped out a lot on the library."

"Like the stone lions?"

"Yes, although I'll thank you to remember that those were a wedding gift to me. I personally own two stone lions that are four feet tall." Glaze rolled her eyes at me, so I shifted back to the topic. "Did I tell you she gave us a healthy-sized grant? New shelving, hundreds of new books. A computer system should be in next month. We'll have to close the library while we get it set up."

"I know. You told me. Several times."

I pointed at her bright yellow tee-shirt. "You dribbled."

"Rats!" She grabbed a paper napkin and dunked the corner of it in her water glass.

While she mopped up the drop of milkshake— and left a palm-sized wet spot on her shirt—I kept talking. "She's set up a trust fund for the library. We get a monthly allocation." I already had a list a yard long of what to buy as Margaret's checks rolled in, and with all the new library patrons from Ida and Sadie's publicity campaign, we were eventually going to have to change to a six-day schedule instead of the three and a half days we were open now. I'd need more volunteers and maybe a paid assistant. Maybe I could just add one day at a time and see how it worked out.

"I didn't know she'd done that," Glaze said.

Annie's long red braid brushed my arm. "Done what?" she asked. I was glad she inquired. I'd forgotten what the subject was.

"Oh, we're talking about Margaret and her fortune," Glaze said. "She's helping the library."

"Well, of course she is."

I slid closer to the window. "You want to join us?"

"Can't," she said. "I have to get back to the store to meet Pumpkin. Just came by for a quick sandwich"—she waved the paper bag in her left hand— "because my tummy was rumbling. Thought I'd stop over to say hello."

I was in a zany mood anyway, so I turned to Glaze and asked, "Have you met my little sister?"

Glaze scowled at me as though I'd gone barmy, but caught the twinkle and stretched her hand out to Annie. "I'm glad to meet you. I've heard so much about you from your big sister."

Annie shook hands, laughed, and pivoted toward the door with her braid swinging out behind her. We both watched her until she was blocked from view by the stocky woman and the man with the holey sweater. Henry and Father John joined the exodus. Everyone seemed to be leaving at the same time. Except Susan. She still sat there sipping her coffee. I smiled at her, but she ducked her head and ignored me. "What were we talking about?" Glaze finally asked.

I thought a moment. "Margaret and her gener-osity to the library. Speaking of which—Marga-ret, not the library—are you sure you can't wangle some extra vacation so you can go on that cruise with us? She said she'd pay everything for all of us. She said only eight have signed up so far."

"Can't do it. I told you. The timing's wrong. Hank sets our vacation schedule, and this year it starts next Monday, whether we like it or not."

"Do you have plans?"

She lifted one shoulder. "Nothing special."

"You know," I said, "Bob's going to be gone all week."

"Where's he going?"

"It's that statewide training for small-town po-lice chiefs."

"Oh, yeah, you told me. I forgot it was com-ing up."

"Well, why don't you come down and stay with Marmalade and me for a few days? We'll have ourselves a sister-week."

"Sort of like a five-day slumber party?"

"You got it."

"What about the library?" She adjusted the rim of the stomach-remedy-pink hat that enveloped her head. I wasn't about to criticize her, but I did think the hat looked silly.

"I'll have to go in on Monday and Friday, but

you can come with me and help laminate dust jackets."

"Whoopee." She was really quite good at rolling her eyes. I guess I gave her lots of practice.

"No, it's fun," I insisted. "I'll show you how to work the machine. Piece of cake. You can even wear your hat."

She drained her glass and wiped her upper lip one more time. "It's a deal, big sister. What about Wednesday, though? Don't you have to be there that day, too?"

"The Petunias can handle it just fine." I chuckled. "I know how to delegate."

She plopped a generous tip on the table. "Will you give Hank some lessons?"

I glanced at my watch and started moving faster. "Gotta run or I'll be late opening the library." I loved my work. "You need a new job, Glaze."

She hunched both shoulders up this time. "Yeah," she said. "Like I'm qualified to do anything else."

Dear Margaret,

Thank you for your generous offer to help me. Yes. I accept. I'll get my average weekly sales figures together for you. Is there any other information you'll need from me?

Annie

SUSAN PUSHED HER long black hair back over her shoulder and laid her palm flat across her heart. She held it there for a moment before she knocked gently on the office door.

"Come in." His face brightened for just a moment and then fell. "Susan," he said and motioned to the chair across the desk from him.

"Hello, Dad. May I call you that?" She closed the door behind her.

"Yes. Yes, of course."

She pulled her hair forward over her left shoulder so she wouldn't sit on it. She was proud of her hair. It puddled in her lap, like midnight under an old magnolia. "I guess you knew I was coming."

He nodded. "I saw you a couple of days ago down on First Street, and I was pretty sure who you were. I suppose I've always half expected you to find me. I just didn't know when, but I figured you had a good reason for taking your time."

She plucked at a loose string near the cuff of her sleeve. "I needed to see the town, needed to hear people talk about you without knowing who I was, needed to find out what the people were like."

"They're good folk in this town." He cleared his throat. "Can I get you a glass of water?"

"No, thanks, Dad." She pulled down on her earlobe and scratched at her collarbone. "I chose 'Dad' because my stepfather, who legally adopted me when I was seven, has always been 'Daddy' to me. I love him a lot, and he's the only father I ever knew, but then you probably know that from Mama's letters."

"She didn't write me that much. Not after she got married. I did know you'd been adopted. Your mother sent me a Christmas card each year with a picture of you." He unlocked a drawer and pulled out a stack of photos. "After she married, she didn't want any more child-support checks from me, and I was afraid she'd quit sending me pictures. But she kept right on." He fanned the photos across his desk and Susan bent forward to look at them. "I've kept up with you, you see. As much as I could. I'm sorry I wasn't there for you when you were growing up. The money probably wasn't enough. And I was…I was sorry to hear of your mother's death. You look like her, you know."

Susan inspected the floor. "Yes. Well. Mama never told me much about you. She never even spoke your name. Almost everything I know I found out from her old diaries after she died. She put a note to me in the box where they were stored. It started off 'If you're reading this, my dearest daughter, then I'm either dead or I've gone barmy in my old age and lost my mind.' She asked me to read about you and apologized for keeping the information from me."

"I wonder why she did that."

"She said—or rather wrote—that by the time I

was old enough to be told, I already was so bonded with Daddy that she didn't want to, as she put it, rock the boat."

He didn't say anything.

Susan began to braid her hair, but stopped as it tangled in her lap. Her hands felt too shaky anyway. "Daddy's remarrying now, and much as I love him, I'm not that fond of his new wife. I've been wandering around the town here, checking everything out. I came here expecting to hate you for what you did, but right now I don't know how I feel. If you hadn't left, I never would have known Daddy, so maybe you did me a favor."

A pained expression flitted over his face.

"I can tell the people here respect you, but I think they might be surprised to find out about me."

"You've stirred up quite a bit of speculation, I hear." He ran a hand along his jaw and pulled on his earlobe.

Susan wondered if she'd gotten that habit from him somehow. Maybe earlobe-pulling was a genetic trait. "I came here to force you to apologize to me. And to Mama, even though it's too late for that."

"Surely you know that I regret—"

"Regret is not what I'm talking about. I want an apology."

"I've already said I was sorry—"

"A public apology, Dad. Public."

She watched the color drain from his face and felt a pang of pity. "When I was just a little girl, my mom used to brush my hair. While she brushed, she'd usually sing that song about wanting to be around when somebody smarter than she was would break your heart. I don't think she thought much about the message she was giving me." Susan gathered a handful of her own hair and watched it slip through her fingers. "I couldn't have been more than five or six when I swore I'd never cut my hair until that man apologized to my mother." She stroked the hair that spread across her lap. "I'll miss it." She looked back up at him. "I mean it, Dad. I do expect a real apology."

"Yes. I am sorry. I truly am. But—"

"I think I'd like to stick around Martinsville for a while, if you don't object. I inherited some money from a trust fund. I want to start a holistic health center for retreats and classes. This looks like a good place, but I need to make some concrete plans."

"I'd be happy to have you here." He moved a yellow pad of sticky notes from one side of his desk blotter to the other. "The only thing—"

"The only thing," she finished for him, "is that you haven't told your wife about me. Is that it?" He didn't answer, so she went on. "Are you still ashamed of me?"

"No! No. It was never you I was ashamed of. It was me. My actions. I wasn't brave enough to go back and marry your mom once she told me she was expecting. I was already engaged, you see."

Susan leaned forward and picked up the framed photo that stood beside the phone. "Do you love your wife?"

He leaned his elbows on the desk and folded his hands, almost as if he were getting ready to pray. "Yes," he said. "Very much."

She stood. "In the meantime, then, I'll hold my tongue. How about one month? Could you tell her in thirty days?"

The earlobe again. "I… Yes. I'll tell her. I can't do it right away, though."

"Thirty days." She smiled. "Dad," she added.

"WHAT IS IT WITH this town?"

I could hear Bob complaining even over the sound of the shower. My shower. I love hot water streaming through my hair and down my back, but I'd already been in there an inexcusably long time. Thank goodness for an extra-large water heater.

Thank goodness, too, that the drought had ended. I sighed and turned off the deluge, reluctantly, I must admit.

"There hasn't even been a bunch of kids racing up and down First Street in a souped-up car," he went on, gesturing with the toothbrush. Marmalade, who sat on the bathroom counter, took a swipe at the toothbrush as it passed her nose. She missed.

I wrapped myself in a dark blue towel. Bob handed me the second one I'd left folded up beside the sink. I bent over to towel-dry my hair and he patted my rear end absentmindedly. Married just a year and used to each other already. "Surely you don't want a crime wave," I said.

"No, you're right. I don't. But it sure would be nice if Reebok could at least write somebody a ticket." He went back to brushing his teeth while I wrapped my hair up in the towel. I hate the feel of cold, wet hair dangling between my shoulder blades. "Anyway, there's other stuff going on."

"What stuff?"

What is stuff?

The toothbrush paused in midair. "I can't say anything yet, but right now it's something only I can handle. Reebok couldn't do a thing about this."

When Bob didn't want to tell me something, I couldn't wheedle it out of him. "Reebok will learn, soon enough," I said.

Bob shook his head. "I'm afraid everybody will."

I headed past him, but he straightened up, tossed the toothbrush into its holder, and pulled me into one of his unimaginably comforting hugs. "You'll get wet," I said, not that I meant him to stop.

Stop what?
"Who cares?"
Who, indeed?

I am grateful for
my humans, even when they are hard to
understand
naps
sunshine
wide windowsills for me to sit on
this soft bed

WEEK THREE

SUNDAY

My Gratitude List for Saturday
(written early Sunday morning because I forgot last night—hee-hee!)
1. Hot chocolate from the Delicious.
2. Glaze.
3. Annie.
4. A hot shower before bedtime.
5. Bob!

MARMALADE HOPPED OFF the couch and stretched.
Fishgiver is coming.
She purred and walked to the front door.
"I'm too busy to stop this and let you out, Marmy. Go use your cat door. That's why we put it in."
Mouse droppings!
She sneezed rather loudly, but stayed there with her tail curled around her toes. My orange-and-white bookend. I went back to plowing through

the mounds of paper that somehow always piled up on the coffee table. Three issues of the *Keagan County Record*, more junk mail than I could imagine, that note from Auntie Blue I'd been looking for.

Marmy meowed at the knock on the door. I motioned Tom in. I love the beveled glass window on my front door. He just stood there, though. The bright sunshine behind him must have made it hard to see inside, especially through the lace curtain. "Come on in, Tom," I hollered.

"Hey there, Furball." Tom leaned over and tousled Marmy's head.

Hello, Fishgiver.

Bob strolled through the kitchen doorway, smoothing down his mustache. "Want some coffee?"

"No, thanks. I'm headed down to Atlanta to look at some new stoves. There's one supply store that's open on Sundays." What was wrong with the stoves he already had? I wondered. I thought CT's had a state-of-the-art commercial kitchen. Before I could ask, though, he said, "Thought I'd stop by with a little something for the furball."

Thank you.

Tom was the only person who called her that. I thought it was cute.

"You skipping church?" Bob asked.

Tom nodded. "The sign says the sermon's

going to be about casting bread on the waters. I cast enough bread at that restaurant of mine." He waited for our appreciative chuckles. "It's a long drive to the city, so I thought I'd start early."

I pushed the papers and the junk mail into two stacks. One to recycle, one to toss. "Drive carefully," I told him.

Marmy followed Bob and the bag into the kitchen.

I HADN'T EVEN SETTLED into the pew yet when Ida squeezed by Bob's knees and mine and plopped down beside me.

"What on earth are you doing here, Ida? You go to Saint Theresa's."

She grunted and bent forward to set her purse on the floor.

Oh, dear. I wondered if she had a problem with Father John. Ida was a good friend, but I knew that if she took a disliking to someone, it was all over for good. There was her long-term feud going with Carl Armitage, Sharon's husband. I didn't know what had caused it in the first place, but she never had a kind word to say about that man, and she avoided him whenever possible. I'd even seen her turn around in the middle of her own grocery store and walk down a different aisle so she could avoid him. At least, that's what it had looked like to me. "You're not mad at Father John, are you?"

She wrinkled her forehead. "Whatever gave you that idea?"

"Well, you're Catholic. And the last I heard, this is still a Protestant church."

"It's not like I have to do penance for showing up here."

"But why would you want to? I've never seen you here before."

"How would you know? You've only been here a couple of years."

"Come on, Ida. There's got to be a reason."

She let out one of those snorts that was halfway between a giggle and a guffaw. "If you must know, it was sheer curiosity. I'm in the grocery business. Figured I needed to hear a sermon about bread."

The signboard. "You're kidding, right?"

"It's as good a reason as any. I'm sure you'd rather hear that than 'I decided to slum around.' And anyway, I was here at Wallace's funeral, and I liked what Henry had to say."

"Right." I turned to check out who else was here. From three-quarters of the way back on the left side of the center aisle, I could see a large percentage of the congregation, all except the ones who came early enough to get a seat behind me.

This town was entirely too isolated, I thought. Too homogeneous, like white bread or cow's milk. Where were the interesting skin tones? Where, for that matter, were the multitudes of churches that showed up in every other Southern town I'd ever seen? Protestant and Catholic. That was it. I scanned the crowd. Nothing but brown and blond hair, with a few sprinkles of red thrown in here and there. Plus all the other tones that Sharon so readily provided. Glaze's hair was white, of course, but the only other silver hair I saw belonged to the helmet-head crowd. Susan, with her shining cap of waist-length blue-black hair and her doe-like eyes, stood out like a baby panther in a litter of orange tabby cats. I could see her on the other side of the church as she slipped quietly into the far end of one of the middle pews. I turned back to Ida, who seemed to be eyeing Susan herself. "Do you know if she's planning on staying?"

"Susan? All I know is what she told me when she came in for some groceries last week. Didn't buy much. She said she's renting a room from Alicia. But I already told you that." Ida smoothed out her program and I noticed the spots on the back of her hand. Ida was too young to have liver spots. "She didn't exactly volunteer the information. I sort of had to coax it out of her."

Uh-huh. The third degree. When Ida wanted information, she never let something like good manners or someone else's reticence stand in her way. "I wonder if she had a reservation." I figured Ida would know by this time.

"At Alicia's? No, she just happened on it. Well,

she had to slow down for that sharp curve, and then there was the sign."

"That driveway's so steep it's a wonder anybody goes up there," I said.

"Yeah, but there's a nice view once you're at the top. She's quite a woman."

"Susan?"

"No. Alicia. Did you know why the highway still has that sharp curve there?"

"There's a reason?"

"You bet. When they were trying to improve the road ten or fifteen years ago, they couldn't dynamite too close to Alicia Rae's house because she refused to get out. Told the county commissioners that if they knocked her house down with their blasting, they'd have to haul her body out of it."

Reverend Pursey wasn't up front yet, and everyone around us was talking, too. Bob wasn't. He sat quietly on my right, reading his program and shaking his head occasionally at the misspellings. "I kind of like that curve," I told Ida. "It's sharp enough to slow people down."

"Yeah, well, I don't like all those ugly yellow warning signs and arrows." Ida patted her sparse brown hair. "Suppose they're necessary, though. After all, the curve is pretty sharp, and there's Alicia's long driveway and another one you'd hardly even notice right there coming out on that curve. Downright dangerous, so I guess they need all those signs." She looked as if she was ready to say something else, but Henry walked up to the pulpit right then, and we settled into the Sunday routine. We *thought* it was going to be routine, that is. A prayer, a hymn, some announcements, a reading, and the sermon.

Henry's sermon title had been posted all week on the big white board out by the corner. Cast Your Bread Upon the Waters. Ida's grocery-store topic. That's what she'd come to hear, if I could believe her warped sense of humor. But bread was not what he talked about. Instead he led off his sermon by saying he'd changed his mind and was going to talk about forgiveness. I heard Ida mutter, "Oh, for crying out loud. I have to sit through this?"

He gave a good talk, though, mostly about how if we didn't forgive ourselves, it would be hard for us to forgive other people or to accept forgiveness from them. "Seventy times seven," Henry intoned. "Seventy times seven is what we're supposed to forgive. Do you know why?" He paused, but nobody hazarded any guesses. "It's because it takes us that long to break through the wall we've built inside that says we may be able to forgive *this,* but we can't possibly forgive that." He paused again. Henry tended to do that a lot in his sermons. "So, do you think this seventy-times-seven idea means we're supposed to forgive—do the math, my friends—four hundred and ninety different people? That would be everybody in this room," he chuckled, a bit ruefully I thought, "and then some."

Ida leaned over to me. "I could forgive maybe half the people in here, but there's a few others I'd have to think about." Bob laughed, and Annie, sitting right in front of us next to Glaze, turned slightly and nodded. Ida's whisper was louder than she thought.

"No, and no again." Henry was in his pontificating mode, which he luckily didn't do too often. Usually he just stood up there and talked. He looked down at his wife. Irene was always so supportive of him in his work. He could count on her to nod her head at the right times, to chuckle out loud at his little jokes, to lead us by example. "What I'd like to suggest," Henry said, "is that you forgive *one* person seventy times seven."

I looked at the back of Glaze's head. I wondered if she could do that kind of forgiving—her sleazy former boyfriend who used to beat her up, and then there was… I brought my thoughts back to Henry. I may have missed a sentence or two.

"…one of those lined notebooks, the kind you get in grade school." He looked back toward us. "Ida will be happy to sell you one, I'm sure." Ida half stood and took a slight bow, acknowledging the plug for her store. "You ought to visit more often, Ida. Just think of the business you could drum up."

"Only one grocery store in town, Reverend." She glanced around the room. "Looks to me like you're all customers of mine."

There was scattered applause before people settled down and turned their attention back to Henry.

"As I was saying," he went on, "get yourself a notebook. Then you have to decide who it is you've got something against." An indistinct rustle went through the congregation. No one person seemed to be moving, but even I got the itchies right then. Grandpa, I thought. I wondered if Bob needed to forgive Sheila, his first wife. The one who divorced him. And what was I going to do about Sally?

"But what, you may ask, about the injunction in the book of Matthew to *judge not that ye be not judged?* I can hear you thinking that. In answer, I say that forgiving is not the same as judging. In fact, it's the opposite of judging. Forgiving allows us to understand that other people, the ones we feel anger toward, the ones we resent, had their own motivation for doing what they did. Most people do what they do because at the time it seems like the right thing to do."

He looked at Irene again and waited for us to catch up with him. Most of us, I imagined, were still right where I was, still thinking about having been wronged. Irene sat in her usual place, on the front row over at the far end, where he could see her easily. She had to have been proud of Henry.

"So, if you say the words *I forgive you* to somebody, do you truly think you'll believe that, right down to the core of your being? No!" he thundered. "No, indeed. Because once is not enough. Saying it one time doesn't even begin to reach what we're really thinking deep down inside. Saying it one time is giving lip service. Saying it only one time is fueling the anger we're feeling inside. It's stoking up the fire of self-righteousness. That is a fire that will burn you, burn you more surely than your mama's woodstove ever did."

I looked down at my right palm. I'd put that against the hot oven door when I was maybe four or five years old and still remembered the shock of it. Ida next to me turned her left hand over and rubbed the pads on the tips of her fingers. Maybe Henry wasn't so far off at that.

"Forgiving," he intoned, "lets you see the blessing in what happened. It does not mean that what happened was okay. It means you've decided that you're not going to let past events continue to hurt you. You're not going to let them run your life."

Grandpa, I thought. I wondered what Glaze was thinking. Could she ever really forgive me for not having protected her when she was so little?

"Now let's go back to that notebook." Henry reverted to a more conversational tone. Good. I was tired of being preached at. "You decide when you're going to start this forgiveness stuff, and you pick one person to forgive. Just one." He grinned. "We'll work on all the others later. Use the first few pages of that notebook of yours to write a list of everything you've been blaming that person for. We're going to bring those lists here and burn them next week, so make them as long as you want. Roger's going to build us a bonfire out in back. We're going to send those unforgiven complaints right up into the arms of the angels, and they'll take care of them for us so…"

He probably would have gone on in this vein for quite some time, except that black-haired Susan stood up and walked to the front of the church. Henry wound down in some confusion, not even finishing his last sentence. "Reverend Pursey," she said so quietly that I strained to hear her. "What if someone does something that is unforgivable? Can you expect somebody to forgive the unforgivable?" She paused, as if waiting for a reply. She must have been talking about her father, the one who had left her before she was born. I wondered if the men in town knew what was going on. Had Ida talked to Ralph? Had Sharon talked to Carl? I knew I hadn't mentioned it to Bob yet.

Henry swallowed. The interruption seemed to

have thrown him off his stride. "There is always room for forgiveness," he said, "and it's never too late."

"Not too late?" she echoed. "Even after twenty-eight years?"

She couldn't have been much older than that herself.

"No," Henry said. "Of course not." He glanced up at the rest of us. "Would you like to sit down and talk privately with me after the service, Miss…?"

"No," she said. She didn't tell us her last name. Instead, she stretched out her arm and displayed a small piece of paper. "I don't need to talk." She looked at the paper. "I read my mother's diaries after she died two years ago. I have a photograph, too." There was another rustle that went through the congregation, something deeper, more primal than the earlier one. I don't know why I thought of this, but for a moment I felt as if I could smell fear. Probably just my overactive imagination. Bob sat up a little straighter and pulled his arm away from mine. It was a bit hot in the church. Someone should have put on the ceiling fans.

"I have come here," Susan said, "to live near my father, the father who left before I was born."

Henry's mouth dropped open. He looked as if he had to make a conscious effort to close it. "Your father didn't abandon you," he said. He seemed to be groping for words. How does one handle something like this? "What I mean to say is...he surely wouldn't have done that."

Have you ever noticed how many different kinds of silence there are? This one felt expectant somehow, with fear mixed in, but with curiosity, as well. Susan looked at Henry, turned to gaze over the congregation, and pivoted back toward the minister. "He's going to acknowledge me." She waved the photograph over her head. "I have proof, and I want an apology."

I'll say this for Henry. He handled the disturbance quite well. "I'd be happy to talk with you," he said. "After the service. Perhaps I can help?"

"Yes," Susan said. "Perhaps you can." She headed back for her seat.

Ida turned toward me. "How's she going to find him?" Of course, Ida's voice was a lot louder than she thought, and the acoustics in the Old Church have always been quite good.

"I'll give him four weeks," Susan said.

WE USUALLY ATE our lunch at the breakfast table tucked into the bay window, but today Bob had set our plates on opposite sides of the long kitchen table. "I thought you weren't planning to leave until this evening," I said. "It's not like they'll give away your room." All the course participants were being housed in an unused dormitory at UGA.

The building was due for demolition in another couple of months, and since the students had been shuffled elsewhere, it stood available. Bob thought the beds probably wouldn't be long enough, but since the police officers would be in class or on the shooting range for long hours each day, it wouldn't matter that much.

He slurped down the rest of his coffee and adjusted the collar of his dark blue polo shirt. "I still have some reading I need to do for tomorrow. It'll be easier for me to leave now."

"Bob, you've barely eaten anything."

"If I get hungry, I'll stop on the way."

I couldn't put a finger on it, but something didn't feel right. "Is something wrong?"

"What would be wrong?"

"I don't know. That's why I'm asking."

He pushed his chair back. "Don't you worry. I'm going to run up and finish packing."

I sat there nursing my cup of licorice-root tea. The sweetness of it was sorely at odds with what I felt. A few minutes later Bob plopped his suitcase on the floor by the front door, strode into the kitchen, and gave me a perfunctory kiss on the forehead. "I'll see you at the end of the week, and yes, I'll call to let you know I've gotten there so you won't worry." At least they'd left the phones in the rooms. We'd have to route the calls through a campus operator, but I knew I could reach him if I had to.

He turned to leave, but I grabbed at his hand. "Bob! Stop! I'm already worried. What on earth has gotten into you?"

"Nothing. I…" He took a good look at my face and must have decided not to lie. "Look. Something's come up. Something I need to do some thinking about. Can we talk about it next weekend when I get home?"

"Can't we talk about it now?"

"No," he said. "I love you, Bisque. And I need to leave for Athens right now, as soon as I stop by my office for a bit."

What else could I say? "Can I have a real kiss before you go?"

"WHY DID YOU MAKE that announcement in church today, Susan? I thought you were going to be quiet about this."

Susan smiled. "Oh, I will be, Dad. I just wanted you to know that I'm serious about the thirty days and the public apology. Don't worry. Nobody knows yet."

"You don't know this town the way I do," he said. "While you were talking, several of the men looked scared, and some of the women seemed to think you were issuing a challenge."

"There's something nasty about secrets," she said. "Maybe this will help clear the air."

"Your intentions may be good, but let's hope the fallout can be repaired."

A COUPLE OF HOURS after Bob left for his first week of classes in Athens, Glaze drove down Beechnut and parked her green Honda headed downhill on the wrong side of the road. It's so nice to live in a small town where people can park any way they want and nobody seems to mind. Glaze pulled far enough downhill that she didn't block the mailbox, though. Marmalade was helping me deadhead a rather bedraggled *Dicentra spectabilis* that grew next to the front walk. I wasn't ready to stop yet. "Grab a lawn chair and pull it over here," I said. "You can keep me company while I piddle around. If I don't get this plant cleaned up, it'll look scroungy." Usually they grew only to about thirty inches, but I'd learned never to be surprised by the garden Elizabeth had planted.

Glaze pulled her blue travel bag out of her car and toted it to the front porch. "I thought you didn't like flowers that needed to be fiddled with," she called over her shoulder.

She was right about that. "I didn't plant these. They reseed if you don't pull off the seed heads before they spill. These were left over from Elizabeth's color frenzy." The unfortunate Elizabeth Hoskins—but that was another story—was a master at gardening and several other endeavors, too. I'd benefited from her landscape planning. All I had to do was keep up with the tidy month-by-month list of garden chores she'd left with me when Bob and I bought her house, and then I looked like a whiz at gardening myself. Not that I was any slouch at it. I'd built my own three-bin compost pile the week after I moved in, and I could spout botanical names with the best of them. But I'd gladly gotten rid of most of her pesky annuals so I had nothing left but native plants, and perennials at that. Still, I looked up at the bush-like foliage that climbed a foot or two above me as I squatted there beside the front walk. The bright reddish-pink, heart-shaped flowers—the ones that hadn't gone to seed already—were lovely. The long, arching stems held dozens of blossoms, about a third of which were in dire need of my help. I thought they were supposed to fall off automatically. Too bad this wasn't one of the sections that we'd lost last fall after all the rain. I wondered what sort of natural fertilizer Elizabeth used on this one. Maybe I could move the whole plant farther from the sidewalk. Maybe I could rip the whole thing out and just leave the *Ajuga reptans,* the creeping bugleweed, that grew around its base.

Marmalade nosed several of the dead blossoms that I'd dropped on the ground. I scooted the heavyily padded kneeler a bit farther to my left and reached for the next set of leftover blooms. Glaze sat down on the concrete next to me.

"What's it called?"

"Dicentra spectabilis."

"Would you mind using English for a change?"

"Bleeding heart. Because of the shape of the flowers. Look." I lifted one of the sprays so she could see it better.

"What a depressing name." She pulled at a stray silver hair on her pants leg. "Do you ever wonder where you'll be ten years from now?"

"Ten years from now, I'll probably still be deadheading this fool plant."

I will help you.

Marmalade oozed her way around my knees and squirmed into Glaze's lap.

"No. I mean it. Don't you ever think about what will happen when you start falling apart?"

I reared back and inspected her. "I don't know about you, but I plan to be going strong ten years from now. Look at Sadie," I said. "She's thirty-plus years older than I am, and she started taking tap-dance lessons last year, for heaven's sake. She stole the show at our recital, remember?" I leaned forward and snapped off another dead flower. "Sadie's more like that oakleaf hydrangea over there than like this *Dicen*...bleeding heart."

I pointed with my nose at the *Hydrangea querci-folia* that graced the corner of the house. Its new wide, pointy leaves shadowed the ground beneath it, and the burgeoning blossoms formed white pod-like lumps at the ends of each stem. There still were a few of the browned blossoms from last season that I'd never gotten around to snipping off. If I were a rabid gardener, I would have cut the whole plant back to eighteen inches once our mild Georgia winter set in, but I liked its structure, with those stark leafless stems and dried-up balloon-sized flowers.

"It just keeps going, year after year," I said, "even though it gets a bit scraggly-looking occasionally." I scouted around for another example. "These *Ajugas*...creeping bugleweed plants here are so hardy. Each individual plant doesn't look like much, but put them all together like this and they form such a soft carpet. Here, feel them."

She reached forward and ran her hand across the reddish leaves. "Uh-huh," she said.

I didn't think I'd made my point yet. "Or look at those wild asters that keep springing up along the curb. They're incredibly hardy. That's what I want to be like." I held my arm out toward my sister. "Look at what my skin is doing," I said. "Kind of getting to be like crepe paper, isn't it?" I wiggled my arms back and forth and jiggled the sagging tissue. "You may think this looks like Jell-O on a stick, my dear, but I call them my angel wings. Hand me that water, would you?"

She shifted Marmy a bit to the side and leaned over to lift my water bottle out of the bucket that spouted trowels and garden forks and such. I took a big glurp of it, and she watched me with those emerald eyes of hers. "I didn't mean you," she said. "I meant me."

"What's gotten into you?"

She wrapped her arms around her knees, and Marmalade squeezed the rest of the way out of her lap and beneath her legs, like a tiny airplane flying under the St. Louis Arch. "What would have happened to Sadie," she said, "if Ida and you and Margaret and everybody else hadn't been there to help her with Wallace? Or what if it had been her dying instead of him?"

"But we *were* there."

I am here.

She balanced her chin on her left kneecap and glanced at Marmalade, who meowed softly. "That's because everybody loves Sadie," she said.

LooseLaces is gentle when she pats me.

Did I miss something? I wondered. "Of course we love Sadie. Don't you?"

She feeds me cream.

She sighed, one of those long, drawn-out exhalations that sounded as if it started at her toes. Her eyes were on the plant, but I got the feeling she wasn't really looking at it. "Of course I do. Of course. But she's so...so sweet."

I gave up on the gardening chores. "What are we talking about, Glaze?"

She dropped her eyes from the halfway-cleaned-up plant to the sidewalk. She picked up one small grayish stone lodged in a crack in the concrete and ran her thumb back and forth across its smooth surface. "Nothing, I guess." She let out another deep breath. "It just all seems so useless."

"Are you feeling okay?"

She looked at me and I shivered. There was something in her eyes. A shadow, maybe. They weren't their usual clear green. They looked...old, somehow. "Just a blue mood, I guess," she said. "I got a job offer."

"A new job? That's great! Where?"

"Oh, it doesn't matter. I turned it down. It was something I wasn't really qualified for." She pushed the stone into the dirt at the edge of the sidewalk.

"You turned down a job offer? I thought you wanted to get out of CelerInc."

"I told you, I'm not qualified for the job."

"But if they offered it to you, they must have thought you could do it."

"Forget it, will you? Just forget it."

I didn't like dropping the subject, but I felt a

wall around her that I didn't know how to get through. "Maybe something better will crop up?"

"Not a chance."

I scouted around for something neutral to say and settled on, "Want some cheese and crackers?"

I will take some chicken.

"Sure." Glaze stood up and dusted off her britches. "Sure. Maybe that's what I need."

My Gratitude List for Sunday

1. Bob, of course. I hope he has a great time in Athens—and learns lots—and comes home fast! I need to talk to him.

2. Glaze. She seems a little down. Maybe it's that time of month.

3. I'm so glad I'm finally in menostop instead of menopause.

4. Those doggone bleeding hearts. They really are pretty, even though they're a pain in the butt to fiddle with. I ought to move them away from the sidewalk.

Stop it, Biscuit. This is supposed to be a gratitude list—not a to-do list.

5. Marmy's soft purrs. I love this cat!

I am grateful for
toys from Widelap

pats from Softfoot
hugs from Smellsweet
cream from LooseLaces
salmon from Fishgiver

WEEK THREE

MONDAY

THE NEXT MORNING Marmy and I padded downstairs to squeeze some juice before Glaze got up. There was a small daybed in the sewing room upstairs, and that was where she'd chosen to sleep. I heard her snoring softly as I tiptoed to the top of the stairs. Of course, that third step creaked, the way it always did, and Glaze joined us a few minutes later, yawning her fool head off. "Didn't you get enough sleep?" I asked her as I cut the oranges in half.

"Yeah, I guess," she said. "I haven't slept well the last few days."

I always sleep well.

"Maybe you could take a nap this afternoon," I said. "Or go on upstairs and tuck yourself back in for a while. You can come on over to the library whenever you want to."

I like naps.

Glaze reached down and patted Marmalade,

who wove underneath her purple bathrobe and back out again, purring intermittently. "No," she said. "Once I'm up, I can't get back to sleep. I forgot my toothpaste, so I used yours. I hope that's okay."

I nodded. Of course it was okay. "Isn't that what sisters are for?"

"Want me to boil some water?" She picked up the teakettle without waiting for an answer, and we did one of those kitchen dances, weaving around each other just the way Marmy had done.

I like to dance, too.

"Why don't you take a shower while I get breakfast made? It'll wake you up."

"You think I stink?"

"No. I think you could use a lift. Try that honeysuckle soap I got at Annie's. It'll brighten your day."

Glaze rolled her shoulders and yawned again. "Okay. Are you still planning to teach me to laminate book jackets?"

"Sure. If you can stop yawning long enough to learn how."

WE WALKED OUT the front door as Celia drove her white mail van up the road, swerved around the Honda, and pulled in beside our lavender mailbox. She waved a bulky bunch of flyers, letters, bills, and who-knew-what-all at me. "Hey there," she said, nodding at both of us. "Wait a minute, Glaze, and I'll get yours, too." She turned to her left and rummaged in the wide white plastic bin that held the various bundles.

"How do you ever keep all that straight, Celia?" I asked.

She held out another packet wrapped in an advertising circular of some type. "The junk mail helps," she said. "It keeps the letters from getting mixed up. You forget to go to work this morning," she asked Glaze, "or you just don't like your house up the road anymore?"

Glaze shook her head. "I'll be here the rest of the week."

"Bob's out of town," I explained, "and Glaze is on vacation, so we're having a sister get-together."

"You want I should drop your mail off here?"

"Sure, if it's not too much trouble," Glaze said. "Thanks."

"Not a problem. Love your mailbox," she added. "Brightens my day." Marmy wove her way through the daylilies at its base.

I see a crawly bug.

I patted the bright lavender box, thinking about its varied history, and stood back to admire the dark green vines and sky-blue morning glories Ariel had painted on its wooden post.

"Earth to Biscuit." Glaze poked me in the ribs, gently. "Are we going to head to the library any time in particular, or are you planning to stand there all day?"

"Just admiring the mailbox," I said, "and wondering why Roger stopped painting it all those ghastly colors."

"It's because he finally got a job he enjoys," she said and headed down toward Second Street. "Unlike some of the rest of us," I heard her add quietly.

MARMALADE LED US to the library. We'd walked that same way so many times before, we could probably both have done it in our sleep.

Why would we do that?

My Petunias weren't ever scheduled on Mondays, although sometimes they showed up just for the fun of it. Sure enough, Sadie and Rebecca Jo were already there when Glaze and I walked in shortly before ten o'clock. We could hear them upstairs. The third-floor office was piled with boxes of gently used books that the town folk donated when the library started a couple of years ago. We were still trying to get them all cataloged. As we progressed, I sometimes brought home the empty boxes for Marmalade. She seemed to enjoy napping in them. It was a good way to recycle.

I like boxes.

Some quirky architectural configuration carried a faint echo of the women's distinctive laughter, like a ghost from an older era, down the elegant staircase that was something of a showpiece in town.

This is where AntlerBagMan died.

I had a sudden inexplicable memory of the young man who'd been killed on those stairs two years ago, shortly after I moved to Martinsville. I'd found the body when I came to work one morning.

I am the one who found him.

I wondered if Marmy remembered. Of course not. What a silly thought.

Mouse droppings!

Marmalade sneezed, then veered to the left just before she reached the landing, almost as if she wanted to avoid the spot where Harlan died. He'd worn an amulet bag that had a small piece of antler in it. Funny how I thought about that after all this time. There had been handmade beads on the bag, beads that were about the same orange color as Marmalade's coat. There is not a super-stitious bone in my body, mind you, but I moved to the left anyway and followed Marmy up the stairs. Glaze walked beside me, on my right, and didn't seem to feel a thing.

"DID YOU HEAR?" Rebecca Jo said as soon as we stepped into the third-floor office. "Margot and Hans are going to start opening the Delicious on Mondays."

"Do they have that much business?" Glaze asked.

"Are you kidding? They'd be packed seven days a week if they were willing to work that long. Especially for breakfast."

Glaze sat down. She looked tired. "You mean I can get cinnamon rolls every morning except Sunday now?"

Sadie wagged her finger at both of us. "If you eat too many of those, you'll end up shaped like me."

"I can't see that it ever slowed you down much," Rebecca Jo said. She looked up at me. "I'm taking Sadie up to Amanda's tomorrow to get a massage."

Sadie raised her arms and waggled them back and forth, like a palm tree in a stiff breeze. "I'm in my eighties and I'm going to get my first massage ever. I can't wait."

"Be sure you tell me how it goes," I said.

Rebecca Jo put down her marker. "If she likes it, I may make an appointment for myself. Polly told me massage is good preventive maintenance." She looked down at her grandmotherly protuberant belly. "I could use all the prevention I can get." We chuckled right on cue. "So what are you two up to?"

"Laminating today. We thought we'd head up to Mable's tomorrow to check out the dress sale."

Glaze nodded. "Biscuit looks too pale. She needs some bright red lipstick, too."

"To match yours?" Sadie set aside the book she'd just finished. A huge stack leaned precariously next to her chair. "I like it, but you'd never catch me wearing anything that bright. What's it called?"

"Wildfire."

Rebecca Jo cocked her head to one side and looked me up and down. "I think Biscuit's more the pink sort. Why don't you both get some lipstick called Bubblegum to match that hat you like so much?"

Sadie started sobbing. Rebecca Jo turned and sent the stack of books crashing to the floor.

"I'm so sorry," Sadie said through the tissue she grabbed. I looked at Glaze. She spread her hands in an I-don't-know motion and shook her head. "Wallace iiked bubblegum"—Sadie sniffed— "right up until he got his false teeth and couldn't chew it anymore."

Rebecca Jo moved around the scattered books and took Sadie's hand. "Don't worry about this mess. It's not your fault, dear. I'm the one who's clumsy."

Glaze and I picked up books while Rebecca Jo hugged Sadie and let her cry it out.

WEEK THREE

TUESDAY

"This one's pretty." Glaze pushed her way between two dress racks and held a frothy pink concoction in front of her. "What do you think?"

"I think you'd look like a piece of Wallace's bubblegum. in high heels. But it would match your pink lipstick." And your hat, I thought, but I didn't say it out loud.

She hung the dress back on the rack, muttering something about throwing out that lipstick. She pulled out an emerald number. "This?"

"Try it on. What about this one?" I held up a dark indigo dress and spread the swirly skirt out to one side. It was what I'd earmarked to be my matron-of-honor dress. At her wedding. I wished she'd get a move on.

"Hmm," she said. Hardly the enthusiastic approval I'd hoped for.

Sarah Watkins—she'd gone back to her maiden name after her husband committed a murder and she divorced him—pushed some dresses to one side and set them swinging on their hangers. "That color is perfect for you, Biscuit. And Glaze, the green matches your eyes." She tilted her head toward the back of the store. "The fitting rooms are empty."

Glaze headed that way, picking up a silky white piece as she went. Large purple-blue flowers wound up one side of it. I didn't have to try mine on. I'd already done so. Several times. "How are the classes going?"

Sarah managed to grin and grimace at the same time. Quite a trick. "College is harder than I thought it would be, but I sure am enjoying myself."

"How do you find time to do all the reading? You must have to write tons of papers."

"Oh, it's not that hard," she said. "Mable lets me work around my class schedule, and I just made up my mind to do without sleep for the next three years."

GLAZE CHOSE THE WHITE SILK. "No, I don't have anywhere to wear it, but I feel like splurging. Are you going to get the blue one?"

"I'll wait. Sarah showed me some more of their his-and-hers line." I held up two polo shirts in a luscious shade of deep indigo.

"You can wear those when I wear this," she said. "You'll match my flowers."

ON THE RIDE HOME, though, Glaze was quiet, distant almost. I tried to keep a conversation going. I wondered out loud how Sadie must be enjoying her first massage and received a noncommital grunt as a reply. I made a delectably nasty crack about Hubbard Martin's recent operation. "Yeah" was all Glaze said. I might as well have been talking to the polo shirts that sat in their bag beside me.

We stopped by the Delicious for half an hour or so. Tom sauntered up to our table with a suspicious white bag in his hand. "Did you just buy what I think you did?" I asked. "I should think that such a world-class chef would make his own cinnamon rolls."

"I'm not going to compete with Margot and Hans." He looked over his shoulder at Doreen, one of his employees, who sat at a nearby table enjoying a cup of coffee, then bent close to me and lowered his voice. "That's because I know I'd lose." He swiveled his head to look at Glaze. "There's a good movie up in Garner Creek tonight. Do you want to go?"

She smiled, rather halfheartedly, I thought. "No. It's tap-dance night. I'm staying with Biscuit this week."

"We're calling it our sister-week," I chimed in to fill the pause.

He backed away in mock alarm. "I wouldn't want to come between two women on a sister-week."

Glaze did laugh at that. Not her usual hearty chuckle, but at least it perked up her eyes a bit. We sat awhile after Tom left, but didn't say too much.

GLAZE PUSHED ASIDE her empty soup bowl. "That was good," she said. "I can't make it through tap class without dinner first, but if I eat too much I feel stuffed all during class."

"I know what you mean. But then again, I get hungry after class."

"Is that why you drink so much iced tea at Melissa's afterward?"

"You noticed?"

"Bet you spend all night getting up to go potty."

"Yeah, but the tea keeps me from eating too many of those cinnamon buns that Dee always brings. They're way too sugary."

Glaze put her elbows on the table, leaned her chin on her hands, and looked at me. "Did you ever measure the amount of sugar in sweet tea?"

She was right. Georgia sweet tea, made with enough sugar to founder a horse, wasn't exactly calorie-free. "Maybe we should take some healthy snacks."

"Bet you nobody but Annie will eat them."

I got up and looked through the fridge. "How about celery sticks?"

She stood and mimed an upchuck.

"Okay, so I won't take celery. What would you suggest?"

"Cinnamon buns, in case Dee forgets," she said on her way out to the front hall. I heard her open that big purse of hers. When she walked back into the kitchen, she held three lipsticks in her hand. "Which color do you think I should wear?"

"You're asking me about lipstick? I'm the one with no fashion sense, remember?"

Glaze grinned. "No, really. Which one is better with my blue leotard?"

It was good to see her looking a bit brighter after the last two gloomy days. "I think the Wildfire looks great on you."

"You don't like the pink?"

"It doesn't have enough pizzazz with that icy blue. Why are you wearing lipstick to tap-dance class? It's just us. Nobody to impress."

"I know." She laid down the lipsticks and began to clear the table. Not much to clear—just two bowls, two spoons, two bread plates. "I guess I wanted a pick-me-up."

"Well, lipstick is safer than a lot of other alternatives."

"Here, big sister. You try on the pink one."

"Me in bubblegum pink? I don't think so."

"Quit being silly. If you like it, we'll get you one next time we're in Garner Creek."

SADIE SHRUGGED OUT OF her bright yellow cover-up. While she sat down to put on her tap shoes—yellow, of course—Ida walked over to where I stood beside the big mirror. "Some lipstick," she said. I couldn't tell from her tone whether it was approving or incredulous.

"Did you get the certificate for the driving class?" I whispered.

"Sure did," she said. "Let's give it to her now rather than waiting till we get to Azalea House. I clued in Pumpkin so she'd know what we were up to."

"Miss Mary," Sadie called out from her chair, "do we have a couple of minutes before class starts?"

"Why, certainly, Sadie! We all want to welcome you back to class! And a big welcome to Pumpkin, our newest class member!" Pumpkin grinned and drummed her feet in a perky rat-a-tat-tat.

Sadie bobbed her head and stood up. "I have two announcements to make. Everybody gather around here. First, I want every single one of you to call up Amanda and go get a massage. I feel wonderful!" We all oohed and aahed. "Secondly, I want to thank Ida and Melissa and Biscuit for driving me everywhere this last week. I do appreciate it, but I'm going to get back on the road." She held up an envelope, opened it, and pulled out a piece of paper. "You're not going to have to worry about me anymore. Look what Margaret gave me. She signed me up for a defensive-driving class."

If she'd been expecting appreciative comments, she was sorely disappointed. I looked at Ida, who squinted at Glaze, who shrugged in Melissa's direction, who nudged Pumpkin with her elbow, who glanced across at Annie, who put her hand on Miss Mary's shoulder. Miss Mary couldn't keep her mouth shut. "But that's the same thing we have for you!"

Ida held out the certificate we'd all signed. Sadie looked it over. "If one certificate will help lower my car insurance, I wonder if two would double the savings."

AFTER CLASS, IN THE dressing room, Annie had a proposal to make. "What about if we invite Connie to join the class?"

Pumpkin, newer to Martinsville than the rest of us, spoke up. "Who's Connie? I don't think she's ever been in the Beauty Shop."

"Probably not," Annie said. "She's that woman who has the glass-blowing studio over on Willow, right up against the south cliff, next to Easton's house."

"Oh, yeah. I've seen the sign outside. It's really pretty, with all those colors. Looks like a whole bunch of fingernails."

Ida humphed as she slipped her tap shoes in a tapestry carry bag. "Just what a manicurist would think."

I spoke up. "I think it looks like a bunch of flowers."

"The produce section," Ida said.

"No." Melissa sounded pretty definite. "Icing on a birthday cake."

"It reminds me of stained-glass windows," Dee said, "like the ones in St. Theresa's."

"There's not enough yellow," Sadie offered.

"Biscuit could offer to plant some yarrow around the post," Annie suggested. "It's yellow. Anyway, could I invite her to join? She's a fun person. She'd fit right in."

"She'd have to be half nuts to fit in with this group," Melissa said.

"Zany."

"Crazy."

"Talented."

When we finally ran out of adjectives, we agreed that Connie would be a fine addition to the class. "I'll talk to her tomorrow," Annie said. "She ordered some honeysuckle soap, and I just got a delivery."

"I have some fresh poppy-seed cake for us to eat," Melissa said. "Let's go."

Sadie patted Ida's arm. "Could you take me home on your way there? It's been a long week."

AS WE FINALLY SETTLED around the long table at Azalea House, Ida asked if any of us had talked to Susan lately.

"Susan?" Annie asked. "The one with the long black hair?"

"Yes. Have you talked to her?"

"She came in my shop yesterday and told me her father lived here, but I already knew that from her announcement in church Sunday."

"Well," Dee said, "who is he? Did she say?"

"No." Annie looked around the table at each of us. "She said her mother got pregnant with her in college."

"Now, wait a minute," Ida said. "That's an awful lot of information to give a complete stranger. Why would she want to tell you that?"

She'd already told the whole congregation that she was looking for her father, I thought.

Melissa smiled over at Annie. "Annie's easy to talk to, and she doesn't judge people for what they say. Did she say anything else?"

"It was like she wanted the word to get around. There were two other women in the shop, and she never lowered her voice. She said she never met her father when she was a kid, but that he'd sent money each month until her mother married when she—when Susan, that is—was seven."

"Well, at least her father was honorable about it," Dee said. "Wonder why he didn't marry the mother."

Annie took a deep breath. "She said he'd married somebody else." She looked at Dee and Ida and me.

Dee threw her hands up in the air. "Are you saying it was Barkley? Not that I care anymore, but I'd hate to have Susan stuck with a real rat for a father."

"I think we're just looking at the possibilities," Melissa said. "It couldn't have been my father. He never went to college. Anyway, he's dead." She glanced around the table in the uncomfortable silence.

Ida spoke up. "It could have been anyone. How do we know she even has the right town?"

Annie shrugged. "I think she's in the right place."

"What about Carl Armitage?" Ida asked. Sounded as if her private feud was rearing its ugly head.

"No," Dee said. "He and Sharon are from New Jersey."

Ida picked up a cinnamon bun, but set it down

on her blue-ringed plate. "That doesn't matter. Susan could have tracked anyone here."

It was certainly tempting to assume Carl was the culprit. Better than thinking it might be Bob, but I did want to be fair. "It's not like Carl came here to hide out. He and Sharon didn't want to raise their girls in a city."

Dee scratched her chin. "Could it be Marvin?"

"No," Ida said. "He's too young to have a daughter Susan's age."

"And Wallace was too old," Annie said.

We walked the streets of Martinsville mentally, looking at every business, every house. Five streets wide and seven streets long.

I have walked them all.

We tallied ages and possibilities. Some of the men were instantly disqualified; some entered that shady realm of suspicion. Ida slammed her palm down on the table, making us all jump. "Why doesn't she just come out and announce who he is? This is ridiculous. Here we are sitting in judgment and we don't even know if Susan's in the right town."

"But," Dee said, "it's not easy to find Martinsville, unless you know it's here. She couldn't have come here accidentally."

"Maybe it's someone from those new houses north of town," Glaze suggested, but none of us could let go of our suspicion that one of our men had been hiding the reality of a grown-up child, the black-haired Susan. Susan's father was one of ours.

I am grateful for
this soft bed
chicken at GoodCook's house
cardboard boxes to curl up in

WEEK THREE

WEDNESDAY

My Gratitude List for Tuesday
(written Wednesday morning)
  I was too upset to write last night.
  The only thing I'm grateful for is that Bob's out of town for the week. How will I ever talk to him this weekend? By the way, I could say, do you have a grown-up child you've been ignoring all these years? Oh, Lordy, what will I do? My grandkids are supposed to be here today. I'm grateful for them. Give me patience!
  Sadie and Esther, too, for holding down the fort at the library so I can take care of Verity and Angela today.

"SEE HOW THE CREAM floats up to the top of the milk?" I held the glass bottle so Verity could inspect it easily.

"I see it! I see it!" She pointed to the dividing

line, clearly visible because of the varying density of the two fluids. She swiveled her eyes at me without turning her head. "Does that happen inside Moonbeam's tummy, too? Is the cream all at the top?"

I looked at Glaze, who sat at the round table with Angela on her lap. "Don't ask me," she muttered.

Why on earth was she so grumpy? "I don't think it does, Verity. Moonbeam moves around a lot and keeps the milk mixed up inside her." While it wasn't a scientific answer, I was fairly certain there was a grain of truth to it. "Maybe we can ask Miss Maggie next time we're there, just to be sure." Passing the buck, of course, Maggie would most likely know the real answer. I hoped it agreed at least partly with mine. I did know that it took a long time for the cream to rise to the top.

Verity helped me spoon the two or three tablespoons of rich cream into a small glass jar. She screwed the lid on tightly. After we washed off the outside of the jar and cleaned up the counter, she began shaking the jar. "Is it done yet, Grannie?"

"No, Verity. Ten minutes. We have to shake the jar for ten whole minutes."

"That's a long time."

"Yes." I looked at Glaze over the top of Verity's head. "A lot can happen in ten minutes."

Glaze frowned and buried her face in Angela's

wavy golden mop. Angela squirmed down. "Me, too! Me, too!" She held out her little hands for the jar.

Verity shook the jar another few times, then handed it to her sister. "Hold it with both hands," she warned before I could say the same thing. She laughed up at me. "That's really hard work. Angie won't be able to do it for very long."

She was right. Between the two of them they managed about three minutes of shaking. Then Glaze took a turn. After less than a minute, she handed it to me. Pretty soon the butter began to separate, making a thumping sound as it bounced around in the jar. The longer I shook it, the firmer the butter became.

"Is it ready? Is it ready?"

Why do children always seem to repeat every utterance? "Not quite. Remember from the last time we made it? We have to pour off the liquid and then keep shaking until more liquid comes out."

"Can I do it?"

"Sure you can." I handed her a wide-mouthed glass and hovered while she took off the lid and tipped the jar.

"It looks like milk," Verity said.

"That's because it is milk, remember?" I told her. "You can drink it if you want to."

"Me, too! Me, too!"

"And give Angela some."

We shook some more and poured some more and finally spread the white goat-milk butter on thick slices of toast.

My Gratitude List for Wednesday
1. Life is good, regardless.
2. Verity and Angela.
3. Glaze.
4. Moonbeam and Noel.
5. Bob, who always remembers to put the garbage out on Wednesday nights. I miss him!
6. And I have to add Marmalade, who sits with me and purrs while I write these lists.

I am grateful for
the couch to hide under when small humans
run through the house
my special door so I can get outside when I
need to
this quiet evening with just my two humans
around Widelap
Smellsweet

WEEK THREE

THURSDAY

"WHERE ON EARTH does all this come from?"

Marmy looked up at me and purred.

You put it there.

"Where does what come from?" Glaze leaned against the bedroom door frame, scratching under her right armpit.

"'Home is where you can scratch anywhere it itches,'" I quoted at her. That was one of Grandma Martelson's favorite sayings.

"So, what were you talking to Marmy about?"

"Laundry. I get it all done and I turn around and there's another full hamper." I picked up the article in question. "Do you have anything you want to add?"

"About a whole suitcase."

"Why not? We'll run a couple of loads and have it all done before lunchtime."

"Okay." She yawned. I guessed home was also where you could yawn without covering your mouth. "I'll get my stuff together and be down in a minute."

Someday I was going to be smart and get a second hamper—one for whites and one for darks. But then I'd need one for the in-between stuff. Oh, nonsense. Who the heck cared? Everything of mine was so old, none of it would fade any more. I invented a new laundry routine on the spot. I took everything out of the hamper, dumped half of it on the floor and put the other half in the washer.

Glaze had enough for a full washer herself. I expected her to want to do two half-loads—she was normally so fastidious—but she surprised me. "Oh, I'll just dump it all in there at once," she said. "I don't feel like fiddling with it."

That was easy. Three loads later I thought we were ready to go. "How about a quick walk and then let's drive up to see Mom for a while. I haven't been there in a blue moon."

"No," Glaze said. "You go ahead. I think I'm going to lie back down for a while."

"I thought you could never go back to sleep once you were up. Are you coming down with something?"

"No," she said, but I didn't hear much conviction in that word.

WEEK THREE

FRIDAY

I TOOK A FINAL BITE and pushed my plate aside. The birds sang lustily outside the bay window; the pancakes were delicious if I did say so myself—light and fluffy with a slight crunch from the organic flour and the nuts and seeds I'd ground in there— and life in general was very good. My sister was another story altogether. She looked out the window without seeming to see anything. "Ellen told me yesterday that Ariel and Easton made a CD of some of Roger's songs."

"That's nice." Glaze sat there slumped over with her arms crossed.

"I told her I'd buy one."

"Uh-huh."

"Roger's garbage-collection business seems to be thriving. I hope he doesn't give up on his song-writing."

"Ummm."

"As long as he lets other people do the recording. He has the worst singing voice I've ever heard."

She uncrossed her arms and scratched her chin.

"Come on, Glaze. Let's walk the long route to the library this morning. We need to perk you up."

"I'm okay."

"Sure you are. You always droop around like a dog with its tail between its legs. Have you been eating well?"

"I eat just fine, thank you." She looked down at her mug. "Besides, you're the one who's been feeding me this week."

"But you haven't eaten much. You didn't run out of your meds, did you?"

Glaze picked up the napkin she'd set to one side and wiped at a spot on the table where some syrup had dripped off the edge of her plate. "I still have plenty of my meds."

She wasn't exactly surly. Just sort of—I don't know—blank. "I'm going to run up and brush my teeth real fast," I said. "We'll both feel better after a brisk walk." No response. "You don't have to work very long at the library if you don't want to."

"I don't mind."

"Wooo-eee! Such enthusiasm! I love it!"

Didn't work. She rolled her eyes at me. But then she sort of chuckled. "All right. I'll get my shoes on."

Marmalade hopped off the windowsill and headed toward the front door.

We took the loop around Third Street and down Magnolia. At the corner, before we turned up Second Street, Annie called out to us from Melissa's front porch.

"Hey, Annie. How's it going?"

TomatoLady is sad.

She shook her head and walked out to meet us. The closer she got, the more awful she looked, despite her long red dress. If I wore something like that I'd look like an overage would-be hippie. On Annie it looked comfortable and casual and truly attractive. "Hey there," she said. "I just finished telling Melissa I'd be gone for a while. She said she'd open the store for me if anyone needs anything. I'm going to leave a note on my front door to have people call her."

"Is it your brother? Did something happen?"

She pursed her lips. "It's a brain tumor. A deep one."

"Oh, no, Annie. What… Can they do anything?"

"At least now we know he wasn't just complaining. Something's really been wrong with him, but nobody found it till now. They can't operate until Tuesday. He has some sort of infection that they're going to treat with antibiotics before they operate."

"So Melissa's going to watch your store?"

I will help.

Annie nodded. "Not that there's much to do. Business is so slow lately, I doubt I'll be missing much income. I'll just close down for a week or two and let people call her if they absolutely have to get something. I already called Bob to ask him to keep an eye on the place. Lucky you stocked up on your tea." Her smile hardly reached her eyes. "I don't relish the thought of sitting in the waiting room at the hospital for five or six hours while he's operated on, but I guess I wouldn't want to go through something like that alone."

"I know. Hospital waiting rooms are no fun," I told her, thinking of all the hours I'd spent in that hospital last year, wondering if Bob would survive. "Do they say what his chances are?"

"He wouldn't say. I think it's really serious. I can tell he's worried, even though he was trying to joke about it. He said the worst thing about being in the hospital was that they told him he couldn't have any of his diet sodas. He's addicted to the things, you know."

I cringed at the thought. I put my arm around Annie's shoulder. When would people ever wake up to the danger? I sure enjoyed my tea—and the deli's hot chocolate—but at least I didn't have to worry about addiction, and I didn't think hot chocolate was potentially deadly the way aspartame was.

What are aspartames?

"He told me not to come down there, but I know he didn't mean that. He's always been good at laying a guilt trip on me, but this seems like something more than the usual whining. I don't think I can leave him alone at a time like this, even though I'd rather stay home and quilt and have him call me when it's all over. Do you think I'm awful to say something like that?"

"Of course not. Nobody in her right mind enjoys sitting around a hospital. And caring for a man who's recovering from surgery—well, let's just say that most men make lousy patients."

She rubbed the back of her hand. "I feel so bad now about all the nasty things I've said about him."

"You didn't know, Annie."

"You're right, but that doesn't make me feel any less guilty. I won't be able to do much while he's in the hospital, but he'll need me once he gets out. I talked with Margaret. She suggested that I bring him home with me once he can leave the hospital. I can put him up in that back room. That way I can keep an eye on him and I won't have to close my store. Doctor Nathan said he'd stop by each day just to check on him."

How lovely to live in a small enough town that the doctor was willing to make house calls. How good of him to help out Annie. Of course, Nathan was a special person in a lot of ways.

He is GoodHands.

I looked at her. Annie was—what?—maybe twenty-three or twenty-four? Too young to have that kind of burden. Why did illness ever have to hit people? "That's a good idea," I said. "It's kind of you to take care of him like that."

"Can I still go to the circus with you two tomorrow?"

I looked at Glaze. She shrugged. What on earth was with her? "Sure you can. We'll be delighted to have you there. It sounds like you could use some cheering up." Just the same as my sister, I thought, but I didn't say that out loud.

Smellsweet is very sad.

"Great. I'll have two sisters to hang out with."

WE LEFT THE LIBRARY EARLY. Rebecca Jo and Sadie had things well under control, and Sadie, I think, appreciated the chance to ease gently back into her routine. When we got home Marmalade did her usual search through the daylilies around the mailbox. Whatever was she looking for?

I already told you. Bugs.

I handed Glaze a couple of bills and a letter from Auntie Blue. That woman sure did like to write. Near the bottom of my stack of bills was a yellow envelope.

Dearest Biscuit and Bob,

You cannot know how much comfort your frequent visits gave me through these final times with Wallace. I particularly enjoyed how often you popped in with a cheery hello, Bob. Wallace looked forward to your conversations, and I'm thankful you had such patience with his slow speech, especially toward the end.

Biscuit, your quiet presence on the day he passed on was such a help. I know I wasn't a very gracious hostess that day, but I'm sure you understood.

I have to admit that I laughed a bit when I saw your flowers at the funeral home. I don't know how you knew, since I don't think I've ever shared this with anyone, but the first flower Wallace ever gave me was from a joe-pye weed. It was considerably more wilted than the one that formed the center of the gorgeous spray you sent. That brought back a lovely, lovely memory, and I cannot thank you enough.

I ate those blackberries you brought from Maggie—every single one of them—the morning after Wallace left. Ida and I sat there in my kitchen while I ate and cried and remembered. I felt he was sitting there with me, watching me enjoy such a homey pleasure.

Thank you, Bob, for loving Wallace so much. Thank you, Biscuit, for loving me so much. I wish you many long and happy years together.

Fondly,
Sadie

I folded the two sheets of yellow stationery back into the envelope and set it on the drop-leaf table in the entryway. So Bob visited Wallace a lot? If there was anything not to love about that husband of mine, I certainly couldn't think of it. Unless it was Susan.

GLAZE WAS, I THOUGHT, getting closer to being willing to think about considering the possibility of maybe getting truly serious about Tom. My sister had some commitment issues. We'd spent the week avoiding talking about Tom. Every time I mentioned him, she'd change the subject. Well, this was as good a time as any. I tried to think of a diplomatic way to ask Glaze about that man in her life. "So, Glaze," I said, throwing diplomacy to the winds as we washed up the dishes after a late lunch, "where do things stand with Tom?"

"What things?"

She wasn't making this easy. "It's just that Auntie Blue and I were talking last week about whether we should think about any wedding plans." That wasn't exactly the right way to put it. Glaze glared at me.

"Not that it's any business of yours," she said, "but Tom proposed last week."

I dropped the dish towel on the counter and threw my arms around her shoulders. "Glaze, this is wonderful! We can head up to Mable's next week to get your wedding dress, and I've got my heart set on that beautiful indigo job we saw Tuesday. Matron of honor—what fun! When are you going to call Mom? Does Bob know? Why didn't he tell me? Have you set the date yet? Late summer would be nice, when it's not too hot but before the autumn rains start. Do you want to have the reception here?" My sister wasn't responding the way a bride-to-be should. She hadn't even turned away from the sink. I'd been gushing on at the back side of her head. "Glaze? Is something wrong?"

She whipped around, knocking me off balance, and I caught at the edge of the counter to keep from stumbling. "Would you for once in your life keep out of my business?" She grabbed up the towel, dried her hands on it, threw it at my feet, and stalked out of the room. I sat down rather heavily at the big table and looked at the empty doorway she'd passed through. I heard her stomp up the stairs. She must have thrown her clothes into her bag without even folding anything because within minutes she clattered back down and poked her head into the kitchen. "Just for your information," she said, "I said no. I'm not ready for this." Her voice escalated to a scream. "I can't take it. I don't even want to think about it. So leave me alone. I'll make up my mind when I'm good and ready, and not before." Was this my sister yelling at me? "And just so you'll know, if I ever decide to get married, I'm going to elope."

"Elope? Are you nuts? Do you know what that would do to Mom? Or to me for that matter? How selfish can you get?"

"Here! Take this." She threw something at me. It careened off the table and crashed into the kitchen cabinet. "I don't ever want to see it again! I hate that color! And you can forget about the circus tomorrow. I don't want to go anywhere with you and that fake sister you like so much." She turned, banged her blue tapestry bag against the door frame, and stalked out of the house. She slammed the front door behind her, and I listened to her leave with a squeal of tires. When I thought to look on the floor by the sink, I found the tube of bubblegum-pink lipstick.

Glaze,
    I'm so sorry I ticked you off this afternoon, but you could at least answer your phone when I try to call you to apol

Dear sis,

Can we get back on track somehow? If you'd only stop being so uptight

My dear sister,

What the heck got into you this morning? And why have you turned off your answering machine? I can't even leave an "I'm sorry" messa

To whom it may concern:

The party of the first part wishes sincerely to convey regrets for having offended the party of the second part. That's me and you, kid.

I balled up my first four attempts and lofted them one at a time into the wastepaper basket. Two points each, except for the one that landed next to Marmalade.

Thank you.

She batted it around the floor while I tried one more time.

Dear Glaze,

Can you forgive me? I know I've offended you royally. I should have kept my mouth shut about Tom. I admit that. I don't want anything to come between us, particularly not something that we could clear up if we'd just talk to one another.

So—can we talk? I know this great deli that serves the world's best milkshakes. Or there's even a second-rate kitchen on Beechnut Lane that whips up edible soup. If you insist, I'll crawl on my hands and knees to your house. Call me?

Epistle number five wasn't great, but it would do. Hadn't she herself said one step at a time? So I signed it, tucked it in an envelope, and wrote *Glaze* on the front with a little heart on each side of her name. If she wouldn't answer her phone, I'd tape this to her front door. That ought to get her attention. Before I walked out of the house, with Marmalade in attendance, of course, I scrawled *Call Me!* across the back where I'd sealed the flap. Then I grabbed the tape dispenser in case she wasn't home.

MADELEINE'S ARMS WERE FULL. This shopping on the way home from work was a pain in the backside after spending so many hours sitting at work. Of course, writing copy at Wish Fulfillment was a better job than she'd expected to get after all those years of slaving for her mother in Atlanta as a glorified housekeeper. Best of all, it gave her time in the evening to write her thrillers. It was hard to keep killing off her mother on the page, though, now that they weren't living in the same house.

Marmalade stood on the top step.

"Hello, sweetie. Did you stop by for some catnip?"

Hello, Curlup.

"Yes, I'll get you some just as soon as I put these packages down. Hold on. I really do have to get the cold stuff in the fridge before... What have we here?" She juggled the handles of the bags until a thumb and a forefinger were sort of free. The envelope taped to the kitchen door had one word dashed across the front of it. "Glaze," she read. "Hmm. Wish you knew how to open doors, Marmy. You sure could help here."

I cannot reach the doorknob.

After untangling her hands from the bags, putting the cheese and ice cream and butter and soymilk creamer in the appropriate places—she left the rest of it on the counter to sort itself—Maddy pulled a jar of catnip from the cabinet that Marmalade pointed out to her. "Smart cat."

Of course I know where you put the catnip.

She handed Marmy a fuzzy cat toy coated with the aromatic leaves, then turned back to the envelope. "Let's run this down to your aunt Glaze. It looks like it might be important."

She is gone.

"If you were a dog..."

Excuse me?

"…I'd tie the note on your collar and send you home, but I guess that won't work, huh? Anyway, I could use a short walk. I've been inside way too long all day. Come on, Marmy."

I am still playing.

"Funny cat. I love watching you toss that thing around. Tell you what. You play for a while and I'll get the rest of the groceries put away. Then I'll walk you home and take Glaze her mail. Why on earth am I talking to a cat?"

I WAS LUXURIATING in the tub, washing off the crud of the day and trying to soothe my soul after the fight with Glaze, when I heard someone knock on the front door. Can't get there in time, I thought. Anyway, I didn't want to drip my way downstairs. Bob wouldn't be home for another three or four hours, and I was just as happy to delay the conversation I felt I needed to have with him. About Susan. So I ignored the knocking and lathered up a bit more. Honeysuckle. Loved the soaps I got at Annie's. I tried to remember the name of the woman who made them. Annie had probably told me her name, but I couldn't recall it. Oh, well. I'd put her nameless on my gratitude list, simply because her soaps were heavenly.

I slipped into some soft gray sweatpants and a dark pink tee-shirt, grabbed a book, and curled up on the loveseat upstairs. Marmalade wandered in and joined me. I was so glad we'd put one of those kitty doors in for her. That way she could come and go whenever she wanted. I did wonder where she'd been mooching today after I'd left Glaze's house.

"Where's my woman?" Bob's voice echoed through the house and brought me running downstairs.

"You're early! Welcome home… Have I told you that you give the best hugs in the… Ooh! And the best kisses, too. Ah, yes, and that, too." I loved nuzzles. It couldn't be him. It couldn't.

"Is Glaze still here?"

"Glaze?"

"Yes, Woman. Your sister. Is she here?"

"No. She… Well, we sort of had a bit of an argument today, and she took off in a huff earlier than she'd planned. Why? Were you hoping to spend the evening with both of us? Wouldn't you rather have me all to yourself?"

"Fine with me, Woman. There's some mail for her, though. I put it on the table."

"That's funny. I thought we'd emptied out the mailbox. Oh, what the heck, it doesn't matter."

"It wasn't in the… Hey there, little one!" Marmalade rubbed her head against Bob's leg, and he bent down to scoop her up. "Did you miss me?"

Widelap and Smellsweet kept me very busy walking all over town.

"Have you been snoozing the whole time?"

Mouse droppings! I just told you I have been busy.

We laughed when Marmy sneezed. Bob set her down gently and wrapped his arms around me again. Ahhh, even better than cinnamon buns. There would be plenty of time to talk to him about Susan. Maybe tomorrow. For now I could concentrate on more pleasant things.

SOMETIME LATER he rubbed a finger across my forehead, smoothing back a few stray strands of hair. "So you and Glaze had a fight?"

"Not a fight really. She got mad at something I said and ran off before I could apologize."

"Call her."

"I did, but she didn't answer."

"She'll call you back."

I slipped into my robe. It was too late to get dressed again. "Her machine was off, so I couldn't even leave a message."

"So talk to her tomorrow at the circus."

"She said she didn't want to go."

He leaned back against the headboard. "Must have been some fight. What did you do?"

"Why do you assume it was my fault?"

He put his glasses back on, probably just so he

could look at me over the rims. "She's the one who ran out, right?"

"Oh, all right. I ticked her off when I asked when she was going to get married."

"That's worth missing a circus for?"

"My thoughts exactly. You know, though, she's been really down all week. I figured she was just in one of those slump times that women get in." He raised one eyebrow. "Don't you say a word!"

"Me? Would I be dumb enough to comment?"

"Smarty-pants! What am I going to do with you?"

He waited a full four seconds before making a suggestion I simply couldn't pass up.

Just before we went to sleep, he said, "If I see Glaze tomorrow while you're at the circus, I'll ask her to give you a call."

TWENTY QUESTIONS. Glaze gripped the steering wheel. Is it bigger than a breadbox? She shook her head. No. Yes. This is bigger than any breadbox. Is it outside Biscuit's house? Yes. Forever now. She doesn't want me back. Is it my hair? Is it Marmalade? Is it the doorknob? Am I crazy?

The needle on Glaze's gas gauge had been pointing almost to empty when she'd left the valley, but she hadn't paid any attention to it. Now the red light was on. She pulled into the next gas station. She had some cash. She had a credit card. There was the pump.

"Are you okay, lady?" The tapping on her window became more insistent. "Lady!"

She looked first at herself in the rearview mirror. There was a stripe across her forehead where she'd been leaning against the steering wheel. When the man tapped once more on the window, she turned her head toward him and said, "Gas."

"It's pump-your-own, lady," he said. Glaze gripped the steering wheel and rocked back and forth. "Uh, you want me to fill 'er up?" he said.

A few minutes, a lifetime later, she handed him her credit card. When he returned with the slip for her to sign, he bent down and looked at her through her open window. "You sure you're okay, lady?"

"Biscuit," she said. "I need Biscuit." It was a tenuous lifeline, but one she felt she could hold on to.

"We don't have biscuits here, ma'am. You head down to that diner just across the four-lane."

Her inborn good manners took over and she thanked him. It seemed like the right thing to do. Pulling out of the station, she turned left, the direction he had pointed in, only vaguely aware that she was headed back the way she'd come. The diner reminded her of something. *Home-Cooked*

Food! Breakfast Anytime! Delicious! The sign featured a crowing rooster.

"Coffee, honey?" The voice seemed to come from a yellow-and-white-checkered blouse just to her left.

"Biscuit," she said.

The blouse breathed in and out. "You want them sausage biscuits of ours? We're world famous for them." The checks leaned a little closer until a face and some blond hair came into view. "Leastways that's what we're supposed to say. Who knows?" She scribbled something on her order pad. "Someday it might get to be true."

Glaze smiled. It seemed as if she should.

She ate half of one biscuit dripping in gravy and pushed her plate away. Cash. She had cash. She had to pay. She left a twenty-dollar bill beside her plate and walked out. The car turned right when she left the diner's parking lot, and she kept driving until she was back in Keagan County. Biscuit, she thought. Biscuit.

She was all the way through Braetonburg before she remembered that Biscuit was angry. Angry with her. Why? She didn't know, couldn't call up a reason. But she did remember one phrase. How selfish can you get? How selfish can you get? How...

She slowed way down for the steep curve. How

selfish. She couldn't go home. Biscuit hated her. She saw a sign. BED & BREAKFAST. Bed. Bed. Biscuit for breakfast. She had a credit card. But Biscuit hated her. Bed. She turned right, and her car headed up the steep driveway.

Twenty questions. Is this my kitchen? No. Is this my bedroom? No. Is this my home? No. Do I have a home? No.

ALICIA RAE KESSLER LIKED to sit on her front porch a few minutes every evening before she ate her dessert. She did like desserts. If she had guests she usually asked them to join her. What was the use of having people there, other than the income, of course, if she couldn't have some good conversation along the way? This particular evening, she'd been wondering if she should get into town more often and try to make some friends. It seemed like too much bother. She did know that Annie person, the one with all the coppery-red hair. The one who bought her sister's honey-suckle soap to sell in that Healthy Place store or whatever it was called.

That train of thought ground to a halt when a car turned in. Awfully late for a guest, but sometimes people had trouble finding a place. If the motels in Braetonburg were full, sometimes folks would ride down the valley until they saw her sign. She liked her sign, with its painted drawing of a bed and a big plate of biscuits, and a silly rooster in between them. Corny, but effective. Drew her a lot of business.

She bustled off the porch and pointed toward the small parking area tucked behind a dense row of Burford hollies. She wanted people to see the house first. It wasn't fancy by any means, but it was unique. Plus, with all the hummingbirds flitting around the feeders from sunrise to sunset, it made the house look downright festive. The sound, too. That was something else. All those teeny bird wings flapping away maybe fifty times a second. She waited until the car stopped. A woman with striking silver hair stepped out from behind the wheel.

"You looking for a room?" Alicia asked. The woman nodded. "Well, honey, you've come to the right place. Come on inside with me. Do you have a bag?"

The woman looked confused. "I've been driving a long time."

Oh, dear, Alicia thought. Was this going to be another one of those tear-jerkers? She always seemed to attract the women who were running away from something or someone. The ones who needed a few days to gather their courage. The ones who were looking for something. What the heck, though, it was company. And income. "I'm just getting ready to have my dessert and you're welcome to join me. We'll get you signed in first."

Glaze McKee the woman wrote in the book and stopped.

"That's okay if you can't remember your license plate. We'll get it tomorrow morning when it's light out. How long will you be staying?"

The woman shrugged.

"Do you know your address?"

She shrugged again.

"Are you just needing some time to yourself, honey? Is that why you came?" She could see the tears start to form, but they didn't spill over. The shrug came again. By this time Alicia had the woman pegged. Probably somebody who'd run away from an abusive spouse. No wedding ring, though. An abusive boyfriend, then. All she needed was some pampering for a few days until she could get her thoughts in order. "I have one other guest, but she's real quiet. In fact, she's already turned in for the night. She said she was going to read for a while. She won't bother you any." Alicia Rae waited for a response. When none came, she plowed on. "This price covers your room and breakfast each day, but I can provide all your meals if you want. It's not that much more." She named a figure and the woman nodded.

"Let's get some dessert. I never charge for dessert. You look like you could use it."

GLAZE EYED THE SWEET concoction in front of her.

"I bet you'd like a glass of milk to go with our dessert," Alicia Rae said as she lifted an old-fashioned pitcher from the fridge.

Milk? Did that mean a milkshake? This didn't look like the way to make a milkshake. Glaze nodded.

The kitchen of the bed-and-breakfast sported an array of rooster-related items—framed prints of barnyard fowl on the walls, a troupe of painted wallpaper roosters that ranged around the room near the ceiling, and rooster-shaped salt and pepper shakers in the middle of the table where Glaze sat with her hands in her lap. A spoon, blessedly devoid of excess design elements, lay beside a bowl decorated with open-beaked roosters that alternated with yellow-rayed suns. She rotated the garish bowl. Biscuit would think it was cute. Those birds marched all the way around it, matching the wallpaper in everything except the direction they were heading. Where was she heading?

Alicia Rae's milk pitcher took the form of an open-beaked rooster. The red comb on the rooster's head surrounded the opening on top. Alicia must have already poured the milk in there. Glaze had never seen anything like it. No. That wasn't true. Grandma Martelson used to have a pitcher shaped like a frog. The orange juice at breakfast time poured out of the frog's open mouth. Biscuit always said *riddip, riddip, riddip* whenever the juice came out. Glaze remembered that she used to think that was funny. Now it wasn't a frog. It was a rooster. She watched the pitcher tilt. A white stream issued from the rooster's open yellow beak. No orange juice. Something colorless. Something sad. There was no Biscuit to call out *riddip*. It wasn't funny anymore.

"Cockadoodle-doo," Alicia Rae sang out and placed the glass of milk in front of Glaze.

Doodle-Doo. The rooster who used to wake her up. She'd never hear Doodle-Doo again. She had to leave the valley. Biscuit didn't love her anymore. She reached for the bowl and moved it a quarter of an inch to the left.

"These are right pretty bowls, aren't they?"

Glaze lifted her eyes to the source of the voice. Twenty questions. That's number one. She nodded, but only because it seemed to be expected.

"I bet you're wondering what I call my dessert, aren't you?"

Two. She nodded again.

"Well, honey, that's my Ice-Cream-Sandwich Chocolate-Chip Oreo CoolWhip Delight. I invented it myself. You go right ahead and dig in."

That wasn't a question. Glaze lifted her spoon.

The woman took a big bite and smiled as she munched. "I do love chocolate, don't you?"

Three. Glaze considered answering that one out

loud, but speaking seemed like more bother than what it was worth.

"Now, you're a quiet one, aren't you? Don't you talk very much?"

How many questions had that been? Was it four and five, or had they gotten to five and six? Glaze looked down at her hands, hoping to find an answer there. It was no good. She couldn't remember. She'd have to start counting all over again. The woman would get free questions. It's my fault, Glaze thought. I lost track. I lost track. I lost... I'm lost.

"...you worry. That's okay with me. I bet you have a lot to think about, don't you?"

One. The woman's voice faded back out again as Glaze took a bite. Vanilla ice cream. Delicious. Milkshakes at the Delicious. Biscuit.

"...Hiram was one of those dapper men that could charm the warts off a bullfrog, if you know what I mean. We figured he must have been kidnapped when he didn't show up for the wedding. Why else would he leave me standing at the altar?"

Two.

"...a lot of years ago, but it seems like yesterday. It was an awful couple of days I spent, wondering what had happened to him. We let everybody keep the wedding favors, and of course we went ahead and ate all the food. It would have been a shame to waste it, don't you think?"

Three. Don't waste food. Glaze took another bite. It did taste good. She kept eating. Kept tallying the questions.

"Do you... Wouldn't it be fine if... Isn't there a way to... Doesn't it seem... Isn't it a shame that... I buy it from that really sweet store in town called Healthy Place. Have you been there?"

Nine.

"Annie, the owner, buys the hand-milled honeysuckle soap that my sister Louisa Mae makes."

Soap. Biscuit's favorite soap. She likes Annie better than me.

"...almost more bother than what it's worth."

Like living, Glaze thought.

Alicia Rae looked at the morsel balanced on her spoon. "I do love chocolate. If I had to do it over again, I would have told Hiram we needed to elope. Wouldn't that be a good idea?"

Ten. Eloping. She'd never elope. Why had she told Biscuit she'd elope? She wanted a wedding in the Old Church. Tom had gone away, though. She pushed him away.

"Are you feeling all right, honey?" Eleven. "You're looking a little pale. My goodness, do you want some more Delight?" Twelve. "Here I am talking your ear off and you've hardly said a thing. No wonder you finished your dessert before I got even halfway through mine, right?"

That was thirteen. Glaze smiled briefly and

shook her head. The woman still had seven questions to go, but she wasn't asking the right kind of questions. Didn't she know how to play? Biscuit knew she was supposed to ask yes-and-no questions. Biscuit would never play twenty questions with her again. Biscuit loved Annie. Annie was her new little sister.

"…and they finally found his body up there on the ridge." The woman paused and gestured vaguely off to her left. "…well, you see, then I knew he hadn't left me at the altar on purpose. They said they could see where the rattlesnake bit him, two swollen puncture wounds on his leg, right through his pants. He'd been dead a couple of days. That's the reason he missed the wedding, don't you see?"

Fourteen. Missed the wedding. Biscuit wants a wedding. She said I was selfish. Selfish. Selfish.

"…and I figure that as long as I carry my shotgun when I go walking up there, I'll be safe. Did you ever shoot?"

Fifteen. Glaze shook her head again.

"…for helping me with the dishes. You didn't have to do that, like I said, but it was fun, wasn't it?"

The woman had been yammering for some time without asking any questions, and Glaze had almost lost count. It had to be sixteen, though.

"I'm glad you saw my sign. You look too tuckered out to drive anywhere else tonight. You said you've been driving all day?"

Seventeen. Glaze shook her head. Not all day. Just since she had yelled at Biscuit. Screamed at her. Just since she had run from the house. Why? What had Biscuit done to her? Glaze followed Alicia upstairs, feeling the woman's chatter fall over her in waves.

"This old house may look tiny on the outside, but it's bigger than you'd think. I've always liked how sturdy it is, with the bottom floor built into the hillside. I have the front bedroom downstairs, the one with windows, and the upstairs front room is taken already by that young woman I told you about. Beautiful long black hair. Susan, her name is. Like I said, she's pretty quiet. You won't mind having one of these back rooms, will you?"

Eighteen. Glaze looked around. The gray feeling in her head made the room look dull, but some little piece of Glaze knew that the white sheets and the soft blue blanket would be comfortable.

"...towels and washcloth are here. The bathroom's right across the hall. You've got it all to yourself. There's another bath up front that the other guest uses. Here's a brand-new bar of my sister's honeysuckle soap. Do you like honeysuckle?" Nineteen. One to go. Glaze shrugged. Biscuit smelled like honeysuckle.

"Is there anything else you need?"

Twenty. They were at twenty questions, and now it was time for the woman to guess the answer, but Glaze couldn't remember what this game was about. Marmalade? The doorknob? Biscuit? That was it. Biscuit was the answer.

"Is there anything else you need?" the woman repeated.

You can't repeat questions. Glaze shook her head. "Toothpaste," she said.

"I'll go get some. I even have an extra toothbrush, and I've got some real nice herbal mouthwash I bought in town. You can swish that around and it'll make your teeth happy. That's what you need. Just get cleaned up and comfortable, and a good night's sleep will put you right back in fine form." The woman was blessedly quiet for a moment. "That's enough talking from me. You sit here and I'll go get that toothpaste for you. I'm really glad you saw my sign in the dark."

Glaze looked at the bed. The game was over. All the questions had been asked. But they'd been the wrong questions, and anyway, there wasn't an answer. Not really. She slipped off her shoes and lay down on top of the blue blanket. She heard the woman come back in, heard the soft bump of something—toothpaste probably—being set on the dresser. She felt a quilt laid gently across her. She knew through her closed eyelids when the light went off. Dark. It was dark. Glaze opened one eye. The soft glow of a night-light whispered through the room. She doesn't love me anymore. She doesn't love me anymore. Glaze slept.

ALICIA RAE KNEW AS WELL as anybody that sometimes healing just took time.

There was still one serving of her Ice-Cream-Sandwich Chocolate-Chip Oreo CoolWhip Delight left. Not enough for two people. The fridge purred when she opened it. No sense dirtying another dish, so she pulled out a long-handled iced-tea spoon and went to work.

I am grateful for
Widelap, who forgot to write her list tonight
Softfoot
Smellsweet
Curlup
this soft bed
my special door

WEEK THREE

SATURDAY

Celia,

Glaze has gone home. Our sister-week is over. You can start delivering her mail back at her house now. Thanks for all the good service you give. You're going on my gratitude list tonight.

Biscuit

THE CROWD SURGED FORWARD when a nondescript fellow wearing a cowboy hat pulled open the three-rail metal gate. Fanning out in all directions, the press of people thinned to a more comfortable level. Annie grabbed my shirtsleeve and pulled me toward a tattooed man who held a long rope and spun it slowly around his head. It looked so easy. I probably could have done it myself, I thought, except that the rope was on fire at the end. The man's bare chest and arms sported tattoos of vivid red, orange, and yellow flames. He must have had a high level of pain tolerance, if not from the tattooing, then from the learning process with the fiery rope.

Before we reached the edge of the circle of gawkers, we passed by a cotton-candy vendor ensconced in a tiny white trailer with a blue-and-white-striped awning. A dozen or so crystals dangled on strings from the edge of the awning, catching the morning light and tossing rainbows around as they twisted in the slight breeze. Two vats of spun sugar, one pink, one blue, whirred in front of a wizened fellow who smiled a missing-tooth grin. "Two for you beautiful lassies on this glorious day?" he said, drawing us closer to him by the sheer force of his salesmanship. He held up two long paper cones. "And what color would each of you be liking the best?"

I'd been fully prepared to ignore cotton candy, but this looked like too much of a treat for me to resist, and anyway, the old guy had a merry twinkle. "Pink," I said, as Annie chimed in, "Blue."

"Annie? You're a health-food nut. Why on earth would you even consider cotton candy?"

"All the rules are off," she said. "This is circus day. Besides, I love cotton candy."

"Don't you worry about it, dearie," the man said, handing her a concoction of sky-blue fluff. He rolled the *r*'s in *worry*. I liked his accent, even though it sounded a bit put on. He was probably from Idaho. "'Tis good it feeds the laughter in you."

Sugar. That's all it was, and food coloring. And a bit of magic. I took my pink magic and handed over an astronomical amount of money, considering that what I bought was mostly air. Then I looked at Annie, who already had some blue sugar crystals on the tip of her nose, and figured that what we held wasn't mostly air. It was mostly wonder, just like the dancing crystals, with a big dose of childhood mixed in.

I pointed to her nose, handed her a napkin, and we wandered over toward the fire dancer who had collected quite a circle of admirers standing two or three deep. Annie tapped a particularly tall man on the arm. "Excuse me," she said to him. "May we stand in front of you so we can see better?"

He looked down at her, glanced at me, and said, "Yes, ma'am," with a courtly Southern air. "You and your friend both just step right here."

"My sister," Annie said and grinned at me.

The tattooed man passed the flames under his leg, over his shoulder, around his head, back under his leg. I hoped his knee-length skin-hugging pants were fireproof. The tongues of fire seemed to glance off his body without effect, but I did see him wince one time when the flaming ball brushed against his bare calf. He covered it well, though. Quite the showman. I glanced at Annie. She stood with her mouth agape, the cotton candy forgotten for the moment. The tall man standing behind her stared, not at the fire dancer, but at Annie. He seemed entranced with the wrist-thick braid of vibrant red hair that draped over her shoulder. I saw him raise his head and scan the crowd, as if he were looking for someone. He nodded once and tilted his head toward Annie. I looked the direction he'd been gazing, but all I saw were the usual circus-goers, gaily dressed in tee-shirts and shorts, in polo shirts and jeans, in sundresses or overalls. A regular crowd, with nothing in particular to distinguish any of them. Maybe I was just imagining things. I recognized a number of people from Braetonburg and quite a few from Martinsville, too. Melissa was there, several of the volunteer firefighters, Marvin Axelrod with his wife, and Sarah from the dress shop in Garner Creek. It was good that Sarah had taken some time for herself. When I looked back, the tall man was gone.

The fire dancer had progressed to acrobatics while I'd been noodling. He leaped into the air and with a tremendous whoosh blew a spout of fire out of his mouth. It fanned upward to the gasps of the delighted onlookers, including me. As he bowed to enthusiastic applause, a barker on a raised platform beside the doorway of the tent called out, "See more, much more, of Firenzo the Magnificent during the main show in the big top, starting at eleven. That's E-LE-VEN sharp! Beat the crowd! Buy your tickets right here, right now! Come back in time and you can be practically the first one in line."

"Yeah," I muttered at Annie, "after the other couple of hundred people," but she seemed to be ignoring me. I caught Melissa's eye and waved her over. "I didn't know you were coming. You could have ridden with us. Having fun?"

"That was amazing! I've never seen anything like it." We followed Annie toward the ticket line. "I bet Firenzo the Magnificent is covered with scars underneath all those tattoos."

I wasn't the only one who had noticed the wince. "Seems like a dicey way to make a living."

"I thought it was wonderful," Annie breathed. "I always wanted to run away and join a circus when I was a kid."

"What would your act have been?" Melissa asked.

"The flying trapeze."

"You have to be kidding."

"No. I thought that would be the most exciting life."

"Well," Melissa said, "it's never too late."

Annie looked down at her feet. "Doubt I'd make it up one of those rope ladders," she said. I pictured a skinny swing far overhead and thought that a rope ladder would be the least of her problems. Annie brandished what was left of her blue treat. "But I could always work for the cotton-candy guy!"

"You have to be kidding," Melissa said again.

Annie didn't answer. Her eyes, I noticed, had gone all soft and blurry.

FLAGS AROUND THE TOP of the tent snapped in the brisk morning breeze. We bought our show tickets, and the three of us wandered aimlessly, greeting friends, urging on the men who vied for prizes at the coin toss, the ring throw, the shooting gallery with its yellow ducks bobbing in a perky and apparently unsinkable line. One particularly hefty fellow managed to send a bright-colored marker almost to the top of the test-your-strength game. *Close, but No Cigar* read the line where the silver arrow paused before it plummeted again to the floor of the column. Melissa shook her head. "What on earth does that mean anyway? People use the phrase all the time, but it doesn't mean anything."

"Yes, it does," Annie piped up. "Way back, when fairs and circus midways were in their heyday, the top prize was a big, fat cigar. All this guy did was get close...*but no cigar.* Get it?"

Melissa swiveled her head to watch the sweaty-faced guy make another try. "It must be one of those man things, because it makes no sense to me." He spit on his hands, grasped the sledgehammer and hefted it until it swung up gracefully, powerfully, in a smooth arc, paused, and crashed onto the pad. Without apparent effort, the arrow rose and rose and rose. I held my breath. Clang went the bell. We cheered, all of us, including Melissa. The man, rather red-faced by this point, handed his prize, a four-foot teddy bear, to a comfortably-built woman who hugged it, hugged him, and pulled him away toward the shooting gallery.

"He still didn't get a cigar," Melissa said. "Maybe they should change the sign to *Close, but No Teddy Bear.*"

"Nope," I said. "It doesn't have the same ring."

Annie pointed to the pretzel wagon. "I'm hungry."

COTTON CANDY, PRETZELS, fried dough. An hour of walking and eating and laughing. We even tried our hands at the ringtoss. Annie won a pack of gum, which she gave to Melissa; I won a super-special, genuine emerald ring, easily the size of a nickel, which I wore proudly; but Melissa pocketed the grand prize, a stuffed duck wearing a vest that proclaimed *I Won the Ringtoss!* There was another message on the back of the vest, a blatant suggestion that made me laugh, Melissa blush, and Annie stare in blank incomprehension. Surely she wasn't that naïve? I was glad she didn't ask me to explain. There were too many children within earshot.

"Oh, look!" I said, glad to change the subject. "Here's a wild aster growing by the fence." I picked two sprigs from the healthy-looking clump and handed them out. Then I turned back and plucked one for myself.

"Dress up in old-timey clothes! Get your picture taken! Step right up here! Think how lovely you'll look in silk and satin! Top hats for the men! Parasols for the ladies! Step right up. A souvenir picture to last you a lifetime!"

Annie's face positively glowed. "Could we?"

"Sure. Why not?" We slipped the open-backed fancy gowns over our casual duds. I chose an outrageous pink-feathered hat. It reminded me of Glaze's crazy pink cap, but I refused to worry about it. We'd patch things up later. The furbelows and flounces on my dress clashed horribly with Annie's hot-orange ball gown and Melissa's fire-engine-red outfit that looked as if it would have been at home in a saloon, or above one. "These clash," I said, knowing that Sally would have approved of my fashion sense for once. "We can't wear them together."

"Yes, we can," Annie said, emphasizing each word.

The assistant handed me a tray of gaudy jewelry to choose from. "The photo's in sepia tones. You'll look fine. This your daughter?"

"No. We're all sisters for the day. My daughter wouldn't be caught dead in a place like this."

The woman shrugged. "Her loss."

She was right. It *was* her loss. So, I loaded myself up with necklaces and rings and helped Annie do the same. Melissa already fairly dripped with the gaudiest of the jewels. Then we struck terribly dignified poses in front of a backdrop that combined the best—or worst if you thought of it that way—of Victoriana, the old West, the Deep South, and some Greek Revival thrown in for spice. I paid for three prints, of course. They gave me a receipt and said to return after the circus show to collect our photos. On the way to the circus tent, we bought french fries. Extra large.

A HAPPY HORDE OF PEOPLE—"All of you are first in line!" yelled the barker—streamed into the big top. I wished Glaze had come along. Surely this would have brightened her up. My super-special, genuine emerald caught a ray of sunlight just before I stepped into the shadow of the tent. The green glint was the same color as my sister's eyes. What was I going to do about Glaze?

Annie led us toward the left, but a clown circulating through the crowd blocked her way with an outsized umbrella. He opened it, took Melissa's arm, and ushered her to a seat in the fourth row. He handed her one of those little white bubble-blowing bottles that you see so often at weddings. He motioned for me to sit beside her and waved Annie in to sit next to me on the end of the row. This must have been his specialty. He kept ushering people to seats all over the place, some on the left, some on the right, handing a bubble thingy to every third or fourth person. Calliope music stuttered away in the background. A muted clamor of happy voices sounded all around us. I sat there, perfectly content, picking out people I knew in the crowd. I felt a particular affinity for the top-heavy woman whose man had apparently kept winning prizes for her. She sat a few rows away from us, her arms filled with teddy bears. Bags of other prizes crowded her feet like a whole litter of kittens around a mommy cat. If Bob had been there, my arms would have been as full as hers. I knew that for sure.

Drums rolled, and a curtain flew open as three feather-bedecked horses charged into the sawdust ring and loped around once before they whirled in perfect time to the accompanying band music. They stopped in the center of the ring when the cymbals crashed. "Ladies and Gentlemen!" The red-coated ringmaster strode into the spotlight. "Welcome to the Biggest Little Circus. It's the big-

gest little circus in this valley, the biggest little circus in the country! This one ring holds a promise
for you—the promise of lights, of action, of en-
tertainment! The promise of thrills, of suspense,
of amazing physical feats never before seen in a
ring of any size, anywhere! You have come to the
right place at the right time. Now prepare to be
delighted by Marla Henderson, horsewoman ex-
traordinaire, and her fabulous troupe of world-
famous, world-renowned Henderson horses, who
have performed before the crowned heads of Europe!" He paused for another drum roll. "The
Amazing Marla and her Henderson Horses!"

Melissa leaned close as the applause rang out.
"Crowned heads of Europe, my foot! They've
probably never been out of the southeast U.S. of
A."

Despite the hokey intro, Marla did put on an
amazing show. She had those horses quick-tim-
ing it to music, dancing, pirouetting, leaping over
barriers. Then she hopped effortlessly, or so it
seemed, onto the back of the lead horse and stood
with her hands raised high above her head as the
horse galloped in a circle. When a second horse
cantered up beside the first one, she stepped from
one horse to the other and back again, ending up
with a foot on each horse, balancing and gyrat-
ing with total ease. She stood on her hands and
did a flip dismount that made me gasp. Her se-

quins razzle-dazzled as she swept into a low bow, the kind that circus performers make with such élan, but would look downright dumb if the rest of us did it.

A whole raft of clowns poured out of a teeny car that came to a screeching halt in the middle of the ring as the last horse flounced out. The band struck up a perky clown-appropriate tune, complete with honk-honks and squeaks and toots. I laughed until I heard a child scream and saw a toddler clamber onto his mother's lap and bury his head in abject fear. The mother dandled the child, cooed, and finally carried the little one out of the tent. So much for clown motifs in nurseries. Those white faces and bright wigs and big red, painted-on lips could be terrifying when you thought about it. The clowns didn't seem to notice. They went on with their inane chaos, chasing around and throwing buckets of water at each other in the center of the ring, and popping each other with enormous foam baseball bats. In the heat of the "battle" a blue-wigged clown grabbed an outsized water bucket and charged at a yellow-wigged clown who stood directly in front of us. Yellow-Wig ducked as Blue tossed the entire contents of the bucket straight at us. Of course we hollered as the bucketful of confetti rained down on us. It caught in our hair, filled our laps, stuck to our arms. Melissa guffawed. Annie laughed so hard I thought she'd fall off her seat.

Next came a trio of jugglers and then some acrobats. A dog act, a contortionist, and a fellow who twirled a lasso around so fast I could barely keep my eye on it. It was exhausting just watching him. What a relief when he exited and the spotlight shone on a solitary clown, our usher, who stood in the back on the top step. The spotlight followed him down the stairs as he blew bubbles slowly and deliberately. He stopped by a small girl and motioned to the bubble jar she held. She offered it to him, but he shook his head, motioning to her bottle again. Her mother leaned in and whispered to her, and the tiny girl pulled out her white bubble wand and blew on it. Four incandescent bubbles fluttered into the spotlight. The clown turned to others and nodded encouragement. Soon we were all blowing bubbles in sheer delight, sharing the little containers, laughing at the misfires. Our clown worked his way down to the bottom, hopped into the ring, and pulled one of those gigantic bubble makers out of a bucket that had materialized while we weren't paying attention. He held the dripping green circle at arm's length and spun slowly, forming a wavering worm of a bubble that expanded in his wake, caught the spotlight, and shimmered in expectancy. Then it burst, and the spotlight shot upward to illuminate a wire high above our heads.

"Ladies and gentlemen! For the highlight of to-day's show, the Biggest Little Circus, which just happens to be the biggest little circus you'll ever see, is proud to present Harry Walker and his World-Famous Wonder Walkers! This is a family troupe of the most amazing tightrope walkers you've ever seen! Please welcome Belinda Walker, whose daring feats have awed this entire country as well as the crowned heads of Europe!"

He paused just long enough for Melissa to mutter something about "those crowned heads again."

"Belinda Walker!" he bellowed. A stunning woman in a shimmering emerald cape—the same color as my ring—swirled her way through the parting curtains and swished to the center of the ring. She raised her left arm dramatically and the cape fell away from her shoulders, revealing a green sequined outfit, about the size of a skimpy bathing suit, that threw a circle of reflections on the floor of the ring.

"She is joined today," the ringmaster went on, "by the youngest of the Wonder Walkers—tiny Theresa Walker!" The curtains parted again, and a child who couldn't have been much more than seven bounced into the ring. She looked as if she was trying to be terribly dramatic, like her mother...aunt...sister? But she had a spring to her step that betrayed her childlike enthusiasm for what she did. She, too, sported a cape, this one in sky blue. She, too, threw her arm into the air. Her cape hung there a moment, until she shrugged her shoulders, and it fell beside Belinda's. Two ropes descended from the murky heights of the tent, and they each grasped a loop with their outstretched hand. Theresa slipped her foot into a second loop at the bottom of the rope, but Belinda didn't seem to move. The ropes started to ascend, and the two performers were pulled upward. Belinda had to have her foot in a loop, but I couldn't for the life of me see how she had gotten it in there. One of the tricks of the trade, I supposed.

As they neared the miniscule platform overhead, the ropes slowed. Theresa stepped onto the wooden square, bent to lift the loop away from her foot, and gave us a brilliant bow. Belinda joined her, bowed, and stepped onto the rope backward. "Silence, please," intoned the ringmaster needlessly. We could barely breathe. Belinda backed her way across the tightrope, stopped halfway, and beckoned to Theresa. Without hesitation, the child stepped forward. "I must repeat myself," the ringmaster said slowly. "We ask for silence as tiny Theresa Walker joins her mother on the tightrope. This is the moment of greatest danger, as she gets her balance for the first step." I privately thought that the greatest danger would be when she was halfway to nowhere on a wire forty feet in the air, but of course I didn't say anything. I did risk a quick look at Melissa craning upward, and Annie, gazing in rapt openmouthed excitement. When I looked back myself, I caught a reflection of light from a wire that seemed to hang above Theresa. Thank goodness. I felt certain it was a safety harness of some sort. I hadn't really believed they would risk a child's life like that, but the illusion of danger was so very real. When Theresa met her mother, the two of them continued across the rope, with Belinda walking backward, testing each step before she shifted her weight, and Theresa trailing behind in sky-blue splendor. When they reached the end, the applause was deafening. This time I saw Belinda reach behind her daughter as they let go of their respective ropes, and give a twitch of her hand. Unhooking the safety harness, I assumed. They got down the same way they'd gone up, with ropes that appeared out of nowhere, Belinda holding her daughter's small hand.

A long, lanky man in brilliant scarlet tights bounded into the ring as Belinda and Theresa whisked out of sight. He leaped onto one of those rope ladders we'd been talking about earlier and scooted his way up to the platform on the left, like some bizarre, bright red monkey. "And now," said the ringmaster, "now we must ask for some help from someone in the audience. Are there any volunteers? Wait! Before you raise your hand, I must warn you that this is not for the faint at heart. This is not for someone who quails at the thought of danger. I ask for someone who dreams of adventure. Someone who saw the circus as a child and longed to ride the flying trapeze, someone who would give anything for a chance to join the Wonder Walkers on the tightrope!" He looked to the right and the left. "Are there any volunteers?" A few hands went up here and there, but he ignored them. "Would you dare to ascend the rope ladder? Just once in your life, would you follow your dream? Have you yearned to be free of the bonds of this noisy earth, to walk in the very heavens of the circus tent? Where is my volunteer? I ask you, where?!" Annie's hand shot up.

"MAY I ASK YOUR NAME?" the kindly, avuncular ringmaster asked.

"Annie," she practically shouted in her excitement. "I'm Annie McGill."

"Are you absolutely certain you are willing to risk this, my dear?"

"Sure am!" Annie said.

"Is this a lifelong dream of yours, Miss Annie?"

"Sure is!"

"And may I ask where you are from?"

"Just down the valley, in Martinsville. I own the herb shop there on First Street."

"Ah! A true saleswoman!" He winked and swept his arm in an arc to include the whole audience. "If you survive today's adventure, we'll all be sure to visit your store."

Annie looked as if she was in her element. Such a change from the quiet person I'd met when I moved to Martinsville. "Mention the circus, and I'll give you a 5% discount," she said.

He waited for the laughter to die down before he asked, "Do you have relatives we can inform in case something goes wrong?"

Annie laughed at his mock-serious tone. "Just my sister, there," she said and pointed at me. A clown materialized to my left, holding a huge parchment and an enormous feather-topped quill pen. "Madam," said the ringmaster, "we must ask you to sign a release form, holding the circus free from possible lawsuit should anything untoward happen to your sister during her death-defying attempt." I looked at the paper, which held a lot of scroll-looking lines. The clown pointed to the bottom, where it said, *Thanks for playing along! You'll get this as a souvenir after the act.* He handed me the quill, and I "signed" rather dramatically with the ballpoint beneath the feather. "Let's hear a round of applause for our self-sacrificing big sister!"

The ringmaster turned back to Annie. "Now, my friend, I'm afraid we must cover that miraculous hair of yours to keep it from getting tangled in the ropes." A black-clad assistant held out a large, floppy hat, and we all watched as Annie struggled to tuck her thick braid into the folds. "Now," he continued, "we want to protect your clothing from the rosin on the ladder, so we will ask you to don this set of overalls." Annie dutifully took the proferred clothing and stepped into the baggy legs, pulling the straps up over her shoulders. She looked up at the ringmaster and said something. He laughed. "Our friend Annie said she'd rather have an outfit like Tiny Theresa's. Perhaps next time, my dear, after you've joined our act officially. Think of this, today, as a job interview."

Annie gave a thumbs-up and looked overhead. She turned when the inconspicuous attendant tapped her on the shoulder and led her to the rope ladder. He murmured a few words to her and helped her climb into a bright blue safety harness. The ringmaster spouted instructions, including "Keep your hands away from the safety latches, and you will be perfectly safe" while the attendant pointed to the shiny gold buckles. Annie grasped the ladder with both hands and put one foot on the bottom rung, then her other foot on the next rung. The ladder quite unexpectedly began to rise in the air with Annie hanging on for dear life. She opened her mouth as if she were taking a truly deep breath, then let go of one hand and waved. The audience loved it. When she reached the platform, Scarlet Tights waited. He helped her off the rope, stood her back against the multicolored curtain that formed a backdrop to the small platform, and turned toward the rope. "Now," bellowed the ringmaster, "Harry Walker, head of the Wonder Walker family, will help to coax our job applicant onto the tightrope." The drums rolled to a crescendo as Scarlet eased his way onto the insubstantial-looking wire. With amazing dexterity, he floated to the center of the wire and turned around, but one foot slipped, and he fell sideways. Several people screamed. He twisted and, at the last possible moment, grabbed the wire. He hung there for a heart-stopping few seconds, pulled himself up somehow so he balanced on the wire with his head on one side, his feet on the other. Must be hard on his stomach muscles, I thought, once my own tummy settled back into place. From there he contorted until he crouched on the wire and gradually stood. The whole event probably took no more than half a minute, but I'd swear I didn't breathe the entire time. We fueled our applause with adrenaline as much as with relief. It's a wonder someone didn't have a heart attack.

Harry Walker in his scarlet tights beckoned to Annie, and the spotlight swung around, illuminating the dark platform. She still stood against the curtain. He beckoned again, and she shook her head, the big hat flopping wildly. Then he called to her. "Annie," we heard him say into the silence. "Annie, trust your safety harness. Take one step. Just one." She gripped the tiny railing beside her and inched forward. Several people began to clap their hands, but the ringmaster called for silence. Outside I could hear that inane calliope on the merry-go-round taking someone out to the ball game. Annie spread her arms out and took one more tentative step toward the edge of the platform. She stopped to adjust the floppy hat that enveloped her head and left her face in shadow. How could she even see the wire with that thing drooping in the way? She patted her safety harness, spread her arms again, and stepped onto the wire.

"Silence," the ringmaster suggested one more time, although he needn't have bothered. The wire rocked back and forth alarmingly. Scarlet, with some effort, maintained his balance, then rotated his left hand quickly. "A rope!" The ringmaster's voice cut over the excited gasps from the crowd. "Harry Walker requests a rope!" A white, snake-like apparition appeared overhead and slithered down from the upper reaches of the tent. When it dangled in front of Scarlet, he took it casually, formed a loop in the end of it, and threaded his right hand through the circle. With this lifeline available, Scarlet motioned once more to Annie. Seemingly reassured, she stepped fully onto the wire. One step, another. She wobbled a bit, but did surprisingly well. The harness seemed to be supporting most of her weight. Scarlet Tights might as well not have existed, for all the notice we paid to him, but after four or five steps, Annie lifted her head and seemed to use him as her focal point.

Halfway to him, Annie stopped and swiveled her head from side to side, as if looking around her at the rarified atmosphere up there. She brought her right hand in toward her chest and fumbled with the latch on her safety harness. It released with a clearly audible click. "Annie! What are you doing!" The ringmaster's voice was incredulous but quiet, as if he thought the sound waves might somehow overbalance her and topple her from the wire. Annie shook her head and unlatched the other side. The harness slipped loose and dangled behind her from the safety wire. She spread her arms slowly and stepped forward, completely unsupported. Scarlet hadn't budged an inch. I noticed he wasn't even trying to balance himself. Instead, he used his grasp on the safety rope to hold himself perfectly still. Annie made it another few feet. When she was almost within arm's length of him, though, she teetered, listed to her right, and almost in slow motion began to fall in an arc, her feet still planted on the wire. I jumped up, screaming. Scarlet leaped for her, grabbed her with one arm—around the waist, I thought—and pulled her tight against him. The spotlight bounced alarmingly, trying to keep them in its circle. The safety rope he held—thank goodness for that—lifted them and swooped them sideways along the wire, governed by some unseen mechanism above. They stumbled onto the platform. Annie went to her knees against the curtain, although it was hard to see because the spotlight hadn't found them yet. Scarlet turned back to the front, still without the light. "She is safe!" he cried. "She is safe!" He pivoted, and the spotlight caught him as Annie rose to her feet. He draped his arm across her shoulder and held her close between him and the tiny railing. Then, with his arm still around her, they both stepped into loops on yet another rope and glided smoothly down to the ring.

Annie swept off her hat, and her bright braid spilled down her back as she and Scarlet took a sweeping bow. The ringmaster chanted her praises, urged the audience not to try anything like this stunt at home, and said he hoped Annie would understand if he didn't offer her a job.

Annie laughed and bowed again as she slipped off the overalls and took one more dramatic bow with Scarlet to the accompaniment of thunderous applause. How could she walk so steadily after almost dying? Before she reached her seat, where I sat ready to strangle her for frightening me so, Firenzo the Magnificent stepped into a solitary spotlight and shot a spout of flame from his mouth. The spotlight went out, and he was illuminated by fire spinning around and over him. He passed the flame-tipped ropes between his legs and wrapped them around his body, then unwrapped them just as quickly.

Another fire dancer joined him, then two more, and yet another one. Each one of them had just one rope, one flame. Firenzo had disposed of his extra rope somehow, but I didn't have time to wonder where it had gone. The five of them spread in a circle around the ring, spinning and twisting and yelling eerie, primal calls that fueled our imagination, as if they were there to invoke ancient gods to descend and bless us. Or feast on us. Without a visible signal, all five of them, at the same time, tossed their ropes toward the fire spinner two places ahead in the circle. Each one then spun around to catch the oncoming rope as the ball of flame passed by their heads, and spin it four, five, six times before tossing it on in the same pattern. The trailing arcs, with the path of the flame momentarily burned on our irises, formed a perfect five-pointed star. One last yell, one last spectacular gyration of flame and half-bare bodies, an energetic surge of curtain calls, and it was over.

WELL-WISHERS AND ADVICE GIVERS surrounded Annie. "Why'd you ever do a fool thing like that, girl?" "You coulda got yoreself kilt for sure!" That came from the woman with all the prizes. "Bet you're gonna run away and join the circus now," her hammer-wielding man said.

"I don't think they'd have me," Annie called back. "Anyway, this was enough excitement for a whole lifetime!"

When Melissa and I got her alone a while later, I was a bit more specific. "You about gave me a heart attack, Annie. Why on earth would you try such an absolutely stupid, foolish, inane, ridiculous…"

"You mean you *believed* it?" she said. "You really thought that was me up there?"

"Of course it was you. I saw you go up to the platform, and just when I was happy you had that safety harness on, you went and…"

"Biscuit, that wasn't me. They hid me behind the curtain the whole time. That stagehand in black told me what was going to happen, so I was prepared for it. That was one of the older Walker kids on the wire, dressed up in overalls and a floppy hat. He knew exactly what he was doing. Can I have some more popcorn? I'm starving."

Melissa shook her head. "Not until you explain how this all worked."

"It was simple. As soon as I was chosen, George, the Walker son, put on a tee-shirt that was pretty close to this green one I'm wearing.

They have a whole stack of different colors up there. We switched places while everybody had their eyes on Harry Walker when he slipped off the wire. It was all planned. Nobody was looking at the platform, so I just stepped backward, and George moved into my place."

I wasn't sure who I wanted to throttle first, the ringmaster and Scarlet for fooling me or Annie for playing along with them.

"There was another stagehand behind the curtain who told me that I'd been selected almost as soon as I came through the gate this morning. They look for somebody with long hair, so they have an excuse to put the hat on." It was a good disguise, I had to admit. "They pick four or five women, and the clowns usher them to seats right on the aisle, so they're easy to get to. If I hadn't volunteered, one of the other ones would have. Just in case nobody volunteers, they have a plant sitting in the back row." She giggled. "There was a hole in the curtain, so I got to peek out. Even though I knew what was going to happen, it still looked pretty scary. Bill, the stagehand, said that George, the Walker son, was the one who came up with the idea to begin with. If he grows much more, though, he won't look like a woman. Anyway, his dad wouldn't be able to hold him through that leap, so Theresa had better grow up fast."

"Theresa?" Melissa was aghast. "They'd do that to little bitty Theresa?"

"Ha!" Annie barked. "Bill said Theresa has more nerve than the other three put together. She'll be the next head of the Wonder Walker family act." Annie gestured with her head. "Now, can we get some popcorn?"

I took a deep breath. She was alive. I'd been thoroughly flummoxed, along with a couple of hundred other people. The sun was shining, and the popcorn smelled mighty good wafting across the midway. "Let's go," I said.

"And then the merry-go-round," she added, "and our old-timey photographs."

SORE FEET, ACHING BACK, tight shoulders, overstuffed tummy. Knees, hips, even my elbows hurt. I dropped Annie off in front of her place and circled around to Beechnut Lane. Had to groan getting out of the Buick. My body didn't want to cooperate. If I was this sore now after a full day walking around the fairgrounds, I'd be a basket case tomorrow. Still, I felt wonderful. Not my achy muscles, but my heart. What a fun day. I patted Marmalade, who had been napping on the front steps.

Hello, Widelap.

She yawned and purred at me as I stepped around her, wondering why I didn't expect her to move out of my way. Hauling myself up the steps was harder than it had been yesterday. A nap, maybe? No. I'd probably never wake up once I collapsed. I hadn't had a chance to talk with Bob about how his week had gone, and we hadn't discussed Susan, either. Of course, we'd had phone conversations throughout the week, but it wasn't the same. I looked back at Marmy. "Is he home?" I asked, as if she could answer me.

No. He went down the street.

All she did was stand up, purr, and stretch. "Bob!" I hollered.

Nobody home.

I told you so.

I pulled the old-timey photo from its bag and set it on the drop-leaf table in the entranceway. Beside it I laid the super-special, genuine emerald ring and my circus ticket stub. Quite a haul. Well, I wasn't hungry, that was for sure, but I was going to have to feed my husband. First, I called Glaze. No answer, doggone it.

Before I could start dinner, Bob walked in with a take-out bag from CT's. I kissed him and reached for the bag. "I knew there was a good reason I married you," I said.

He pulled it out of my grasp. "Oh, didn't I mention? This is for Marmalade."

All for me?

I slapped at him until he handed me the bag. There was a little treat in there for Marmy. Salmon.

"Sometimes my cat eats better than I do," I said. The white folded-over containers looked promising, though.

"Let me guess." Bob poured himself a big glass of buttermilk. "So far today your balanced diet has included popcorn?"

"Yes."

"Cotton candy?"

"Uh-huh. Annie had some, too."

"Annie? I thought she was a vegetarian."

"There's no meat in cotton candy last time I looked."

He peered at me over his glasses, confirming my suspicion that he wears them so he can look at me over the rims. "I mean I thought she eats only health food."

"Well, she ate the cotton candy anyway and enjoyed it thoroughly."

"Soft pretzels? Boiled peanuts?"

He wasn't going to stop his quiz. I nodded.

He grinned at me. "Fess up. What else?"

"Would you believe fried dough?"

"No wonder the cat eats better than you. She's smarter." I poked him in the arm again, but he just laughed at me. "Let's eat some real food," he said, "and then I'm going to give you my super-special massage."

That sounded even better than my super-special, genuine emerald.

"A LITTLE LOWER DOWN," I said. Bob moved his hands four or five inches farther down my back and dug in. "Ouch!"

Are you hurt?

"Don't you want me to fix it, Woman?"

"No. I don't want you to *fix* it. I just want you to make it feel better."

"Same thing. Scoot over, Marmalade. You'll get lotion in your fur."

"No, it's not. It feels better when you just sort of smooth the ouchies away."

"Isn't that what I'm doing?"

"No, you're trying to fix me, and you're hurting me."

"But I have to push." He stopped for a moment, and the bed wiggled. "Marmy, get out of the way. Pushing is what massaging is."

"Maybe so, but not that hard."

"This is what you get when you spend all day long traipsing around the county fairgrounds." He didn't add *serves you right,* but I could tell the thought was there.

"I don't care. I had a… Ooh, that feels good. Just hold the pressure there for a little bit."

"You had a what?"

"What?" I asked.

"You said, 'I had a—' and then you didn't finish it."

You two are hard to understand.

"I had, in case you're interested, a perfectly lovely time."

Marmalade nuzzled at my nose, and I reached up to scratch her head. Why wasn't I asking him about Susan? No, I just couldn't. It would have to wait. I couldn't face that right now. Later this evening. This week. This year. "Perfectly lovely," I repeated. "I haven't laughed that long or that loud in quite a while. Most of what we laughed at wasn't even that funny."

"It never is," he said and slopped another glob of herbal pain-relief lotion across my right hip.

"If you'd been there, would you have won lots of prizes for me?"

His hands slowed down. "I've never won a single one of those things."

"Why not?" My vision of multiple teddy bears crumbled around me. "Why not?" I asked again.

"I couldn't win at them. I always tried when I was a youngster. Must have paid those carnies a minor fortune a quarter or a buck at a time." He rubbed my back absentmindedly, then stopped again. "Now I'm smarter, and I don't waste money on that foolishness."

By this point he sounded distinctly self-righteous, but then he found another knot that needed some coaxing, so I forgave him for not winning me a four-foot teddy bear, and I decided not to brag about the nickel-sized genuine emerald ring

I'd won. I wanted to ask him about Susan, but I didn't want to know the answer if it was a yes. Instead, I settled for saying, "I wish Glaze had been there."

Smellsweet.

He eased off the pressure. "Uh-huh."

"I tried to call her again when I got back."

"Yeah?"

"She wasn't there. Or she wasn't answering the phone. I can't see why she's so angry with me. It seems all out of proportion."

"Did you leave a phone message?" He smoothed his hands all the way down the bundle of tight spots I used to call my spine. "Maybe she'll call you back."

"Didn't."

"Didn't what, Woman?"

"Didn't leave— Oh, golly, that's wonderful. Keep doing exactly that. I'll give you about three hours to quit it."

"What didn't you leave?"

"Huh?" My mind wasn't functioning. "A message. I didn't leave one. Her machine's still turned off."

"You'll see her tomorrow in church. Patch things up then."

"Ow! Stop pushing so hard."

He broke contact. "If I remember correctly, you told me to keep doing what I was doing for three hours." I sat up. I wasn't expecting to cry. Must have surprised him, too, because he scooped his arms around me and pulled me onto his lap. Not the easiest thing to do considering our relative positions on the bed. "Did I hurt you, Woman? I didn't mean to."

I blubbered a bit onto his shoulder. Nose goo is not the most appetizing thing in the world to add to a husband's biceps, but I couldn't reach the tissue box with my hands pinned to my chest like that. "Glaze must be so angry with me." I took a breath. "Sally's furious, Glaze is upset, I'm afraid to ask— Oh, I can't do anything right."

I love you.

He let me keep crying for a while. Marmalade wove around both of us, purring. Then Bob whispered, just above my right ear, "I love you, Woman." There was a sweet emphasis on the first word. For now, that was enough.

We decided a snack was in order. I hardly limped at all heading downstairs. In fact, when we got in the kitchen I felt good enough, after that gorgeous rubdown, to lean over and fluff up Marmy's bath towel, the stained one. Something rustled underneath it. "What's this?" I held up an envelope, the one I'd written to Glaze.

"There it is! I looked for it to take it up to Glaze this morning, but it wasn't on the table where I left it." He scowled down at Marmy—a thoroughly fake pirate-type scowl. "What be ye doin' absconding with ye oldie proclamations, wee varmint?"

"Your pirate sounds Scottish," I said and turned the envelope over. She hadn't even bothered to open it. "Where did you find this?"

"Last night, you mean?" He rummaged in the fridge and pulled out a hunk of Romano. We both loved hard cheeses. "It was taped to the front door when I came in. Why?"

The *Call Me!* was still intact. It wasn't disturbed in any way. She'd ignored it. She'd returned it. She didn't want to talk to me. She wasn't even willing to meet me halfway. She was pissed off big-time. So much for my fun day. So, I did the best thing I could think of. I cried for a bit longer, drank a cup of tea, and nibbled some paper-thin slices of salty Romano cheese. I asked Bob about his week, scratched a few lines in my journal, and then we went to bed.

Me, too.

My Gratitude List for Saturday

Humph! What's gratitude got to do with anything?

I guess I'm grateful for Bob. I refuse to believe he's Susan's father. He would have told me. It could be Tom. Maybe that's why Glaze is upset—she found out and she doesn't want to admit it. Maybe I should throw on some sweats and hand deliver that note right back to her.

No, it's too late. Marmy goes on the list, too, although she's making it hard for me to write around her right now.

I am grateful for
Widelap, even when her face is wet

WEEK FOUR

SUNDAY

EITHER NOBODY HAD WRITTEN that anger letter Henry had told us to write—I certainly hadn't—or else nobody wanted to admit it. That didn't slow Henry down one bit. The ushers handed everyone a slip of paper about the size of a three-by-five card. "Write a name on it," he told us. "Be sure it's someone you feel a need to forgive or even somebody you think you might be willing to consider forgiving."

Then we trooped outside and dropped the papers into a fire Roger was tending over near the cemetery fence. When we filed back into the sanctuary, there was another assignment waiting for us. Henry stepped up to the pulpit and looked down at Irene as she settled herself onto the front row. Once she looked up at him, he spoke. "Remember those notebooks you were supposed to buy from Ida?" he asked. "This week you're going to use them. By the way, it's nice to see you again, Ida," he added. "Father John's going to have to forgive us both if you keep showing up here."

"Just curious, Reverend," she said. "So you can get on with it."

He waited a moment for us to quiet down. "Take the first page of your notebook and draw a line down the middle of it. To the left of that line you're going to write the same thing over and over again, seventy times a day for seven days." Several people groaned at that, but Henry plowed on. "What you write is this. *I forgive so-and-so completely.*" He paused. "To give you an example, my lovely wife might write *I, Irene, forgive Henry completely.*" Some of us chuckled gently. Some laughed outright. "That is," he added, "if she'd be willing to consider forgiving me." Irene waved her hand at him in a dismissive gesture and shook her head. He turned back to the rest of us. "Now, don't you go writing the words *so-and-so*. You fill in the name of that person you want to forgive."

Sally, I thought. Followed in close second place by Glaze, doggone her. Did that mean I'd have to do two of these infernal things?

"Just pick one person to begin with," Henry said. I hated it when he read my mind like that. "You can write it thirty-five times in the morning and thirty-five times before you go to bed. Or you can do it all at once, just so you write it seventy times each and every day for seven days."

"I wonder what the center line is for," Ida said.

He heard her. The acoustics in this church were frightening.

"It's there for a very good reason, that center line," Henry said. "You use the right-hand side of that line to write down the objections your brain is going to come up with. You see, I may write *I, Henry, forgive my father* ten or twelve times, but then the next time I write it, something in my head is going to say, 'Now why on earth would I do that? He's a skunk.' As soon as I hear that, I'm going to write *He's a skunk* on the right-hand side of that center line. That simply acknowledges that I've had that thought and it clears the way for me to go right back to forgiving him."

Somebody—I couldn't tell who—let out a derisive snort from the other side of the aisle. Henry laughed. "You don't believe me, do you? Well, I'm asking you to trust me on this one and give it a try. Remember that forgiving someone doesn't mean that what they did was okay. It means you're not going to let the negative charge around your resentment rule the rest of your life."

Did that mean I'd have to stop making wisecracks about how Sally thought I had the fashion sense of an aardvark? Did that mean I'd have to figure out why Glaze had been such a pill for the last week? No. I'd concentrate on Sally first.

I could always wait till later to deal with Glaze. There was plenty of time.

REEBOK GARNER, NAMED FOR the antelopes long before his parents heard of the shoes, took out his handkerchief and looked around as unobtrusively as he could to be sure nobody was watching through the open door. He rubbed a speck of dust from the badge that adorned his dark blue uniform jacket. *Martinsville* formed an arc across the top half of the oval. *Police Force* rimmed the bottom half. In the center the town motto, *Integrity & Community,* was superimposed on the outline of a leaf. The story was that the leaf pattern came from the enormous maple tree that towered over the gazebo in the middle of the town park. It might have been an old tree already when the first settlers came in 1745. Or it could just as easily have been planted by Homer Martin himself, the founder of the town. Either way, it was a proud tradition.

While he was at it, he inspected the name tag beneath his badge. GARNER on the top line and DEPUTY in smaller letters just below it. Once his badge was in order, he sorted through the sticky notes his boss had lined up around the edge of the desk. Reebok pulled a yellow legal pad out of the second drawer and turned it sideways as the phone rang.

"Deputy Garner here…Hey there, Tom. How's it going?…Any idea how much longer?…Don't worry about your house. I'll keep an eye on it."

Who's Gone, he wrote on the yellow pad and underlined it.

WHO'S GONE—AND WHY	WHO'S LEFT IN THE HOUSE
1. Tom Parkman—staying in Nashville longer than planned. Didn't say why.	Nobody—call Nathan (next-door neighbor) for emergencies.
2. Bob Sheffield—in Athens for police training, leaving today.	Biscuit (wife)
3. Brighton and Ellen Montgomery—in Florida, part business/part pleasure, leaving tomorrow.	Call Biscuit (neighbor)
4. Annie McGill—in Atlanta with her brother, leaving tomorrow.	Nobody—call Melissa (friend)
5. Irene Pursey—in Ohio, visiting her sister, leaving tomorrow.	Henry and daughter Holly

When he finished, he looked over his list and added one more name before he pinned the list on the bulletin board.

6. Wallace Masters—in peace, finally.	Miss Sadie—call Ida and Ralph (friends)

My Gratitude List for Sunday
1. Celia. I was in such a twit last night I forgot to put her on the list.
2. Bob, although I do not understand that man. Why am I afraid to ask him about Susan?
3. Marmy.
4. Henry, I suppose. Not sure what I think of his seventy-times-seven idea, but I'll try it. Not that it was his idea to begin with. Is that plagiarism? Can it, Biscuit. You're acting dumb. It's my gratitude list. I can act dumb if I want to. So there.
5. I think I'll put Reebok on the list. He's trying so hard.
6. Maggie. She's such a dear. I hope her new baby goats grow up to be as nice as the others in the group. I wonder if Maggie would let me attend the birth?

I am grateful for
Widelap
Softfoot

bugs
catnip
LooseLaces, who gives me cream even though
SlowWalker is gone

My 70 x 7 for Sunday

1. I, Biscuit, forgive Sally completely	Like heck I do.
2. I, Biscuit, forgive Sally completely	Why am I doing this?
3. I, Biscuit, forgive Sally completely	
4. I, Biscuit, forgive Sally completely	
5. I, Biscuit, forgive Sally completely	
6. I, Biscuit, forgive Sally completely	
7. I, Biscuit, forgive Sally completely	No, I don't. This is a silly exercise.
8. I, Biscuit, forgive Sally completely	
9. I, Biscuit, forgive Sally completely	Ha!
10. I, Biscuit, forgive Sally completely	
11. I, Biscuit, forgive Sally completely	
12. I, Biscuit, forgive Sally completely	
13. I, Biscuit, forgive Sally completely	Fat chance.
14. I, Biscuit, forgive Sally completely	
15. I, Biscuit, forgive Sally completely	She's the one who's being snippy.

16. I, Biscuit, forgive Sally completely
17. I, Biscuit, forgive Sally completely
18. I, Biscuit, forgive Sally completely
19. I, Biscuit, forgive Sally completely
20. I, Biscuit, forgive Sally completely
21. I, Biscuit, forgive Sally completely   She's always been unreasonable.

22. I, Biscuit, forgive Sally completely
23. I, Biscuit, forgive Sally completely
24. I, Biscuit, forgive Sally completely
25. I, Biscuit, forgive Sally completely
26. I, Biscuit, forgive Sally completely
27. I, Biscuit, forgive Sally completely   It certainly would be nice if she'd meet me halfway.

28. I, Biscuit, forgive Sally completely
29. I, Biscuit, forgive Sally completely
30. I, Biscuit, forgive Sally completely
31. I, Biscuit, forgive Sally completely
32. I, Biscuit, forgive Sally completely
33. I, Biscuit, forgive Sally completely
34. I, Biscuit, forgive Sally completely
35. I, Biscuit, forgive Sally completely   This is dumb.

36. I, Biscuit, forgive Sally completely
37. I, Biscuit, forgive Sally completely
38. I, Biscuit, forgive Sally completely   This
                                            is very
                                            dumb.

39. I, Biscuit, forgive Sally completely
40. I, Biscuit, forgive Sally completely
41. I, Biscuit, forgive Sally completely
42. I, Biscuit, forgive Sally completely
43. I, Biscuit, forgive Sally completely
44. I, Biscuit, forgive Sally completely
45. I, Biscuit, forgive Sally completely
46. I, Biscuit, forgive Sally completely
47. I, Biscuit, forgive Sally completely
48. I, Biscuit, forgive Sally completely   She sure
                                            was a cute
                                            baby.

49. I, Biscuit, forgive Sally completely
50. I, Biscuit, forgive Sally completely
51. I, Biscuit, forgive Sally completely
52. I, Biscuit, forgive Sally completely
53. I, Biscuit, forgive Sally completely
54. I, Biscuit, forgive Sally completely
55. I, Biscuit, forgive Sally completely   I'm still
                                            mad at
                                            her.

56. I, Biscuit, forgive Sally completely
57. I, Biscuit, forgive Sally completely   This is
                                            boring.

58. I, Biscuit, forgive Sally completely
59. I, Biscuit, forgive Sally completely
60. I, Biscuit, forgive Sally completely
61. I, Biscuit, forgive Sally completely
62. I, Biscuit, forgive Sally completely   I don't even like my own daughter.

63. I, Biscuit, forgive Sally completely
64. I, Biscuit, forgive Sally completely   What kind of awful mother am I?

65. I, Biscuit, forgive Sally completely
66. I, Biscuit, forgive Sally completely
67. I, Biscuit, forgive Sally completely
68. I, Biscuit, forgive Sally completely
69. I, Biscuit, forgive Sally completely
70. I, Biscuit, forgive Sally completely   Done! Whew! Six more days to go.

WEEK FOUR

MONDAY

ANNIE WALKED DOWN the porch stairs and leaned into her car. Then she heard someone behind her and started to turn. That was all she remembered until she came to with her ankles hobbled, her hands tied, and her eyes covered. She smelled the cinnamon buns. She'd bought some at the Delicious to take to her aunt Martha's house in Hastings, a spur-of-the-moment visit on her way to Atlanta to be with her brother. She should have called first. Then Aunt Martha would have expected her.

Now nobody knew where she was. Nobody but the woman in the driver's seat and the little kid who asked, "Mommy, is that lady sleeping?"

"Yes, Willie. Don't you worry none about her. You just finish that sticky bun I brought you."

"It's good, Mommy."

Oh, well, then, Annie thought. It was all right. She was tied up and blindfolded and her head throbbed, but a little boy was enjoying the cinnamon buns. She was obviously losing her mind.

Now, STILL TIED UP, but thankfully not gagged or blindfolded anymore, Annie perched sideways on an old wooden chair, the only way she could sit with her hands trussed behind her. Hollering hadn't helped, she was too angry to cry, and her stomach woke up at the thought of those cinnamon buns. She hadn't even taken one single bite. Rats! The only thing worse than her empty insides, and her tied hands and her hobbled feet, and the fact that she had no idea why she was here or even where she was, worse than all that was her bladder. One plain wooden door, no doorknob. When she looked through the hole where the knob had been, all she saw was a long, depressingly bare hallway with several closed doors, and one old-fashioned light fixture. One bulb in it, maybe as much as 40 watts, covered by a formerly white globe with a dark cluster of dead bugs settled at the bottom.

She stood up and made her way slowly back to the door. They'd taken her shoes, and the carpet felt faintly gritty. Turning around, she hooked her fingers as best she could through the doorknob hole and pulled. The door rattled a bit, gave maybe half an inch, then stopped. Sounded as if there was one of those hook things holding it closed on the other side. Maybe more than one. Her head hurt like the dickens, but she forced herself to explore the room once more. Two windows, but those were boarded up. She could see dents in the heavy plywood where the hammer had driven the nails deep. A recent remodeling. No rust on the nail heads. No cobwebs stuck to the miniscule splinters that poked up around the nails. That meant they'd been expecting to grab her and stash her here, like excess meat stuffed in a second freezer in someone's garage. She didn't like that thought at all. Dead meat. She shivered, even though the room was warm, stuffy.

No pictures relieved the tedium of the four bare walls. A brown stain spread out on the ceiling from one corner. One lonely lightbulb hung in the center from the end of what looked like a dangerously frayed cord. A faded sleeping bag lay stretched out against the wall kitty-corner from the door, adding an incongruent sense of adventure to the general ambiance. The threadbare carpet, like a dog with mange, had outlived its usefulness probably thirty years ago. It was most likely olive green originally, but she wouldn't have sworn to that. There were distinct dents in the carpet where furniture used to sit. A narrow bed here, maybe a dresser there, a chair perhaps? She spent a few idle moments imagining what the many and various stains and dents may have held, like a kid lying on a newly cut lawn, finding dragons and schooners and teddy bears in the clouds. Talk about useless, but it helped calm her. This nightmare couldn't be real.

She fought back a growing sense of claustrophobia. No matter how hard she pulled at her hands, the cord held. She was lucky, she guessed, that the knots didn't tighten. Whoever tied her up must have been a Boy Scout once, like her brother had been. Oh, God, she thought, what was happening to him? She needed to be at the hospital.

She shifted her weight from one foot to the other, hoping that would relieve the pressure on her bladder, but it didn't. She shuffled back to the chair, wondering if she would contract plantar warts from the olive shag. The chair was the sturdiest item in her twelve-foot-square world. Heavy, in a 1940s sort of utilitarian way. No loose rungs. Nothing she could break apart and use to defend herself, even if she could have figured out how to do that with her hands tied in back.

"Sit down." The voice startled her so much she almost fell. An eyeball stared at her through the doorknob hole. She sat and listened as something rattled on the other side of the door. She had a screen door with one of those hook latches on it. This sounded the same. Except that there were three, maybe four of them. Each one alone sounded insubstantial. But together, they would provide enough of a barrier to prevent her from breaking free.

A heavyset figure wearing a ski mask pushed the door back against the wall, as if to be sure nobody was hidden in that neglected corner. Fat chance.

The good news was that ski mask didn't carry any weapons. The bad news was that he—or was it a she?—had sturdy bare hands that looked strong enough to throttle her.

"Who are you?" Annie asked. "Why am I here?" Nothing. The figure just stared at her.

"If I promise not to try to run away, would you untie my ankles, just so I can move around comfortably?"

"Not a chance. I don't trust you." It was a woman's voice. Gruff, but definitely female. The same voice she'd heard in the car.

"We're in the middle of nowhere. I couldn't possibly get far barefoot through the trees."

"How do you know there's trees around here?"

"I heard them when we got here. The wind was blowing. There aren't any traffic sounds. Also, I felt the car bumping over ruts as you drove."

"Don't get smart on me. I have to keep you safe, but I won't take any guff off you. You're worth a lot of money."

"What? You've got the wrong person. I'm not worth much at all."

"That's what you think, Gale."

"Gale? That's not my name. You've got the wrong person."

"Ha! You can't fool me."

"But my name is not Gale. It's Annie. Annie McGill."

"I may have the name wrong. My brother's not too smart. But you're the one we want all right. I've been following you and the library lady."

"Biscuit? What does she have to do with all this?"

"She's going to pay to get you back."

"But she's not rich. Neither one of us has money."

"She knows somebody who is. Now you be quiet."

"Can I at least have my shoes back? And maybe a bathroom?"

Something went thump far down the hall, and the woman turned without another word and left the room, latching the door. Three latches at least. It was hard to tell for sure.

Annie sighed, stood as best she could with a great deal of sympathy for hobbled horses, and shuffled to the corner, taking three-inch steps. The sleeping bag was slightly softer than the threadbare carpet. At least it was clean. As long as she lay on her stomach, her hands didn't get too cramped behind her. Her bladder was another issue. She wasn't sure which was worse—the fear she felt or the need to pee.

The sound of the door scraping across the thin carpet woke her from a dazed almost-sleep. She hoped she didn't have a concussion. Her head throbbed. The crick in her neck kept her from seeing more than a pair of sturdy work boots approaching. She assumed the ski mask was still in place. Everything felt numb. Even though her hands weren't tied tightly, she couldn't guess how many hours they'd been behind her back.

"I'm going to untie you, you hear?"

She made a faint sound.

"You hear me?" the voice repeated.

"Yes."

"Nothing funny, now. You lie there and be real still."

As if she could move anyway. It sounded like scissors that cut the inch or so of cord between her wrists, then dug under the knots where the cord looped each wrist tightly. Her arms fell to the floor at her sides. Even that slight movement hurt. Her shoulders burned, and her wrists screamed.

"Hush that whimpering. You stay still now while I do your legs."

Another cut between her feet and two more to remove the tight loops that circled her ankles. She'd read once that kicking an attacker if you were on the ground was a good way to incapacitate them. That might have worked if she'd been faceup and if she'd had any feeling in her legs.

"I put a pot over yonder. You can use it to go to the bathroom. Don't try to stand up until I leave the room. The door's going to be locked. You understand?"

"Yes."

"I put you some food by the door. It's not much, but we have to wait till payday. There's two wet washcloths there so you can clean yourself up a bit. One of them has some soap on it. It's important to wash your hands before you eat."

"Thank you." You conk me on the head, she thought, tie me up, dump me back in my own car, blindfold me, haul me into this godforsaken place, and leave me here starving for hours and hours and don't tell me anything. You give my cinnamon buns to a little kid, and I don't even complain, and now you lecture me about hygiene and I say thank-you. Wouldn't Miss Manners be proud of me.

Annie stretched, moved her arms tentatively, then with more vigor. The pins-and-needles feeling gradually subsided. She explored the lump on the back of her head. Not as big as one of the eggs she bought from Maggie each week, but extremely tender. There wasn't any blood as far as she could tell. She supposed she should be grateful for that, but somehow gratitude wasn't high on her priorities. The chamber pot came first. She stumbled only slightly when she stood up. After relieving herself, she wished briefly, and uselessly, for a sink and a real bar of soap. The washcloths were better than nothing, though. Then she dove for the food.

She should have saved her energy. Two peanut-butter sandwiches on limp white bread and a Coke bottle with water in it. She hated grape jelly. Her stomach lurched at the thought until she reprimanded it out loud. "What you get is what you get. This beats starving." Not by much, she thought. But it was food, of a sort. Once she considered the alternative, the food didn't taste quite as bad. She quit thinking and ate.

IT MAY HAVE BEEN EVENING when she heard the woman's voice again, but with no watch and only a bare lightbulb for illumination, it was hard to tell. "Back away from the door and start talking loud so I can tell where you are. Go on. Get on the far side of the room and say something."

"I can't. I'm using the chamber pot." Is that what they called it? Grandmother used to call it a thunder mug. Granddad called it a piss pot, and Grandmother always said, *Now, you hush that language, you hear?*

"What? Talk louder."

"I'm going to the bathroom. Please wait a minute." Thank goodness there was some flimsy toilet paper beside the pot. The windowless room reeked from the stench, but there was no lid for the pot, probably because she could have used it as a weapon. "All right. You can come in now."

"No. You're too close to the door. Move away and keep talking."

Okay, if that's what she wanted. "'We the people of the United states, in order to form a more perfect union'"—the room wasn't that big, so she took her time—"'establish justice'"—that phrase came out extra loud—"'insure domestic tranquility, provide for the common...'"

The door swung open and her captor sidled in, crouched in a parody of a kung-fu movie. "You crawl in the sleeping bag and lie there. I'm going to take that stinking pot out, and I don't want you moving till I get the door locked."

She considered trying to make a run for it, but the woman outweighed her by at least fifty pounds. She knew she could make a weapon out of the Coke bottle, but the woman wouldn't let her get close enough to use it. She considered begging, too, but didn't think it would get her anywhere. The books she'd read all said to try to make friends with your captor. They were novels, but surely there was some truth there. "So, what's the weather like outside?" The tremor in her voice didn't help.

"Don't get cute with me. Get your legs inside that bag. I'm not taking any chances on losing you."

"Why not?" She really was curious, in a morbid sort of way. The good news was that it sounded as if they weren't going to kill her.

"You're my ticket out of this rotten valley, honey. My ticket out."

"You don't like the valley?"

"I don't like living close to starving…"

Didn't look as if she was starving with that kind of weight. Poor nutrition, probably, so maybe she did feel hungry all the time.

"And I'm tired of scraping for a living."

"I'm so sorry. What kind of work do you do?"

"I've got me a job on a— Wait a minute. Nice try, but I'm not dumb. I'm not telling you anything. Now get all the way in that bag."

Annie watched the woman lean over to heft the chamber pot. Her back hurts, she thought. I can tell by the way she favors one side when she straightens up. What on earth am I doing feeling sorry for someone who knocked me out and kidnapped me? Still, she couldn't help but wonder how hard the woman's life had been to bring her to a place like this.

My 70 x 7 for Monday:
1. I, Biscuit, forgive Sally completely   Here we go again.

2. I, Biscuit, forgive Sally completely…

REEBOK LOVED RIDING around Martinsville when everyone was asleep. He drove out past the fire station. All quiet. George and Wilena and Martin and Bill must be on duty. All four of their cars nestled against the concrete curbs in the fire-station parking lot like a rootle of baby pigs against a sow's belly. He considered going in and having a cup of coffee—they always had a fresh pot brewing. The last thing he needed, though, was one more cup of coffee. All was quiet, and Reebok felt thoroughly content.

WEEK FOUR

TUESDAY

JEFF SPENT A LOT of time waiting for the guards to walk farther along the corridor, out of earshot. Tuesday morning was no exception. "Your sister going to pick you up?" he asked his cellmate.

"Naw. It's too far for her. I'm hitching my way."

"I'm out of here on Thursday. I'll be hitching, too. You be there Friday morning, early, to get me, hear?"

"I will. The Barbecue Barn in Russell Gap."

"Don't be late. I don't like sitting around."

"What if you're not there on Friday?" Gordon's long, lone eyebrow bent in the middle. "The phone's disconnected."

"Then come back on Saturday."

"What if you're not…"

"Look, just keep showing up at the Barn. I'll get there when I can."

"And then we split the money, right?"

"Right. And don't try to pull anything fast, you hear?"

"I wouldn't do that. We're partners, like."

"Auntie Blue?" The limp phone cord hung over the edge of the kitchen counter. It looked about as perky as I felt. Pretty pathetic.

"Well, if it isn't my favorite niece. How you doing, honey? You sound lower down than a snake's belly."

"How could you tell after only two words?"

"I don't listen with just my ears, hon. I listen with my heart."

"Oh. Are you going to be around this morning?"

"You want to come up for a heart-to-heart?"

"I'll bring cinnamon buns."

"Now, I'm not going to pass on an offer like that, but you know you're welcome anytime, even without a bribe. When are you coming?"

"I could leave now."

She welcomed me into her house and enveloped me in a big, motherly hug. "Let's go out by the pool. I dragged a chair for you over into the shade." She bustled me out the back door. "You still having problems with sunburning so fast?"

"I'm going to have that all my life, Auntie. I don't have any pigment in my skin."

"You need yourself a good tanning lotion, then."

"It doesn't work that way. There's no melanin to come up to the surface and turn brown when the sun hits."

"Well, that just doesn't make sense. A body's meant to tan. But you didn't come to hear me blather on about that stuff. Let's look at these cinnamon rolls. Gotta keep myself from starving." I tried not to laugh. Auntie Blue was an ample woman, built so much differently than my slender mother I sometimes wondered if they came from two different gene pools. "Don't you laugh," she said. "It's been two hours since breakfast, and I did forty-five laps this morning instead of my usual twenty."

"I don't see how you do it. Even two laps would do me in."

"That's because you don't like to swim. Fair skin like yours, you probably spend more energy worrying about burning when you're in there than you spend swimming." Her droopy jowls were leather-like after so many years in the sun. "Maybe you should come swim with me at night." She looked around her fenced-in backyard. The sun-loving flowers I'd helped her plant flourished. "It's so peaceful here after dark."

"I don't know. I've never been able to relax in the water."

"It's warm, and we put the lights on under the water. Or leave them off so you can see the stars better." She brushed at some crumbs and laughed. "This built-in shelf of mine does catch the most amazing assortment of food. Maybe that's why I like being in the water so much. I weigh a whole lot less in there than I do out here." She picked up another cinnamon bun. "When are you going to tell me what you came for?"

"It's Glaze," I said. "Why did you call me your favorite niece when I called this morning?"

"Are you two at odds?" I nodded. "I love both of you more than the dickens, but your sister is distant somehow. She's never even once stopped by with cinnamon buns."

"That's not true. We were going to come up two weeks ago, but then Wallace died."

"But the drive up here was your idea, right?"

"I'd love to take the credit, but Glaze is the one who suggested I talk to you about Sally."

"Was she planning to come up here with you?"

I thought back to that walk we'd taken. "Well, no."

"My point exactly. You would have had to talk her into it." She wadded up her napkin. "She was gone, too, for so many years."

"So were you." Why was I being so defensive about a sister who was mad at me?

"You've got a point there. Your uncle Mark's job always came first. I'm glad he wanted to retire back here. Colorado was beautiful, don't get me wrong, but it never quite seemed like home with all that snow. Guess you can take the girl out of the South, but you can't take the South out of the girl." She looked at me and grinned. "I know what you're thinking. Ain't much girl left in this great big, old body of mine." Auntie Blue had the best laugh imaginable. "Your uncle Mark loved Colorado. All those mountains and the sweeping plains. He would have stayed there in a heartbeat, but we didn't have any family there." She smiled at me, and I had the feeling she knew a lot more than she let on. She reached across the table and patted my hand. "I guess I should treat your sister like that prodigal-son guy, the one whose daddy was so happy when he came home."

I couldn't think of anything to say to that. I still felt so angry at being shunned, and yet I knew if Glaze would take just one step in my direction, well, I'd feel like celebrating. Same way I felt about Sally. "I guess I see what you mean."

"Do you? Do you really? I've always wondered about that snippy older brother, the one who stayed home. *What about me?* he kept asking. But he'd had all those years of the family connections while his brother was off painting the town."

"Glaze wasn't exactly painting the town, Auntie Blue."

"I know she tried to kill herself, but that was the depression stuff taking over her mind. Thank goodness she takes that medicine. Hmm. Maybe one more cinnamon roll. You want to split this last one?"

"Sure." We munched companionably. The water did look calming. Maybe I'd take her up on her offer.

"Uh-huh," she said. "I think maybe I'd better take a lesson from that daddy. Your sister needs more loving than you do right now."

But I was the good one.

"Even if you don't think so."

"Am I that transparent?"

"Well, honey, all I can say to that is, don't you ever think of taking up poker and hope to make a living at it."

ANNIE FELT SOMEONE watching her. The doorknob hole was blank, though. No, wait. She could see something moving there. A little finger reached in and wiggled in her direction.

"You get away from there, Willie." The woman's voice sounded from down the hall. "It's not polite to peek at people when they don't know you're watching."

"You do, Mommy."

"Only because I had to. You're really smart, Willie. Did you know that?"

"Uh-huh. You told me."

"Now, you stay out here for a minute."

There was a knock on the door. As if Annie was being given a choice in the matter. Click, click, click, click. The latches rattled one by one. This time, though, no ski mask.

"You forgot your mask. Aren't you afraid I'll recognize you?"

"It was making Willie ask too many questions. Anyway, by the time you get home, we'll be out of this place. Out of this valley."

"When will you let me go?"

"As soon as I get the money and my brother shows up. Him and a friend of his, too."

"I hope it's soon. My brother's having surgery, and I need to be there."

"I'm sorry about your brother," she said. "There's nothing I can do about that. You'll be out of here by the end of the week, most likely."

Could she last a week on peanut-butter sandwiches? Oh, sure, why not? Could her brother get along a week without her? She didn't even want to consider the problem.

"I came to ask kind of a favor."

That's a good one, she thought. I'm a prisoner here, and you're asking me a favor?

"I know, I know. You got every right to say you won't. But I had to leave my car in town when I…" She had the good sense to look shamefaced. "When I brought you here. Please don't look like that. This ain't…I mean isn't anything personal. We need the money."

"So what do you want from me, other than money I don't have?"

"I want you to watch Willie for me while I go to work. I'll pick up my car after my shift ends. I have to show up for work so they won't come looking for me, and I have to get my car." She scratched her fingers back through her curly light brown hair. "It's too far for me to carry him, and he's too little to walk all that way. If I had anywhere else I could leave him where he'd be safe, I would. But there's nobody else."

"If there's nobody else, where do you usually leave him when you go to work?"

"The town pays for a child-care place."

"I didn't know that. I don't have children."

"Yeah, well. Maybe someday. I'm on the three-to-eleven shift today, so I won't be back till late tonight. Willie will be asleep then."

"You could take my car."

"Not a chance. They'll be looking for your car. I don't want to get caught in it. Anyway, I need to get my own car, and then where would I leave yours? See?"

"Oh. I didn't think of that." She was truly curious. "Why would you trust me with your son?"

"Because I think you're a nice person." A nice person. A nice smelly person. One day and one night, and she already felt stinky. What she wouldn't give for some honeysuckle soap right now. "I'll leave some food for both of you, and he's pretty well potty-trained. He'll think the pot is a lot of fun. I'll bring you a lid, too. I have to leave real soon to make it to work on time. Should take me half an hour to get there if I walk fast. Then I've got an eight-hour shift. I'll drive my car home. Willie still takes a long nap every day. Maybe you two could lie down together?"

Half an hour to walk to Martinsville. So they couldn't be too far up the valley road. "Okay. I'll watch him for you."

"I'll have to lock the door. I hope you understand. I'm real sorry about all this."

What am I supposed to say to that? Annie wondered. The woman carried her son into the room and set him down near Annie's chair. "You get to stay here with Gale today while Mommy's at work. She's going to play with you. You'll get to take your nap on a real sleeping bag. Won't that be fun?"

Willie looked doubtful about that. He studied Annie and reached out to finger the end of her long red braid. Annie winked at him and smiled. "I'll take my hair down," she said, "and you can help me braid it again."

Before the woman left she brought in some sandwiches, some water, and Annie's purse. "I figured you might want this. I had to look through it first. I hope you don't mind. But there's your hairbrush in there. You can use that." She ran her hand across her son's brown curls. "Sometimes Willie brushes my hair for me." She lowered her voice to a whisper. "Makes a bit of a mess of it, but he has a lot of fun." She bent down to kiss Willie. "You be a good boy. I'll change you into your pajamas when I get home tonight, okay?"

Annie picked him up and held him while the latches dropped into place. Click, click, click, click. "You have a nice name," she told him. "My name is Annie."

"No," he said with the assurance of a three-year-old. "You is Gale."

Gale. This was insane. "That's close enough, Willie. What's your mother's name?"

He looked at her as if he thought she was nuts. "Mommy."

"Right." Sigh. "Do you want me to tell you a story?"

"No. Brush hair."

AUNTIE BLUE HAD BEEN more helpful than she knew. Maybe I'd have to do that anger list of Henry's on Glaze, too, just to let it all out so the forgiveness could start. I'd been behaving an awful lot like that stuck-up older brother. I did wonder if Glaze was going to feel like writing an anger list on me. Of course, I'd have to finish my week with Sally first.

I braked as a bright red sports car barreled around me on a solid yellow line, way too close to the big curve in the road. Some people were insane when it came to driving. He could have slid off the road—there weren't guardrails for quite a stretch beyond the curve—and nobody would have found the car for days. Plus, all the quick reflexes in the world wouldn't help if somebody were coming from the other direction. Thank goodness Sadie never drove outside Martinsville. She'd be all over both lanes and we'd have another funeral on our hands. It was a good thing I'd slowed down. There was a pedestrian ahead of me, just past that hidden driveway. No room to walk very far off the pavement because of the deep ditch on that side. She turned around and lifted a thumb. I motioned to her and pulled into the next driveway beside that cute bed-and-breakfast sign. The one with the plate of biscuits on it.

"Thanks, ma'am," the hitchhiker said through the open window before she opened the door. "That guy ahead of you almost blew me off the road." She sank heavily into the seat.

"Me, too. Some people shouldn't be behind a wheel. Could you fasten your seat belt, please?"

"Yes, ma'am." She fumbled with the strap above her right shoulder. "I always strap my little boy in whenever we go anywhere." She pulled the belt across and looked at me. "Oh, crap!"

"Is something wrong?"

"Uh, no. I, uh…I twisted my finger or something."

"Here," I said, "let me help." I took the seat belt from her and snapped it into place. "Now everybody's safe."

"That's right. Safe."

She seemed nervous. "Haven't I seen you around town somewhere? You look familiar."

"Yes, ma'am. I think I've seen you, too, at the circus. I took my little boy. The town paid for all the firefighters to go. Me, too. We went on different days so the station would be covered."

Margaret paid for that, I thought. It would be just like her, but I didn't say it out loud. "Are you a firefighter, then?"

"No, ma'am. I drive the ambulance for the department. Never got the training for the fighting. I'm too short to qualify."

"That's too bad, I guess, if it was something you wanted to do. But firefighting is such dangerous work. I can't imagine what it would be like."

"It's just as well. I've got my little boy. I wouldn't want him to wonder if his ma was coming to pick him up each day. There's a town day care where I leave him when I'm working. There's even a lady they hire to be there at night if any of us single parents are at work."

That blessed Margaret. It was amazing what she'd done for the town. "My name's Biscuit, by the way."

"Pleased to meet you, ma'am. I'm…uh…I'm Wilena."

"That's a pretty name. Are you the only female on the fire-department staff?"

"Yes, ma'am. But there's another single parent. Bill. He leaves his two little girls there when he's working."

"I'll bet you're very grateful for that. But you're not working now. Where's your son?"

"I…uh…I'm on my way to work. I left him with a…a friend. Had some car trouble, so I left my car at work the other day."

"Well, I'll drop you off right at the station so you won't be late. Do you live nearby? How far have you been walking?"

She cleared her throat. "Up the road a ways."

"Well," I said, "you let me know if your car won't start. I'd be happy to drive you home this evening." I told her my phone number, and she seemed downright embarrassed. I always thought it was a shame that some people had such trouble accepting help.

"No, thanks, ma'am. I don't think I'll need you to carry me home."

Alicia Rae stood by her front window looking out across her porch at the hummingbirds flitting around her feeders. Most people thought the hummers were cute, but she'd seen enough of them to know they could be real bullies. Not a one of them wanted to share the sugar water with anybody. Maybe when you're so little, she thought, you feel like you have to fight for everything you get. That was why she'd put fifteen feeders out across the whole length of her front porch. That way the birds could always find somewhere to take a sip before the bullies closed in.

The lawn needed mowing. One more thing to do, but she didn't feel like going out there now. Hiram would have mowed the lawn for her if he hadn't died. But there was no sense in worrying about what was done and long gone. A green car turned in at the foot of her driveway. Another guest? She still had one room available. She was going to have to stop airing out that unused bed. It was just an excuse to put off making up the rooms. Before she could scoot upstairs, though, someone got into the green car on the passenger side. Must be a hitchhiker, she thought. After a few moments, the car backed out and headed down the valley toward Martinsville.

Alicia Rae looked over at Glaze, who sat unmoving in the rocking chair by the bookcase. It was probably just as well. The last thing she needed was another guest sharing the breakfast table with someone so uncommunicative, so gloomy. "How about a nice game of old maid?"

Glaze shrugged. Alicia Rae was getting mighty tired of that method of communication.

ORDINARILY I WOULD HAVE BEEN at tap dance on Tuesday evening, but Miss Mary was sick, so she'd canceled the class. I decided to have a late dinner at CT's even though a heavy storm was moving in. I hooked my extra-wide umbrella, the one I'd gotten for donating to public radio, over my arm and set off, pausing only long enough to admire the indigo iris, the one I'd transplanted from my grandmother's garden. The first iris to bloom this season.

I looked up at the clouds, gauged the speed of the wind, and backtracked into the house…

I thought you were leaving.

…to get my garden knife and a vase of water. The iris would never make it through the storm. I might as well enjoy it inside. Marmy followed me back out the door and watched me cut the long flower stalk. Then she followed me inside and hopped onto the windowsill when I set the vase there.

Is this for me?

Bad idea. Marmy ducked her head to nuzzle the

blossom, but I pulled it out of her reach. Where could I set it so she wouldn't knock it over?

I want to smell it.

I settled on the middle of the counter near the sink. The water wouldn't do much damage there, even if it spilled. I sighed. Cats! Just to be on the safe side, I pulled out the heavy four-quart sauce-pan and set the vase inside it, tucking a dish towel around it to keep it upright. Now she couldn't tip the vase all the way over. "Don't eat the flower, Marmalade."

Humans!

She humphed at me as I walked out the front door. She sounded very much like Grandma Martelson.

DOREEN SEATED ME at the small table where Bob and I usually sat. If Susan really was Bob's daughter, we'd have to pick a larger favorite table. Half-way through my eggplant parmesan, Madeleine walked up and asked if she could join me. My mouth was full, so I nodded and wiggled my fingers at her.

"Why didn't Glaze come with you?" She pulled out the chair opposite me and curled one leg underneath her. How could she sit comfortably like that?

I didn't want to air our dirty laundry, so to speak, so I settled for "I didn't even think to ask her." That sounded better than *She doesn't ever want to speak to me again.* "Why didn't she come with you?"

Doreen set Madeleine's place with utensils and a glass of water, then proffered a menu. "Don't need one," Madeleine told her. "My dad sent me a check, so I'm splurging. I'd like the salmon, with asparagus and a Caesar salad."

"Yes, ma'am. Can I bring you some sweet tea?" That Georgia staple, iced tea so sugared you could put in a sprig of mint and it would practically stand up by itself, graced most of the tables around us. I'd chosen hot tea for myself. I was something of an anomaly. Must have been from my ancestors in Scotland.

Madeleine nodded and rearranged her silverware slightly. "I haven't talked to Glaze in more than a week."

"You two mad at each other?"

"No. I just haven't seen her since—" She paused and took the tall, icy glass from Doreen, then turned back to me. "Haven't seen her since she went to visit you."

"Visit me? What do you mean?"

"You know. Your sister-week."

"Sister-week?"

Madeleine took one more long swallow of tea. "She said since Bob was out of town, you and she were going to have a sister-week." She sounded like a kindergarten teacher explaining why we have to wear our shoes on the playground. "She packed up her blue carry-on bag. Seemed to be looking forward to it. Guess you turned it into two weeks instead."

I put my fork down. "But that was Monday before last. She stayed…" I counted on my fingers. "She stayed four nights and then went back home Friday afternoon. Last Friday. To your house. Her house. You know what I mean."

"No, she didn't."

"Didn't what?"

"Didn't come back home."

"Of course she did."

"Biscuit, I live there, remember?" Madeleine gripped the edge of the table and leaned forward. "I haven't seen her since that Monday."

I did another quick calculation. If Madeleine was right, Glaze had been gone for four solid days and nights. Dinner didn't taste so good anymore. I waved Doreen over so she could go get Tom. If anyone knew where Glaze was, he would be the one. By the time I'd reached the end of that thought, Doreen was at my elbow. "How are you two this evening?" she asked. "Everything okay with your dinner?"

I ignored her question. "Would you get Tom, please?"

"You sound like a Yankee," she said, "jumping into a question without even a 'Hey, how you doing?'"

"I'm serious, Doreen. Please go fetch Tom."

"Well, honey, I can't do that. He's not here, remember? He's at that big restaurateur's convention in Memphis." Oh, shoot! I remembered now. "Been there since Saturday. Is there anything I can help you with?"

"We just wondered if he'd seen Glaze lately."

"Why? Did you lose her?"

I lowered my voice, even though the tables were far enough apart to ensure some privacy. "We haven't seen her since last Friday."

"Last Friday?" she echoed. She looked at Madeleine, who nodded.

"I saw her Monday morning a week ago," Maddy said. "Biscuit was with her from then until last Friday."

"Has she been in here?" I asked, hoping against hope.

"Don't think so. I haven't seen her since that day last week—was it Tuesday or Wednesday?— when I ran into the three of you at the Delicious."

"That was Tuesday, I think. Glaze and I were there after we went dress shopping in Garner Creek," I told Madeleine. "Tom joined us for a while. He asked Glaze if she wanted to go to a movie up in Garner Creek, and she said no, she couldn't. Then he took off." I looked back up at

Doreen. "We sat there for a while longer, just talking and laughing." But Glaze hadn't been laughing very much. I guessed she was sad about Tom. "She and I were having a sister-week," I added. "That's why she couldn't go to the show."

"A sister-week?"

"Sort of like an extended slumber party. But it was only five days, from Monday to Friday. Then she left to go back home, but—"

"But she never showed up," Madeleine said.

"Wait a minute, Maddy," Doreen said. "Don't you and she have a carpool thing?"

"She took her own car," Madeleine said.

Doreen tapped her fingers on the menus she held. "Wouldn't CelerInc have called if she didn't show up for work?"

Madeleine shook her head "I never heard from them."

They both looked at me. "They wouldn't have called," I said. "They were closed last week. This week, too."

Doreen's face went blank, that look that people get when they've gone within, when they're really thinking. She clapped her hands, startling people at the next tables. "I know exactly where Glaze is," she said. She lowered her voice to a conspiratorial whisper and looked from me to Maddy and back again. "Yes. I know exactly where she is. Yesterday," she said, "I was posting the receipts in the office, and Tom called to see how things were going. 'I may stay an extra day or two,' he told me. 'Why?' I said, and he said, 'Something's come up.' Just like that, no explanation whatsoever."

Madeleine put a hand on Doreen's arm. "What does that have to do with Glaze?"

"Can't you see? They've eloped!"

"How can you possibly be sure of that?" Maddy asked. She must have been reading my mind.

"Come with me, ladies." Doreen swept out of the dining room like the lead dog in that circus act and ushered us down a hall and into the office. "I check the mail each day," she said. "Something came for Tom last Saturday, the day he left." She rummaged through a pile of papers in the overflowing in-box and extracted a postcard. We both leaned in close to take a look. Addressed to Tom. A single word—*YES*—in block letters.

"Oh, Doreen, don't be ridiculous," Madeleine said. "That could mean anything."

"Is it Glaze's handwriting, I ask you? Is it?"

"Good grief," I said. "You can't tell anything from one printed word like that."

"But could it be?"

I took another look. The postmark didn't help at all. It looked as if it might have ended with *ville,* but I couldn't be sure. Even the address looked anonymous, printed as it was in all caps. "I suppose so, but it just as easily could be someone else's altogether."

Doreen straightened her back. I could see a capital-*P* pronouncement on its way. "Wait till I tell you what else happened." She paused, apparently trying to build the suspense. It worked.

"What?" Madeleine prodded her.

"Tom called that evening. Saturday it was. He's staying in that hotel where they have the ducks. He asked if any mail had come for him. I thought that was a little strange. I told him that we'd gotten a stack of bills and a whole bunch of junk mail. 'That's not what I mean,' he told me. 'Was there anything else?' 'Like what?' I said. I guess I felt like pulling his leg a little bit. 'Come on, Dori,' he said." She turned to Madeleine. "That's what he calls me. Dori. Even though I'm almost old enough to be his mother."

"Well?" Madeleine sounded irritated.

"I told him he'd gotten a postcard and he got real excited, but like he was trying not to let on. 'What did it say?' he asked me, and I told him it had just one word on it. As soon as I said *yes,* you'd think he'd won the lottery. Well, now, I ask you. What else could it be? He proposed. She said yes. He was happy. And then she joins him in Memphis and they get a license and get married as soon as his conference is done. So now they're on their honeymoon. Oh, I think this is so romantic!"

I turned the postcard over. It was a picture of the Atlanta skyline. Hardly a romantic way to accept a proposal.

Madeleine went back into the restaurant to finish her dinner. I paid for mine and left. The storm had hit with a vengeance. Thank goodness for my wide umbrella, but even so, I got soaked from the knees down.

I DIDN'T EVEN TAKE OFF my raincoat when I walked in my front door. I just headed for the phone. "Melissa?" I said, as soon as she picked up. "Have you seen Glaze?"

"Today? No."

"No, I mean this week."

"This week? Last time I can think of was when you two were talking to Annie out front. I was up to my elbows in flour, otherwise I would have come out to talk with you. When was that? It was the day Annie asked me to watch her shop for her so she could be with her brother. Last Thursday or Friday." She yawned. "Why? Is she lost?"

"I don't know." I went through the whole story. "So Doreen thinks she eloped."

"Eloped? How could she? What about that dress you wanted?" Leave it to a really good friend to put me first. "How could she do that to you?"

Yeah. My thought, too, but I didn't say it out loud. "What if she didn't elope?" I pushed the saucepan with the indigo iris in it out of my way and drummed my fingers on the counter while I thought. "What if she's lost or something?"

"She could always get to a phone, couldn't she?"

"Well, yeah. I suppose so. Maybe she's had a car accident, though."

"No." She sounded so definite. "They would have found her."

"Are you sure?"

I heard something rattle in the background. "I'm getting out my car keys right now. I'll pick you up and we'll go looking."

"It's storming out."

"So what? I'll put on a raincoat over my pajamas. You're worried. Let's set it to rest. She probably *has* eloped, durn her hide. But just in case, we'll look along the sides of the road all the way to Surreytown if you want to."

THERE WEREN'T MANY CARS on the road. The guardrails were all intact. The vegetation was undisturbed as far as we could tell. Melissa drove her light blue car as far as Russell Gap, then turned around, and we checked the other side of the road all the way back. The ditches were empty except for the flowing rainwater.

"I feel silly doing this, Melissa."

"Don't. Now you can stop worrying. Go on in and get a good night's sleep. You'll probably hear from her in the morning. She'll be married, and then you can cuss her out."

Before I opened the car door to the rain, I turned back to her. "Thanks."

"BOB? I KNOW THIS MAY sound crazy, but I can't find Glaze." Marmalade wove around my ankles as I stood in the kitchen. The counter blocked some of the light from the yellow lamp, so Marmy's tail alternated between orange and shadowed gray.

Bob mumbled something or other, and I heard a click in the background. Turning on the light, I supposed. "What are you talking about, Woman?"

I waited to answer until he'd finished yawning. "I saw Madeleine this evening," I started and told him everything I could remember. "So, when I came home, I called Melissa and we went looking along the sides of the roads. Then I called Dee and Maggie and Irene and even Miss Mary. Nobody's seen her. I'm getting worried. Do you think Doreen might be right or should we be concerned about this?"

He asked me to repeat some of the details. I could hear him scratching notes. "Tom said something a couple of weeks ago, about how something big was in the works."

"Why didn't you tell me?"

"Because I didn't know for sure what he was talking about. He seemed to want to keep it quiet, like he was just giving me a warning." Bob thought for a moment. "He said his whole life was going to change."

A huge thunderclap shook the kitchen windows. "Like how?" Marmalade levitated onto the counter and stuck her head under my elbow.

"I don't know, Woman. He didn't give me any details. Is it storming there?"

Yes. It is very loud.

"Yes, it is. Didn't you ask him?"

"Why would I do that?"

"Maybe he wanted to tell you."

"If he'd wanted to tell me, he would have."

Men! How did they ever get anything accomplished in life?

Take a breath, Widelap. Your face is turning red.

I took a deep breath, which calmed me down a bit, and rubbed Marmalade's ears. "So you don't think we should be worried?"

"I didn't say that. There's one more session tomorrow morning. I have to stay for it so I can get the arms certification. But I'm going to call Reebok. What are you wearing?"

"What do you mean, what am I wearing?"

"Answer me, Woman. What are you wearing?"

"My pink pajamas, if it's any concern of yours."

"It *is* a concern of mine. Put on some real

clothes. Reebok's going to be there in five minutes to ask you some questions. I'm finally going to put that kid to work."

REEBOK WAS DELIGHTED to be of service. I answered the door wearing hastily donned tan chinos and my dark blue polo shirt with the library logo over the pocket.

You forgot your shoes.

Marmalade licked at my toes as Reebok walked past me through the wide doorway.

"Can I get you some lemonade," I asked, "or coffee?"

He pulled off his raincoat and hung it on the coatrack. "No, thank you, ma'am. I don't drink while I'm on duty." He sounded so earnest, I didn't have the heart to set him straight. I led the way into the living room and switched on one more lamp. Everything felt dark. He pulled a small black notepad from his shirt pocket. "I understand your sister is missing." Bless his heart, I could tell he was excited about this, but he did his best to sound duly serious. After I ran through my story, he asked some questions—rather good ones, I thought. "Have you checked her closets? Are her clothes all there, or is something missing?"

"I never thought of that." I looked at the clock. Ten. Madeleine would probably still be up. She answered on the third ring and scoffed at my apology for calling so late. "I'm a writer, remember? Got home from CT's and went to work on one of the chapters I'm having trouble with. I can't figure out how to kill Mother this time. Anyway, I hadn't even looked at the time. What's up?"

"Reebok is here," I said. "Can we come over and look through Glaze's closet?"

"You think this is serious? Don't you think she could have eloped?"

I had to admit it made sense. "What if Doreen is wrong about that, though? What if we wait and find out she's wrong?"

"Come on over. The door's unlocked."

MARMALADE SAT ON MY LAP as we drove to Upper Sweetgum Street. From what I'd heard, Marmy was as at home in Glaze's house as she was in mine.

I am a cat. I am at home wherever I choose to be.

"I looked for her purse and keys," Madeleine said as soon as we walked in the kitchen door. "Nothing."

"Wouldn't she have stopped by here to get some clean clothes if she were headed off on a trip?" Reebok asked. I couldn't help but be impressed by his good grammar, a crazy thing to think about under the circumstances.

"No," I said. "We ran a big load of laundry at my house on Thursday. When she left on Friday, all her clothes were clean."

"What time?"

I thought back. "Late afternoon. It was after we left the library. Maybe four or five?"

"We'd better check her clothes anyway, in case she took something else with her." Reebok blushed. I don't think he relished the idea of pawing through a woman's dresser drawers. I was right. "Maybe you could do the honors," he said to me. "After all, you'd know what her wardrobe was like."

"Maddy," I said, "would you look along with me? I'm not sure I'd recognize what was missing."

We gave her closet a fairly thorough search, then rummaged around in her bureau. Madeleine mentioned a couple of shirts, but they were ones I knew she'd been wearing at my house. "What about those white capri pants?"

"Nope. She had those. In fact, I think she wore them on Friday when she left."

We both looked at Reebok. He looked at his notebook. "Are you sure there's nothing missing except what she had with her last week?"

I glanced around the small room again. "It's hard to tell. What do you think, Madeleine?"

"I'll bet she has her blue suitcase with whatever she packed for the sister-week, and that's it."

She paused. "Is that enough for a wedding and a honeymoon?" She went through the closet again. "Here's her dressy green outfit. Did she have anything fancy with her?"

"You know," I said, "she did buy a dress at Mable's last week. I wondered about that at the time. She said it was just because she liked it and hadn't splurged on anything in quite a while. But it didn't seem like the kind of dress she'd wear anywhere around here."

"What was it like?"

I made some swishy motions around my hips. "It draped beautifully. Of course, on her figure, everything drapes beautifully. It was a tea dress, mid-calf length, with one of those uneven handkerchief hemlines." The kind that would look as if I'd made a mistake if I wore it. "White silk," I added, "with dark blue misty-looking flowers. Kind of an indigo color. When we got home she hung it in the back seat of her car."

"Sounds like a good outfit for a wedding," Madeleine ventured.

"You're right. Except for the indigo flowers."

By the time I got home I was too tired to write the seventy list, but the thought of having to start all over again was daunting, so I wrote it as quickly as I could. It made no sense whatsoever. I was too grumpy to even consider a gratitude list. Anyway, I couldn't think of anything to be grateful for. Except Melissa. And Bob. And Marmalade.

I am grateful for
this dry bed on a wet night and Widelap

"WHEN MOMMY HERE?"

"I don't know when she'll be back, Willie. It shouldn't be too much longer."

"Want Mommy." One tear dripped down his cheek.

"You love your Mommy, don't you?" Annie didn't have a lot of experience with small children, but she did have enough compassion not to blame this child for what his mother had done. She picked him up and rocked him quietly. "Mommy loves you, too. She'll be back soon. Don't you worry."

Mommy had better be back soon. The pot was full and they'd eaten the last crumbs of the peanut-butter sandwiches. She'd run out of stories to tell and couldn't think of any more games to play.

He'd just fallen asleep when she heard a car. It sounded loud. Good. Maybe somebody was coming to get her. Somebody with a noisy car.

Willie's mother stumped in a few minutes later. "Everything is going wrong," she said. "Everything. First I forgot to take the letter to mail it.

Then I forgot to go to the grocery store before work. Then something goes wrong with the engine when I turn in at the bottom of the driveway."

No food?

"The engine's making a horrible noise."

Annie nodded. "I heard it."

"Yeah. Well, it's too hot to touch now. I'll look at it later."

"Maybe it just overheated or something."

"Yeah. That'd be good. Here, I'll take Willie. He gets pretty heavy when he's all slumped over like that. Sort of like a sack of potatoes."

Speaking of food? "That's all right. He was a really good boy. But he missed you a lot."

"Did he go potty before he fell asleep?"

Annie nodded.

"Let me go lay him down in my bed, then, and I'll find us something to eat. If you don't mind canned soup, I can heat some up. Then I'll check the car again. The funniest thing happened on the way into town. I got a ride with… Oh, never mind. It doesn't matter." She paused. "Thank you for watching Willie. And you can call me Wilena." Annie nodded and Wilena carried Willie into the hall.

Annie waited a moment and tiptoed to the door. She hadn't heard the latches. Of course not. Wilena's arms had been filled with a totally relaxed little boy. If only she knew which way to head once she got down the hall. Even barefoot, she didn't care. If she could just make it to the road. Wilena wouldn't follow her; she'd never run out and leave Willie alone.

Annie eased the door open and saw her captor walk from one room—probably the bedroom where she'd laid Willie—into the room at the end of the hall. Probably the kitchen. Where the door was. Rats! By the time Wilena knocked gently on Annie's door, Annie was back on the sleeping bag.

"Can I come in for a few minutes?" Annie didn't say anything. She was too disappointed at having missed her only chance for escape. "I brought you some soup." She offered a big mug, and Annie took it, hoping it was hot enough for her to throw in the woman's eyes. Then she could run out, fast. But the mug was only lukewarm. Anyway, she couldn't do that to Willie's mother.

Wilena held out a paper plate. "They gave us some food at work. They do that sometimes. Some sandwiches and stuff. I brought you half of mine."

Annie looked at the fat sandwich and shook her head. "I can't eat it," she said. "I'm a vegetarian."

Wilena frowned and bit at her lower lip. "I thought you were supposed to have protein. They feed Willie good food at the day care. He always gets plenty of hamburgers and stuff like that."

Annie sincerely hoped they weren't feeding those children nothing but hamburgers. When she got out of here she was going to do some checking up on the menus. "Hamburger isn't always the best source of protein. Our bodies can digest beans and seeds and things like that much better than meat."

"Beans? You mean like string beans?"

"No, I mean like pinto beans and black beans and kidney beans. Things like that." She took a sip of the tomato soup. "There's even protein in peanut butter; your body can use it as long as you combine it with some kind of bread."

Wilena's frown melted a bit. "Like peanut-butter sandwiches?"

"Yes. I suppose so."

"That's good, then. Willie's doing just fine, isn't he?" Annie thought about the tearstained little bundle she'd held and rocked.

"Yes, Wilena. You're a good mother." When she got out of here, she was going to be sure this woman took a class on child-rearing. She needed to learn about the value of vegetables. Maybe she'd talk to Margaret about it. "Wilena?"

"Hmm?"

"I could talk to Margaret, the rich lady in town, about helping you and Willie. I bet she'd be happy to give you a loan so you could fix up this house or even get your own house. For you and Willie."

"She wouldn't do that for me."

"You don't know her like I do. She's really thoughtful. She paid for all those circus tickets you got." Annie wasn't a hundred-percent certain of that, but it made sense. "She'd be happy to help you. She just doesn't know you need the help. Maybe you could pay her back a little bit each week from your paycheck. She's really nice."

Wilena looked up at the stained ceiling. "She bought the circus tickets?" She looked down at her sturdy work shoes. "My brother wouldn't like it much if I let you go."

"You don't have to let me go. Wait until he gets here, and I'll talk to him and explain about how generous Margaret is."

"But look what we done. How's she going to forget about that?"

Annie reached out and touched the back of Wilena's hand. "You haven't hurt me. Well, except for the lump on my head, but that's almost gone."

"I'm real sorry about that."

"I think you just wanted to make a better life for you and Willie, right? Well, this is a way you can do it legally."

Wilena stood up. "I need to think about this," she said and then left the room. The latches clicked back into place.

WILENA'S CAR SAT UNLOOKED AT all night long. The storm that had billowed up out of the south buffeted the car, and the wind howled through the night. The rain washed away the dust and grime that the dirt driveway had deposited on the sad, old car and the run-down house. Willie slept the rest of the night away beside his mother. Annie didn't sleep at all.

WEEK FOUR

WEDNESDAY

"I CALLED THE MEMPHIS hotel, Sir. They won't give out any information on their guests. I did ask to be connected to Tom's room, but they said they had nobody by that name at this time."

"Well, it was worth a try. Keep this under your hat, Garner, but there's a guy in my class here who mentioned he has a brother who works security there."

"At the duck hotel?"

"Right. I'm going to talk to him and see if he can find out when Tom left and where he might have gone. Did you check on that other matter?"

"Winslow? Yes, Sir," Reebok said. "He's still locked up tight."

"When's he getting out?"

"Sorry, Sir. I didn't ask. Do you want me to call them back?"

"Not a problem. As long as he's locked up, Doreen's probably right. Glaze doesn't have any enemies."

"Bob? It's me."

"Well, of course it is, Woman. Reebok didn't have time to redial the phone yet."

"Is he bothering you?"

"No, we've just been having some discussions."

"About Glaze, you mean?"

"That and some other stuff."

"Listen, I just thought of something. Do you think there's a chance Jeff Winslow is involved in this?"

"That's what we were talking about. I already got Reebok to check on it. Jeff's completely out of the picture. He's still locked up. Look, I have to get to the morning session now. You've got that emergency number for me. Call if you absolutely have to."

"Have I told you lately that I love you?"

"Not lately."

"Well, I do."

Wilena knocked before she opened the door. "Doggone it," she said without preamble, "do you know anything about cars?"

"Not much," Annie said. "Why?"

"I can't get this one to start without that horrible racket, and I can't drive a car that noisy. I'd get stopped for sure."

"I suppose I could take a look, but I don't know how much help I'd be."

"I'm gonna let you walk out to the car, but don't try anything funny. I'm a whole lot heavier than you, and I can run pretty fast. All I'd have to do would be to tackle you, and you'd probably have a broken back or something."

"Do you think I could have my shoes back?"

"Better not. We gotta be on the safe side."

"Right."

THEY WALKED OUT the front door. A sharp piece of gravel poked into Annie's foot. She took a deep breath. Outside for the first time in two days. Never again would she take her freedom for granted, and she was going to go barefoot more often to toughen up her feet. Not that she ever wanted to go through anything like this again. She looked around quickly, hoping for a clue as to where she was. Straight ahead of her a cliff, easily fifty feet high, loomed up on the other side of a small gravel parking area. From behind her, the morning sun slanted over the house and warmed her back. That meant she was facing west. A gravel driveway curved down to the left, skirting the inside of the ridge that bordered the property on the south. The tree-lined driveway probably went directly down to the main road. She listened closely, but couldn't hear any traffic sounds. Of course, with all those trees, the clatter of the road would be muffled.

Her gray car sat there, nosed up against a prickly-looking holly bush of some sort. The other car was a few feet behind it with the hood wide open, like a baby bird begging for food. She could see Willy asleep, strapped into a car seat. They leaned over the engine. "Do you feel comfortable leaving him alone in the car like that when you're inside?"

"I left the window open, and it's not hot out. He sleeps real sound once he starts his morning nap. He can't get out of that car seat yet. Never figured it out. You see anything in the engine yet?"

"I told you, I don't know much about cars. Why can't you find the problem? You look like somebody who'd know mechanics."

"Nah. Willie's father, he was the one who knew about cars."

"Did you ever ask him to teach you?"

"Only thing he ever taught me about cars was what to do in the back seat of one."

"Oh. I can see how that wouldn't be much help."

"Got me my Willie, and that's about it. Haven't seen his sorry hide in a couple of years, so now my car never gets worked on."

"That's too bad. I wish I could help."

Wilena leaned against the fender and waved her hand at the house. "My brother and me rent this house from the lady who lives on the other side of that ridge there."

"It looks like she doesn't take very good care of it."

"She's kind of peculiar, but she's a good sort. Sometimes she watches Willie for me, but she has guns, and I don't like leaving him there." She looked back at the house. "This house is old. That's most of its problems. It needs some work. My brother and me were going to try to fix it up some, but we didn't have time. He bought a whole bunch of stuff to do the work, but that was before he lost his job."

"Is that where the plywood came from?"

"The pieces I put over the windows?" Wilena nodded. "Yeah. I wish I'd known how to keep you safe without doing that. Willie didn't like me covering up the windows. That was his bedroom."

"Once I'm gone, he can have his room back and you can take the plywood off."

"No way. Once you're gone, Willie and me, we'll be in another state." She thumped the fender. "If we can get this car working."

"Couldn't your brother come back and help you with the car?"

"He coulda. But he's…he's been away for quite a while." Her voice dropped almost to a whisper. "Why me? Everything's going wrong. I was supposed to grab you last week, but it took me a while to find you. Then I shoulda mailed this letter a long time ago, but I forgot to take it to work with me yesterday. You better be glad I'm doing this. The quicker they get the letter, the quicker you'll get out of here."

"You could use my car."

"Not a chance. Like I said before, they'll be looking for it. They see the car, they nab me. I gotta use this one."

"I keep telling you I don't have any money, and no family with that kind of money, either."

"You've got friends, Gale."

"It's Annie."

"I'm used to calling you Gale." She looked Annie up and down. "Gale kind of suits you."

"Yeah, sure. Tell you what, when I get home, I'll change my name."

Wilena chuckled. "You do that. Gordon said he and me are gonna have to change our names, too."

Annie threw her braid back out of her way. "Wilena, you don't want to do this. Not really. Think of what sort of life you'll be subjecting Willie to. You'd have to be on the run all the time."

"Not a chance. We're going to get a big chunk of money out of that friend of yours. Enough to set Willie and me up for life."

"I don't know if Margaret's that good a friend."

"You said she was real generous."

"She'd help you get a house, Wilena, but I don't think she'll cave in to a kidnapping scheme."

"Don't you worry none about it. Your sister's gonna talk her into giving us the money."

"My sister? What are you talking about? I don't have a sister."

"Yes, you do. I saw you at the circus and at that deli. We got this all figured out."

This was absolutely screwy. They didn't even have her name right. She leaned back under the hood. "Oh! There. See that wire thing?" She lifted it, and the spark plug on the end of it knocked against the engine. "Isn't that supposed to be screwed in?"

"You got it!" Wilena pushed her aside. "I think I can get it back in, at least far enough to hold for a while."

"Would that make the loud sound?"

"Dunno for sure, but I bet it's what the problem was. So you get back inside now. I have to lock you up while I'm gone. We'll get some food and bring it back. You hungry?"

"Starving." Wilena motioned her back toward the house. Just at the porch, Annie paused, wondering if she could make it to the woods, but the gravel was sharp on her bare feet, and her captor was close behind.

"You go on back in, now, you hear? I'm gonna lock the door."

"You wouldn't have any books, would you? So I could read?"

"Books? All I have is ones for Willie."

"Never mind."

"You got an empty pot there in case you gotta go before I get back."

"Thank you. I appreciate that. Uh, do you want me to watch Willie for you while you're gone?"

"Nah. He's asleep. I'd hate to wake him up. I'm going to leave you some crackers. They're a little bit stale, but I'll get us some real food after I mail this letter."

"Wilena, will you think about what I said? Once you mail that letter, you're committing yourself. It's a crime, what you're doing. But it's even more of a crime, the example you're setting for Willie. He's such a good little boy. If you don't mail that letter, you could live without being afraid."

Wilena shook her head. "Gordon would kill me," she said.

Annie tried one more time. "Maybe you could think this out on paper. That always helps me when I'm trying to figure out a problem."

"What do you mean?"

"Before you leave, will you sit down and write a list of what you have to be grateful for? I'm sure one of those things would be Willie. You can't possibly want to bring him up with his mom as a criminal. What if you get caught and sent to jail?"

"I won't get caught. Gordon said we'd go far away."

"Wilena, they're going to look for you, and they're going to find you. Then what happens to Willie?"

The four latches rattled into place. Annie sank onto the chair and listened to the newly quiet car start and pull away.

She hadn't gotten through. Wilena hadn't stopped to write a list before she left. Annie cried a bit in self-pity and raged a bit in impotent anger. Finally she settled down and imagined her own gratitude list.

1. I'm alive.
2. I still have some sense of integrity if I can try to help someone who kidnapped me.
3. I'm learning to appreciate good wholesome food more than ever.
4. I can fix cars. Well, this one car this one time, but it felt good to find the problem.
5. I had a chance to go up on that ladder to the high wire.
6. I have a good friend—a big sister!—who taught me about gratitude lists. I'll have to remember to thank her when I get out of here.
7. I'm learning how to tap dance.

She stood and did a modified buffalo step across the room. It was hard barefoot and on the carpet, but she did it anyway. Then she sat and watched the mildew stain on the ceiling, wondering if she could design a quilt called "Mildew Mania" or "Fungus Among Us," or one with an image of Willie asleep in his car seat. She'd call it "Kid Napping."

"MOMMY? WHY WE STOP?"

"You go back to sleep, honey. You haven't had a long enough nap." Wilena reached over and brushed a tumble of dark brown curls back off his forehead. "Mommy has to write something, and then we're going to go get some food."

Willie didn't say anything. Wilena watched him sink quickly back into the sort of slumber only a three-year-old could manage. His little body skewed sideways in his car seat. She brushed her broad fingertips over his soft curls and his head dropped forward over the safety straps across his chest.

Wilena sat there at the end of her driveway and wrote for a while. She made sure Willie's car seat was buckled in tightly, then turned left, up the valley toward Braetonburg.

A BRIGHT RED SPORTS CAR picked up speed as soon as it passed through Braetonburg, and headed toward Martinsville.

THERE HAD TO BE A CLUE. I felt as if I knew at some gut level below consciousness that Glaze would have left something to point the way to what might have happened. I knew she was in the valley. She had to be. Surely if she were in real trouble, my heart would feel it. But where could she be? She wouldn't have eloped. That would have killed Mom and Auntie Blue and cheated all of us out of the fun of helping her with her wedding. She just couldn't be that selfish, could she?

I called Madeleine at work and moved the saucepan with the iris in it to the round table while I waited for her to answer. Indirect light from the bay window brightened the indigo petals. I wished my spirit would lighten up as easily. "Maddy? Can I drop by your house and look at Glaze's stuff?"

"You think we missed something last night?"

"No. I'm not talking about clothes. We know she must have still had her blue overnight bag with her because it's not at your house, and she didn't leave it here. I know that for sure. I just feel like I'm missing something, so can I go look?"

"Sure you can. Just walk on in anytime. I'll be back at 5:30 or so."

Marmy and I paused on the front porch. I felt reluctant to barge into her house, knowing she wasn't there. Knowing she wasn't anywhere I knew about. I watched Marmalade sniff the mat, changed my course, and walked around to the left of the house, the downhill side. A fat gray squirrel hung upside down from the wooden lid on top of the bird feeder, gaily stuffing his face with sunflower seeds. Several nondescript brown birds fluttered in a nearby oakleaf hydrangea, and a black-capped chickadee twittered and fidgeted in the small Rose of Sharon I'd helped Glaze transplant shortly after she moved in. I clapped my hands and watched in momentary delight as the startled squirrel catapulted himself—or was it herself?—off the feeder, executed a frenzied shoulder roll in the grass, and raced for the mountain-ash tree beside the street, chattering at full voice.

You do not want to know what he is saying about you right now.

Bob's old shed, where he still maintained his fly-fishing workshop, listed slightly to one side, like a tired old gardener leaning on a hoe. The Sweet Autumn Clematis vine clambered up its left side along the lightweight wire fencing we'd suspended from the eaves. Give it another year and that entire east side of the shed would be a living wall of vanilla-scented glory in late summer. I'd have to plant a scarlet-flowered *Lonicera sempervirens,* a trumpet vine, on the other side. Red and white. That would look festive. Glaze would like the bright colors.

That reminded me why I was there, and all thought of festivity drained out of me like so much dirty dishwater down a kitchen sink. The work-shop door was always locked except when Bob was there, but I looked inside just in case. There were three windows, one on each side and one at the back. They gave me a clear view. All I saw was what I expected to see. No Glaze.

I kept on walking around the house. I had no clue what I was looking for, which was just as well because there was nothing out of the ordinary. A coiled-up hose. A watering can that leaned against the concrete foundation. I smiled at the yellow-striped king snake sunning himself—or was it her-self?—on the wide, flat rock that stretched along a good quarter of the back wall of the little house. "Marmy, don't go over there," I warned.

I do not get close to snakes.

The thing must have been eight or ten feet long. The rock, not the snake. Bob had tried to dig it out once a long time ago, but couldn't find a bottom to it. A deep ledge of bedrock underlay this valley. Here and there it projected up above the soil. There was a big, pointed rock that stood a good three feet tall at the rear of our fenced-in backyard. This one, graced by the black-and-yellow snake, rose five or six inches above the grass at its downhill end, and sank gracefully into the soil at the other end where ground-hugging weeds abounded. Not enough soil there to nour-ish grass of any kind, I supposed.

I was delaying. I wasn't sure I wanted to paw through Glaze's belongings again, but I couldn't put it off much longer. I said a silent good-bye to the king snake, who ignored me and kept on digesting the mouse-sized lump that distended his body way behind his head.

Bob's old house had two front doors, for God only knew what reason. The one on the right led into a boxy living room that Glaze and Madeleine had brightened with celery-green paint, strategically-placed mirrors, and white slipcovers over the ancient but still serviceable couch and chairs. I chose the left-hand door instead. It ground on its hinges as I pushed it inward. Marmalade stepped in ahead of me and turned left. The homey kitchen smell of coffee and cinnamon wafted out toward me. The cinnamon reminded me of Annie, for some reason. I hoped her brother was doing okay. She'd said she would call if there was a problem. Oh, well. No news must be good news, as Grandma Martelson used to say, before she lost her marbles. I watched Marmy paw at the lower cabinet where I knew Glaze kept a jar of catnip. "Not now, Marmy," I whispered.

Why are you whispering? Smellsweet and Curlup are gone.

I tiptoed past the potpourri bowl on the otherwise empty white counter on my right, then turned back to stir the mixture of coffee beans, cinnamon sticks, ginger, and who knew what else Madeleine had put in there. It smelled like Madeleine, but I wanted Glaze's vanilla perfume. She always used to smell like a cookie. Why was I thinking in past tense? She smells like a cookie. I laid the longest cinnamon stick, the one I'd been stirring with, across the top of the spicy potpourri and headed up the stairs.

Her bedroom, the one at the left that overlooked the bird feeder, felt so ordinary. I paused at the threshold, trying for one melodramatic moment to conjure up a cloud of suspense that would match the fear, the bewilderment inside me. But her room refused to buy into that. There sat her bed with the spread pulled tidily into place. A fat pillow covered with a flouncy blue sham leaned against the white-painted headboard. The delft-blue lamp that had been our grandmother's squatted beneath its white shade on the maple bedside table. An ordinary ballpoint pen sat on top of her journal beside the lamp. A slight indentation of her bed-spread brought to mind an image of Glaze sitting there, pulling on socks and tennis shoes. Her slip-pers weren't in their usual place beside the table. No, of course not. She'd had them with her dur-ing our sister-week. I strode across the room to her closet and rummaged through shirts, slacks, dresses, jackets. Nothing that she'd worn during our sister-week was there. I opened her wicker laundry hamper. Some undies and her bright yellow tee-shirt. I picked it up. She'd gotten out the milkshake stain. A white towel. A blue washcloth. Capri pants, the denim ones. Nothing else. Marmalade wandered in and hopped up onto Glaze's bed. She kneaded the bedspread several times and settled in, snugged up against the pillow.

The desk did double duty as a dressing table. Across the back edge was the usual assortment of lotions, combs, brushes, her medicines, a notepad with a few pages torn out, some lipsticks, a prism about six inches long. It reminded me of the crystals on the cotton-candy stand. Why on earth hadn't Glaze gone to the circus? She would have had such a good time. Toward the front of her desk, some artist's pencils lay in multicolored abandon. A tidy stack of what looked like bills was topped with her checkbook. I looked around, as if I expected Madeleine or Glaze herself to pop in and catch me, picked it up and looked at the balance. It was slimmer than I would have hoped. I'd have to figure out a way to see if she needed some financial help. When I set it back down I noticed the lipsticks again. I checked the colors. No Wildfire in sight. No purse. No car keys. Well, of course not. Those would have been in the kitchen, where she always plopped them on the counter right inside the door, beside the potpourri. Anyway, Madeleine had already looked for them. The image of that empty counter hovered a moment in my mind. I will not give in to despair, I told myself firmly. I will not.

There were some letters and postcards. No. I would not read her letters. But I did glance at the return addresses on the envelopes as I shuffled them aside. Nothing too interesting. Below them, though, was a brochure for a hotel in Atlanta and another one for the restaurateur convention. The one where Tom was. And still another for that hotel in Memphis, the one with the ducks that traipse through the lobby twice a day. Funny. She'd been talking about that place while we were on one of our walks a couple of weeks ago. She stumped me with those ducks in the twenty-questions game.

I set down the brochures, picked up the prism, and walked over to the window. The noontime sun barreled onto the floor and landed in a puddle of warmth that I could almost sense through my shoe soles. The prism caught the light, funneled it into a brilliant rainbow, and splayed it across her bed, the maple table, and a drawing thumbtacked to the wall above her desk. I hadn't noticed it last night. It was a pencil sketch of Tom, just his head and neck. Quite a good sketch, as a matter of fact. She had signed and dated it. The middle of last month. She'd captured that diffident air of his and his sparkly eyes. His open collar showed just a hint of dark hair that joined with her signature. She even got the scar at the base of his right ear. I knew from Bob that he and Tom had both fallen out of a tree when a branch broke. They were eight or nine. Bob broke his arm. Tom tore his ear in the process. It never stopped them from tree climbing, but they did learn not to put two boys on one branch at the same time.

I couldn't get over the feeling that I was missing something obvious. There was this nagging suspicion in the pit of my stomach. I looked around the room one more time. Nothing jumped out at me.

So I set the prism back down and picked up the letters again. One from Auntie Blue. A postcard from Yuko Tanaka, her former roommate in Philadelphia. There was no such thing as privacy around a postcard. Yuko had completed her midwife apprenticeship and paired up with another midwife. Good for her. Oh, and she was also enjoying being married. Good again. There were two letters from people I'd never heard of, and one with no return address and a postmark from Augusta. The final postcard was from Tom. It was a picture of the hotel ducks. Instead of a message, on the back he had written a string of question marks and his name. What on earth was that about? The postmark was smeared, the date completely illegible.

I plopped down on the bed beside Marmalade

and reached for her journal. No. That was truly invading her privacy. On the other hand, maybe there was a clue of some sort. I thumbed through to the last entry. *Tom asked me again,* it said.

Doggone her hide, I thought. She really did elope with Tom, and now I won't get to wear that dress from Mable's. Of course, she'd been moping around off and on during the four days we spent together. We'd had our fun moments, but a lot of the time she was off on another planet. Why didn't she give me a hint? Nonsense. She *did* give me a hint. More than a hint. She was trying to prepare me. She told me she'd just as soon elope. And I'd told her she was nuts. No wonder she left in a huff. Doggone it. Now she was gone and married, and the next time I saw her she'd have a ring. It should have been a happy thought. Instead, I picked Marmy up and cried into her fur.

ANNIE STRETCHED AGAIN and groaned again. Nothing but stale crackers to eat. Yuch.

"If only I could live the last three days over again." She tried to curl into a reasonably comfortable position on the thin sleeping bag. "I'd fight like crazy when she dragged me into the car instead of going all frozen like a wimp." That was ridiculous. She'd been hit on the head. "Well, then, I'd be more aware of my surroundings, and I'd hear her coming and I'd turn around sooner and see her. Then I'd scream and duck and run so fast she couldn't catch me."

She gave up trying to talk out loud. Her voice sounded thin, like tea that hadn't steeped long enough. What she would give for a cup of tea.

How long could it possibly take to mail a letter and buy some food? I wish I had a watch, she thought. It had to have been hours. Maybe Wilena had to go to work and forgot to mention it. That was it. She'd be home after dark.

She looked through the doorknob hole. There was light at the end of the hallway, coming from an unseen window. How much longer? Her stomach rumbled in protest. If Willie was at the day-care center while his mom worked, he'd get good food to eat. She hoped it wasn't just hamburgers. Maybe she'd talk to Margaret when she got free, just to be sure the day-care diet was well-balanced.

SHE WOKE WHEN FOOTSTEPS stomped down the hall. It didn't sound like Willie and his mom. Maybe rescue was on the way. An eyeball showed briefly in the doorknob hole and the latches clicked one at a time.

"Who are you?" For such a wide man, he seemed surprisingly tentative despite the gun tucked into his belt.

She didn't like the look of that. "Where's my sister? Where's Wilena?"

So much for rescue. "I don't know." She stood and backed away from him as unobtrusively as possible. He didn't seem to notice the movement. Instead, he looked around as if he expected his sister to be hidden in the bare room. Under the sleeping bag perhaps? Behind the chamber pot?

"Where'd she go?"

"She drove out of here this morning and I haven't seen her since."

"Hmm. She left her purse on the counter. There's no money in it. She's probably picking up the loot."

Annie didn't particularly want to be the one to tell him the bad news, that the letter was only now being mailed. She made a noncommittal sound and left it at that.

He looked her up and down. "Did you dye your hair?"

"What kind of question is that?"

"I just want to know, see?"

"I did once, but I didn't like it. What does that have to do with anything?"

"That your car out front?"

This was not a promising conversation. If he hadn't had only one continuous eyebrow, he might have looked a tiny bit like her brother. He was certainly as self-centered. "Yes, that's my car." Why did Wilena seem so loyal to him? Of course, why had she herself headed off to Atlanta again—as if she could ever get there—to be with her own brother, who never appreciated what she did for him? Good questions, both of them.

"Gimme the keys."

"I don't have them."

"Where are they?"

"How would I know?"

A few minutes later he was back. "I'm gonna take your car to go get some food."

There's food in the kitchen, Annie thought, but stopped herself from saying it. If he took her car, somebody might recognize it. "Drive safely," she said. "Could you bring some food for me, too?"

"You got any money?"

Annie sighed. As if I have an option, she thought, and picked up her purse. "There's not much in here." He grabbed the bag and pulled out her wallet. She thought about asking him to buy some gas. She'd forgotten to do that before she left town. No. She wouldn't mention that. If he ran out of gas it would serve him right.

FRENCH FRIES. The smell reached her nose at the same time the locks started clicking open. "Stay back away from the door." Who cared? French fries. She sniffed. Stretched, moved her arms tentatively, then with more vigor. Not even three whole days yet and she was already out of shape.

He opened the door and shoved a bag inside. She attacked the food before he snapped all the latches back in place. Crispy fries with way too much salt. Hamburger. Extra salt packets. Mustard. Three napkins. Paper bag. Visions of a dead cow slowed her down for an instant, but her stomach insisted that just one cow wouldn't make that much difference in the grand scheme of things. She started to take a bite and stopped. What was she thinking? A few days on low rations and she was turning into someone she didn't like very much. She would not sacrifice her principles over one lousy meal. She would not. She peeled back the bun. The ketchup and lettuce stuck to it. Two slices of dill pickle adhered to the meat. She lifted those and the thin slice of anemic tomato, removed the slab of ground-up meat, and replaced the pickles. Maybe it would all taste more nourishing if she thought of the pickle and the tomato as her daily dose of vegetables. Even without the meat, it was way better than peanut butter and jelly. She hoped her brother was being fed well in the hospital. Then she quit thinking and ate.

"MARTINSVILLE POLICE DEPARTMENT. Deputy Garner here."

"Sir, this is Ms. Emma Brody. I'm calling from the Simmonds Blaine Hospital north of Atlanta."

"Yes, miss? How can I help you?"

"That's *Ms*."

"Sorry, ma'am. What can I do for you?"

"Could you help us locate Annette McGill? We've been trying to call her for two days, but there's no answer. She's listed as the next of kin for Peter McGill."

Reebok smiled. This one was easy. "She may be at his house in Atlanta. She went there to be with him while he was operated on. I can get the number for you."

"I have that number. She's not there. She never came to the hospital. Her brother died on the operating table yesterday. We've been trying to locate her ever since."

"You're sure of this?"

"Of course I'm sure." She sounded as if she was pulling a wad of hair from a bathtub drain, the way she drew the words out like that, making sure he caught her irritation. Reebok could almost see her slash a red line through his name.

Why did some people, he thought, need to grind other people into the dirt? "Give me your number," he said. "I'll check around and call you back."

Reebok straightened his badge and stuffed thoughts of Miss...Ms. Brody into an envelope he kept tucked in his mind. Maybe he'd think about putting her on that forgiveness list Reverend Pursey had talked about.

He toyed with the idea of turning on the siren that he'd never used. No. That was uncalled for. He did hurry, though, rounding the few corners at a higher speed than perhaps he should have. Police business after all.

He pulled into the small parking area behind Annie's store. Her car wasn't there, of course, but he walked up onto the small porch and tried the back door. Locked. The windows were secure. What he could see inside looked undisturbed.

He walked around toward the front door.

"Reebok? What's up?"

"Oh, hey there, Melissa. Someone called trying to locate Annie. Have you seen her?"

"No. She's in Atlanta. I thought you knew that. Sharon needed some of that special shampoo for the Beauty Shop." She walked past him and slipped a key into the lock. "I told her I'd pick some up for her. I hope Annie ordered a lot of it. A lot of people who saw Annie at the circus have been coming by and asking for their five-percent discount. I hope it's okay to give it to them."

Reebok looked at the sign on the door. GONE TO ATLANTA. CALL MELISSA IF YOU NEED ANYTHING. The phone number was there for all to read. "We may have a problem, ma'am," he said.

"Biscuit? Have you seen Annie?"

"Of course not, Melissa. You know she's in Atl—"

"No, she isn't. Reebok told me the hospital called…"

"Martinsville Police. Depu—"

"What's this I hear about Annie being missing?"

"I was getting ready to call you, Sir. How did you hear about it?"

"Biscuit just called me in a panic. What are you doing with this?"

"I checked the shop. Melissa was there to get some shampoo, and she let me in. Nothing seemed amiss."

"Front and back doors locked?"

"Yessir."

"Windows?"

"Closed and latched."

"Cash register?"

"Fine, Sir. Sir? You don't suppose she eloped, too, do you?"

"Deputy, this may seem like a lark to you, but somebody's going to be pretty worried until we find out where she went."

Reebok pulled himself to attention, even though nobody could see him. "Sorry, Sir."

"These are real people we're dealing with, Reebok. Always remember that. You start phoning her relations. Annie has aunts and uncles all up and down the valley."

"How will I find them, Sir?"

"Call Clara. She knows everything about everybody."

"But won't she tell everyone in town?"

"Well, that way we'll have more people on the lookout."

WEEK FOUR

THURSDAY

ONE MORE CAR whizzed past Jeff Winslow. He swore loudly, using sheer volume to make up for a lack of imagination. Why bother with other words when one worked just fine. Four letters. Rhymed with *duck*. That was the extent of his lexicon. He'd never needed much more than that. His height, regular features, stark black hair, and fund of ready jokes had always served him well in getting what he wanted. His willingness to fight had, too. Whether it was drugs or girls, he'd had what he needed. Until Glaze. She'd broken his winning streak. He came up with another word or two that fitted her.

Another car passed him by. He'd been lucky to get a ride as far as Toccoa, but now the roads were narrower, less traveled. He hated the thought of walking all the rest of the way to Russell Gap, but he would if he had to. It really sucked, he thought. You do your time and finally get out and there's no way to get anywhere except hitching, and nowadays people were too chicken to stop and help a guy.

His thumb was getting sore from sticking out like that. He used a different appendage and yelled at the next woman who drove past. People sucked. That was all there was to it. He turned and kept walking.

70 x 7. WHY AM I STILL doing this when Annie's missing and Glaze is gone?

   1. I, Biscuit, forgive Sally completely…

WEEK FOUR

FRIDAY

"I'M NOT GOING to empty that pot for you. You cart it down here and empty it yourself."

She lifted the chamber pot. Thank goodness Wilena had given her a lid. He stationed himself halfway down the hall and motioned her into the bathroom. Dingy, she noticed, with years of wear, but not completely bleak. There were curtains on the tiny window. A small bouquet of those wild asters that grew along the roadsides sat, a bit wilted, in a blue plastic cup. The rust-stained sink was clean and dry. She wondered if her male captor ever washed his hands. Probably not. A yellow rubber duck sat on the edge of the tub, waiting for Willie's next bath time. The towel that hung above the tub was worn but clean. Thank goodness. She added some water to the aster's cup.

When she came out after having washed her hands with the cracked bar of soap, he still stood there, filling up the narrow hall, stolid, unmoving.

There was no way she could make it past him, and his single-eyebrowed head would probably dint the lid of the pot if she threw it at him. Anyway, he still had that gun.

"You go back in there. I'm taking your car to go pick somebody up."

"Did you find Wilena and Willie?"

"Who? Oh, you mean the brat. No. They must be waiting for the money to get delivered."

Not likely, she thought, and hoped that Wilena had simply driven away with her child, leaving the valley and her sleazebag brother behind. If she'd stayed, though, I would have helped her get out of this, she thought.

The only thing she was sorry about was that Wilena hadn't cared enough to let her loose first. She had thought Wilena was nicer than that.

"MARTINSVILLE POLICE. DEPU—"

"Reebok? Clara Martin here. How you doing?" The voice was so loud he pulled the receiver away from his ear. Naturally, she didn't wait for him to answer her question. It wasn't really a question after all. "You can stop searching for Annie. She's back."

"Is she at her store?"

"Not yet. I was driving up in Russell Gap this morning and I saw her drive into that barbecue place on the corner of Star Farm Road."

Annie was a vegetarian, he thought. She wouldn't go to the Barbecue Barn. "You're sure you saw her?"

"Of course I'm sure. I even waved at her."

"Did she wave back? Did you definitely see her?" A lot of people owned nondescript gray cars, and Reebok wasn't sure of Clara's attention to detail.

"Those windshields are too dark nowadays, but it was her car, wasn't it? Who else would be driving her car?"

He took a deeper breath than usual. "Now, Clara, if you didn't see her, it could have been somebody else. Or a different gray car."

"Nonsense. It had that stupid bumper sticker on it, the one that says BE A LITTLE KINDER." Reebok could hear the capital letters in her voice. Why such scorn? He thought the bumper sticker made a really good point. Maybe he should have been kinder to Miss...Ms. Brody.

"Now quit asking questions, *Deputy*. I need to call everybody and tell them she's okay."

He was putting two people on his forgiveness list, the one Reverend Pursey told him about. Maybe he'd put himself on it, too. His thoughts weren't very kind at the moment.

"BISCUIT? HOW'RE YOU DOING?" Maggie sounded out of breath. Maybe Vampirah had drowned in the pond. No. Maggie would have been crying, rather than panting.

"Fine, Maggie. How are you?"

"I just ran down from the goat barn. I had a good idea and wanted to call you about it. Did you hear from Glaze yet?"

"Not yet."

"Don't you bother about it. She'll call."

"I wish she'd hurry up so I could stop worrying. What's that good idea you mentioned?"

Maggie took a couple of deep breaths. "I got to wondering if you might be interested in coming up here when Joy gets ready to deliver. If you're not on Margaret's cruise at the time."

"Oh, Maggie! I'd be delighted!"

"It might could be four in the morning, you know."

"That wouldn't matter. Will there be anything I could do to help?"

"Probably not. Goats drop their babies without much fuss. I just thought you might like to see it."

It wasn't a grandchild, but then again, I'd never have to worry about a goat trying to psychoanalyze me. I'd have a grand-*kid*. Bad joke, Biscuit. I wondered if Maggie was doing this to get me so used to her farm animals that I'd start to like chickens. Fat chance.

"...usually have twins, and we don't expect this to be any different." Her placid comments brought me back to present time.

"Twins? That's great, Maggie. Will that make them my grand-kids?" It was too good a line to waste.

I could almost see her shaking her head and rolling her eyes. "You call me as soon as you hear from Glaze, okay?"

"Will do," I said. "And, Maggie? Thanks." I hung up the phone and scooped up Marmalade in almost one motion. At least somebody wanted me around, even if it was only a goat.

And a cat.

"AUNTIE BLUE?"

"Did you hear from Glaze?"

"No."

Auntie Blue let out a deep sigh. "You probably won't," she said, "until she's through with her honeymoon. Are you going to come swim with me?"

"How'd you know?"

"Well, it wouldn't take a magician. Glaze isn't home yet. Here it is after dark, and Tuesday afternoon when we were talking about swimming, you took a long look at the pool and I felt you pull in a big breath, and I think you just might be ready to get a little less scared of the water. Am I right?"

The iris in the saucepan was beginning to look a bit wilted, rather like the way I felt. "I don't have any cinnamon buns this time."

"You come on anyway."

"Oh, and, Auntie, one more thing."

"Yes, hon?"

"Clara called. She said she'd seen Annie up in Russell Gap this morning."

"I wonder where she could have been for the past few days. Do you think she knows about her brother, yet?"

"Maybe she's on her way to Atlanta. She has a bunch of aunts and uncles. She could have been staying with one of them."

"Well, we don't need to worry about her anymore, then. You come on up for that swim."

THE WATER *WAS* WARM. The stars were spectacular. Even with the light of the town, we could still see a couple million or maybe more. I floated—that I do know how to do—and thought a lot.

"Auntie Blue?" I pulled my legs underneath me and stood in the shoulder-deep water.

"Uh-huh?"

"Would you be willing to invite Sally to your house? And me, too?"

"You want a referee, honey?"

"Sure might help."

"After we get you and Sally squared away, do you want me to invite your sister, once she gets settled in?"

"Settled in?"

Auntie Blue turned to face me. "If she just got married, don't you think she'd want to move into her husband's house?"

"Oh." I hadn't thought about that.

"So, do you think you'd like to talk something over with her?"

"Might be a good idea."

"That's settled, then. You ready to get out of the pool?"

"Nope. I think I want to stay here for another year or two."

"Uh-huh. I'll have some hot tea waiting for you next year when you get inside."

"Give me five minutes."

"Take as long as you need."

My Gratitude List for Friday
1. Auntie Blue.
2. Melissa.
3. Marmy.
4. Glaze.
5. Annie.

6. Maggie and the goats (but not the chickens).
   Oh, what the heck—Sally.

70 x 7—Day 6
1. I, Biscuit, forgive Sally completely. This is
                                          the first
                                          time
                                          I've
                                          written
                                          it that I
                                          sort of
                                          believe
                                          it.

2. I, Biscuit, forgive Sally completely....

WEEK FOUR

SATURDAY

DOODLE-DOO HADN'T even crowed yet when I woke, bleary-eyed and dreary-minded. I lay there before dawn, unwilling to think too much about the discussion Bob and I still needed to have. I tried snuggling down farther under the comforter and I put my arm around Marmalade, who had her head on my tummy. How could she breathe under a blanket?

Through my nose.

My brain didn't seem to give a hoot that I wanted to ignore the upcoming discussion. It went on thinking anyway, at full speed. So much for sleep. The only thing I could think of was unthinkable. Susan, that young woman looking for her father. Hadn't she spent the whole week walking around town, peering at every man available? It wasn't the kind of looking someone like Easton Hastings did, with her come-hither glances. No, it was more of a searching look. She hadn't claimed anyone yet, and only two men had been unavailable for her scrutiny this past week. My husband and Tom. Brighton was gone for the week, but he'd probably been in grade school when Susan was born.

Would I be able to accept her as a daughter? Did she even *want* a family? What was she really seeking? How would we ever find out? She hadn't shown her photograph to anyone, which was ridiculous. If she had, we would have known. Any man would have changed a lot in the past twenty-five or thirty years, but the people he grew up with would recognize him. Unless—maybe she didn't have a photo. Or maybe it was someone else altogether.

That was beside the point. What was truly at issue was that my Bob felt threatened somehow by this black-haired invader. That could only mean that she *could* have been his daughter. Whether she actually was—or not—wasn't the point at all.

With a fenced backyard and heavy woods beyond it, we'd never bothered with curtains on the bedroom windows. The predawn light spread an insubstantial presence across the space between the bed and the outside. I turned and tucked my right arm under my pillow and stared at Bob. There wasn't enough light to read by. Just enough for me to study the face of the man breathing quietly beside me. Did I want to hear him say, "She could very well be my daughter, the child I never raised"? Is that what I wanted? Would I be willing to have him love another person the way I loved Sandra or Scott?

You forgot the other one.

I stopped breathing for a moment when I realized I'd left out Sally. So the question now wasn't what I was going to do about Bob and his possible daughter. It was what I was going to do about my ambivalent feelings toward my own child. Marmalade wiggled out from under the covers and stretched herself on top of my left side. The two of us stared at Bob while I wondered just why I loved him…

Softfoot is gentle.

…why I loved anyone, in fact. I had always assumed I loved all my children, until one of them started acting like a turd. Even then, where did the love go? Was it still there? If Bob and I developed problems, if we stopped listening to each other, would my ability to love be so tenuous that I might somehow stop caring?

Glaze was right. Sally and I did need counseling. We couldn't keep talking, or not talking, the way we were doing and expect anything to improve. I'd ask around and see if anyone could recommend somebody. Somehow I thought that Auntie Blue, even with all her love and all her good sense, wouldn't be enough to help us heal this rift.

You feel soft now.

I wrapped my left arm around Marmalade and pulled her down snug in front of me. Goats and cats were easier than people. She kept on purring, and we continued to watch Bob sleep until I felt I could honestly say to myself, "If she is truly Bob's child, I can—I will—accept her as my daughter as well. If she wants me." But then, of course, I wondered what Sally would have to say about all this.

I rolled onto my back and Marmalade shifted with me, almost as if we were tango partners changing direction. The last thing I felt before slipping back into sleep was Marmy sneaking beneath the covers on my left, and Bob vibrating quietly on my right as he snored in the reckless abandon of that sound-asleep state. Maybe this would be a good day after all.

The phone call, when it came, was thoroughly unwelcome. I wondered, illogically, and angrily, too, if it might be Susan saying good-morning to her daddy. So much for acceptance.

I ran my hand along Bob's spine as he reached for the phone.

He sounded only slightly bleary. "Sheffield here." After a moment or two, I felt his back muscles tighten. When he sat up and groped for a pen, I sighed. It sounded as if he'd be heading for the station early instead of enjoying that leisurely Saturday breakfast and the long talk I had planned.

I was sure it was Reebok. I could hear his tenor leaking out of the receiver. That young man was proving to be entirely too energetic when it came to making reports. Telephone reports.

Bob and I did a bit of a dance as I reached for my robe that had fallen on the floor and he stretched the phone cord so he could grab his pants from the back of the chair. "Are you sure it wasn't…" He sat down on the side of the bed, which squeaked alarmingly. Where had that squeak come from? "No ID?…What shape was the car in?" A car accident, I thought. Oh, dear. I hoped nobody was hurt. I handed him his socks, and he gripped the phone between his shoulder and his jaw line while he pulled them on. "What shape is he in?" He looked pretty grim. Somebody must have died. He reached out and grabbed my arm, effectively preventing me from heading downstairs to make him some coffee. "Read it to me." He must not have liked what he heard, because his fingers tightened on the pen until his knuckles went white. "I'll meet you at the station in ten minutes."

He pulled me down onto the squeaky bed beside him and gripped my shoulders. I didn't like the feel of that. "It's about Glaze," he said.

Before I could flood him with a barrage of questions, though, he shook his head. "Reebok got a call from the Braetonburg police a few minutes ago. They found a car smashed into a tree this morning, with somebody—not Glaze," he added quickly as I gasped and tried to jump up. "There was no identification, no driver's license, nothing, except a stamped, unmailed letter in the driver's jacket pocket. It was addressed to you. They opened it."

"Don't stop talking. Tell me. What was it? Where's Glaze?"

"It was a ransom note, asking you to produce a quarter of a million dollars."

"She's been kidnapped? That's nonsense. We don't have that kind of money."

"Apparently they knew that. The letter said"— he looked at the notes he'd made—"'If you want your sister back in one piece, you better borrow the money quick from that rich friend of yours.'"

"Margaret? How would they know about Margaret? Where's Glaze?"

"Calm down. We'll find her."

"Well, ask the stupid driver! He must know."

"She. The driver was a woman." He ground his teeth together. "She's dead. Looked like the car went over an embankment two or three days ago. A jogger spotted it this morning." He pulled me down again. "Don't go rushing off when we don't have information, Woman."

You need to breathe.

I felt as if a fist had slammed into my stomach, but I forced myself to take a deep breath. Marmalade appeared in my lap, somehow, and began kneading my tummy.

"That's better. There's more."

"More?"

"There was a child in the car. Strapped in a car seat. A little boy. Couldn't be more than three or four. He's alive, barely. Critical condition."

I WILL SAY THIS for myself. I did think to slice off two thick slabs of my oatmeal-dill bread for Bob's breakfast. Some meal. I couldn't eat a thing.

Take a breath, Widelap.

Marmalade wove around my feet and yowled as I handed Bob the bread and gave him a quick kiss. She probably wanted to be fed, too.

"Don't worry, Bisque. We'll find her."

The only time he ever called me Bisque was when he was worried himself. I didn't trust myself to say anything. He pulled me into a bear hug that felt full of fear. His arms, usually so strong, trembled. For one long moment I could hardly breathe, but I clung to him in desperation. "Find her for me," I said.

He touched my cheek. "I'll call when I can."

He headed down the front steps, and I ran for the phone. "Melissa!"

"What's wrong?" Friends, real friends, listen with their heart, just as Auntie Blue had said. One word was all it took. Of course, the note of panic in my voice may have helped. "Did something happen to Bob?"

"No. It's Glaze. She's gone. She's been kidnapped. They want money."

"Is she okay? They didn't hurt her, did they?"

"I don't know. The note didn't say where she was."

"We can ask Margaret for help. You take a big breath, now, and don't—"

"You don't understand. The kidnapper is dead and there's a little boy and the letter was dated a week ago and—"

"Biscuit! Settle down a tad, okay? You're not making any sense. You sit down. Don't go anywhere. Let me turn off the oven and I'll be right there."

As soon as she hung up, I dialed the phone again. "Mom?"

"Yes, dear. What's wrong?"

"Mom?"

"Are you okay? Has something happened to Bob?"

"No. No. Are you sitting down?"

"Tell me. Just tell me, whatever it is."

"Is Dad...?"

"He's gone down to the diner to have breakfast with some of the guys. They do that every other Saturday, remember? Oh, my God, has something happened to your dad? They should have called me first."

"No, Mom. It's nothing like that. It's…it's Glaze. She's been kidnapped. They want a quarter of a million dollars before they'll give her back."

"Is she okay? Did they hurt her? Where is she?"

"We don't know. It's a long story, Mom."

"I'll go pick up your dad right now. Don't you go anywhere until we get there."

"No, Mom. Don't come here. Stay there in case Glaze calls you." I filled her in with what little I knew. "So, can you call Auntie Blue?"

"Of course I will. I'll get her and Mark to come over here. Does Rebecca Jo know yet?"

"I didn't even think of her."

"Don't worry, honey. I'll handle it."

"I've got to call around town. Mom? I love you."

"I know, dear. Bob will find my baby. Don't you worry. Call me as soon as you hear anything."

Melissa ran in the front door as I dialed Margaret.

"Margaret, it's Biscuit. I've got some bad news."

"Oh, no, did something happen to Bob?"

"Why does everybody think it's Bob?"

"He's a cop."

"Oh. Well, no. Bob's fine. It's Glaze. She's gone. Kidnapped. They want you to pay a quarter of a million dollars before they'll give her back."

"That damn money! If I didn't have it Glaze would be safe."

"Oh, Margaret, no! That's not what I'm saying. It's just that, well, the kidnapper died and we don't know where Glaze could be. I knew she was gone, but we thought she'd eloped with Tom."

"Tom? Of course not. He doesn't have time to get married. Not with the new school."

"New school? What are you talking about?"

"Oh, it's all very hush-hush. He talked to me months and months ago about funding a vocational school for at-risk teens. It's a cooking school, where they'll learn to be cooks in family restaurants and diners."

"But somebody saw him leaving the hotel in Memphis with a white-haired woman. We figured that was Glaze."

"No, hon. That was Cecily Carpenter. She was his mentor when he was in culinary school, and she's retired now. Lives in Doraville, near Atlanta. He asked her if she'd come out of retirement and head up his school. She said yes, so they met up in Memphis. They've been having planning sessions for the past couple of days. It wasn't Glaze. I'm sure of that."

"Then, where is Glaze?"

"I don't know. I've gotta run, honey. Your husband just drove up to deliver the official news.

Don't worry. He'll find Glaze for you. Oh, wait! Call Madeleine."

"Madeleine. I forgot about her." I set the phone down. Melissa had been standing there with her head near mine, listening in as well as she could. She got the gist of the conversation.

"Why the heck didn't they elope? If they had, she'd be safe."

I shook my head. I needed a cup of tea, but it seemed heartless to think about that while Glaze was missing. "Are you blaming Tom for this?"

"No. I just think it would have been a whole lot happier if he'd taken her off into the sunset. Now, you sit there and tell me everything, and I'm going to make you a cup of tea."

"I have to call Madeleine first."

"Okay." She sounded as if she was humoring me. "But then sit down and tell me the whole story. I need to know so we can plan something."

"How can we plan anything when we don't know where she is?"

"Just call Maddy and don't worry about anything."

"Don't worry, the woman tells me."

"You're muttering."

Thank goodness I had all these phone numbers memorized. "Maddy?"

"What is this, Grand Central station? First, Tom here, then you."

"What do you mean? Is Tom there?"

"Yeah." She yawned. "He just walked in the door."

I could feel my eyes narrow. "Put him on the phone." She mumbled something, and the phone rattled as she handed it off to Tom.

"Hey there, Biscuit. How—"

"Don't you 'hey there' me, you rat. Why didn't you marry my sister?"

"What?"

"She'd be safe if you'd taken her off to Memphis, and now some dead kidnapper has her and we don't know where she is and you come waltzing in here and— Stop that, Melissa!"

She grabbed the phone and glared at me. "Tom? This is Melissa. Why don't you and Maddy come down here?…Yes, now…Biscuit's a little bit distraught." She glowered at me. "We need to plan… Yeah. Glaze is missing and they heard from the kidnapper. But the kidnapper is dead or something like that. I haven't been able to get a straight story out of Biscuit yet…Just what I told her. I'll make a whole pot of it. It should be ready by the time you get here." She set the phone down but grabbed it out of range when I reached for it. "You sit there," she said and pointed to the chair at the head of the long table. "If we're going to have a war council, we need to have room."

"I need to call Ida."

"You're not calling anybody, not after what you just did to Tom."

"But he—"

"Biscuit." Here came her Reasonable Voice. As if I was a four-year-old throwing a tantrum. "Sit down and wait for your tea. You'll be a lot more human then." I stuck my tongue out at her. "That's more like it," she said.

THE FRONT DOOR SLAMMED open and Maddy and Tom flew into the kitchen. Melissa took charge and sat everyone down, making sure Tom was on the other end of the table from me. "Now, Biscuit," she said, "start at the beginning and tell us what you know."

"It started with our having a fight."

"Who?" Tom asked.

"Glaze and I had a fight last Friday, a week ago, and she left in a huff. I thought she'd gone home—"

"And I thought she was staying here," Maddy broke in. "Anyway, the point is that nobody's seen her since that Friday. We figured it out on Tuesday, but Doreen saw that postcard you got at the restaurant, the one that said *yes* in big block letters, and she decided you'd asked Glaze to elope."

"I wouldn't do that," Tom said.

"Don't you want to marry my sister?"

Melissa put her hand on my arm. "Settle down, Biscuit. He didn't mean it that way."

"How would you know?"

Tom held up his hand for quiet. "It's the eloping I wouldn't do. Glaze would want a pretty church wedding, with you there and her mom and dad. She'd never consider eloping."

I opened my mouth to tell him just what she'd said, but Melissa poked my arm. I might have kept objecting, but the front door banged open again, and Ida charged into the room. "Rebecca Jo called us. What can we do to help?"

Dee was right behind her with her cat-like eyes wide and staring. "What happened?"

Melissa made me start all over again and tell the whole story.

"MARTINSVILLE POLICE Department. Garner here… Just a moment, please. Sir? It's Captain Hopkins from the Braetonburg police force."

Bob motioned to Reebok and turned to a new page in his notebook. "Hopkins? Bob Sheffield. I've got you on speaker phone so my deputy can listen, if that's okay. What have you got?"

"We traced the car to a Gordon Harvey who's been doing time. He was released this past Wednesday. Now, listen up. His cellmate was that Jeff Winslow that you sent down last year."

"Oh, crap! Does this Harvey live here in the valley?"

"We haven't figured that out yet. His address of record is a Braetonburg P.O. box."

"Can you stake it out?"

"We're a little shorthanded."

"This is a kidnapping!"

"I know. We still have only a few officers. There's some sort of flu bug going around."

"If I send Garner up there, can you assign him as a temporary duty officer for your department and let him do the stakeout?"

"How soon can he get here?"

"Well, he looks like he's headed out the door right now." He beckoned to Reebok to come back and sit down.

"One other thing, Sheffield. The dead driver? We're pretty sure she was Wilena Harvey."

"Wilena? She's an ambulance driver for the town here. Was she Harvey's wife?"

"His sister. Would you check and see if she's been to work in the past couple of days?"

"Will do." He scribbled a note. "Any other relatives?"

"Just the little boy."

"Sounds like somebody needs to talk with Jeff Winslow."

"That's the other bad news. They released him two days ago. Got out early on good behavior.

I've put out an APB on both of them, but no luck so far."

Bob Sheffield didn't believe in swearing. He thought it indicated a poor grasp of the English language. This time, though, he swore.

"One other thing," Hopkins said, and his voice sounded tinny through the speaker. "We found a piece of paper under the driver's seat. It was lined, like from a kid's school notebook. Wilena signed it. That's how we first figured out who she was. Unusual name."

"What did it say?" Bob asked.

"I'll read it to you." He shuffled a few papers around. Bob and Reebok could both hear that clearly. "Here it is. It says"— his voice took on that artificial tone that some people use when they read—"'My brother got me to kidnap Gale to get money, a lot of money—'"

"Gale?"

"That's what it says. We figured she didn't know how to spell." He went on reading.

It wasn't Gordon's idea. He's not smart enough to think of that. The guy he shared a cell with it was his idea. He said we'd split the money. It took me a while to figure out how to catch Gale, so I didn't get the letter mailed yet. That's good. She's nice. She said that rich lady in town would help me get a house for me and Willie. I'd pay her back. My paycheck isn't much, but I could do it somehow. Gale said if I run away and they catch me Willie will be left without a mommy. Even if they don't catch me, I'd be raising him to cheat and lie and be scared all the time. Gordon's going to kill me when he finds out, but I'm going to let Gale go as soon as I get back from buying some food. I'm going to burn this letter, even though it already has a stamp on it. She said she'd help me talk to that rich lady, and I trust her. She likes Willie a lot.

I'm going to sign this so it's kind of like a contract. A promise to myself.

What I'm thankful for most of all is Willie, and Gale.

Hopkins stopped reading. "That's it," he said. "Plus the signature."

Bob cleared his throat. Something seemed to be caught in there. "So where is Glaze?"

"She didn't say."

JEFF WINSLOW HAULED the car door open and threw himself into the passenger seat. "Let's get out of here. I don't like sitting around."

"I'm the one who's been sitting, and I was here yesterday, too. Sitting."

"Yeah, well, I was thumbing rides yesterday.

Let's go." Gordon circled the Barbecue Barn and paused before turning onto the main road. "I oughta go by the post office and check my mail."

"Leave the frickin' post office alone. You'll have plenty of time to check it out later after we split. You got the gun?"

"Right here."

"Give it to me."

"Why?"

Jeff lowered his voice to a near growl. "I said give it to me. I want to check it over."

"Okay, but I want it right back." Gordon pulled the gun out of an improvised holster and handed it to Jeff before he turned left, heading south on the road that ran the length of Keagan County. "I want it back," he repeated.

"Sure."

"It's mine."

"Right." Jeff made sure the safety was on and slipped it into his waistband. Awkward. Bulky. Efficient.

"Wait a minute. Give it back!"

"I'm keeping it safe for you while you're driving." Gordon gripped the steering wheel but said nothing. A dozen or so miles down the road, Jeff broke the silence. "Did you count the money yet?"

"Well, there's…sort of been a…kind of like a…holdup."

"Whaddya mean, a holdup?"

"Wilena's gone. Settle down, now. She's staking out the pickup place. She could already be back there waiting for us."

"You should have had the money by now! What's the hangup been?"

"Calm down. That rich lady probably stalled some. Are you sure she's a good enough friend?"

"Don't you worry about that. Glaze always said her big sister could talk anybody into anything."

"Glaze? I thought her name was Gale."

"Harvey, you are dumber than a bucket of mud."

"You don't have to say that. I do just fine."

"Yeah? If you do so fine, what were you doing locked up?"

"That was just bad luck."

Jeff turned from watching the road to watching the man beside him. He pulled out the pistol and held it across his lap. "You and your sister weren't planning on taking off with the money all by yourselves, were you?"

"I told you, she's probably back by now. I waited a long time at the Barbecue Barn."

"She better be. How much farther?"

"Maybe ten miles."

"I'M GOING TO MAKE some more of my Delight for dessert tonight. Won't you enjoy that?" Alicia Rae's two guests sat across the breakfast table from her. Susan murmured a quiet monosyllable. Glaze nodded mutely.

"I've been thinking about what we could do today, this being a Saturday. Not that Saturday's any different than any other day, but I decided you both need to get out in the fresh air, and it won't do me any harm, either. I packed up a picnic lunch and we're going to hike up to the top of the ridge and over to where the cliff is. There's a wonderful view up there. As long as we watch out for rattlesnakes we'll be okay." She looked at the grimace Susan made. "Oh, don't you worry. I never go up there without my double-barreled shotgun all loaded and ready to go. That's where Hiram Knelson was killed, don't you know, and it doesn't pay to take chances. I've never seen one up there, and it's been fifteen years since I moved from the little cabin on the other side of the ridge. I rent it out now. It's kind of dilapidated, but I don't charge much rent. There's some families can't afford a lot, you know. It looks like it may need a new roof, although I can't say for sure. I haven't walked over there in quite a while. That driveway's awfully steep. One of them always comes here with the rent money. Real dependable they are."

"I'LL LET YOU CARRY this basket." Alicia Rae directed Susan as the two younger women gathered in the kitchen. "You carry this other one, Glaze.

I put the lunch up in two parts so we could share the load. It's easier that way. You two carry the food, and I'll carry the shotgun. Now, walk kinda heavy once we get on the path. If the snakes feel us coming they'll most likely move out of the way, but just in case, I've got Bertha here. A shotgun scatters shot pretty wide, so you don't have to aim real well if you're shooting at something close-up. Something like a rattlesnake." She patted the stock. "The two of us have been through a lot together."

She led the way past the three cars that were tucked in behind the tall hedge of hollies. A few cars flowed past on the road far down the driveway, but the women paid them no attention as they crossed the yard to where a steep path wound up through the ferns on the side of the ridge.

ONCE I'D FINISHED answering everybody's questions with what little information I had, Melissa pulled out a map of the county and spread it across the kitchen table. I was momentarily daunted by the number of roads. Glaze could be anywhere. Melissa must have read my face. "Don't you worry," she said. "We're going to do this logically. Look here." We gathered around her. "The car wreck was about in here somewhere, right?"

Dee and Ida shrugged. I gave a tentative nod.

"Looks right," Tom said.

For heaven's sake, how would he know? He wasn't even here when it happened.

"The car looked like it was headed up the valley toward Braetonburg, where she was most likely planning to mail the letter. Isn't that what you said, Biscuit?"

"I think that's what it sounded like."

"Well, then, that means Glaze must be somewhere from here"—she drew a pencil mark halfway between Martinsville and Braetonburg—"to here, 'cause that's where the closest post office is."

Dee pointed to Martinsville on the map. "Why couldn't she have been going to mail it here?"

"Because it looked like she was headed away from Martinsville when she ran off the road, and she hadn't mailed the letter yet. Doesn't it make sense she'd drive to the closest place?"

"Maybe she didn't want to be seen here in town," I said. "Maybe she was somebody we'd recognize."

"That's what I meant," Dee said. "She might have lived a hundred yards out of town but had to drive up the valley to get away from here."

Tom nodded. "That means we just doubled the search area."

"Okay." Melissa tapped her chin with the eraser end of the pencil. "We need to go in pairs." I was glad she'd taken charge. I didn't feel up to it. "Ida, you ride with Biscuit." Melissa looked at me. "On second thought, Biscuit's in no shape to be behind a wheel. Dee and Ida go together. Biscuit and Tom. I'll take Maddy."

We divided the main road into thirds, from Martinsville to the location of the wreck, and agreed to check every single driveway.

"But she could be off in the woods somewhere in a hut," Dee said.

"Don't complicate matters." Melissa started folding up the map. "We'll do what we can."

"Her car's missing," I said, "so if we see it, we'll know she's there."

Tom laid a hand on my arm. "Hold on. We can't go storming in. They might have guns."

"I don't care," I snapped. "I want my sister."

"You're missing my point. They might panic and hurt her."

"Oh."

"Tom's right," Melissa said. "If we see her car, we turn around and let Bob know so he can handle it. Do we all agree?"

My Bob. Going into a house with guns? I sat down rather unexpectedly. This was way more than I wanted to deal with.

IDA AND DEE TOOK the first section as far as the scenic overlook. Tom and I took the middle one, which went up as far as the big curve with all the orange warning signs. Maddy and Melissa agreed to start just beyond the curve and go north from there to where the car was found. We formed a sort of train leaving Martinsville with Melissa leading the way. Tom and I were the caboose. He slowed down as Dee turned off into the first long driveway outside of town. "I hope they'll be okay," he said.

We passed the scenic overlook and started watching carefully for driveways. "I think we got the easy section," I said. "There aren't many houses along here."

HALFWAY UP THE SLOPE, Glaze switched the picnic basket to her right hand. A rough spot on the handle irritated her index finger. She stopped abruptly and Susan's basket bumped into the back of her legs.

"Sorry," Susan said.

Glaze turned and looked at the woman's black hair. Like my mood, she thought. No. Her hair is shiny, sparkly, like Annie's red hair. Biscuit loves Annie better than she loves me.

"Is something wrong?" Susan asked.

Glaze shook her head. Just everything. Biscuit won't forgive me. Mom and Auntie Blue love her better. Biscuit hates me.

"Do you want me to carry your load for you?"

You wouldn't want my load.

Alicia Rae bustled back. "Something wrong here?"

"She just stopped walking."

"Glaze, honey, I'll carry the basket for you. It's a lot bulkier than Bertha here. Of course, Bertha's got a lot more kick to her than a picnic basket does." She laughed and patted the shotgun.

Glaze reached for the gun, but Alicia Rae shifted it to her left hand, away from Glaze. Glaze saw her look at Susan. Susan stepped forward. "I can carry both baskets. I'm a lot stronger than I look."

JEFF FINGERED THE GUN in his lap and watched a small, light blue car drive by, headed up the valley. "What are you slowing down for?"

Gordon Harvey rounded the sharp curve and slowed even more as he downshifted into second gear. He turned into the driveway, shifted into first, and started up the graveled incline. "This here's the house."

"I thought you said this place was hidden," Jeff said.

"Heck, nobody comes up this way. The driveway's way too steep, and you cain't see the house from the road for all the trees." He stopped talking so he could concentrate on the sharp turns as the drive zigzagged up the hillside.

"I thought you said this was a cabin. It looks like a regular house."

"Yeah? Well, it's not much on the inside, but

Wilena and me, we've been trying to fix it up some." Gordon drove up close to the overhanging cliff and pulled the car into a tight circle, stopping directly in front of the door.

Jeff practically snarled. "Where's her car?"

Gordon shifted his hands on the steering wheel and turned off the engine. He left the keys in the ignition. Nobody stole cars around here. "Maybe she went to get some food or something."

"I don't like this one bit," Jeff said. "That money better be waiting inside."

Gordon ran his index finger around the neck of his tee-shirt. "Don't you worry none. Wilena's real dependable."

Jeff opened the car door. "Let's get a look at our white-haired little bird."

"White? No. She dyed her hair. Didn't you know that? It's red."

"So what?"

"Just thought you'd want to know."

"All I want to know is what she's gonna say when she finds out I'm rich." Jeff headed up the stairs and opened the door into a small kitchen. "Where is she?"

"Down that hall. The room at the end."

ANNIE HEARD VOICES, two male voices. She didn't like the feel of this. She retreated to the far side of the room as the latches went click, click, click,

click. A tall man with a full head of black hair strode into the room. "Who the hell are you?" he said.

"I'm Annie McGill. Who the hell are you?"

He didn't waste time answering her. He spun around and grabbed Gordon's arm. "You nabbed the wrong person."

"That's impossible!" He yanked his arm from Jeff's grasp. "Look at that hair. You could spot it a mile away. That's what you said."

"This is not Glaze."

"Glaze?" Annie said. "What's going on?"

Jeff glowered at her. "What's going on is this idiot grabbed the wrong one."

"Wilena done it," Gordon said. "She's the one who got it wrong."

"But you're the one who told her who to nab."

Gordon stomped across the room and grabbed Annie's braid. "Look at this. You said to look for the hair."

"Where's my money?" Jeff shouted at him. "You and that sister of yours cheated me out of my money."

"We didn't cheat you."

"Then where is she?"

Gordon looked around as if his sister might pop out of the woodwork. "She'll be here," he said. "She'll be here."

"She left Wednesday," Annie said. "I don't think

she's coming back. I think she took Willie and ran away." She would have said more in defense of Wilena's character, but Jeff's eyes narrowed.

Gordon dropped Annie's braid. "Don't get mad now." He held up his hands and stumbled backward toward the far corner. "It's okay. Wilena knew what she had to do. I told her to nab the library lady's sister and then mail the letter."

"But she didn't mail the letter," Annie said. "Not till Wednesday when she left."

Jeff ripped the gun out of his waistband and took two long strides toward Gordon. Annie sprinted for the door. She was halfway down the hall before she heard the shot. She ducked left into the kitchen and fumbled with the doorknob. Her hands were sweaty and slipped twice before she wrenched it open.

She sailed down the steps and hit the gravel running. The trees. The heavy pine trees. She could hide there. No. She ran straight toward the steep drive. The sharp gravel was the least of her worries.

"THIS LOOKS LIKE a perfect spot for a picnic, doesn't it?" Alicia Rae scanned the ground one more time. No snakes, but she kept Bertha ready just in case. Some people might think it was disrespectful of her, having a picnic right where Hiram Knelson died all those years ago, but the view up here was so pretty. She glanced down at the little house across the gravel parking lot fifty feet below her. That was a good place to live when she was growing up, but she liked the bigger house much better, especially since her driveway now was much shorter and wider than this one.

"Susan." Alicia Rae pointed to a relatively flat spot. "You spread the picnic blanket right there, and Glaze and I will get the food out, won't we, honey?"

Glaze didn't say anything. She walked to the edge of the cliff and peered down. Alicia Rae felt nervous about that. She stepped up beside Glaze and took her arm in a gentle, but firm grasp. "You come on over here and help us with this picnic now."

Susan motioned to the second picnic basket. "Please help me put out the food," she said. Glaze shrugged and knelt on the edge of the blanket. Alicia nodded at Susan. *Thank you,* she mouthed, but she didn't say it out loud.

She was halfway down to a sitting position herself when she heard a car grinding its way up the drive below them. She smiled. "That's probably Wilena," she said. "She's a real nice lady. Have I told you about her?" Susan shook her head. Glaze did nothing. "She works for the town driving the ambulance. She and her brother rent this place from me. Well, he's been in jail for a while, but I think he should be getting out soon." She straightened back up. "Let's go over and yell hey at her." She reached down and took Glaze by the hand. "Come on. You need to move around more." Glaze pulled away and shook her head. Alicia Rae couldn't get over it. "You haven't said hardly a word in more than a week. You'll feel a lot better if you start connecting. Let's go holler down to Wilena. Later on I'll take you over there and you can meet her for real. I think you'd like her. She has a real nice little boy." She wasn't willing to put Bertha down. "Here, Susan, help me get her moving."

Susan took Glaze's other elbow and lifted. Glaze pulled her arms away, but then seemed to give in. She stood and turned toward the cliff. By the time the three of them made it to the edge of the precipice, the car was at a standstill with nobody in sight. "Well, now," Alicia Rae said, "we're just going to have to go for a visit. Maybe tomorrow." She turned away, but stopped at the sound of a gunshot. Someone screamed. It sounded like a woman.

That nice woman from the healthy store ran down the steps with her long braid flying every which way. "What on earth," Alicia started to say, but a man ran out from the house. Annie was almost at the tree line, headed down the driveway, when he stopped, raised his arms, pointed a gun.

Alicia and Susan both screamed as the gun exploded. Annie fell, and Glaze stepped forward. "Jeff," she said. "Jeff." She grabbed the shotgun from Alicia Rae, pointed it down at Jeff Winslow, and pulled the trigger. The kickback threw her off balance and she stumbled backward.

The man below them grabbed his arm, barked an obscenity, and dove for the car. Alicia Rae felt too stunned to do anything except watch him tumble into the driver's seat and peel off down the driveway. She turned to her right and looked at Glaze. Glaze stood there with the gun barrel pointed at the ground. Susan hooked her hand into Alicia's left arm and leaned against her. "I think I'm gonna be sick," she said.

TOM SLOWED DOWN as we approached the sharp curve. Alicia's bed-and-breakfast sign looked rather perky at the end of her driveway. He turned on his left blinker and waited for an oncoming car to go past. As he made the turn, we heard what sounded like a gunshot. I grabbed his arm. "Where did that come from?"

"Hush," he said. "Hush." He rolled down the window. I rolled down mine, too. "It could have been up at Alicia's." There was another shot, closely followed by a boom from what sounded to me like a different gun. The sound came from my side of the car, up the hillside. "There," I yelled.

"There's another driveway farther up the road." Tom backed out onto the highway and headed for the narrow gravel drive. We got to the base of it just as a car came screaming down the hill and careened into a turn in front of us. The car looked familiar, but I couldn't place it.

"That's Jeff Winslow," Tom shouted.

"What? It can't be. He's in jail."

Tom swung the car in a tight turn and hit the accelerator. "I helped Bob arrest him. I should know that face. He gave us quite a fight before we could get him under control."

"Wait, Tom! Wait! What about Glaze?"

Thank goodness I had on my seat belt. Thank goodness there weren't any other cars coming. He did a U-turn, barely missing the guardrail, and headed up the narrow gravel driveway, scorching his way around the sharp turns.

WE COULD SEE ANNIE lying at the edge of the gravel road just below the crest of the hill. You could spot that hair a mile away. Had Jeff Winslow hit her with the car? What was going on? I know I was screaming, but the sound seemed to come from somewhere far outside me. I bolted from the car before Tom stopped completely and stumbled over the dozen or so feet of gravel until I reached her. Her arms were flung out to the side as if she hadn't had time to try to break her fall. It was clear that the murder weapon hadn't been a car. Tom pulled me off her body and tried to turn me away from her, but I clawed at his arms and wrenched my way free. I couldn't bear to move her, in case I might hurt her somehow, even though that sane side of my brain knew, knew beyond guessing, that she was gone. Somewhere in the back of my mind it registered that she lay in a patch of creeping bugleweed. At least they would have been soft beneath her when she fell. I lifted the end of her long braid and brushed out a few pine needles that had caught somehow between the coppery strands.

Tom knelt beside me, slipped his hand under her neck and felt for a pulse. "I have to check the house, Biscuit," he said. "We still haven't found Glaze."

That got through to me, finally, but I couldn't leave Annie lying there alone. I looked at Tom and saw, over his shoulder, three figures on the top of the ridge. You could spot my sister's hair from a mile away. She stood there with a malevolent-looking gun in her hands. I stared back down at Annie. "No," I screamed. "No! How could you, Glaze? Why? What did she ever do to you?"

One of the women standing beside her took the gun away and shouted something, but I was beyond hearing. Tom held me until a car ground up the driveway behind us. Bob and Reebok and half the police force of Braetonburg showed up. They must have traced the dead driver. Little good that did any of us at this point.

WEEK FIVE

SUNDAY

SUNDAY MORNING, I asked Melissa to go with me to Annie's to help pick out a dress to bury her in. I felt like an interloper. I'd never been in the shop when Annie wasn't there. Melissa unlocked the door and stepped inside to the clash of the jangling bell.

The shelves held an orderly array of health and happy times, good smells and gentle memories. I'd hidden behind the shampoos once to avoid a woman I hadn't wanted to meet. Annie had called me a coward. She was right. There was so much I didn't want to see in life.

"Do you have any idea what will happen to her shop? It would be a shame to let all this go."

"I don't know. They'll put it up for sale, I guess." Melissa pushed on the back of the rocking chair by the front window. The first quilt Annie ever made, one square a month for eight years, swung softly in time to the creaking of the rocker. "She was seven when she started this," she said. "Did you know that?"

"Yes. Yes, I did."

"Do you think we should wrap her in it for the burial?"

"No!" I surprised myself as much as I startled Melissa. "We can't put that underground."

Melissa ran her finger over what Annie had called her self-portrait square. The one with the figure of a red-braided little girl in the middle of it. "Maybe we should frame it."

"Yes," I said. "Yes. We'll hang it in the library."

"Her aunts and uncles may have something to say about that."

"Do you see any of them here helping us?"

Melissa looked at me. "You're pretty bitter."

"You're darn tootin' I am." I pulled Annie's quilt against my chest and sank into the rocker. "Why? This is all so senseless!"

Melissa laid a hand on my shoulder. "Yeah," she said, and I had the feeling she'd seen beyond my words. "It's not her fault, you know."

I buried my face in the quilt and inhaled that healthy herb scent that was, that had been, so much a part of Annie. "My head knows you're right. But my heart says it doesn't want to listen."

Melissa knelt on the wooden floor beside me. Her knees creaked. "Biscuit, this is not your heart speaking, and you know it. This is your stubborn streak. You're embarrassed because you accused her of murdering Annie."

"How did you know that?"

"You don't think people talk? Come off it, Biscuit. You probably think she'll never be able to forgive you."

"She couldn't. I don't know how I'll ever face her." Melissa was quiet a long time.

"If she'd done that to you, do you think you could understand?"

"I…I don't know. It wasn't, though. She'd never do anything like that to me. Never."

"Will you at least think about it?"

"You think I've been thinking about anything else since then?"

"It's okay. Settle down. I'm here to help, remember?"

"I keep seeing her face looking down at me and I hear me shouting at her and screaming those awful things. And that Alicia woman putting her arm around Glaze and turning her away from me, the same way Tom turned me away from looking at Annie. It was like something died between us right then, and I'm the one who killed it."

Melissa put her arms around me. She would have held me forever if I'd needed it. "I could forgive you, I'm sure," she said. "I'd be willing to bet Glaze can, too. The real question is whether you can forgive yourself."

We stayed there for a long time before we got up the nerve to go upstairs.

IN HER CLOSET, an old-fashioned bird's-eye-maple wardrobe, we found Annie's long, shapeless dress in that lovely, deep Irish-setter red. She'd worn it so often. We left her quilting frame and all her supplies in their tidy stacks. We left her bed, made up with a checkerboard quilt in browns and ivories. There was a poem in a lovely frame hanging above her bed. I looked closer. It was the text of Roger's song about Martinsville. Maybe we could give it to him after the funeral. We left it there for now, along with the CD that Easton and Ariel had made of the song. Roger had been planning on giving them away, but Sadie made everyone in town buy the CD. Everybody including Annie, it looked like. Too many decisions to make. A pair of cow-headed slippers, with *Moo* written across the insteps, sat expectantly beside her bed where she would never step into them again. There would be time later to deal with all of these things. We took only the dress and a length of matching ribbon to weave through her long braid. But what could I possibly take that would stitch together my broken heart?

WEEK FIVE

MONDAY

> Notice:
> The Martinsville Library
> will be closed this week.

*Dear Biscuit, Dee, Ellen, Esther, Glaze,
Ida, Irene,
Madeleine, Maggie, Margot, Melissa, Miss
Mary, Mom,
Myrtle, Pumpkin, Rebecca Jo, Sadie,
and Sharon,*

*I called the cruise line today and canceled.
Maybe we can go in the fall.*

*I love each of you, and I plan to tell you
on a regular basis from now on.*

Margaret

WEEK FIVE

TUESDAY

GLAZE WASN'T AT AXELROD'S for the viewing. The women in the tap class had been taking turns, two by two, sitting with Annie at the funeral home so she wouldn't be alone. Ida and Sadie, Dee and Pumpkin, Melissa and I. Glaze hadn't taken part. I think she was afraid to face me, but there was a deeper, clinical reason that we tried to make known through the town. Glaze was still coming out of the aftereffects of having gone without her medications for two weeks. Bob told me she didn't remember a lot of what had happened, only that she had quit taking them just before our sister-week, hoping against hope that she was somehow cured of her depression. That was why she'd gone steadily downhill all week until that Friday when she screamed at me and left the house. She'd driven for hours, finally decided to come home, but instead found her way to Alicia's where she stayed, almost entirely speechless, for the ensuing week. The only thing that snapped her out of it was seeing her old boyfriend Jeff Winslow shoot Annie in the back.

If only I'd noticed her medications sitting there on her desk. I'd looked right at the pill container and then looked past it. How would things have been different if I hadn't been so blind?

Annie looked like an alabaster goddess with the red ribbon in her long braid. We all had a chance to hold her hand. Her cool hand. Her hand that looked so fragile now. I could still see the strength in it, though. She should have been quilting. She should have been laughing at the circus. She should have been standing beside me now, mourning someone else, someone older and more ready to go. But all the should-have-beens were empty words.

Marmalade hadn't come inside with me. Even my cat blamed me.

I am waiting for LooseLaces.

She had stationed herself, with her tail wrapped around her feet, outside the front door of the funeral home. Through the floor-to-ceiling glass panes beside the door, I saw a few people bend to pat her, but she pretty much ignored them. That was distinctly unlike Marmy, who was usually so friendly. The only time I saw her move was when Sadie walked up, leaning heavily on Ida's arm.

Marmalade stood, reared up onto her back legs, and placed her front paws above Sadie's knees, her orange-and-white feet standing out against Sadie's yellow slacks. Sadie reached with her free hand and caressed Marmy's head. I could see her murmur a few words, but of course I couldn't hear what she said.

Ida stooped to try to pat Marmy, but Marmalade oozed her back into that U shape that cats get when they want to avoid human contact and stepped back out of Sadie's way. Sadie had almost a smile on her face when she came up beside me. I motioned to the chair I'd pulled up for her. "I think Marmy's going to miss the fresh tomatoes she used to eat at Annie's," she said. I'd forgotten that. Melissa fed her chicken. Tom gave her salmon. Sadie gave her cream. Glaze and Maddy supplied catnip. Annie had been Marmy's source of fresh tomatoes. I wondered what else I had already forgotten about Annie. I couldn't let her slip away like this. Sadie patted my shoulder when I sank onto the chair and slowly, and not so quietly, dissolved. I hardly even noticed when Marmalade hopped onto my lap.

AFTER THE VIEWING AT Axelrod's, Bob went home. He said he needed to call Margaret about something important. The five of us women that were

there from the class walked with Miss Mary to
the dance studio.

Me, too.

Ida had chosen to stay with Annie.

Miss Mary put a CD in the player. The voices
of Easton and Ariel filled the room with Roger's
song about being home and loving home and feeling at home. Without directions, without conscious
planning, we formed a circle and began swaying to
the music that Annie would never again hear. For
once, Miss Mary was subdued as we all danced
out our pain. Marmalade sat beside the mirror
wall and watched us.

Later, at Melissa's, we went through a whole box
of tissues while Marmalade ate chicken from a
tiny plate and then rotated from one lap to another,
purring at each of us and licking away our tears.

My Gratitude List for Tuesday
1. Melissa.
2. Bob and Marmalade.
3. All the women in this town. except for
   Easton. No. Even her. I do love her voice.
4. Mom, Dad, Auntie Blue. And Uncle Mark,
   too.
5. I'm grateful for the times I had with Annie.
   I'm grateful for her level head and her sense
   of integrity and her sense of fun and the circus and her rocking chair and those quilts and

I am grateful for
Widelap
Softfoot
LooseLaces
GoodCook
Smellsweet
TomatoLady
bug sounds
this soft bed

WEEK FIVE

WEDNESDAY

DOODLE-DOO SOUNDED bright and perky. Didn't that rooster have an ounce of sense? How dare he, on a day like this?

I raised my head and peered over Bob's sleeping form. Five? Five o'clock? That little voice inside told me I wouldn't be going back to sleep today. Annie wouldn't have the choice of whether or not to get up. Ever again.

I knew that Bob needed to sleep, but I needed him more. I snuggled into his arms and sobbed until I was all wrung out.

FIVE O'CLOCK? That bird was insane. Melissa groaned. She remembered this feeling. This hollow in the pit of her stomach. Hollow except for the rage. It was like this when that drunk guy hit and killed Jake. Her fun, funny, life-filled, bicycle-riding nephew. Jim, Melissa's twin brother, had never really recovered from his son's death. Maybe you didn't get over something like that. Maybe you just piled life on top of it and kept going. But how was she going to handle Annie's death? Or deal with Biscuit's anguish? Had she said the right things, or was her foot in her mouth big-time?

She stumbled out of bed and slipped her feet into her scroungy old slippers. A mistake. That brought to mind the black-and-white cow slippers that Annie left so expectantly beside her bed that last morning before she was stolen away. Melissa walked downstairs and into her kitchen. Thank goodness she didn't have any B&B guests right then. She couldn't face making breakfast even for herself, much less anyone else. She sank down onto what she always thought of as Annie's chair, at the foot of the long table, laid her head down on her arms, and cried until there weren't any more tears.

FUNNY, MARGARET THOUGHT in the predawn quiet, how a rooster's crow could carry so far in the early morning air. Of course, all this way down the whole length of Fourth Street, Doodle-Doo sounded more like an echo than a cockadoodle. She'd been awake anyway, lying there wondering how she could have stopped all this. For a long time she'd done so much to help the town. What good was a fortune if you couldn't use it to help? But she'd missed the mark somehow with Wilena.

Biscuit had told Sadie, and Sadie had told Ida, and Ida had come straight over to Margaret's house to let her know about the scribbled sheet of paper the police found in the car with the dead woman and that sweet little boy.

Wilena had kidnapped Annie, thinking she was Glaze somehow. Margaret wasn't sure they'd ever figure that one out. But Annie had told Wilena she could get some help. Wilena had stopped at the end of her driveway, apparently, and written out a statement, almost like an affirmation, that said she was going to go get some food and then she was going to come home and let *Gale* free. She was going to burn the letter that asked for a ransom and ask for Gale's—Annie's—help in getting Margaret to help her buy a little house.

The waste of it all. Margaret had turned funds over to the town to pay for the fire department and the ambulance and the child-care facility. She wondered just where her money was going if Wilena hadn't been able to live decently or feed her child well enough on her paycheck. If only Glaze would take on the job of supervising all this. Margaret had heard from Bob yesterday. He'd been investigating some complaints and found out that something fishy was going on with the town's money. He wanted to look into it more closely. They finally decided that Margaret should call

Bushy, Bagot & Green today, and then she and
Bob and her friendly lawyer would visit Hubbard
Martin's office and demand to see the town's pay-
roll information. Hubbard had better have some
real good answers, backed up with receipts.

PUMPKIN FELT LIKE turning over and going back to
sleep, but Doodle-Doo seemed more insistent than
usual. She hadn't known Annie for very long, but
Annie was the one who'd brought her into the tap-
dance class. Annie was the one who'd taught her
so much about the herbs. Whatever was going to
happen to that wonderful store? Pumpkin felt as
if she'd lost a lifetime of friendship. She reached
for the tissues.

ROGER JOHNSON STARTLED AWAKE when Doodle-Doo
crowed. It was way too early, even for Doodles.
Roger could tell that from the light, or rather the
lack of light, coming in through the window. He
was in his early twenties, and he could still feel the
effects of digging that grave yesterday. He wondered how Tom and Bob, and Ralph, were feeling.
They had to be at least fifty. Old.

He remembered Annie from when she was just
a little thing. They'd grown up together. He used
to pull her braid when they were out on the grade-
school playground. Had there been someone wonderful right at his elbow all this time and he'd

never even noticed? He'd been so busy writing his songs and starting his garbage-hauling business, and what had it gotten him? A big zero. What had he lost?

MAGGIE WAS HALFWAY OUT to her car when Doodle-Doo crowed. "Hush, you silly bird. You're going to wake up the whole town." She paused and looked down Beechnut Lane. There was a light on at Matthew's house. Biscuit's house, what she could see of it through the trees, was dark. Maggie had left strict instructions with Ida about what to offer as her gift to Annie. She sure was glad Ida wasn't afraid of Almyra the way Biscuit was.

The trees between her and the river hardly swayed at all in the stillness before dawn. When she was in high school she'd had old Mrs. Gatch for English. She'd drummed that poem into their heads, the one about earth being so fair early in the morning when nothing was moving. Just like now. Of course, Wordsworth had been talking about London, and she was talking about little bitty old Martinsville. But the feeling was the same. Maggie breathed a thank-you to Annie for all the friendship and laughter over the past decade or so, and then she headed downhill to spend some time at the intensive-care unit sitting with Wilena's dear little boy. It wouldn't do to leave him alone. Two, maybe three days strapped in a car seat with his dead mama beside him. That poor child.

DOODLE-DOO WOKE Miss Mary from a deep dream about dancing on clouds. She certainly hoped that was what Annie was doing right about now. How sad that it took Annie's death for her to feel like a real, close part of that tap class. Was that self-centered of her? She hoped not. But, enough of that! It was time to wake up and get up and keep living! They'd lay Annie to rest today, but they wouldn't ever forget her!

DEE LOOKED ACROSS the table at her mother-in-law. Neither one of them had slept well, and they'd each crept to the kitchen around four o'clock, surprising each other. She supposed she could still call Rebecca Jo her mother-in-law even though the divorce was finalized. Rebecca Jo was certainly the closest thing to a mother that Dee had ever experienced. Coming here when she'd left Barkley was as natural as breathing. It felt like home. On a sad day like today, she wanted to be surrounded by family. Her family of choice.

Doodle-Doo's saucy announcement caught them both at the kitchen table in a pensive mood. Rebecca Jo shook her head. "Nobody that young should have to go. I watched that child grow up, and she lighted up the world in a very special way. I'm so glad you're here, Dee. Nobody should be alone right now."

Dee just nodded. What else was there to say? She reached across the table and held Rebecca Jo's hand.

SADIE LAY QUIETLY in her lonely house and listened to Doodle-Doo crowing his fool head off. Wallace used to love that sound. She looked over at the pillow beside her. Thank you, Wallace, she breathed. Take good care of Annie until I come to join you both. She sank back into a gentle sleep.

THE FIRST THING IDA SAW when she opened her eyes was Ralph lying beside her. Poor thing. He was tuckered after that grave digging yesterday. They should have let Roger do the whole thing. He was young enough not to feel it. Doodle-Doo let out a trumpet call, and Ida breathed a sigh of relief that she didn't live right across the street from Maggie Pontiac. From this far away, Doodle-Doo sounded plaintive. *Annie McGill is gone, Annie McGill is gone,* he seemed to be crowing. She wished he'd shut up. She also wished she knew for sure about Susan. Could she possibly be Ralph's daughter? Damn. There went any possibility of going back to sleep.

GLAZE PROPPED HERSELF up on one elbow and reached for a bottle of water and her meds. Never again. If she hadn't stopped her meds, she wouldn't have gone downhill. If she hadn't left town, maybe Annie would be alive. If she hadn't gone nuts, maybe that Wilena woman would have taken her instead of Annie. If she'd never started dating that creep Jeff Winslow in the first place, he never would have known about Martinsville and never would have come here, and they'd all be safe and Annie would be alive. Biscuit was never going to forgive her for killing Annie. Oh, she hadn't pulled the trigger, but she'd killed her. She could see it in her sister's eyes. She fingered the bottle of capsules. How could she live with herself after this?

MADDY BRIEFLY CONSIDERED rooster soup until she remembered what day this was. Annie's funeral. She heard Glaze crying down the short hall and padded that way, barefoot, to see if she could offer some comfort. Crying together worked just as well as anything else.

BOB CAME HOME FROM the station to walk with me to the cemetery. Marmalade trailed along beside us. When we stepped out on the front porch, I saw that the violet irises I'd transplanted from my grandmother's garden had begun to bloom. They usually opened a few weeks later than the other varieties. These light violet flowers were blossoming way ahead of their time. They were far too bright for my mood. I felt more in tune with that indigo iris, the one that opened just before the big storm last week. It was hard to appreciate anything around me.

I appreciate you.

The Old Church was packed. I sat there feeling stunned and angry and sad and furious and hopeless and helpless and dejected and just generally wretched. I was so glad Glaze was alive and so angry that she'd run away and let Annie be kidnapped in her place. I knew that was stupid. It wasn't Glaze's fault. But if she'd never taken up with that Jeff Winslow in the first case, Annie would be alive. My God, how could I even be thinking that? No wonder I'd never felt a need for a dog. I did my own barking—at the people I loved. I reached for Bob's arm and hung on as if my sanity depended on it. Maybe it did.

Glaze and Madeleine walked in together and moved down the outer aisle to a place on the far side of the room. She didn't turn around. She barely moved once she sat down. I saw Madeleine look back at me and quickly avert her eyes. Other heads in the congregation swiveled from Glaze to me. It was humiliating. I was the talk of the town. The big, bad sister. No stepmother in a fairy tale could be any worse.

I looked from the coffin to my sister and back again. I couldn't even begin to fathom the agony Glaze had gone through in her life. What had I ever done to help her? Here, at the end of Annie's life, when Glaze had to have known how much I missed my young friend, was she aware, too, of my resentment? How could she not be when I'd flung my blazing hatred...yes, it had been, at that moment, hatred. And bewilderment. I'd flung it in her face in front of everyone. How could I do this to my very own sister? What kind of monster was I? Bob took my hand and lifted it gently away from the stranglehold I had on his arm. "Go on over to her, Woman. Now's as good a time as any."

So there, in front of the whole town, I walked down the center aisle, the same walk I'd taken when I married Bob. I looked at Annie's body lying among the flowers. Then I turned and circled around to where my sister, my dear sister, sat in wooden silence with her head down. I think I stepped on Maddy's feet because by that time I couldn't really see where I was going. I pulled Glaze to her feet and drew her into a bear hug.

AT THE GRAVESITE IN the Green Cemetery, Easton and Ariel sang "Amazing Grace" as a duet. Sadie had asked them to, although I didn't see how Sadie was going to make it through two funerals in so short a time. Maybe the song helped. Henry said a few more words, probably an embellishment of what he'd said in the Old Church. I hadn't listened to that talk, either. I'd been too conscious of my sister sitting and breathing beside me. Now, standing between Glaze and Bob, I felt lines of magnetism from me to each of them. Lines of love. Of acceptance. If we couldn't accept each other just as we were, what good was living?

As if summoned by my thoughts, Auntie Blue spoke from just behind me. "Is there room for a little bit more family here?" Glaze and I widened the space between us, but Auntie Blue didn't step forward. Instead, she moved aside. Behind her stood Sally.

"Mom?"

I thought I was all cried out, but when Sally stepped into my arms, I found out differently. The two of us held each other for a few moments, for a whole lifetime. When I glanced up to thank Auntie Blue, I caught her making a thumbs-up sign at someone down the line. Following the direction of her gaze, I met Melissa's smile, and I knew who all would go on my gratitude list.

Henry finished his speech, stepped away from the grave, and nodded at Bob. Bob looked at Tom. Together they walked to the long, lightweight casket that sat balanced on the quilt-covered sawhorses. Roger and Ralph steadied the box. Tom bent to pick up Annie's body, but Roger stepped forward and pushed Tom aside. Without a word, he lifted Annie's limp body, wrapped in the soft yellow blanket that Sadie had offered. "I have no idea if she would have had me," he said. "But I realized this morning when Doodles crowed…" He paused for a moment to let the ripple of laughter die down. "I figured out this morning that if I'd been a little smarter, I might have seen the value that was right in front of me. As it is, since we were never anything more than friends, I'd like to be able to say that I treasured her friendship. But that wouldn't be true. I took her for granted." He hugged her closer to his heart. "I'm sorry, Annie. Forgive me?"

Bob and Tom helped him slip her body into the flower-bedecked grave. A woman I didn't recognize stepped forward. "I'm from the quilting group that Annie started. She taught a bunch of us to quilt. We live in that new section north of town, and she used to come out once a week to help us." She indicated a cluster of women gathered on the fringe of the crowd. "We're going to rename our quilting group the Annie McGill Quilters." They filed forward one at a time, bent down, and placed seventeen quilt squares over Annie's body.

Madeleine turned to face us and waved a fat sachet of her cinnamon potpourri. "She did love this smell," she said and dropped it into the open grave.

"Honeysuckle soap," Pumpkin said. "She adored this stuff."

Sadie held out a length of handmade lace. "I taught her how to tat lace when she was just a little thing. This is the last piece I ever made." Tom took it from her and reached down to place it gently along Annie's braid.

An enormous poster showing a bright red Duesenberg was Margaret and Sam's gift. Margaret couldn't bring herself to speak, but Sam told us, "She loved that car almost as much as I did."

Miss Mary dropped in two tickets to a dance program at the Fox theater in Atlanta. "We had planned to go together," she said.

Melissa added a glass bottle of water. "She never would drink my iced tea, and she didn't think much of plastic, either."

Once we'd stopped chuckling, Glaze stepped forward and handed her pink hat to Bob. She didn't say anything, so he reached down and perched it at a saucy angle.

Ida brought a paper airplane. "She taught me how to fold these blessed things," she said. "I'd hate for the skill to go to waste." She tried to sail it into the grave, but a stray burst of breeze lifted it and sent it skittering just above our heads. One of Sharon's daughters caught it and started over to the grave with it, but Ida stopped her. "You go ahead and keep it. Annie would have liked that."

Dee moved forward, but Ida held up her hand and reached in her pocket. "This egg is from Maggie," she said. "She made me go get it this morning." She grinned over at me. "Almyra laid it special." Glaze reached behind Sally and tapped my shoulder. Maggie and Ida weren't the only ones who knew I was afraid of that dadblamed chicken. "Annie always got three eggs from Maggie every week," Ida went on. "She said it was okay to eat eggs if you knew the chickens had been loved." She handed the egg to Bob and nodded at Dee, who took her place.

"I couldn't figure out how to make this napkin look like a cruise ship, so I had to fold it like a sailboat, but I think Annie would have enjoyed the trip."

Margot and Hans brought Annie a fresh cinnamon roll. "She loved these," Margot said when we laughed.

I gave her my super-special, genuine, nickel-sized emerald ring. It fit her finger perfectly.

Her aunts and uncles stood to one side, as if they didn't quite belong in the family.

GORDON HARVEY HAD NO FAMILY except his sister. Margaret agreed to pay for their burial side by side in the green cemetery. The tree roots there didn't make any distinction between good and bad, between happy and miserable, between loved and unlovable. Wilena's little boy was still in the hospital, hovering in that twilight realm between life and death. Ida and Maggie and Dee and Melissa had taken to visiting him, rotating shifts each day so he always had someone there. We didn't know if there would be need for another, smaller grave soon. But I sincerely hoped not.

Funny, isn't it? My indigo iris, the one I got from my grandmother, bloomed the day we found out that Glaze was missing. The violet iris, another one that came from Grandma's old garden, bloomed the day we buried my little sister. Life goes on.

The end
Not quite

* * * * *